6/22 NORRIS ELLOYER

CURRENCY
WAR

CURRENCY WAR

A NOVEL

LAWRENCE B. LINDSEY

NEW YORK TIMES BESTSELLING AUTHOR

Forefront
BOOKS

ACKNOWLEDGMENTS

ALTHOUGH I HAVE WRITTEN FIVE NONFICTION BOOKS AND WRITE almost daily on nonfiction topics, this is my first attempt at fiction. *Currency War* has been five years in the making, and that has meant countless numbers of people were asked for feedback as the book progressed. During those five years a book that began as pure fiction inched closer and closer to reality. So the nature of the people who were asked for their feedback changed from friends and family to individuals with a more professional bent. Some of these people are not acknowledged as a result of their profession, and any others I have omitted have my apologies.

First and foremost, I want to thank Joe Clifford Faust for his outstanding editorial help. He was the go-to man to answer the question, "Does this work?" Of course, behind every good man is a good woman, and his wife, Connie, has read the book so many times that she probably has it memorized.

Second, I want to thank all of the folks at Stansberry Research and Stansberry Asset Management for their help in the publication process, especially Mark Arnold, Fawn Gwynallen, Marco Ferri, and Brett Aitken, and Erez Kalir, formerly of Stansberry Asset Management. The folks at Forefront Books, particularly Jonathan Merkh and Lauren Ward, were indispensable.

Third, I want to thank all of my friends and colleagues for their insights. Christine Frates and Theresa Perfetto, who read major sections of several drafts, went above and beyond the call of duty. Karolin Junnila, whose organizational talents make all things possible, did the same on this project. Barry Jackson, in addition to his kibbitzing, found me Joe Clifford Faust.

Fourth, I want to thank my children. Tommy, my youngest, was a major inspiration for this book, though he did not know it at the time. Emily and Ashley provided terrific insight on some of the more sensitive parts of the book—the kind you don't find in nonfiction works. All of them, especially Troy, had to put up with a grumpy and preoccupied dad quite a bit.

But the book also would not have been possible without the real-world men and women who make our global political and financial systems operate. This is a work of fiction, and as such, any resemblance between those individuals and the characters in this book are purely coincidental. But the nature of their work is not fictional, even if it is gussied up a bit to omit the day-to-day activities that consume the lives of all of us. Though fictional, *Currency War* takes place in a world that is all too real.

DEDICATION

*To the real-life Bernadette, who, like her fictional namesake,
absorbed a lot of her father's tradecraft from an early age.*

PART ONE

THE MONEY GAME

CHAPTER ONE

"**Stop the car.** *Now.*"

It was the third time Ben Coleman said it to the man behind the wheel of the limousine, but his companion, Zhang Jin, told the driver in Mandarin to ignore him. She was a classic government worker drone with the requisite long black hair and piercing dark eyes, not even five-foot nothing and a hundred pounds—well, forty-five kilos—soaking wet.

"Jin. I mean it. Stop the car."

She shook her head. "No. We have to get you to the airport." She spoke in a vaguely British accent. Most Chinese learned English in Hong Kong, Australia, and even India. The sun still never set on the British empire.

The desire to investigate the gathering crowds was gnawing at his gut. All the signs of what he was seeing were familiar to him, but he wanted to make sure.

His trip to the airport started off strictly routine through the beginning of another workday in Beijing. The early morning crowds were slowly building, traffic starting to congeal with automobiles and bicycles competing for space on the asphalt.

Then he started to notice the lines. Small crowds forming outside certain buildings, a few scattered here and there. As the trip went on, he could see the crowds growing. Passersby seeing the crowds quickly joined in. Fifteen minutes into the drive, the crowds were covering whole blocks.

Then civility began to vanish. The crowds were turning into mobs. As people spilled into the street, traffic was slowed even further. Then it clicked. The central banker in Ben's mind realized he was seeing in person what he had only read about.

"I mean it. Stop the car."

"I cannot let you miss your flight."

"Look at these crowds. I'm going to miss my flight anyway." Zhang Jin said nothing. Ben continued. "Look, we're going so slowly I could get out of the car now."

Jin spoke to the driver, who barked back. They were both loud and animated.

Ben was thinking, *Damn, when do I get my chance?*

As if sensing Ben's thinking, the driver slammed his foot down on the gas, laying on the horn, forcing workers to get out of the way or be run over.

"If you're not going to stop, at least tell me what's going on." Ben lurched sideways in his seat, away from Jin and toward the door as the driver made a hard left, horn blaring and tires squealing.

"It appears," Jin said, not looking at him, "that there has been a power failure and people are lining up to wait for it to come back on so the stores can open."

Ben rolled his eyes. The lines weren't at every building, and the stores were clearly open, their colorful neon signs advertising they were ready for business.

He said, "There's no blackout. They're only queuing at certain places, one every few blocks. But there're so many people trying to get into them they're spilling into the streets. They're not stores, are they?"

Casting a worried look at the driver, she said, "Do not do this, Ben Coleman. You don't understand the trouble you would be making for yourself."

He looked at the worry in her eyes knew exactly what was going on. *You don't understand the trouble you are making for me by asking this.*

Then he started to shake his head in resignation, not wanting to put Zhang Jin in trouble with her superiors. He'd come to look on her as a friend during his many trips to China. Though she was officially his translator, he knew she was actually his minder. She was employed by Chinese internal security, but she treated him well, knew his preferences for food and drink, and knew how long it took him to sleep off jet lag. She loved to hear about his life in the United States. She inquired about his family, particularly his wife, and said she'd love to meet her in person one day.

The driver slammed on the brakes. There was a bump and Ben caught himself on the rear of the front seat. When he looked up, he could see an old woman on the hood of the car, her bloodied head up against the windshield. Then another thump as she rolled off.

"Shit! What the hell—"

The driver stared back at the bloodstained spiderweb on the windshield. Jin picked herself up from the floor and gasped at the sight.

The driver burst into more Mandarin, faster than Ben had ever heard it, his arms waving.

Then the car started to sway.

Ben's stomach dropped.

The crowd outside was no longer concerned about queuing. They turned their attention to the limo, covering the front with their hands and rocking it, pushing and pounding on the driver's side window.

"Don't be afraid," Zhang Jin said, looking right at Ben. "They don't want you."

The driver looked back at them, fear in his eyes.

There was a loud crack and the driver's side window gave way, shattering into hundreds of tiny crystals. Hands poured in through the opening, grabbing the driver by the hair, neck, and left arm. He looped his free arm through the steering wheel to try to stop himself from getting pulled out, then threw himself across the front seat to get away from the grasping mass of arms. But they grabbed his legs and pulled him from the car.

The crowd moved their attention away from the car. Ben seized his chance, threw open the door, and climbed out into the street. Zhang Jin had been right. They hadn't been after him. They were taking turns punching and kicking and spitting on the driver, who had curled into a ball on the street.

Jin jumped out Ben's door. "We have to get out of here."

Ben, still staring at the bloody driver, said, "Jin. What the hell?"

"This happens." She looked over at the crumpled body in the street. "Somebody's grandmother."

She put a death lock on Ben's arm and pulled him away from the limo, backtracking down the street. The scene of retribution was quickly obscured by crowds of people mobbing around glass-framed doors. An even larger crowd was growing ominously in the direction they were headed.

They stopped in their tracks.

"They're banks, aren't they?" Ben asked. "This is a bank run. But it's bigger. They've lined up on every bank I've seen. Is it all the banks, Jin?"

She surveyed the growing chaos in the street and looked afraid for the first time.

He looked at her and could feel his heart in his throat. "It doesn't matter. You didn't tell me. I figured it out. But that doesn't matter now. We have to get the hell out of here."

Jin grabbed his arm and started leading him away from the growing crowd, more interested now in the bank than the limousine driver. But less than a block away was another crowd, another bank, another street blocked off. Then the mob surged toward the bank with an animal groan and its front windows gave way. People jumped up and into the building, and as Ben turned back to the street, he realized he was now caught up in the middle of the mob, streaming toward the broken windows.

He felt himself go off balance, the crowd packed around him so tightly that he couldn't move. Ben kicked to keep himself up, but it did no good.

Zhang Jin shouted, "Lift your feet!"

Ben picked his feet up and to his surprise, he did not fall. They were packed in so tightly that they flowed with the crowd, inching toward the breached bank.

Then the crowd stopped. Ben felt himself start to sink as the mob around him loosened, and he realized the people packed around him were turning away from the bank. He shifted to see what had drawn their attention.

A truck had pulled onto the street. It was military issue with blocky front ends, canvas-slung cargo beds, and now, troops pouring out of their backs.

The crowd began to scatter and then momentarily stopped. Another truck pulled into the next intersection. Assessing the situation, Ben saw that all points of egress were being blocked. He and Jin were now in a no-man's land, caught between the mob and the troops.

Jin was facing the soldiers, a resigned look on her face. Her hand slid out of a pocket and she brought out a mobile phone and began to thumb the screen.

Like dozens, no, *hundreds* of other members of the mob, holding their phones up, taking videos of the troops.

"Jin, there's no time—"

Ben never finished the thought. As if it had a single brain, the crowd rolled toward the soldiers, their voices rising into a din. He couldn't be sure if anything was being said, but the sentiment was there: *The banks closed and took our money and now you bring out our own army to protect those bastards.*

Jin bending her arm, bringing up her cell phone.

The line of troops was now obscured by the advancing crowd. Ben grabbed Jin's hand as the phone reached her ear and pulled it away, then pulled her away from the scene and started to drag her back toward the limousine, now visible as the crowd dispersed in all directions.

Then the noise from the crowd pitched upwards into a terrible cry of pain, so loud that it took Ben a moment to hear the gunshots causing it. The cry became louder, and the crackling sounds disappeared beneath it. Ben stood, stunned, not believing what was happening, hand still clamped to Jin's arm.

Then something angry buzzed past, mere inches from his ear.

He started to run again, pulling Jin with him, scanning the streets looking for somewhere safe to go. There was nothing. People were piling up at the doors of open shops, fighting to get in. As they neared the limo Ben heard a wet smack and a young man in front of them spun around and fell to the ground, a fresh red blossom in the center of his chest.

Ben changed direction again. He had been thinking the limo might be bulletproof like the one he rode in back home, but there was no safe place—

Until he spotted the alleyway.

People were running past it, a few had the presence of mind to turn and run down it, and there were bodies in the street between them and the entrance. Ben grabbed Jin's arm and he ran for it, wishing she would drop that damn phone.

Someone else was knocked down by the gunfire, and as Ben and Jin reached the entrance to the alley a bullet ricocheted off the brick of a building and Ben felt a sudden burning near his right shoulder blade. He led her deep into the alley, stopping when he realized that a crowd of people were blocking the way out. At the end of the alley, between the two of them and the sunlight he had seen, a truck pulled in to block the way.

Behind him, people were streaming into the alley and behind them Ben could see an advancing line of troops, double-timing it, weapons aiming from their waists.

He thought, *I'll be damned if I let things end this way.* He began to scan the alley.

As the next volley of shots rang out, he spotted a dumpster next to a stained and decrepit metal door. He wasn't altogether certain that the thin metal sides would stop a round from an AK-47, but in the moment, it was all he had.

By the time he dragged Jin over he had abandoned the idea of getting behind it. There was too much chaos around him. He flung one lid open, grabbed Jin around the waist, and flung her toward the top of the dumpster. She scrambled onto the top of the second lid. Ben reached up, took her by the shoulders, and shoved her through the opening down inside. Then he clambered up the side and jumped down in next to her, pulling the lid shut as he went.

And when he stopped, he promptly threw up. The smell was overwhelming. He was sitting in a sludge of sour grease, rotting vegetable matter, bones, and entrails, and he was staring into the cloudy eyes of a large carp.

Jin raised that damned phone to her lips again. He reached up to silence her, but the Mandarin started pouring out of her mouth, so fast that he only recognized some of the phrases.

Chairman Ben Coleman.

Federal Reserve Board.

United States of America.

Send help.

A loud ping deafened him as a bullet slammed through the upper part of the metal. Jin dropped the phone and threw herself flat, curling into a fetal position. Ben thought that was smart and forced himself down, on his side to keep his burning shoulder out of the sludge. Jin scooted toward him, hands still cradling the phone. He put one arm around the ball she had wound herself into and could feel her trembling.

Ben realized he was trembling as well. And to try and regain control of himself, to drown out the sounds of screaming and gunshots from the world outside, he began to hum a song to himself. An old one from a musical, that recent revival of *The Music Man.*

¥ $ €

Lying in the dumpster amid fish scales and rotting food, only half of which were in garbage bags, Ben said to himself, *How the living fuck did I get here?*

Barely an hour ago, he was meeting with Li Xue, the governor of the People's Bank of China. While the United States and China were strategic competitors, their central bankers had no choice but to get along.

China was vying to become the world's only superpower. That goal had been formally adopted by Xi Jinping early in his term as president of China in a program called China 2049. He had ruthlessly consolidated power and China was now governed by a small group of men in the politburo.

Li reported to them. This limited Li's ability to speak completely freely, but central bankers have their own little language; a combination of a few well-placed technical phrases, accompanied by just the right body language, got the point across.

The geopolitical battle had first taken an economic turn with a trade war during the Trump administration when Xi Jinping was in office.

That war had been painful for both sides, but in the end, the pain was too much for the Chinese to take. They struck a deal. China capitulated. In the process, Xi Jinping, who had viewed himself as president for life, was now in "retirement" in a remote city in central China.

Still, the humiliation stung. The new Politburo decided to follow a different tack. The U.S. had beaten them on the trade front, but they were going to follow an approach that had long worried many U.S. politicians. The trade surpluses that China had run up were used to buy U.S. Treasury bonds and China now owned one and a half trillion dollars of U.S. government debt. This was going to be their new weapon.

Used intelligently, the Chinese yuan would become the world's dominant currency, replacing the dollar. It would be a painful humiliation for America and reestablish China on its path to become the world's only superpower.

Li and Ben both knew this was the grand strategy. Li wanted to advance it. Ben wanted to fight it. But both men wanted the war to be conducted with as little collateral damage as possible. If something went wrong, both countries could be sucked into another Great Depression, pulling the entire global economy down with them.

Ben told Li, "Look, if you dump your Treasuries on the market, you're going to take a hit. You can't move all your Treasuries on the first day. Your selling will drive the price down on the remaining U.S. bonds you hold, and you'll end up with a loss. They'll lose value, making China poorer."

Li responded, "Mr. Chairman, you are talking in the interest of the U.S. That is your job. My job is to look out for the best interest of the people of China."

Ben knew from the formality of the answer that Li had understood his point perfectly well.

Then Ben asked Li, "Why have you been accumulating so much gold?"

Li said, "Gold has always been a store of value and along with silver, something treasured by the Chinese people for thousands of years. Our gold holdings signal to the people that the yuan should be treasured as much as gold." Li's mouth turned into a tight-lipped smile.

Ben knew he was facing a worthy adversary. Li had obviously

thought through his strategy and Ben knew that if Li played his cards perfectly, he very well might win. The only comfort Ben took was that Li would not be left alone to play his hand. The politicians in China, like politicians everywhere, thought they knew better. Ben knew that his best chance was having the Chinese politicians, not Li, play the hand. Ben also knew that if U.S. politicians took charge, he wouldn't be able to play his cards well either.

Li sat quietly, assessing Ben. The American's work as both an academic and financial adviser was legendary. He was not some mere academic economist caught up in theories from the middle of the last century. Ben was a practitioner. His clients got rich in part by using his advice. He would know how to confront China's moves in global markets. Li knew Ben must have some trick up his sleeve. But he also knew that the American political system was even more complicated than China's. That meant more politicians seeking the limelight by grandstanding about Federal Reserve policies. In the last decade, Trump's constant threats against the man he had appointed as chairman were legendary. Li was hoping that Ben would face the same obstacles with President Turner, considered a legendary grandstander in his own right.

Finally Li said, "Ben, thank you so much for coming all this way. I know you have a plane to catch. I believe we understand each other well, and this meeting helped in that regard. Fortunately, we did not have our first meeting at one of those G20 summits, where there are too many prying eyes and ears. I hope we continue to be able to have frank and candid conversations." He stood and extended his hand to Ben.

"Governor Li," Ben said as they shook, "I share your desire to continue to have frank and candid exchanges. I think we both agree that despite our countries' differences, we both want to minimize the needless pain they could suffer in this conflict."

Li nodded in tacit acknowledgment and began to escort Ben to the door, which opened well before they got there. It was all too convenient. Ben knew that someone had been listening in on the entire conversation and knew exactly when to open the door.

The men shook hands one last time. Zhang Jin escorted Ben down the elevator to their car in the basement.

There was something in Ben's mind about Li's body language that hinted at a touch of insecurity. He thought about Li's comment that if the People's Bank of China was holding gold, then the common people would treasure the yuan. That suggested they weren't treasuring it all that much at the moment.

He had read CIA briefing memos about what was happening in some of the more remote Chinese cities. Sporadic reports of bank runs and heavy-handed responses by the authorities were becoming more frequent. With any luck, the politicians would become nervous and force Li to move more quickly than he otherwise would. That would deprive Li of the time he needed to get things ready to roll.

Ben continued to analyze the conversation with Li as he rode to the airport. Li was nervous. He was reticent to talk freely and clearly hoped they could reach an understanding that benefited both of their people without either resorting to what amounted to an economic nuclear option. To Ben this meant that Li knew he didn't hold all the cards.

Then he glanced out the window of the limousine to see those mobs forming in the streets, realized why they were forming, and then got out of that damn limousine so he could see a bank run in real time.

¥ $ €

What the hell had he been thinking? Had he been driven by a vision of himself as an aged academic, regaling his students with the story he'd tell every year? *I was in Beijing during their great bank run, the one where the troops fired on the crowds. And I hid in a dumpster with—*

He hoped that was not it. His psyche demanded relevance in the present and not some reminiscence of past days of glory.

He started to cough but fought to keep it silent. The stench in the dumpster was getting to him. Jin didn't even look up, still curled against him, phone clutched in her hands, still shivering. He tried to swallow but couldn't. At least, for the moment, the shooting had stopped. He did nothing to reveal their position, still feeling that even the relatively thin wall of metal provided them with some semblance of safety.

I'd better survive this, or Bernadette's going to kill me, he thought.

Never mind that. She's going to kill me anyway after I tell her how I survived. Not enough that I stepped out into the middle of a riot. I had to do it with my minder in tow.

Maybe it was a male thing, but he suddenly realized how few of the details about Jin he had shared with Bernadette. But he couldn't hide this one and in telling his tale it would become clear how much he had neglected to tell her.

Yeah. Forget the rioters. Forget the soldiers firing on the crowd. Bernadette's the real hell I'm going to have to face.

¥ $ €

The pounding on the outside of the dumpster nearly made Ben wet himself.

He had resigned himself to lying there in his disgusting, dire state, thinking maybe if he could sleep the time would pass. But insistent pain from his shoulder wouldn't allow it. He ended up staring at the shaft of light beaming in from the hole left by a round from an AK-47.

He wasn't sure how long it had been since things had grown quiet. The shooting was the first thing to stop. Then the crying and whimpering, the shouting of orders in Mandarin. Ben was in shock and couldn't bother even to get the gist of what was being said. The trucks had come, with their huge diesel motors. They sat and idled, men grunted, people groaned. Then the trucks left, and it grew eerily silent. Ben thought for certain that there should be something else out there, the sound of propaganda music from loudspeakers, or the sounds of a broom sweeping up broken glass and spent bullet casings. But there was nothing.

That was, until the banging on the side of the dumpster, rhythmic and intentional. Ben didn't know whether this meant the end of his life or a return to the one he had left behind forever when he and Jin had hopped into the dumpster. Shouts in Mandarin came from outside the metal walls that had once provided shelter. Jin shouted back and there was a squeal as the rusty hinges of the lid started to move. Ben was blinded as light streamed in.

A face appeared at the opening, a young soldier with an official

People's Army helmet. His expression changed from *mission accomplished* to *damn, that stinks* in an instant and he stepped away.

Zhang Jin stood slowly, trying at first to shake off the stuff that clung to her, but quickly gave up and began to give orders to the soldier, who in turn passed her commands on to someone nearby.

Ben stood now, realizing the futility of trying to shed the putridness that had soaked into his clothes. His head popped out of the opening and he saw that the alley had been cleared with the exception of a single military truck and a limousine, this one different from the one he had been riding in. A dozen or so soldiers occupied the alley, picking through debris and inspecting other dumpsters. When they saw the tall Caucasian stick his head up, they all quit working and made their way toward the truck.

He looked at Jin. Clothes disheveled, covered in grime and hair askew, she looked like a chewed rat. He was sure he didn't look much better.

"Sorry," he said.

She didn't say anything, just started trying to climb over the walls of the dumpster. He bent down, cupped his hand under her raised foot, and boosted her up, a more elegant solution than the one that had gotten her in there hours before. Ben hoisted himself over the top of the dumpster, putting most of the weight on the arm and shoulder that was not throbbing. He did a vault into the alley. *Not bad for someone my age,* he thought, and then vowed to double down on his workouts. There was a real advantage to upper body strength.

A man in an officer's uniform stalked up and was having a heated discussion with Jin as Ben tried to scrape grease and fish intestines off his suit. He was so numb that the Mandarin still wasn't clicking with him. All he could tell was that the conversation was not a happy one.

Seeing Ben, the officer motioned at him and looked at his injured shoulder. More yelling at Jin, who appeared not to be giving any ground. They appeared to be of roughly equal rank but in different silos of the state's security apparatus. This battle was as much a contest between competing bureaucracies as between two individuals.

When the tirade was over, the officer walked them out of the alley toward a waiting staff car. Ben didn't need any arm-twisting. Jin gathered as much dignity as she could and followed in a way that told the officer she was doing her job and not merely following his orders. The soldiers around them were quick to step out of the way, turning their faces as the grimy pair passed. Another soldier emerged from the driver's seat and started to open the door for them, but his face puckered and he said something to the officer. The officer shouted, and in a moment, two more soldiers appeared, each with a tarpaulin that they hesitantly wrapped around Ben and Jin.

More conversation and Jin said, "We are to ride in the truck instead."

"Makes sense, I guess," Ben mumbled. Detailing the staff car after they had been in it would be a thankless task. Better to ride in something that could be hosed off.

The soldiers carefully boosted the two of them up and they took places on the bench next to the driver's compartment. The benches then filled up with soldiers, although they took care to keep their distance from the duo. The engine fired, vibrating the soles of their feet, their butts, and their backs, and pulled out of the alley. Looking past the soldiers out the rear of the bed, he could see the street was deserted.

"Can we talk," he said to Jin in a low voice.

She nodded. "They're mostly boys who don't care to know English."

Ben nodded at the street. "Curfew?"

"Most likely."

"How long?"

"Until the insurgents who caused this unfortunate uprising can be identified and any survivors punished."

Ben gave her an incredulous look.

"There's something you Americans say, 'It is what it is.'"

"What happens now?"

Jin didn't look at him. "Our finest doctors will treat your shoulder. Probably after you have had the chance to clean up."

Ordinarily Ben would have laughed, but her growing distance alarmed him.

"What about you?"

Her expression didn't change. "Well, the crowd burned the limousine.

And our driver did not make it. He was the lucky one. I have brought shame upon my organization and my superiors."

He waited for her to say something else. She didn't. He felt a sudden pang of regret, afraid she was looking at a life of indentured servitude, making tennis shoes or iPhones for the rest of her life. He wanted to tell her he was sorry again but wasn't sure it would mean anything in the moment.

He asked, "Is there something I can do for you to help your situation?"

A long pause from Jin. "Please do not."

"I should have let you make your call when you first had the chance. I didn't realize what you were doing."

"You thought I was doing what every other poor citizen was doing out there on the street." She finally looked at him. "I am grateful to you, Ben Coleman. If I had stood there talking on the phone, I likely would have been killed. You saved my life."

"But did I really?"

She broke eye contact to stare at the flapping canvas side. "It is what it is."

Ben wanted to smack whoever had taught her that expression. "Listen, Jin—"

"No," she said. "It is time for you to listen. You need to go home and do your important things, things that are bigger than what happens to me. Things the world needs to know." For a moment she showed that same tight-lipped expression that Li had hours ago.

"But I know people. Important people. I can—"

"No," Jin said. "You are so typically American. When you see a problem, you want to jump in and fix it. You want to make everything better, but you don't realize that what makes things better for Americans doesn't always work in the rest of the world. But still you go on, trying to make the world American.

"So do not make those promises, Ben Coleman. You Americans, your films, your television, your culture, are all full of them. 'I can help you. I can come for you. Be faithful. Wait for me. I will find you.' And the solutions they show are all so ridiculous. They have no idea how things work, let alone how things work in my part of the world."

The truck lurched to a halt. The solders sprang to their feet, as did Jin, leaving Ben sitting. For the first time in ages he was at a loss for words as the soldiers helped her out of the truck, eyes rolling at her smell, laughing as she walked away.

He rose to his feet, his shoulder reminding him it needed attention. She was right, he realized. He wanted to do that American thing, to shout out at her that it was all right, he'd pull the strings, he'd fix it.

She disappeared through a door. The soldiers helped Ben off the truck next, and he could hear their snickers and grunts of disgust from the stink he was giving off. Once off, he started to walk, but they shouted and pointed, directing him to a different door than the one that Jin had used.

CHAPTER TWO

"Honey, I'm home."

Ben dropped his suitcases on the floor. There was a deafening silence in return.

Bernadette entered the foyer from the living room, the faintest of smiles on her lips. Her red hair was brushed back off her shoulders and her green eyes flickered uncertainly.

"A bit late, aren't you?" After all these years, he still found her British accent delightful, but today it did nothing to mask the undercurrent of anger in her voice.

"Let's say a bad day at the office." Ben chuckled to break the mood. It didn't work.

Bernadette said, "The State Department already briefed me. Let me get you to bed."

"Don't get any wild ideas," Ben said. Another attempt at humor.

"I know. You need your sleep. I know how jet lag hits you, and the office will need you first thing in the morning."

He slogged to the stairs and once they were in the bedroom, he threw his bag on the bed and started to undress. Bernadette opened his suitcase and began to unpack.

"Where's your pinstripe suit?" she asked.

"No amount of dry cleaning would've solved that problem."

"Do tell."

Ben pulled his shirt off. "Well, there was this little riot and I ended up in a dumpster for safekeeping along with the discards from half a dozen restaurants."

"You poor darling. You must have been so lonely and frightened in there."

Ben dodged. "Yes. I need a shower to get that fourteen-hour flight off of me."

Bernadette finished inspecting his luggage and turned down the sheets on his side of the bed.

While he was in the shower, she began to unpack his suitcase. From the top drawer of her nightstand, she took a small handheld device and carefully ran it over his clothes and the suitcase. Then she double-checked the seams between the inner lining and the outer part of the case.

Ben emerged from the shower toweling off his hair, thinking it would take four or five more before he could live with himself.

Bernadette said, "They didn't bug you this time."

He slipped on a pair of boxer shorts and sat down on the bed.

Bernadette opened his toiletry case and thought, *No condoms*. She knew he wasn't the cheating type, but she had more than the usual wife's interest in the matter. Given his job, he would be a natural target and she knew he would be naïve. She had to be his protector.

"Sleep at all on the plane?"

"I may have dozed off for a few minutes. Adrenaline was still pumping, and I knew I was in a vulnerable position. It might have been a Gulfstream Five, but it still belonged to the Chinese military."

"Honey, you know you were vulnerable during your entire stay. In more ways than you might imagine."

"What do you mean?"

"Dearest, I love you, but in some matters you're hopeless."

Ben knew he had married a strong, independent woman, but he always became disconcerted when she reminded him of that fact. He still believed he wore the pants in the family. Like many wives, Bernadette let him pretend that this was the case. Every now and then, however, she reminded him there were limits.

"I was safe the entire time. I knew what I was doing."

"Do tell. Getting out of your car and running into a mob outside of a bank is the sign of a man concerned for his own safety? That was reckless, Ben. There's a reason why VIPs are transported around in limousines with bulletproof glass and a touch of extra metal in the doors. You knew your driver was professionally trained for that purpose. And you doubtless had someone with you to make sure you were safe."

"But I've never seen an actual bank run. Only in pictures."

"And there's a very good reason for that. A picture is worth a thousand words. What was it that the pictures didn't convey? Does a bank run have a particular smell to it? Do the rioters look any different in a bank run than they do in a standard riot?"

"Actually, they do. They were more desperate than angry. You could see the desperation on their faces. Rioters are angry and out to destroy. People in bank runs are there to protect everything they've worked their lives for."

Color rose in her face. "There you go again with your literal interpretation of things. What I really want to know is why you felt you had to get out of that fucking limousine."

Ben looked into her eyes. "Okay," he said. "How many videos of the Stones in concert do you have, bootlegs and all?" He waited a beat. "You don't know, do you? And we've watched them how many times, and yet you never reacted to them like you did when I got us those tickets on the fifth row. It was all I could do to keep you under control. I thought for sure you were going to throw your panties on the stage."

"I never—"

"No, I'm exaggerating, but that's the point. It was the emotional contagion. The need to get in there, get closer, not just see what was going on, but be immersed. Feel the people moving as one, hearing their shouts, and, yes, the smell of sweat and desperation."

Bernadette nodded. "Okay. Then what about jumping into a dumpster? Did that help you observe the bank run?"

"There was a riot going on around me. What should I have done?"

Her eyes narrowed. "For starters—" She caught herself and stopped.

"That's it," Ben said. "You know exactly what I should have done, and I didn't do it. So you're upset because—" He looked in her eyes. "You're jealous. I went out and did something you're trained for and made a hash of it, and you know you could have done it better."

Her nostrils flared. "I don't know what I could have done. All that training was so long ago, it's like muscles that haven't been used in a while. They've atrophied. Maybe if I'd been there, I would have gotten us both killed."

"That's not the case and you know it."

She set her jaw. "No. The case is that you should've listened to your handler when she told you no and let them drive you to the airport. It was more than a bank run you were stepping into. If something had happened to you, it could've led to an international incident."

Ben knew when he was licked. "Honey, you're right. You're not jealous. I was foolish and reckless. I'm sorry you were worried for me."

Bernadette knew he hadn't learned his lesson but decided to press her point. "If you had the chance to do it all over again, would you have done the same thing?"

Ben knew that Bernadette wanted the truth. "You know I would. And I am not the only person in this room who is like that."

"Touché," said Bernadette. "But there are unavoidable risks and ones you can prevent. You're married to me and I love you, and I can't imagine life without you. So if there are risks that are avoidable, I expect you to avoid them in the future."

"You know I can't promise that."

"Then you're being damn selfish."

"Who is being selfish here? You've had your share of preventable, unavoidable risks and I've been nothing but a policy wonk. Why shouldn't I have some moments of risk-taking?"

"Is this a midlife crisis rearing its head?"

"No. I'm not seeking it. If I were, I'd take up wingsuit flying. I'm saying if risk comes my way in the line of my work, I'm not going to run from it."

Bernadette gave him that tight-lipped look. *Time to backpedal*, he thought.

"Besides, I'm a policy wonk, remember? This is probably the only time in my life something like this will happen."

"It had better be." She gave him a perfunctory kiss.

"Me too."

Then he put his head down on the pillow and she covered him up, tucking him in for a sleep she knew he needed.

¥ $ €

Ben leaned forward to get up, his high-backed chair protesting at the request. Stretching his lower back, he moved to the window passing the collection of family photos documenting toothless grins and graduations, all organized on bookshelves holding tales of Washington's evolution. He watched at the traffic on Constitution Avenue, contemplating his next move. He removed his glasses and rubbed his deep-set blue eyes with the heel of his hand.

He had spent the last hour at his desk, staring at his computer screen, trying to get information on the Beijing bank run out of Google. He was surprised at how little information there actually was. The Chinese were clamping down on the information flow, and it didn't help that Google was working with the Chinese government to enhance their censorship capabilities. *Don't be evil, my ass*, he thought.

Ben tossed his glasses on to his desk and opened the door to his secretary's office. "Peggy, get me the Secretary of the Treasury on the phone. I suspect he's going to want a personal debriefing before I submit to the CIA's proctological exam. Please check my calendar, see what kind of openings we can make."

"I'm on the case." Her voice was bright as it always was. Ben wondered how she could keep that tone, day in and day out, with the hours that were often required of her.

"And a heads up," he added. "The next few days are going to be a meat grinder until everyone's done reaming me out for my Cub Scout antics. Fair warning."

"Don't worry Mr. Chairman. You can count on me to have your back." Peggy pulled her well-pilled cardigan together and set to work.

"Thank you," he said. "I don't appreciate you enough."

She peered at Ben over the top of her glasses, her bright pink lips revealing a crooked smile. "Mr. Chairman, is there anything else I can do for you?"

They had known each other for almost thirty years. He preferred she call him "Ben," but titles played a critical role in Washington. They showed respect for the office, but more importantly, put officeholders in their place. It was a way of being reminded, *You've got a job to do and those who report to you expect you to do it. That is what you are here for. Don't make it personal. This is duty.*

As he returned to his desk, Peggy's voice came through the intercom. "It's Governor Li on the line."

He raised his eyebrows as he picked up the phone. "Governor Li. So good of you to call."

"Mr. Chairman. I am calling to apologize for everything you went through during your visit. Not only did you take the time to fly to Beijing for our first meeting, but your trip turned out to be more eventful than anyone might have anticipated. Your visit convinced me that we are going to have to work together more than I had ever anticipated. To reciprocate, I want to follow the American custom and ask that you call me by my first name. Please, call me Xue."

"I like that custom, particularly in this case," Ben said. "And please call me Ben."

"It would be a pleasure and a great honor to do so," said Li.

"So, Xue, I reflected on your comment about the importance of the Chinese people coming to treasure the yuan as much as they treasure gold. I think now I understand how complex your situation is."

"Ben, you should have been a diplomat. *Complex* is a word that covers a host of sins."

"I understand the nature of bank runs. The closest America has come in recent times was on 9/11."

He thought back on that day, the rush on ATMs as people tried to get cash to hold them through the emergency. It was particularly rough in the New York metropolitan area. The staff at the Federal Reserve Bank of New York worked as fast as they could to deliver cash to bank branches to satisfy the demand and keep ATMs filled with twenties. They knew what would happen if, on top of seeing buildings collapse, people couldn't get access to their money. They would lose confidence in their banks, and subsequently, American currency.

"What I learned then," he continued, "is that money and banking are both based on confidence. So the need for the Chinese people to treasure the yuan is now painfully apparent to me."

"I chose the word *treasure* deliberately," said Li. "We both have an interest in minimizing the collateral damage that might occur from an economic conflict between our two countries. As you know, when emergencies begin, time is never on our side. Perhaps we could commit to each other to communicate the possibility of an emergency developing as soon as we become aware of it."

Ben said, "Xue, I completely concur. I can assure you at this time that the U.S. has no intention of increasing the strain on the Chinese banking system. I hope that the politicians in your country understand that certain actions they might take could exacerbate your problems."

"I suppose politicians are the same everywhere," Li said. "They seem to think that desperate times require desperate measures. But you and I know that desperate times require calming measures."

"So we have a personal agreement to work together as much as possible to calm the waters. Agreed?"

"Absolutely," said Li. There was a brief pause, then he continued. "Please forgive my rudeness. I should have inquired about your shoulder at the beginning. I hope you are okay. Economic wars are one thing. Damage to one's person is quite another. You have gone above and beyond the call of duty for a central banker for your country and to promote global calm."

"Thank you. It was nothing. Just a little blood drawn. Fortunately, your doctors did a good job. Their expertise meant that it only required three stitches."

"It's good to know you weren't in any real danger," Xue said. "I look forward to our next conversation."

"And I as well."

They exchanged goodbyes and Ben hung up the phone. He exhaled slowly. With all the chaos of his leaving Beijing under less-than-ideal circumstances, he hadn't had much opportunity to worry about the unsure footing that had begun his relationship with the Governor. And while Li's comments had sounded natural, it was obvious that the two were not alone in their conversation. Still, Ben felt secure in knowing that he and Governor Li Xue were seeing eye-to-eye on their need to manage the relationship between their nations. Putting it into play, however, would be quite another matter. It would start with explaining his actions to his own government.

¥　$　€

Li Xue hung up his phone and looked at the two people who had been listening in on headphones. The first was a diminutive man, small even by Chinese standards. Except for his ostentatious uniform adorned with insignias that bore witness to the many honors bestowed upon him as a commander of the People's Liberation Army, he was nondescript. The other was a slight woman with a downcast look, not a surprise considering what she had been through in the past forty-eight hours. She removed her headphones, carefully folded them, and put them on Li's desk.

General Deng pulled his headphones off and tossed them down without regard. It was a loud gesture, like everything he did. "Li Xue," he said. "Are you confident you have Chairman Coleman where you want him?"

"I am, Comrade General."

"You had better be. Personally, I found your groveling for his favor to be distasteful. Humiliating." He looked over at Zhang Jin, who kept her eyes on the floor.

Deng stared at her. He didn't like her, didn't like the way she deferred to him, more fear than the respect he deserved. Yet there was more respect in her voice when she spoke of that American, Ben Coleman. Her relationship with Coleman, he felt, was suspect. Did she see him as an eventual way out of China? Worse yet, did she love him? That had happened before with handlers. And what people thought of as love could make them do very strange things. Even betray China. He learned that at an early age.

He remembered his first lesson in love and treason. It happened when he was eight and the Cultural Revolution was in full swing. The

Red Guards came for his father and dragged him into the town square along with his mother. The mob surrounded the stage where his father was being paraded around with a dunce cap on his head and a big character sign hung around his neck proclaiming, "Traitor to China."

The mob was shouting *"Traitor! Traitor! Traitor!"* Deng and his mother were put in the front row below the stage and forced to watch the proceedings. The chanting went on forever, or so it seemed.

Then his father was brought forward at bayonet point. He was forced to confess his faults. Whenever he hesitated one of the guards would push a bayonet point just far enough forward to hurt but not to break the skin while the other guard shouted in this ear—*"Traitor!"* The mob would resume its chant of *"Traitor! Traitor! Traitor!"*

Finally his father broke. "Yes. I am a traitor to China. I am deeply ashamed."

"Louder!" screamed the guard into his left ear. His father confessed his crimes at the top of his lungs.

Deng felt so ashamed. His father had betrayed China. He had betrayed Chairman Mao. He felt the anger well up inside. His father had betrayed him. He had been tricked into loving a man who was an enemy to China and an enemy of the people.

The guards shouted to the crowd, "What should we do to the traitor?"

The crowd dutifully responded, *"Death, death, death! Death to all traitors!"*

Deng felt his mother squeeze his hand harder. Was his mother a traitor too? He knew that she loved the man on the stage before them. Was she part of his father's conspiracy against China? He had no evidence but knew he could never trust her again.

The guards forced his father down on his knees. They removed the dunce cap and pulled his hair forcing him to bow his head. He stared down at his son as the guard put his revolver to the back of his head. Deng joined the crowd's chant.

"Death, death, death! Death to all traitors!"

It was the last thing his father ever saw as the bullet pierced his head.

The next day the guard who had pulled the trigger came into Deng's classroom. He motioned for Deng to come to the front of the room and put one hand on each of his shoulders. "Deng Wenxi is the son of a traitor. But he is not a traitor! He denounced his father's crimes and rightly demanded his death!" His classmates all applauded. Then they began to chant, "Deng! Deng! Deng!" Each student pulled out a copy of the little red book, *The Thoughts of Chairman Mao*. In truth, it was the only book in the classroom and reading Mao's thoughts was the curriculum. With each chant of Deng's name, they thrust the book upward toward the ceiling.

His head filled with that moment. There he was, a hero to his peers, a hero of the Ancestor Land. Tears ran from his eyes, at first, he thought, from the image of his father's body being dragged off, leaving a trail of blood on the ground. But no, he told himself. It was because he loved China, more than Mother, more than Father, more than anything.

But that glory of love was short-lived.

It was only a few nights later when Deng was wakened in the middle of the night by his mother's sobs. This was nothing new since the execution of his father, but there was more to it now. Pleading was part of the sobbing, her voice in distress.

Deng hopped out of bed and wandered to her room to find a man standing over her bed, clad only in his underwear and gesturing wildly at her. She was curled up in a corner of the bed, the sheets wadded up before her.

"Mama?"

The word slipped out of his mouth. She saw him and said *No*, and the man turned to face him.

It was one of the soldiers who had dragged away his father's body.

"Get out of here," the man said, "bastard son of a traitor."

"I am no traitor," Deng said. "I am a hero of China."

The man cuffed him in the side of the head. Deng went down to the floor, hand clutched over his left ear. Then, swearing, the man kicked and slapped at him, cursing his father, his mother, his name, and it went on and on until he wasn't in the room any longer and awoke, bruised and sore, in his bed the next day, confused.

Why had the soldier treated him that way? Was his mother a traitor as well? He would never figure it out. All he would figure out was about love. No matter who or what it was for, it had gotten him nothing. All there was to be had was duty.

It was something this Zhang Jin needed to learn. But even if she did, he knew that he could never trust her. Like his mother.

"It was not groveling."

Deng was thrown from his thoughts by Li's voice. "What?"

"It was not groveling, Comrade General. I wanted to express concern for his welfare and build a bridge of trust we can exploit later. We did not get off to a great footing in our first meeting, especially due to the events that surrounded his departure, and this allowed me to extend an olive branch."

"If I knew it would come to this, we could have arranged for him not to make it out of the country. It is beneath our dignity." He turned to glare at Jin. "I don't understand how this could have gotten out of our control."

"It was fortunate for us that it did," Li said. "Remember the expression, 'Better the devils you know?' Chairman Coleman is a known quantity. I have read his papers, know how he thinks. And, of course, there are other advantages to gaining his favor that we all know." He looked at Zhang Jin, offering her a hopeful look. With her eyes still on the floor, she didn't see it. "If something had happened to him, it would have multiplied our problems."

"As long as the situation is back in control." Deng turned his icy glare from Zhang Jin to Li. "You both understand the roles you're going to play, don't you? Li, you are to keep the Chairman from doing anything rash and explaining away any actions on our side that might cause him alarm.

"Zhang Jin, were it up to me, you would be in permanent exile for the grief you brought us. But I also see the protocol division's wisdom in promoting you. You have great skills and useful information about the Chairman, so you are still valuable to us, at least for now."

"Of course, Comrade General," said Jin. "I am most grateful for your compliment. I am proud to be able to serve the people of China in this capacity."

"I expect the both of you to do your duty to the people with the utmost of your ability," Deng continued.

Li said, "Comrade General, my devotion to our cause is complete. We need to project calmness until the moment is right to strike. That moment is still some time away."

"Comrade Governor, that is for the Politburo to determine."

Apparently, my line about desperate measures did not sink in, Li thought. *Subtleties apparently don't work on Deng.*

General Deng stood, signaling the meeting was over. He turned and left Li's office, not bothering to shake hands.

When he was down the hall, Zhang Jin finally looked up. They exchanged a look, neither one liking what they saw on the other's face.

¥ $ €

Ben had barely hung up with Li when Peggy's voice again crackled over the intercom.

"Mr. Chairman, I have Secretary Steinway on the line."

"Perfect timing, George," Ben said, picking up. "I just got off the phone with Governor Li."

"Calling to offer a make good on your last trip to Beijing?" asked Steinway.

"As it turns out, yes," Ben said. "The reason I'm calling is to schedule the inevitable debriefing—"

"Let's call it a briefing," interrupted Steinway. "The President has asked me to organize one for him on your trip to China. Peggy has already confirmed one o'clock."

Ben glanced at the analog clock on his wall. Washington moved fast, and there was no tolerance for creature comforts such as hangovers or jet lag.

To Ben's non-answer, Steinway continued. "I know you've been through a lot in the last couple of days. And I know there are details that didn't come through the usual channels, so we all want to hear more. It will be you, me, the President, and Hector Lopez. We each have an interest in how this will play out."

Ben perked up at the mention of Hector's name. Lopez was the director of the Central Intelligence Agency. He found himself thinking that perhaps Bernadette was right when she searched his luggage. It was one of those spy games moviegoers thought was fiction but was uncomfortably close to reality. Also telling was who was not invited to the meeting—neither the Secretary of State nor the Secretary of Defense. The way Washington worked, those omissions ruled out the President thinking that this situation was to be handled through normal diplomacy or something that might lead to a more conventional—and deadly—confrontation.

He said, "Thank you, George. I hope that having Hector at the meeting will eliminate the need to for a normal debrief with some CIA staffer." One of the things that irritated him was the need to deal with low-level officials when there was so much else to do.

"Technically, that's up to Director Lopez. But I'm sure he'll see it your way. He knows your time is particularly precious."

"Supply and demand," Ben said. "Makes slaves of us all if we're not careful."

"Spoken like a true central banker," said Steinway. "See you at a quarter 'till."

"Always," said Ben. After he hung up, he paged Peggy and asked her to fire up the Nespresso machine, hoping one of those magical pods would have enough caffeine to get him through the next couple of hours.

¥ $ €

Ben stopped at the first of two security checkpoints three blocks away from the basement entrance to the West Wing of the White House. Even the car of the Chairman of the Federal Reserve had to be sniffed by dogs and scanned by the underground cameras at the entrance to make sure there were no bombs attached. The risk was not from the Chairman or his drivers, but that someone had attached something to the car along the way.

Ben's limousine had been part of a motorcade with two side vehicles, an SUV in front and one in back. They broke off as soon as he entered the security perimeter. His driver pulled up at the awning that reached out from the entrance of the basement entrance to the edge of West Executive Avenue. The presidential seal was affixed to the end of the awning. Ben waited, marshaling his thoughts as the guard at the desk, the well-hidden metal detectors, and the cameras did their jobs. Like everyone else, he had to lock his cell phone in a bank of cubbyholes that resembled the old-fashioned mailboxes in a rural post office.

When the guard waved him on, he ducked quickly to the left and passed an elevator to head for the stairs up to the main floor where the Oval Office was located. Ben was a habitual user of stairs and on some days the climb was the only exercise he got. Then a right down to the corner where the chief of staff's office was located, a left past the Roosevelt Room and on to the official entrance to the Oval. Finally, he reached the office of the President's secretary, through which meeting attendees entered.

Ben joined Secretary Steinway and they stopped to wait their turn. He thought it odd that Hector Lopez wasn't there yet. There was no rush at this point. While protocol said it was inexcusable to be late for a meeting with the President, the President could take his time if he needed it. Even Cabinet members and Fed Chairman had to wait their turn. As the saying went, you might wait on the boss, but the boss won't wait on you.

After two minutes of the usual chit chat, Alice, the President's personal secretary, said the magic words. "The President will see you now."

The door to the Oval Office opened to reveal that Lopez was already with the President. *A private meeting before the general meeting?* Ben thought. *That's odd.* This was a matter of etiquette and a signal to be closely watched. When supposed equals go to a group meeting with the President, the appearance that some were more equal than others was disconcerting. But Lopez was a professional, a man who'd paid his dues and moved up through the ranks of the Agency, so Ben was not too worried. Still, it was not as if the CIA never played interagency politics.

The President interrupted his reverie with a warm handshake, putting his arm on Ben's uninjured shoulder and saying, "How are you, Ben?" His brow furrowed in deep concern.

"I'm fine, Mr. President. It was just a flesh wound."

The President led Ben to the standard seat of honor. Presidents may have many different personalities, but they always arrange the Oval Office the same way. It was built that way. The President sits in a chair in front of the fireplace, facing the Resolute desk. Two couches flank the President's chair with the person intended to lead the briefing on the couch to the immediate left of the President. The other attendees sit on the opposite couch where they can most easily observe the briefing and participate as necessary.

"You've had quite a trip," said the President. "We've all read the details, but I'd love to hear them from you personally."

Ben went into his story, describing the level of violence he saw, the worry that Li had projected, and a bit of an apology. "I know it is a breach of protocol and security to be flown home on a military jet from a foreign power, much less a hostile power. But the Chinese wanted me out of there as quickly as possible. I wasn't in the mood to stick around, either. I was told that our ambassador had been notified in advance."

"After events like these, nobody is going to question that," said the President. "But aside from the obvious, why would the Chinese want you gone so quickly?"

"Sir, the Chinese are far more desperate than I ever imagined," Ben said. "This was not a run on one bank. This was a run on all the banks I saw in that neighborhood. I've been trying to find news about it, which is hopeless, but I'm assuming if this was happening in Beijing, the scene was repeated throughout the country."

"So what made this unique? What possessed you to get out of the car for this?"

Ben ignored the latter half of the question. "When you look at situations such as the Greek crisis, people lined up at ATMs in an orderly fashion. This was pushing and shoving to be the one to the ATM first and pounding on the doors of the banks. These people have no confidence in the most fundamental part of the economy—the money.

"This was not happening in some remote industrial city. This was Beijing. It's the place that is pampered by the state and always given first priority. If the public is worried there, they are even more worried elsewhere in the country. Also, shows of force only happen in Beijing in extreme circumstances because everyone knows it when it happens. A police action somewhere in Szechuan province is like a tree falling in a forest when nobody is there to hear it. All eleven million residents of Beijing, including the Central Committee and Politburo, have had this rubbed in their faces. These are increasingly desperate men.

"Governor Li said something interesting to me on the phone. 'Most politicians think desperate times require desperate measures. We central bankers know that desperate times require calming measures.'

"I don't think the political leadership is going to let Li have the time he needs to play their cards in the best way. In the long run, this is an advantage for us. In the short run, I am worried about things getting out of hand. I think we have a need to prepare soon."

The President said, "When you say 'desperate,' what exactly are you talking about?"

"Well, we know two things about the Chinese leadership. First, they are still marching toward global supremacy under the China 2049 program. They are particularly driven due to the humiliation Trump inflicted on Xi during the trade war. Second, we know that hubris is almost an infectious disease in anyone who occupies the seat of power in China. Emperors thought of themselves as ruling the Middle Kingdom for a reason. They saw China as surrounded by vassal states. Overreach was a common practice."

"What will all this lead to?" the President asked.

"Mr. President, Churchill said watching the Soviet Union was like watching a riddle wrapped in a mystery inside an enigma. China is no different. I have learned two things from Li. He stressed the importance of the people of China coming to treasure the yuan as much as they treasure gold. See, the dollar is backed by the full faith and credit of the United States government. However, nobody has full faith in the government of Beijing. That is why they have been accumulating so much gold over the last ten or fifteen years. I think they are moving toward a gold-backed currency."

"You've got to be joking," said the President. "Nobody's on the gold standard now. It's been decades since it's been used."

"And the last time it was put into play," said Steinway, "was what?

Churchill, post-World War One? And when he did, it was such a catastrophe that it set his career back by a decade."

"And won't that limit what they can do with their currency?" the President said.

"Sir, that is exactly the point of gold."

"Ben, I don't get your meaning."

"People choose gold because it limits the government's ability to do something with their currency. Don't ever quote me on this, sir, but money is the biggest and oldest Ponzi scheme on Earth." Ben could see the look of shock and disapproval on the President's face. Steinway, by contrast, seemed to grasp where Ben was headed.

"Here's how it works, Mr. President. You want to spend money on some government program. There aren't enough tax receipts to cover the cost. So you ask George to issue some debt and he calls me up and says, 'How'd you like to buy some bonds?'

"Now, in reality, it doesn't happen like that. It goes through banks and other intermediaries, but that is the essence. In the end George prints a piece of paper, a government bond, and swaps it with me for another piece of paper we call money. The Treasury is then free to spend that money on the government program."

"But isn't something backing that money?" asked the President.

"Yes. The government bond."

"The one that Steinway printed?"

"That's right."

"So what stands behind the government bond?"

"It's called the full faith and credit of the United States. A better name would be the unlimited taxing power of the government."

The President pondered this. "You mean the only thing that stands behind money is the ability of the government to take it back from the people who hold it through taxation?"

"Yes, but it never quite comes to that. There is something else—the willingness of someone to accept the money in return for goods and services. It started with the government. It had the money and gave it to someone to get what it wanted. That person took the money because they knew they could turn around and give it to someone else in return for something they wanted. And that person knew they could spend it as well. That's the Ponzi scheme. The real value of money is the ability to buy things with it."

The President took it all in. "That's how we got through the pandemic in the early 2020s. We issued bonds, got money, and then handed it out to people in stimulus checks."

Ben nodded. "And we did that year after year until what happened?"

"Inflation," said the President.

"Yes. But what happened psychologically was that people came to distrust the value of the money in terms of its ability to pass it off to someone else. They demanded more and more money for each thing they sold. Confidence began to drop. And those bonds that the Treasury were issuing also began to be questioned. People demanded higher and higher interest rates on the bonds. Finally, the Fed and the government had to call a stop. It ended with a painful recession, but that was necessary to preserve confidence in the dollar. This has happened all through history, all the way back to the Ming Dynasty in China. Remember, the Chinese are credited with the invention of paper money."

"And all those excesses let the Chinese gain on us," the President said. "Because they didn't print as fast as we did."

"Until recently," Ben said. "The current Chinese regime is impatient and started going too fast. They wanted to push themselves into the global leadership position well before their 2049 target date. They revved up their money machine to do it. They pushed their banking system—particularly the state-owned banks, which are a big part of their money operation—to lend freely to expand the economy. Pushing out all that money haphazardly meant a lot of the loans went bad. At first the government just printed more money, but then the public figured out the game. That is how their bank run started."

"Where does gold come into the picture?" asked Steinway.

"The Treasury and the Fed can print money freely. So can the People's Bank of China and the Chinese government. It's just too easy. Governments do it to excess. Financial crises happen, and the confidence in the money collapses.

"The only way to restore confidence is to have money become

something the government can't fiddle with. From the beginning of human history that has been some form of precious metal—often silver, but usually gold.

"This goes right back to your initial point—what government would use gold when it would limit what they can do with their money? They go to gold because they have so abused paper money that the people lose confidence. They want something that the government can't monkey around with."

"If they do this," Steinway said, "if they're successful at it, what does that mean for us?"

Ben sat back in his chair. "Our discussion was always in terms of a conflict between our two countries. This means that accumulating the gold is not just to gain the confidence of the Chinese people but is intended as a potential weapon to be used against us. Make no mistake, Li is totally on board with making China the world's only superpower. But he thinks of it as the superpower in a prosperous world. Some of his colleagues think of China as a superpower dominating impoverished vassal states."

"So how would they use it as a weapon?" asked the President.

"We both have the same problem," Ben said, "it is just a matter of degree. If the world somehow gains confidence in the Chinese yuan, then they may go to it as the world's currency of choice. That gain is at the expense of the dollar. Now all those dollars out there in the world are backed by our bonds. If folks don't want our dollars, then they won't buy our bonds, and Steinway is shit out of luck trying to sell them.

"The U.S. government then has a financial crisis on its hands while the Chinese have smooth sailing. They are accumulating gold to make their play at turning the yuan into the world's preferred currency."

"Then they run the Ponzi scheme and we don't?"

"Precisely."

"Gold is all about confidence then," said Steinway.

"Exactly. When people stop trusting government with doing the right thing, they will only have confidence in something the government can't manipulate."

"For better or worse," said the President.

"And that," said Ben, "depends on our response to this situation."

¥ $ €

By the time 5 p.m. rolled around, Ben was exhausted. Since the meeting with POTUS, he had either been on the phone with Steinway or Lopez or had his nose in Microsoft Word and Google. On top of all this, the last dregs of jet lag were catching up with him. So a little after five he told Peggy he was calling it a day and told her not to stay too late.

On the drive home he tried to do what he did best: synthesize information. But his physical and emotional exhaustion had pushed him to his limit, and it was all he could do to keep the names Li and Lopez separate. A few minutes into the drive he gave up and told the car to play what was in the CD player, and he let the original Broadway cast of Meredith Wilson's *The Music Man* escort him home.

When he finally arrived, he was happy to see Bernadette waiting for him in the kitchen with two jiggers of his favorite bourbon. She sat on the granite countertop inside of her big robe from the upstairs bathroom, sipping on her own measure. A serious look on her face, she picked up one of the jiggers and held it out to him. As he closed in to take it from her, she moved her hand back until he was right against her.

"Does this mean I'm forgiven?" he asked as she relinquished the drink.

"I should kill you, Ben Coleman, for the hell you put me through these last few days."

He sipped the bourbon. "I think I've already expressed my regret and remorse over my actions."

"Hector Lopez sent someone to the door to talk to me. Did he tell you that? They'd gotten word about the Beijing riot from one of their sources, and when you weren't on your flight, they did the math. 'Mrs. Coleman, we're adding up two plus two here, and we're praying that it doesn't add up to four.'"

"Darling, I am really, truly sorry."

"That's not enough. I'm going to have to kill you."

"You'll never get away with it. I have too many friends in high places."

"I'll find a way to make it happen." She finished her drink.

He finished his first drink, put the glass down, and put his hand inside her robe. "And how to you propose to do that?"

"I am most skilled in the ways of *la petite mort*."

"I'm terrified."

"You should be."

They kissed deeply. He could taste the bourbon on her lips. He picked up the second glass and threw it back. Bernadette took the glass out of Ben's hand and put it aside. Then she slid down from the countertop and led him up the stairs.

¥ $ €

Sometime in the middle of the night, Ben woke to find Bernadette no longer asleep on his shoulder. He reached over toward her pillow, feeling for her, but she was not there. He sat up, propping himself on his elbows. She was sitting next to him, cross-legged.

"You okay?" he said.

"Wondering how much I have to worry about."

He didn't speak. Many responses went through his head, *You don't have a thing to worry about. Shit, not this again. Honey, I thought we settled that. Dearest, you're worrying for nothing.* None of those seemed appropriate. Then it came to him.

"For what it's worth, my biggest worry was that I'd never see you again."

"Even though you were spooning?"

"Yes, and it was very romantic." Pausing to reel in his sarcasm. "Cooking grease. Fish scales and guts. The biggest damn carp head I've ever seen. Oh, and my own puke. I don't know if she threw up or not."

Bernadette shifted closer to him. "Show me."

"Show you what?"

"How you held Ling Ling."

"Dammit, honey, Ling Ling is a name for a panda, not a government worker drone."

"Getting a bit defensive, are we?"

Ben closed his eyes and pushed himself to be more awake. "Okay.

Lie down."

Bernadette complied, putting her back to him.

"Turn around," Ben said.

"She was facing you," she said, turning. "You said you were spooning."

"We were face-to-face. But not really."

"Face-to-face isn't spooning. What else are you lying about?"

Ben held his tongue. In the dark, not being able to read her face, using her accent to sound curt and businesslike, he couldn't read her in this moment. It felt like an interrogation.

"Curl up. Fetal position."

Bernadette drew her knees up and bent her back.

"Now clasp your hands together like you're holding a cell phone and that you'll die if you lose it."

After waiting for a moment, he slid down next to face her, one arm tucked under his head, the other one around her upper arm and back.

"This is what it was like?" Bernadette said.

"Two differences," Ben said. "We both had clothes on. And she was trembling so hard I thought the dumpster would rattle."

They laid like that for a while, Ben unsure if she had gone to sleep or not, wondering where she was going with all of this. Then, as his eyelids were again starting to get heavy, she stretched out and pushed against him.

"So. How many times have you been with Ling Ling?"

He sat up. "Look," he said, "if we're going to keep going over this, at least call her by her name." He stopped, drew a slow breath, and eased back down in the bed. "Lover, I have never been with Zhang Jin, not in the way you're worried about. Except for not spooning in the dumpster, it has always been proper and businesslike. I hope you're not jealous because at no point has our relationship ever been a thing."

Bernadette gave a long sigh. "I didn't mean it that way. What I meant was, how many times has she been your minder?"

An odd question for now, Ben thought. "I don't know. I don't think I've ever thought about it. Eight or nine times. Whenever I've gone there in the last seven years or so."

"Since we've been married."

"I guess."

"Ever bump into her on one of your visits to Hong Kong?"

Now Ben was fully awake. "Funny you should mention that. About three years ago I was there staying at the Four Seasons. I was walking through one of those high-end indoor malls that connect all the buildings in Central and there she is, three or four shopping bags in her hand. Versace, Gucci, that kind of stuff. Like many Chinese women, she was there on a long weekend shopping spree."

He felt her muscles tighten under his arm. She said, "Did she say anything? You say anything?"

"Oh, God. Not this jealousy stuff again."

She turned and sat up. "No, Ben. This is strictly professional, like you say the relationship was."

"I thought we took care of this. You still don't believe me about Zhang Jin?"

She leaned down toward him, so close he could feel the warmth of her face. "No, Ben, I do believe you. I also believe that you are hopelessly naïve. So answer my question. Did either of you say anything?"

"Um." Trying to replay the scene in his mind. "She said something about drinks later at the hotel."

"Did you?"

"No, sweetheart. I can tell a pickup line when I hear one. It's not like I was a monk before I met you. Besides, I wasn't going to—I mean, not when I have you to come home to."

"How did she know the hotel?"

"Are you kidding? Everyone in that part of the world knows—"

"How did she know *you* were staying there?"

"Hell, I don't know. It was a few hundred yards away, I was walking—"

"Ben." Her voice urgent now. "There are half a dozen hotels within walking distance through those malls."

"I don't understand."

"Dearest, you are the most important thing in my life. But before you became Fed Chairman you were not the most important thing in the life of Chinese State Security. You wouldn't have been in the top hundred or even the top thousand."

"You sure know how to deflate a guy's ego."

"My poor, clueless baby. The reason I want to know what was said between the two of you is to find out whether I ever came up in any of your conversations."

"You did," Ben said. "And she knows how important you are to me, and why she didn't have a chance with me. In fact, she told me on more than one occasion how much she'd like to meet you."

He could feel her nodding as she settled back down on his chest. "That's what I thought. You see, your friend Jin isn't there to get information on you. She is there to get information on me."

CHAPTER THREE

BERNADETTE MURPHY WAS THE BEST THING THAT HAD EVER happened to him.

That was not only Ben's opinion. It was that of his children and all his friends as well. His first wife had died of cancer at thirty-seven, leaving him with four children aged eleven to sixteen. Each was gifted in their own individual and wonderful way and, due to the heartache experienced by their mother's death, wise beyond their years.

Still, the whole family had been devastated. He had stitched things together as best he could. There was plenty of money so household help was not an issue. Nor were therapists. But the experience had taught Ben there were some things money could not buy. Despite the relentless work schedule, he ensured that he saw his children grow up. He rarely missed an event that his children deemed important, be it karate class or writing letters to the Tooth Fairy to explain a lost tooth and ensure the payout. When the youngest left for college Ben Coleman was alone. Most empty nesters have each other, but single parents do not.

Twice a week he took the train north to New Haven to teach classes at Yale. The other three days he took the train south to see clients in New York. Then came an offer of a new gig—to do what he was doing from Connecticut, but in London, England. It was a combination of a visiting professorship at the London School of Economics and some consulting in the City, mostly for the London offices of his current client base. The children would not hear his protests about wanting to be near them. They knew he needed a change of scenery and frankly, they needed to get on with their lives in college.

Ben threw himself into his new life. The apartment in Westminster gave easy access to everything including a real life, something single parenthood had denied him. It was easy. His reputation had preceded him, so the invitations poured in.

One night in early October he went to a cocktail party at the behest of Hank Borstead, an odd duck colleague at LSE who was an American expat like himself. A woman standing at the bar captivated him with her stunning red hair, her self-assured manner, and the way her eyes lit up when she listened to someone talk, even about the most mundane of subjects. She was smiling politely at the person speaking to her and holding what looked like a gin and tonic. She was wearing a black wrap dress with three-quarter-length sleeves and nude heels. Her porcelain skin highlighted her red hair and beautiful green eyes. Ben looked away quickly, worried that he had been caught staring. It had been a quarter century since he had been in the dating game, and his lack of practice was paralyzing.

As if reading his mind, the hostess, Edith Spensley, came right over and pushed a glass of bourbon into his hand. She was a slight woman who typically wore earth tones and tended to keep her hair piled up on top of her head. Ben's first impression of her had been that she was a typical British prig, stuffy with no sense of humor. But it didn't take long for the ever-present twinkle in her eye to win him over, as he realized there was likely more to her and her stuffed-shirt husband, Graham, than met the eye.

"Ben," she said. "So good of you to come."

"I wouldn't have missed it for the world. Have I ever turned you down? You and Graham are the world's best, and your place is stunning."

"How good of you to say. Ben, let me be direct. I couldn't help but notice your gaze."

Ben's face reddened. He never thought he was being obvious. As he would learn four years later when Graham and Edith visited America and finally came clean, he hadn't been obvious and Edith wasn't a mind reader. It was a set up. Edith was very good at all things social. Placing her arm around his elbow as if she were his escort, she half-guided and half-dragged him across the floor whispering, "Do let me introduce you."

In a heartbeat he was standing before the redhead and was being introduced. "Bernadette, my dear, I would like to introduce you to a wonderful American friend of ours. Ben Coleman, Bernadette Murphy."

For a moment Bernadette appeared to feel as awkward as Ben did. "Welcome to London, Mr. Coleman. Any friend of Edith must be a man of distinction."

"It is Edith and Graham who have the distinction. They invite me along as their way of promoting trans-Atlantic relations."

An odd look appeared ever so briefly in Edith's eyes, but ever the gracious hostess, she had her escape planned. "You two are full of flattery," she said. "And flattery will get you everywhere. So before you feel the need to pay me even more compliments, let me assure that you both will be invited back. But now I must attend to my other guests." It was as skilled an exit as Ben had seen, with the right touch of disarming humor to leave the two guests alone together before either could protest.

Realizing what happened, Ben decided that it was his responsibility to take up the slack. "How long have you known the Spensleys?" It seemed safe enough.

"Believe it or not, since boarding school. Edith and I were on the field hockey team together. It seems like a lifetime ago. I suppose it has been."

Ben caught himself staring. Her eyes were green and gorgeous, and contrasted sharply with her red hair. Bernadette's accent was also as intriguing as she was; Ben could not quite decide whether it was English or American or whether she was deliberately mixing the two. He moved to cover his stare, "And where did that intervening lifetime take you?"

"Oh, from one thing to another. Turns out I am good at organizing. I am a wedding planner."

"Nothing like the movie, I assume."

"Movies are made to be entertaining," she said. "I'm afraid most of what I do is rather tedious. Lining up this and that. Making sure that the bride and her mother are happy. Making sure Dad is not put off by the cost. Tedious, but necessary. So many people have no idea how to pull it off. And what do you do, Mr. Coleman?"

"Please, call me Ben." He suspected that Ms. Murphy was down-playing her role and no doubt arranged the weddings of Britain's many lords and ladies. He chose to be modest as well. "I'm about as dull and tedious as one can get. I'm an economist. I suppose that beats being a lawyer, at least in America where we have far too many of them. But just barely."

"From what I read in the papers, economists are quite necessary given the state of things. Like wedding planners, the world wouldn't get on without them."

He raised his glass. "Here's to us, then. Bearing the world's tedium so others don't have to."

She laughed, showing perfect white teeth, and clinked her gin and tonic against his bourbon. Then the small talk commenced, covering what anyone listening would have considered a conversation between two good friends, and continued for another twenty minutes. Ben became more intrigued with each passing moment.

It was Bernadette who ended it. "I'm sorry to cut the evening short, Mr. Coleman, but I have four florists to interview in the morning. As I said, quite tedious. And I must review their price lists before I go in. When one's floral bill is ten thousand pounds it is quite amazing how much bargaining power the buyer can have."

"Might I walk you to your door?" Ben thought this was the right way of saying it, but a flash of insecurity welled up inside of him. *I'm so damn out of practice at this.*

"Why, yes. It's just a few blocks. Sadly, here in London a woman can't be too careful."

As things turned out, *walk you to your door* was exactly the right phrase, even though Ben found himself wishing for more. The chatter continued on the walk home, but once there it was, "Thank you so much, Ben. It was a pleasure to make your acquaintance. I expect that we will be seeing each other at one of Edith and Graham's famous dinner parties." That was followed by a quick peck on his cheek and then a beeline past the bellman and through the door.

He spent the rest of the night replaying the episode, wondering where he had gone wrong. He had put a lot of effort in making sure he looked good and was pleased with his choice of a light blue checked shirt that was now crumpled on the floor of his closet. He never really needed to worry about any of this when Ellen was alive. *Maybe I'm out of practice*, he thought as he closed his laptop and leaned to turn off his bedside lamp. He had his doubts that the next dinner party would lead to any different result.

He could not have been more wrong.

Four days later Bernadette called him, having gotten his number from Edith. It caught him completely off guard when he answered the phone to hear Bernadette's voice on the other end. "I know this is quite forward, but I need a favor. Edith said you wouldn't mind."

His heart sank. "Of course." Then trying to sound both humorous and gallant at the same time, "How might I help the damsel in distress?" He smiled, pleased with his flirtatious response. The mysterious Bernadette had been on his mind ever since she planted the kiss on his cheek four days earlier.

"Would you accompany me to the reception at the Saudi Embassy tomorrow? I am trying to get the contract for the wedding of the ambassador's niece. His brother will be there, and the ambassador was very impressed with the arrangements I made for a friend. I'm calling you because, well, it is not such a good idea for women to go to these things unaccompanied."

I'm being used, Ben thought. *For business, no less.* But she was a damsel in distress, and one that he was quite interested in. "It would be my honor to accompany you," he said. They discussed details for a few more minutes, then ended the conversation.

Pacing through his apartment, Ben found himself walking with an unexpected spring in his step. Business or not, he was getting a second chance to see Bernadette—at her request, no less. He put the phone back into his shirt pocket and let out a long sigh.

The reception itself had been quite boring. Ben was used to forced conversation and making a martini last for several hours, but he now understood why Bernadette had described her job as tedious. It had been ninety minutes of standing and making small talk with strangers. Bernadette had left his side exactly twice, to go to the ladies' room she had said. Twice in ninety minutes. He filed that fact away for future use. But being around her made the tedium bearable, so he was able to wait patiently during her absences. However, as they got into the cab on the way home, Ben was faced with what he considered another disappointment.

"Let me drop you off at your place. I have to go back to the office. I think that I may have landed the contract and I really should start working on it straight away. Thank you so much for accompanying me, I really appreciate it." His thanks amounted to a brief kiss on the lips as Bernadette got out of the car.

Getting closer, was all he could think.

Then a reprieve. Bernadette turned back to the open window of the cab and said, "We will do this again. I promise. But you pick the event. Please, no embassy parties. I am tied up this weekend, but perhaps the one after?" She smiled genuinely and all of a sudden Ben felt like he was sixteen all over again.

This woman was an enigma, keeping him where it seemed she wanted him, and he obliged. He wanted to get to know her and was willing to do it on her terms. He stole one last look at her as the car pulled away and sighed as he loosened the tie he had bought with help from his support network.

That feeling lasted until he got to the London School of Economics the next morning. Hank Borstead poked his head in the door to his office. Ben had met Borstead during his brief stint in government years before. He had retired from the CIA two years before and now lectured at LSE on diplomacy—albeit the kind that never made the papers. Ben and Hank were two of six Americans who taught there at the time, a small enough clique that a natural and much-needed bonding had occurred over homesickness, the lack of traditional American food, what passed for football in England, and the absence of the Thanksgiving holiday.

Borstead hovered in the doorway. The man wore pleated pants and insisted on loafers with tassels on them in varying shades of black. Today a blue blazer complemented the ensemble, if one could call it that. He shoved his glasses up on to the top of his head and stepped inside Ben's office, closing the door behind him.

"Everything okay?" Ben said.

"I am fine," said Hank. "I was wondering about you."

He shrugged. "Never better."

Hank parked himself on Ben's couch. "Never better or *never better*?"

Ben studied the man. "Did I miss something here?"

"Trying to ascertain how *never better* you actually are. As in, have you been in successful pursuit of some horizontal refreshment?"

Laughing, Ben said, "If I was, I'd say you'd have to mind your—" Then he stopped. "All right, what's this all about?"

Hank slid his glasses back down onto the bridge of his nose. "Rumor mill around here says you were recently seen in the company of a red-headed bombshell."

Now Ben was baffled, wondering who might have been at the Saudi Embassy who was part of the rumor mill here.

"Was this a first date?" Hank asked.

"I'm not sure if it was even that," Ben said. "I met her at a party a couple of weeks ago, and she asked me to accompany her to a social function. Who wants to know?"

Hank said nothing, but a smile grew on his lips, revealing a gap between his two front teeth.

"What the hell," Ben said. "You guys have a bang pool on me or something? How many dates it's going to take me to score?"

"I didn't say anything."

"You're a bunch of incorrigible bastards," Ben said, laughing. "I don't even know where I stand with this woman. She puts me back in high school where I was even more awkward with women. So what do I do? Ask a friend to ask her if she likes me? Send her a note, 'Check one, yes or no.'"

"I never had that problem," Hank said. "I played varsity basketball. Just wanted to check in on you. Rumor mill says she's a real looker."

"She's a wedding planner," Ben said.

"Then you really are screwed." Hank rose from the couch and opened the door. "Well, I've been out of The Company for too long. My interrogation skills have failed me. Check you later."

"Who sent you?" Ben gave him a mocking look.

"I still have my cyanide tooth. You ask me again, I'll have to bite down on it." He stepped outside the door, and then popped his head back in. "I've got fifty pounds on third date. Don't let me down, buddy."

Ben grabbed a pencil from his desk, throwing it at him as he ducked down the hall.

That's the thing with academia, no matter where you are, he thought. *It's such a damn small town.*

¥ $ €

After finishing up classes and his office hours, Ben decided to walk to his apartment, the closing of the day being suitably cool and breezy for a brisk walk. His mind raced with thoughts about Bernadette's words. *Your choice.* He wanted that to entail something he thought she might enjoy, yet he thought it appropriate to offer up something that told her something about himself.

He bounced several ideas around in his head as he walked, and when he passed a kiosk selling tickets to West End theater productions, a playbill for one leapt out at him. He considered it as he walked and realized that it was perfect.

He turned to go back to the kiosk and ran into a man his height who was close behind him.

"Excuse me," Ben said, trying to step around him.

The man replied with a strong hand on his shoulder. "No, excuse me." The hand turned Ben away from the kiosk, back the way he had been going.

On impulse, Ben caught the man by the upper arm. Beneath the man's coat, his arm felt like it was made of steel cords.

"Listen—"

"No. You listen." The man's grip tightened. "Keep going."

Ben would marvel later how these threats sounded so polite with a British accent. But in the moment, it seemed so absurd. Walking down a London street, surrounded by passersby, being roughed up by a well-dressed larrikin.

He dropped his hand down, elbow into the crook of the man's arm to try and break his grip, but the man shouldered him and pushed with his free hand. Ben couldn't help but turn and take a stumbling step away from the kiosk. He drew a breath, thinking a shout for help was in order, but the man pressed up against his back and something hard pushed into his side. Ben didn't have to look to know what it was.

"You got balls," Ben said. "My wallet's in the upper left pocket of my coat."

"We'll have a look in a bit," the man said. "Keep walking, Mr. Coleman."

Now Ben felt his own balls tighten. This guy knew his name and that changed the relationship completely. "Look," he said, "you want my wallet, I'll give it to you. Can't say it's worth your while, but—"

"Quiet."

Ben complied and they walked, a block, then another half of a block, where the man pushed his shoulder with his free hand and steered him into a gyro shop. The place was small and untidy and smelled heavily of grease and Tabasco sauce. Two small tables with matching wire chairs sat empty while a sallow-looking man behind the counter looked up from his copy of *News of the World*.

Ben's escort said, "Evening. Are you still out of your famous almond baklava?"

"Sorry. Won't have it until Thursday."

"We'll wait. Table for two, then?"

The counterman reached down and tossed a can of Coca-Cola to the escort, and he caught it quick as lightning with his free hand. Then the counterman opened the door and the escort encouraged Ben to start walking again, through a disheveled kitchen and around the corner to a set of stairs that led down, illuminated by a naked incandescent bulb.

"After you," said the escort.

Ben fought back his panic and descended, the escort taking him past boxes of restaurant supplies that looked like they'd never been opened, then a cramped looking restroom, and into a short hall. The escort stopped at the first door on the right, opened it, and gave Ben a gentle nudge.

He was surprised to see the room outfitted with a concrete floor, a metal table, and three metal chairs, two on one side, one on the other. The escort motioned to the lone chair and Ben sat, seeing a mirror that took up a good chunk of the wall he was facing. His stomach rolled. He didn't have to do any hard thinking to realize where he was.

The escort placed the can of Coke down in front of Ben, then slipped the small pistol into a shoulder holster. "Back in a flash," he said, and stepped out. There was a metallic click from the door after it closed.

Ben stared at the can of soda as it sweated. The room smelled musty and was lit by a fluorescent panel in the ceiling. The walls were concrete, the door was metal. He put his hands between his legs and clasped them to keep them from shaking. He kept staring at the Coke can, thinking how much comfort it would bring him, but having seen plenty of television police procedurals, he refused to touch it.

The door clicked again and a half-second later the escort returned in the company of a shorter, jowly man who carried a sheaf of file folders under his arm.

"How are we doing this evening?" The jowly man sounded cheerful, like he was about to take his dinner order.

"We're wondering what in the hell we are doing here," Ben said.

The jowly man took a chair opposite Ben and plunked the folders down between them. The escort continued to stand.

"My name is Spivey." The jowly man offered his hand. Ben just stared back. "And you've met my associate, Kellen." He motioned at the can. "Please, have a drink. It's meager, but we are trying to be hospitable."

"I'll keep my fingerprints and DNA to myself, thank you," Ben said.

Kellen didn't say anything, but crossed his arms, keeping his eye on Ben.

"We have them already," Spivey said, "but no matter." He opened the top folder. "Benjamin Augustus Coleman. Forty-seven years of age, currently an instructor at the London School of Economics."

"Is that really my middle name?" said Ben. Deep in his heart he knew he shouldn't be so sarcastic, but he couldn't help himself.

"Simply trying to get a feel for your situation," Spivey said.

"Well from my point of view, it sucks," Ben said. "Look, this isn't a robbery. It's obviously not a kidnapping. Why don't you ask what you need with the third most boring person in the world so I can get back to the ticket kiosk?"

Spivey exchanged a look with Kellen. "Red Ninja?"

"No," said Ben. "The revival of *The Music Man*."

"I'm not talking about a West End musical," said Spivey. "I'm asking what it means to you."

"Red Ninja?" Ben said. "Isn't that a Schwarzenegger movie? Jackie Chan, maybe?"

"This use of humor is going to make your evening very long if you persist."

"Fine," Ben said. "My apologies. But could you tell me what this is all about? If I could get a little context here .... "

Spivey drummed his fingers on the tabletop, then reached over and closed the folder, sliding it to his left. "Let's say it was a matter of our national security and leave it at that. I'm sure you understand."

"I'm free to go, then?"

"Not quite." Opening another folder now. "While we have you here, I need to ask you if you know this woman." He slapped an eight by ten glossy on the desk and turned it toward Ben.

It was a picture of Bernadette. Not a good one either. The colors were murky, and the image was hazy, like it had come off a driver's license.

Ben's stomach lurched.

"Before you say anything else .... " Spivey laid down another photograph. Ben holding the taxi door open for Bernadette, the night of the embassy reception. Ben getting into the taxi with her. And then another, the taxi at the Saudi Embassy, him climbing out, holding the door for her, walking to the doors, his hand on the small of her back.

"What the hell?"

"Care to comment, Mr. Coleman?"

"She's just a woman I met at a party some friends of mine were hosting."

"Graham and Edith Spensley, yes," said Spivey.

"Am I in trouble because she's in trouble? I had no idea. Like I said, she's—"

"Just a woman?" Spivey slapped down another photo, this one of Bernadette kissing him as she got out of the cab.

"Okay, look." Staring at the picture. "We just met. Look in your file, I'm a widower, I assumed she was single." He looked at them. "Wait a minute. Is this a shakedown? If it is, you should know a couple of things. We haven't done anything yet, and if we had, we're consenting adults. And I don't do blackmail. So as far as I'm concerned, you can take your two-way mirror and the rest of this James Bond shit of yours and—"

Ben dropped his eyes to the picture again. A little on the grainy side, obviously taken with a telephoto lens, but still detailed. The wind had caught Bernadette's hair as she kissed him and made it look like—

For a moment, all he could see was her hair, tossed in the wind, the lovely red hair.

"This isn't unrelated," Ben said, "is it? Red Ninja. That's Bernadette. Or something she's tied up with."

Spivey and Kellen both stared blankly back at him.

Now the room started to swim around Ben. There was fear and anger and adrenaline and the overwhelming need to know what was going on.

Ben stood. Kellen took a step toward the table, stopping next to Spivey.

"All right, gentlemen, you're going to tell me what the hell this is all about, and you're going to do it right now. You might be pussyfooting around because of British national security, but my personal security is at stake, and I want to know what kind of danger I've put myself in by letting this woman kiss me on the cheek."

Spivey and Kellen exchanged another of their enigmatic looks. Then Spivey gathered up the photos, put them back in their folder, and stacked all the folders together, bumping them on the tabletop to square them.

"Well," Ben said.

"If you will give us a moment," Spivey said, standing, "we will see if we can accommodate you." Kellen opened the door and the two of them walked out.

It seemed like he was in the room forever. He paced and walked over to the mirror and cupped his hands around it, trying to peer through to the other side. When he turned back, that damn Coke was still sitting there on the table in a puddle of its own perspiration. He wondered if it had been doctored with something, or if it really was their meager attempt at hospitality.

After an eternity the door clicked. Ben balled his hands into fists, wanting to build his outrage back. The door opened a bit, and he could see Spivey in front and Kellen in back, talking to someone.

A familiar voice with an American accent said, "There's no danger, I swear. I'll handle it. Wait outside the door if you're worried."

Ben steeled himself, ready for anything. But he wasn't ready to see Hank Borstead walk in the door.

"Hi, Ben," he said in his affable manner.

"Hank? Is this some kind of joke?" He pointed at the mirror. "You got the rest of the faculty watching through the mirror?"

"It's no joke," Hank said. "Sit?"

"I'll stand."

"Fair enough. So will I. You no doubt have a lot of questions."

"Yes," Ben said. "Let's start with why you're the one who's going to solve my problems."

"You don't have any problems. Well, maybe one. But it's minor. As to what I'm doing here, I'm going to solve that problem for you."

"You? How?"

"Ben, there's a special relationship that exists between Great Britain and the United States, and that often extends to intelligence. Let's say that I'm here to help as a spook."

"You're retired."

"You never entirely retire from the CIA," Hank said. "Now if you'll allow me." He sat, gestured at the can on the table. "You going to drink that?" When Ben shook his head, he picked it up, cracked it open, and took a long sip. "That's better. Are you sure you don't want to sit?"

"I'm good."

Hank nodded. "Ben, the gentleman who escorted you here and his colleague are both MI6. You'd best forget you met them. The reason you were invited here—"

"Invited?" Ben said, cutting him off. "Dragged off the street like a criminal. Why didn't they ask me in?"

"In our business, inviting people to come in usually means they'll take a runner before accepting the invitation. It might not seem like it, but this was for the best.

"As for the reason you are here, it is because you were seen at the Saudi Embassy with someone we call the Red Ninja."

"So we're back to that now. Guilt by association? Tell me, which of the many guests there was your Red Ninja? Did I make the mistake of talking to him?"

Hank studied Ben. "They told me you caught on. You honestly don't know?"

"Know what? Are we talking about the same Saudi Embassy? I was there, but with Bernadette. You know, the wedding planner. She went to try and land a contract for the upcoming nuptials of the ambassador's niece."

"A wedding planner. Clever." Hank took another drink. "Your date, or whatever you call her, is one of the top analysts at MI6. She is called Red Ninja because of her ability to sneak into the collective mindset of any organization, break it down, figure out how to infiltrate it with misinformation and/or human moles, and get out without ever being detected. That's the ninja part. The red is obvious."

Ben sat in shock, lost for words. A sense of anger washed over him. He had been duped and felt like a complete fool. That was when Bernadette's two disappearances came into focus. She was getting her job done there all right. Ben sat down. "Hank, we first met at Graham and Edith Spensley's place for cocktails. Do they know?"

"Graham may not, but Edith almost certainly does. Edith's father, Lord Covington, was head of MI6 in the seventies and hired Bernadette right out of school. Edith might have put her on her father's radar, but Bernadette's father was the chief of wet operations both in Hong Kong in the late 1960s and early 1970s and in Riyadh right after the Iranian revolution. He then got posted to Paris. Young Bernadette went to boarding school back here in England when things got a bit too hot in Hong Kong. Remember, it was the time of the cultural revolution in China. Red Guards and others were infiltrating Hong Kong and Whitehall was quite worried about losing the place. Viper was sent there—"

"Viper?" Ben asked

"Sorry. Viper was the code name for Bernadette's father, may he rest in peace. He must have, shall we say, neutralized scores of threats to Great Britain over the course of his life.

"Of course, when Bernadette visited dad, she picked up Mandarin and Cantonese. She has a passable command of Arabic, and of course, French. Degrees from Oxford both in psychology and organizational behavior. Perfect for the job, don't you think?"

Ben put his hand to his forehead. "How ... perfect?"

"Dad kept her out of wet work, if that's what you mean. She was his precious little angel. But not outside the business. He was the kind of agent who quickly read the enemy's mind. Had to if you're going to kill them, I guess. He understood Bernadette's talents from an early age. Doubtless in her genes. He specialized in individuals. She applied the same skill set and insights to organizations. Absolutely brilliant."

Ben's mind was spinning. He really didn't know what to say and blurted out the first thing that came into his head. "Any men in her life?"

"A legitimate question. Not currently. And not for a long while. She had an in-house romance about twenty years ago. Wrong end of the shop though. He was one of her father's favorites, but he cautioned her not to get serious. So did her mom. They were inseparable for over three years, planned on tying the knot. Then the hunter became the victim. He probably had twenty kills to his name by that point but lost the one that mattered most. All it takes is one.

"She was devastated. But it was stiff upper lip and a refusal to let Mom or Dad get away with 'I told you so.' She threw herself into her job, went from being one of the best to *the* best. And not just MI6. Her reputation is worldwide, at least among the people who count in the intelligence community."

Ben didn't know how to take what he had been handed. *Need to know* was the watchword. But did he really need to know all of this?

Did it really matter? A brief fling was one thing, but he knew that it would matter if he was going to get serious. The physical attraction was there when he first laid eyes on her. But he had been used for the Saudi Embassy dinner. He didn't mind doing a favor, but now he knew the whole thing was a lie. She had taken him there as cover for some clandestine operation, and he was not a man who liked being put in that situation. What angered him more than anything was that he hadn't seen it coming. He had been played for a fool.

Ben realized that he was putting himself in a downward spiral of self-flagellation. What had Hank said? That she was internationally recognized as the best at her job? Not his fault. She could fool the best, so why not him? But he was still pissed. He may not be the best in the world at what he did, but he was no slacker. It was a matter of pride that he had to come up with a plan to deal with this.

"Listen," Hank said, "I've convinced my colleagues here that you're not trying to get next to Bernadette for nefarious means—perhaps other than to get laid. They're good at reading people, too, that's their job, and they agree, but they've let it be my call. And I did try to prevent this from happening."

"Our little visit today," Ben said.

"Pretty much. I couldn't get what they wanted, so they decided to try and get it themselves. Anyway, I think we're done here. One more little matter and I'll see you out."

"I don't like the sound of that."

"We just need you to sign an NDA."

"A non-disclosure agreement. What for?"

"You've heard a lot of information that shouldn't leave this room. A risk we had to take, but we're in the business of risk. It's a pretty standard paper, used by many corporations. Except for the part where we kill you if you leak any of it out."

Ben was in no mood to find out if Hank was joking about that or not.

He rose from his chair. "And if there's anything we can do to make up for the inconvenience, short of having someone killed, let me know."

"Actually," Ben said, rising, "there is. I need you to get me a couple of theater tickets. Really good theater tickets."

¥ $ €

"Bernadette, it's Ben."

"Yes, Ben." Her voice sounded bright.

"Hey, you said I'm supposed to pick the third date. You free on Friday? How about a show and a light dinner after?" The question was rhetorical; she had no choice but to say yes. She had proposed it, even if it wasn't out of guilt. He had gotten two tickets, third row in the orchestra for a revival of the 1958 hit *The Music Man*.

He hadn't been home two hours from his interview with MI6 and he had still been pouring down bourbon to calm his nerves when there was a knock at the door. Kellen was standing there with an envelope in his hand. He held it out to Ben and said, "Compliments of Her Majesty."

Bernadette was thrilled, saying that she hardly ever got to a West End show, and when she did, the seats were less than optimal. "You must tell me how you got these," she said.

"Well," Ben stalled. "There is a great story, though you might not believe it. But that's for later."

After the show on the way to dinner in their taxi, they discussed how revivals were very much in vogue, probably because of the lack of new creative ideas for live theater. There wasn't money in it anymore. Too many people could call up whatever movie they wanted from their sofa at any hour of the day and night.

"Besides," Ben concluded as they reached the restaurant, "the 1950s and 1960s were the Golden Age of the musical. They were entertainment, not spectacle. Songs you could leave the theater humming instead of watching falling chandeliers and singing cats."

As the conversation continued at dinner, Bernadette's curiosity got the better of her. "But why *The Music Man*? You don't strike me as being the type for sentimental Americana. And Iowa? Really? Professor at Yale, global consultant, IQ off the charts?"

"I love that show," Ben said. "Dad used to play show music at home so I heard it all the time in my childhood, before I got into rock. It stays with you." He smiled, knowing he'd set his trap.

"But it's so, well, corny, as you Americans would say."

"Iowa does have a lot of corn, but if you want real corny shows you might go with *South Pacific* and 'I'm as corny as Kansas in August.' Or *Oklahoma*. 'The corn is as high as an elephant's eye and it looks like it's rising clear up to the sky.'"

"But aren't show tunes so ... old-fashioned?"

"I guess I'm an old-fashioned guy. And you're an old-fashioned kind of gal."

"How so?"

"Well, take 'Shipoopi,' " he said, naming one of the more unique songs from the show they had just seen. "Remember, you don't want a girl who kisses on the first or second date. But the girl who waits till the third time around is the girl you're glad you've found. This is our third date." Ben was enjoying putting his plan into action.

He could see Bernadette start to blush. "Ben, I don't know what to say. Are you saying that you're glad you've found me?"

"Oh, I was glad I found you the first time we met, when Edith pushed us together. No, the more interesting part is that you waited until the third date."

"Okay, you found me out. Frankly, I plan so many weddings in which people rush into things—"

Ben cut her off. "Oh, do tell. Who was your most famous client who rushed into things? Someone I may have heard of? Is the Saudi ambassador's niece rushing into things?"

Bernadette looked at him quizzically.

"Did you leave me alone at the party while you tried to get the niece to slow down and consider her marriage carefully? Or did you have some other rendezvous to make? Is the ambassador's niece even getting married?"

Bernadette could not meet his gaze. And for the first time in decades, she couldn't find the words to explain her way out of this one.

"Bernadette, I didn't take you to see *The Music Man* because of 'Shipoopi.' I took you to see it because one of the lead characters isn't who he says he is. The other lead finds him out about the phony cover with the help of a little research. She is Madame Librarian after all."

"Ben, where are you going with all of this?"

"I very recently had an interesting visit with a couple of your colleagues. It was very enlightening. For example, I learned you have an interesting *nom de guerre*, but if I tell it to you, they'll probably kill me. Tell me something, do all the men in your life have to be vetted that way?"

"I am so sorry. I had no idea—"

"But you're not surprised?"

She shook her head. "No. Not really. And you're right. I'm not who I said I was. But I really can't be, now can I?"

"Some of us more than others."

Bernadette paused. "Perhaps you should take me home."

"Perhaps I should," and Ben signaled the waiter to bring the check.

"All my life men have been scared of me," she said. "When I was a teenager, all the way into my twenties. My father made them disappear, or that's what I thought. He was one scary man. He didn't try to be, but all the young men I saw could sense it. He could read their minds. Not that the young male mind is particularly difficult to read. But when my father got inside your head you knew it, and you knew that if you stepped out of line there would be consequences.

"I used to blame him for scaring them off. Then I began to realize that I actually didn't mind all that much. He was special and I wanted someone special. I suppose your interview left you well briefed. But did you know about Sam?"

"My source didn't mention him," Ben said.

Bernadette sighed. "When he came along, he reminded me so much of my father. Same line of business, same thought pattern. He was what I wanted. Most young women secretly want someone like their father. My parents warned me of what might happen. But I didn't listen. Why should I? I had finally found what I wanted and a part of me still blamed them for making it so difficult. But the day I found out he had been killed—"

"Bernadette, I'm sorry."

"Don't be. That needed to come out." She stared intently at her well-manicured hands. It had been a long time since she had felt vulnerable, and she wasn't used to it. She could not be upset with Ben. She realized how unfair she had been to him and felt terrible. Her experiences were unique. She didn't have any girlfriends that she could "whine and dine" with. How do you start a conversation about your boyfriend being killed when he was a MI6 agent? None of her training had covered that.

"I haven't been this candid with someone in a long time. Perhaps it says something about you. And you're right about 'Shipoopi.' Only most men never get to the third time around. Being a wedding planner helps. One date is all it takes, and when men find that out, they think I'm out to plan *our* wedding. Let's face it, commitment is not the male long suit. So it's an outstanding cover. Between parents, career, and Sam, I suppose I wanted men to fail.

"Three who made it past the first date turned out to be moles. They were trying to infiltrate my brain and perhaps MI6 as well. It didn't take much research. I could usually tell on the second date or whenever it was when we first slept together, if it got that far. I was too good. Too trained. The Soviets in particular were quite good at that. Honeypot was the name for the women. Not sure what the right name for the men was. One Russian, one French fellow, and one German. Strange, isn't it, how even allies try and infiltrate one another? I never had to break off any of the relationships. Not face to face, mind you. All I'd do is let my colleagues know and they vanished. The Russian, for good. The Frenchman and German were reassigned out of the United Kingdom. I guess being an ally does have its privileges. So you see, it's not like my colleagues were acting like big brothers, trying to scare sister's new suitor off. And I'm sorry you had to find out about me that way." Bernadette was measured and unemotional as she spoke, and Ben understood that this was, in part, what made her an incredible agent.

"So MI6 plays the role my father had played. And as you found out, they can be intimidating. But here's the good news: you've checked out." She smiled, raised her eyes, and looked straight at him. "At least, so far."

This had not gone the way Ben had thought it would. He knew that part of Bernadette's job meant that emotions were never involved, but now he could see the real Bernadette for the first time. It was a moment of vulnerability, and far from creating a little emotional distance for himself, he was now in deeper than he ever had been since Ellen died. He respected Bernadette for being honest with him, albeit under duress, and he wanted to finish the evening on a positive note.

"Listen. Bernadette. I also picked *The Music Man* because of the ending. The duplicitous character is totally forgiven and the two ride off happily into the sunset. Bells on the hills and a magically transformed band parading them down Main Street in celebration. Wouldn't you like to try for a similar ending?"

She nodded.

"I'll take you home like you asked," he said. "You need some time. And frankly, I do too. I've been unfair to you as well."

He helped her into her coat and they made their way out of the restaurant to a waiting cab in reflective silence. Then, as they pulled up to her flat, came the real kiss. Long and passionate. Ben couldn't tell if it were thanks or goodbye or something else. He was done with overanalysis for now and enjoyed the moment before bidding Bernadette good night, not knowing if he would hear from her again.

He didn't have to wait long. His phone rang at ten the next morning. "All right, Mr. Coleman. What does your song say about waiting till the fourth time? Be at my place at six tonight. And dear, it is your job to bring the wine. Two bottles. One simply will not do."

He barely had time to reply to her request before she ended the call. "I must dash. I have a wedding to plan."

Ben chose a Margaux and a Pouilly-Fumé. Bases covered. But it wouldn't have mattered. They didn't eat dinner or even open a bottle of wine. Saturday night turned into all day Sunday, and at six on Monday morning both realized they had to get to work. For two workaholics, even passionate romance had its limits, at least in the short run.

¥ $ €

That had been ten years ago. Nine years ago had come the mutual decision that they wanted to spend the rest of their lives together, and Bernadette used her background to plan a modest but well-attended wedding for the two of them. Eight years ago, Washington called Ben back to the United States and Bernadette made the decision to walk away from MI6 and travel across the pond with her husband.

But she had no plans to be idle. After taking up residence with Ben in Virginia, she realized that while she had wanted to escape that old job, she couldn't give it up all together. She began to write. This time it was fictional accounts of the spy business. They were thrillers and written, as nearly all such novels were, from a masculine point of view, prompting her to take the *nom de plume* of Edmund Whitehall.

By and large the novels were compilations of her father's life as best as she could piece them together. It was her way of posthumously paying tribute to him. Of course, they were advertised as fiction, in which "any resemblance to an actual person is purely coincidental."

While the link between Bernadette and Edmund Whitehall was not public knowledge, it was well known in intelligence circles. As the public gobbled the novels up, thinking they were getting a really good story, the intelligence community read the books with great interest. And MI6 was thrilled—the novels served as an opportunity. They collaborated with Bernadette to interject certain key pieces of disinformation that she incorporated as plot points in her work. Since the intelligence community knew that most of the stories were close approximations of reality, the disinformation was also believed, and her MI6 career lived on, albeit in an unexpected way.

Leave it to her, Ben thought one day, perusing *The New York Times Book Review* to again find Mr. Whitehall on the bestseller list, *to find a way to stay by my side and stay in the work that meant the world to her.*

And wistfully, Ben thought again that Bernadette was the best thing that ever had happened to him.

CHAPTER FOUR

AT A QUARTER TO FIVE THE NEXT EVENING, BEN, HECTOR LOPEZ, AND George Steinway were gathered in the anteroom outside the Oval Office.

The three men had been on the phone together off and on almost the entire day. By the time they arrived at the White House, Lopez and Steinway had blessed ninety percent of Ben's presentation. There were bells and whistles that needed to be discussed, and the President might not like the whole thing, and they would have to start over. But the three of them doubted that would happen.

Promptly at 5 p.m., the President opened the slightly rounded door that completed the look of the Oval Office to let the three advisers in.

"Gentlemen, thank you for coming." He directed them to sit in the same places they had occupied the day before. "Okay, let's see what my brain trust has come up with in the last twenty-four hours."

Ben led off. "Mr. President. We believe what is happening now is part of the China 2049 strategy that is intended to make them the world superpower by the hundredth anniversary of the communists coming to power in Beijing.

"We also believe that they have agreed to win the inevitable war with us to become the lone superpower by economic means. If that fails, the military option is always available.

"Further, we believe they are seeking an economic tool other than trade relations, having failed at that in the last decade. That leads us to think that the most likely battlefield will be in monetary policy. Specifically, the Chinese intend to make the yuan the world's reserve currency. The dollar holds that position now."

"Why does that matter?" asked the President.

"A reserve currency is the one in which most international transactions take place. It's also the one that countries keep on hand in case of emergency. Money isn't free. To get a dollar, a country must sell something of value to America and get this little piece of paper in return. That's a pretty good deal for us. Right now about seventy percent of all the money we've printed is in the hands of foreigners. Yearly, that's three trillion dollars. In other words, we have, over time, gotten three trillion dollars' worth of other people's goods for free."

"You mean we swapped money we can print for free to live a better life? Isn't that like living on a credit card?"

Ben said, "That's a very astute observation, Mr. President. Technically that money is a loan of sorts. The foreign holders can always take the three trillion and buy something that we make. So instead of them getting a piece of paper in return for their hard work, it will be Americans who have to work hard to get that piece of paper back."

"That doesn't sound like a recipe for a happy America," said the President. "It sounds like we'd be working harder and enjoying it less."

"Precisely. What the Chinese want to do is be the ones who can get goods from the rest of the world in return for little pieces of paper. Only in yuan, not dollars. In doing so, they will force those three trillion dollars that are out there back to us. Americans will feel the pain quickly."

"So it's a win-win for them? They get the goods for free with the yuan and we have to work harder to get our dollars back?"

"Exactly," Ben said.

"So why does the world hold dollars now instead of yuan? What gives America the advantage?"

"In a word, Mr. President, confidence. Remember what I said about currencies being a Ponzi scheme? It's a way for the government to get something for nothing. All those dollars are printed by us. Then others, be they American or foreign, are willing to take them in return for something tangible because they have faith that they will be able to use that piece of paper to buy something from someone else. That next person takes it because they also expect to be able to pass it on. The game ends when the last guy holding the piece of paper has nobody to pass it on to.

"Mr. President, you've probably seen pictures of people in Germany in the 1920s carting wheelbarrows full of paper money just to go shopping. Currencies decline in value. Not necessarily all at once, but by people demanding more and more pieces of paper for everything they sell. The faster confidence declines, the more pieces of paper are demanded. This creates a vicious cycle where everyone starts demanding more and more money for everything they sell."

"Meaning inflation," said the President.

"You've hit the nail on the head," said Ben. "The trick is to keep the money game going as long as possible. Usually this means allowing a little more inflation every year. A little inflation doesn't destroy peoples' confidence. The extra money being printed again gives the government more money to spend."

"So inflation is a way for the government to make ends meet?"

"Yes. The government can get money through taxing people, borrowing, or printing money. You might think of money as an interest-free loan to the government. People get interest from a bank because the bank can lend it to someone else. But the money has to be created in the first place. When it is, the person who gets it is making an interest free loan to Uncle Sam.

"The trick is to find the right amount of inflation that won't destroy confidence. When congress passed the Federal Reserve Act, it said one of the missions of the Fed was price stability. Remember, however, it's Congress that gets to spend that money. So we've always taken that mandate as being tongue in cheek. The Fed and most of the other central banks of the world decided that price stability meant two percent inflation. This meant the Fed often pursued a policy of trying to increase inflation in order to get to price stability. However, two percent inflation means the purchasing power of a dollar drops seventy-five percent during a person's lifetime and about eighty-five percent in a century."

"You mean," said the President, "if we have price stability, then a dollar printed today will only be worth fifteen cents a hundred years from now?"

ıd history is full of stories of governments doing exactly that.

me their money was called the denarius. It started out being almost all silver. Then they first began to make it a little bit smaller, still calling it one denarius. Then they began to mix bronze and lead in with the silver. By the end, there was almost no silver in the denarius."

"Didn't Gibbon mention in *The Decline and Fall of the Roman Empire* that inflation was one reason for the collapse of the Roman Empire?" the President asked.

"Economic historians argue that the real mystery is not why the Roman Empire fell, but why it took so long. Inflation was actually one of the ways they stretched it out. The money the government saved by debasing the denarius like that let them make more coins for the same amount of silver. Those coins were used to pay the army until the solders got wise to what was going on and started demanding more and more of these debased coins in return for their labor. That turned inflation into hyperinflation. The same thing happened to Germany's Weimar Republic in the 1920s.

"But it wasn't just Europeans who did that. When the Conquistadors took the silver from the Incas, about half went across the Atlantic to Spain, where it caused inflation. Most of the rest went to China.

"The Chinese invented paper money and ended up printing too much of it. Inflation turned into hyperinflation. To restart the economy and run the government, the Chinese began to circulate the silver the Conquistadors took from the Incas. Of course, they had to give the Spanish goods in return. To show how attractive inflation is, the Ming Dynasty went through that entire cycle twice while they ruled. They introduced paper money along with the silver, the silver began to disappear, so more paper was printed. They again had to import silver from Peru."

"They never learned," said the President.

"It's a hard-learned and easily forgotten lesson, Mr. President. During our Revolution, each state printed its own money to pay the militias. These pieces of paper were called Continentals. By the end of the Revolution, the phrase 'Not worth a Continental' became common-place. So Alexander Hamilton assumed all the states' debts, including the Continentals, and put the country on a mixture of gold and silver. This was called specie, and Hamilton replaced paper with it like the Ming did.

"Since then it fell in and out of favor. During our Civil War, money was printed to pay the Union Army. Naturally, it caused inflation, so America went back to specie. Eventually, in 1913, Congress created the Federal Reserve to take us back to paper money. At first they were cautious. The Fed had to have forty cents in gold for every dollar that circulated. But during the Great Depression FDR's economists wanted to create inflation, so his government forced people to sell all their gold to the government for $20.67 an ounce. If you didn't, the government simply seized it. When they had control of all America's gold, Roosevelt declared that each ounce of gold was now worth $35 an ounce, a seventy-five percent increase in the amount of money in circulation. Prices stopped falling and started rising."

"He did that just by decree?" asked the President.

"That's why they call it fiat currency," Ben said. "Eventually President Ford, a guy with a lot of common sense, decided this was ridiculous and repealed the prohibition on Americans owning gold. We could print money freely once again."

"How does all this relate to what the Chinese are up to?" said the President.

"Confidence," Ben said. "The Chinese plan to bring the dollar down and have yuan take its place by destroying confidence in the U.S. dollar."

"How?"

"If I put myself in Governor Li's shoes, I would force the American economy to inflate. I think the Chinese are going to dump one and a half trillion dollars' worth of U.S. government bonds onto the market."

"How did we get to this point?" asked Steinway.

Ben said, "For nearly three-quarters of a century, the U.S. government spent more money than it took in, so it had to borrow to cover the shortfall. So the U.S. Treasury issues bonds to raise the money. The bond promises the lender that he or she will be paid back at a certain point in the future and the government will pay them interest in the meantime. Some of these bonds, technically called bills, last only three months. Long-dated bonds can be outstanding for as many as thirty years. Usually the markets demand less interest when they are going to be paid back in the short term than if repayment is many years in the future.

"Sometimes the Federal Reserve buys those bonds. It is often said that the Fed simply prints money, and in a sense they do. But each of those dollars they print is backed by U.S. Treasury bonds. So paper money buys something that pays interest, and at the end of the year, the Fed gives all of the interest it received back to the government after covering its cost of operations. Money is not backed by gold. It is backed by government debt.

"Sometimes foreign governments and banks buy U.S. bonds as an investment. When a country like China runs a trade surplus with the U.S., when they sell more to us than we buy from them, they end up holding more dollars. Like anyone, they want to earn interest on those dollars. The best way to do it is buying U.S. Treasuries. Foreign banks may choose to hold U.S. Treasuries as an investment because they might pay a higher interest rate than bonds issued by their own country. That's why nearly a third of all U.S. government bonds are owned by foreigners.

"In responding to such a dump, we would have two choices. We could let interest rates rise to entice others to buy those bonds. The problem is the much higher interest rates would knock our economy into a recession. Or we could print money to buy the bonds. In fact, when I was asked about this possibility in my confirmation hearings, I said what I would do is ask the Chinese whether they wanted large bills or small."

"You're recommending a policy of deliberate inflation?" The President gave him a hard look.

"It's the lesser of two evils," said Ben.

The President took a deep breath. "So much for my chances of reelection. Ben, when I appointed you, I thought having a smart guy as chairman was the politically shrewd thing to do. I guess I was wrong."

"Mr. President, I am not a politician—"

"Bullshit, Ben!"

"Sorry, Mr. President. But history has put both a challenge and an opportunity in your hands. If we play our cards right, you will be the man who derailed China's march to superpower status. That should not just reelect you, it'll give you a great place in the history of America."

The President smiled. "You butter me up like that and wonder why I called bullshit when you said you weren't a politician. So how do we get from here to there?"

"Mr. President, remember—knocking down confidence in the dollar is just one of the things the Chinese have to do. They also have to create confidence in the yuan. And, well, *nobody* has confidence in a little piece of paper issued by a communist dictatorship. But they do have confidence in us.

"The way the Chinese are going to build confidence is age-old. They are going to back the yuan with gold, at least partially. When I asked Governor Li why they were accumulating so much gold, he said he wanted the Chinese to treasure the yuan as much as they treasure gold.

"Right now, they're having a bank run because their people don't have confidence in the yuan or the Chinese banking system. If the people get their money out of the banks, the banks will have to call in their loans. That will wreck the Chinese economy."

"Why doesn't their government print the money and give it to the banks?" asked the President.

"They could," said Ben, "but that would totally destroy confidence in the yuan. Instead, they're going to use their gold stockpile to create public confidence in the yuan, and by extension, their banking system."

"So it all comes down to gold."

"Yes, Mr. President, it does. China has been accumulating gold for several decades. If its price keeps going up, in probably five years, they will have enough gold to cover sixty to seventy percent of the yuan they have printed. That will be more than enough to restore confidence in the yuan and make it a plausible alternative to the dollar."

"That's how they'll wreck us economically and become the world's only superpower," said the President. "We can't let that happen, can we?"

"No, we can't." said Ben. "And there are things we can do to stop it. Our biggest hope is the impatience of the Chinese leadership. Governor Li said something very interesting. He said politicians think desperate times require desperate measures, but to a central banker, desperate times require calming measures. Li knows that today is not the time to implement this plan. It is five years from now. But what I saw in the bank run were troops shooting people in the middle of Beijing. That sounds like a desperate measure to me. And the Chinese long-term plan seems a lot less desperate than shooting people."

"So your hunch is that they'll act too soon."

Hector Lopez joined the conversation. "Our intelligence indicates that may be a possibility. But frankly, our analysts are divided over the situation."

"Hector," said the President, "you're doing a great job, but frankly, this wouldn't be the first time the CIA has not come to a definitive judgment."

"You're right, Mr. President," said Hector. "Our best guess is that if these bank runs continue, they will have to make a move in the next six months to a year."

The President looked to Ben. "Is that your time frame?"

"Sir, I don't think it's my place to question the CIA on its ability to guess the behavior of a foreign government."

"Again, bullshit. That's a political answer. It is not the answer of someone with a reputation as a straight shooter."

"Mr. President," Ben said, "I don't think anyone knows when the Chinese government is going to act. I saw a lot of desperation in that bank run. And that was happening in the middle of Beijing, the most pampered city in all of China. When bank runs start, they rarely go on for six to twelve months. Weeks, maybe?"

The President nodded. "That's my instinct too. From my days in business, I know what you have to worry about is your stock price. Once the selling starts and you don't have good news to give the market, the selling accelerates."

"As long as America wins this fight in the end," Ben said, "confidence in the dollar and in the U.S. government will surge. I think once the Chinese initiate their action, we will be in desperate times. Central bankers have one big calming measure. It doesn't last forever. In fact, it's a dumb thing to do forever. But it works in the short run, and I think this crisis, when it happens, is going to be a quick one.

"So as cynical as I am about the history of monetary policy, I think the best thing for us to do would be to buy all of the bonds the Chinese dump on the market and hint that we'll do the same if there's trouble in the treasury market. If people think we're credible, Wall Street is not going to take us on. We don't have to buy all the bonds for very long. But for a while Wall Street will never fight the Fed. They know it's a battle they're going to lose."

"Well, Ben," said the President, "I appointed you chairman, so I am going to trust your judgment. But there's an old story about why politicians don't interfere with the Fed. It's the great narrative that it's an independent institution. If we didn't have you to blame, what would we do?

"As the writer said, with great power comes great responsibility." He smiled at that. "So the ball is in your court. But if you fuck it up, it's going to be your head on the chopping block, not mine."

"Fair enough, Mr. President. Let's all hope that this crisis doesn't happen anytime soon."

The others nodded in agreement.

The President rose from his chair, signaling that the meeting was over. The other three followed the President's lead as he led them to the exit. The President put his hand on Ben's shoulder.

"I'd like to have a quick word with you before you go."

"Certainly, Mr. President."

Steinway and Lopez took the hint and the President closed the door behind them.

"Ben, the First Lady and I would like to have you and Bernadette over for dinner tomorrow night up in the residence."

Ben knew what a rare honor this was, and said, "Of course, Mr. President." But he could only think, *Something is up.*

Opening the door, the President said, "Great. We'll see you tomorrow night at six-thirty."

¥ $ €

Ben's first impulse was to call Bernadette about the White House dinner as soon as he got in his car. Then he remembered he was springing something on her at the last minute. There would be the inevitable complaint about not having anything to wear. She'd get over it, but there was a trade-off. A few extra minutes of preparation versus the possible miscommunication inherent in using the phone. Ultimately, he opted to do it in person since after Beijing his goodwill with her was still a little thin.

So it was when Ben walked in the door and accepted the glass of wine she had waiting, he broke the news and waited for the reaction.

"Darling, I love you, but why didn't you call me from the car? You know I need time to prepare."

"I wanted to see the look on your face," he offered.

"Well, this is the look of a woman who has less than twenty-four hours to prepare for one of the biggest events that can happen to anyone in Washington."

"You're going to be fine." He sipped the wine. "And beautiful." *I got that one wrong,* he thought. *Or would I have been wrong no matter which decision I made?*

"Easy for you to say. You don't have to get your hair and nails done. You can throw on a blue pinstripe, spend forty seconds picking out a tie, and you're done. I don't have anything to wear."

Ben held back a smile. Her accent even added charm to her complaining. Besides, it made it exponentially easier for him to decipher if he was in trouble, and if so, how much.

"And shoes. *Shoes.* Dammit, Ben, this is the President and First Lady we're talking about and I will never be able to find anything to wear on such short notice."

Despite the accent, the message was clear. She was trying to make him feel that he was in big trouble. Deep inside the flattery of the invitation was taking hold. But she wasn't going to let him off the hook that easily.

"You'll find something perfect," Ben said. "I have no doubt. And don't worry about your hair—"

"Wipe that stupid grin off your face," Bernadette said, a little too quickly. "This is no laughing matter."

Ben tried to swallow his smile. Between the accent and the way she became flustered at times like this, he couldn't take her seriously. To him it was adorable. When he showed such obvious signs of amusement, it angered Bernadette even further, because her facade was fading.

"Well," Ben said, trying to maintain a serious look. "The President is going to fall for you no matter what. But if he falls too hard—"

"Then I will have to assault him in a manner and place so embarrassing that he won't be reporting it to anyone."

"Nobody is more capable of that than you. But I don't think that will be necessary. My suspicion is that he is after your mind, not your body, although he doubtless wouldn't mind that either if he thought it was available."

"My mind?"

"I'm pulling a few things together. A suspicion not fully formed. Let me give it some time to gel."

"By the time it gels, I'm going to be at a table in the White House without proper hair, shoes, or dress." Bernadette studied him, then crossed her arms and glared. "You're doing it again. Get that smirk off your face."

"I—"

"And don't try to sweet talk me with promises of fidelity and devotion. You're going to be in trouble over this for a week."

Ben decided to back off and let Bernadette organize her battle plan for the dinner. Besides, he really did need for his thoughts to gel. It was still a hunch, but it might explain why Hector Lopez was in the room before the meeting and why Ben had the floor for virtually the entire time.

Welcome to Washington, he thought, *where even an invitation to dinner is fraught with intrigue.*

But at the moment the intrigue was limited to the Coleman household, where Bernadette was walking quickly about the house, talking loudly about the situation at hand. Ben had learned early in their marriage not to speak to her at moments like this, even though her ravings were directed at him. She would pass it off as women often did, and prying would only bring him more grief.

Finally she wandered up the stairs, muttering something about what was in her inadequate wardrobe, and soon was out of earshot. Ben took this as his cue. He wandered into his den *cum* office and poured himself a bourbon. He heard the closet door slam from upstairs, picked up the decanter again and made it a double. Then he settled in his recliner and used the remote to turn on CNBC World.

On the flat screen, the Singapore-based anchor seemed more animated than usual. Ben watched with the sound off, his usual custom. He wanted to focus on the numbers in the Hot Box, the stock, bond, and currency prices from around the world. The numbers finally scrolled to the Shanghai market open, and it was down over three percent.

News of the riots, Ben thought. *They've probably reached the trading floor in spite of the authorities' best efforts to keep it quiet.* He mused, *I guess mass shootings in the nation's capital are hard to keep quiet.*

He turned the volume up to hear what the anchor was saying.

"The big story of the day is that Xinhua News Agency has confirmed rumors of a riot and army intervention to suppress it on Tuesday. The report said anti-social elements had tried to create trouble and were stopped by PLA troops. Xinhua did not report any specific number of casualties, but we understand from many sources on the ground that over eighty people are dead."

Yeah, Ben thought. *That would be enough to send Shanghai down three percent.*

The screen switched to a real-time measure of the Shanghai losses. The numbers kept dropping. *This is going to be interesting*, Ben thought.

He picked up the phone to call George Steinway. "Hey, turn on CNBC World. Shanghai is down almost four percent. Xinhua has confirmed the riot I was in. Now they're in damage control mode."

"Already there," Steinway said. "I don't know how long they're going to let this go on."

After some time, the numbers on the screen stopped falling and reversed direction. Within ten minutes, the decline had been reduced to one and a half percent.

"George, did you see that? Their government's obviously trying a price-keeping operation." But the rise seemed half-hearted at best. Eventually the market began to drop once more. "The smart money is betting they won't be able to hold it today and decided to pocket what the government just spent by selling at the temporary high price."

For a couple of minutes there seemed to be a classic standoff between the bulls and the bears. The bears finally won. Now Shanghai was dropping like a stone.

"That didn't work."

"More trouble," said Steinway. "Can't say I'm sad to see it."

"Let's see what their next trick is."

By the time of the hour-long lunch break in Shanghai, the market was down almost eight percent.

"Now comes the die roll," Ben said, "to see if they can revive things when people come back from lunch."

He soon got his answer. CNBC's correspondent in Shanghai burst onto the screen.

"It has just been reported that an electrical fire has broken out in the room where the main server for the exchange is located. Exchange spokesmen reported that they are working hard to fix the damage, but caution that it may be possible that trading will not resume in the afternoon."

Steinway's voice came over the speaker. "Ha! No one is ever going to believe that."

"Spontaneous combustion," said Ben. "Some red ink got too close to a stack of sell forms. But when an exchange is closed, it's closed. The big question is going to be, what happens when they reopen on Monday?"

Bernadette entered the room carrying two of her classic black dresses—one that showed everything off in the best way possible and another, more modest wrap.

"Which one?"

"Honey, you know I'd love to see you all night long in the short one. But a visit to the residence requires a bit more modesty. I don't want to be distracted, and I don't want the President staring as well. I know that he and Cynthia are devoted but no adult male can keep from staring when you wear The Sure Thing."

"Okay," Bernadette said. "I'm doing this one for you. But don't think for a minute that you're forgiven for the short notice. You'll be making it up when I visit Tyson's Galleria on Monday."

Ben knew the shopping spree would easily run five figures. All he could do was hope for a low five figures. Then he heard a chuckle from his phone.

"Who is that?" Bernadette asked.

"George Steinway."

She motioned to the phone and Ben put it on speaker. "Shame on you," she said.

"I'm sorry," Steinway said. "Your husband and I were following the antics on the Shanghai market and I couldn't help overhearing."

"That's fine, George. I didn't want to go shopping alone. I'm sure that Dora would be happy to accompany me."

Steinway sighed, "I guess our bank accounts are both in for some punishment next week."

"Yeah," Ben said. "But it'll be worth the peace at home."

CHAPTER FIVE

BERNADETTE WALKED ELEGANTLY INTO THE OFFICE OF THE Chairman.

"Mr. Chairman your date for the evening has arrived," Peggy announced. Then, to Bernadette, "When did you have time to get ready? That dress is stunning." Peggy loved it when Bernadette came to the office. The two had become good friends over the years, having bonded over their joint role of managing Ben Coleman.

"Ben isn't one for giving lots of notice," Bernadette replied, smoothing her dress down. "I had to pull this from my closet."

"In his defense, I don't think he had much notice either," Peggy said.

Ben stepped through the door with his jacket slung over his shoulder. "You ladies talking about me again?" Then taking Bernadette in, he said, "Wow. I told you that you'd pull it together."

"Tell me, Peggy, is he always this self-centered at the office?" Bernadette inquired. "I'd like to think I have him trained better than that." Then she gave Ben a discreet peck on the cheek. "Looks like I have more work to do on that score." Bernadette reached up to straighten Ben's tie out of habit.

"Don't worry, Mrs. Coleman, he is always a gentleman."

Hoping to take advantage of the moment and escape further scrutiny, Ben took her hand saying, "You look seriously ravishing. My male ego will be in full protective mode when you are in the presence of the President."

"Assaulting the President is a serious offense," she chided back. "Besides, I have a handsome stud to protect me."

Peggy chuckled as Ben guided Bernadette to the elevator down to the garage. He knew when he was being managed but would never admit that, sometimes, he actually enjoyed it.

It was only nine blocks to the East Executive Avenue entrance, so Ben knew he would have to talk fast. He said to his wife, "Hector Lopez was in the Oval before our meeting yesterday. Apparently only a few minutes. I'm suspicious and insanely jealous, of course, but we all know the CIA has been caught flat footed on China. Dinner in the residence is a very unusual thing. I mean, why not a slightly larger gathering downstairs? The State floor is much more impressive. This is something private."

"Your synthesizing mind is working overtime, as is your imagination," Bernadette reassured him. But she knew Ben was on to something. He always was. And while she could probe and analyze a situation from the bottom up, Ben was the expert at top down, pulling together seemingly unrelated facts and linking them, as if he had a view of all that was going on from 37,000 feet. It was one of the many things she admired about him.

The corridor through the East Wing was endless but surprisingly homey and inviting. The First Lady's offices and Congressional Liaison were located behind the paneled walls on either side. This fed them into the receiving floor. Straight ahead was the path to the West Wing and the Oval Office. The Diplomatic Reception room, where heads of state entered, was to the left.

The guards motioned Ben and Bernadette up the stairs on the right to the State floor. The President and First Lady stood at the top in the great entrance hall of the White House. It was an ornate and surprisingly regal space for a country that prided itself on being a republic. The white banquettes accented in crimson and gold matched the walls. Ben and Bernadette walked across the highly polished Truman-era marble floor arm in arm. Bernadette made sure to take note of the skillfully crafted columns and detailed plaster ceilings and the warm light emanating from the pristine chandeliers, showcasing the overall beauty of James Hoban's modified design.

"Ben, thank you so much for coming." The President began the greetings welcoming Ben and Bernadette with open arms and a warm smile. "But you didn't tell me how absolutely gorgeous your bride was. Where have you been keeping her?"

Bernadette said, "Mr. President, you are far too generous. Mrs. Turner, you are so kind to have us to your residence."

"Where did you get that dress, Bernadette?" said the First Lady. "It is absolutely stunning."

The black satin stood out against Bernadette's red hair and green eyes to create a collage that would draw any man's attention. It was a truly wonderful dress. It was plain but didn't need embellishment. Perfectly tailored, the Queen Anne neckline and the simple sheath shape were exceptionally flattering on Bernadette. Finished with simple pearls and peep toe heels, it looked as though Bernadette had hardly tried.

"I can tell that you and I need to compare notes," continued the First Lady. "I saw something similar in *Vogue*, but it wasn't the right cut for me."

"Mrs. Turner," said Ben, "thank you so much for your kindness in that regard. The one thing I can't stand is clothes shopping. Somehow, I always have something to do around the house when that happens, even if it is mowing the lawn or washing the car or something I haven't done in years."

All four laughed, then the President said, "Okay, folks, first it's cocktails in the Red Room, then upstairs for dinner." He extended his bent elbow toward Bernadette. "Mrs. Coleman, would you be kind enough to accompany me?" Ben did the same for the First Lady, thinking, *This is turning into a best-of-friends evening. Turner must have something up his sleeve.*

The charm offensive continued upstairs over an appetizer of a lobster and avocado timbale, during which the President used the opportunity to butter up Ben. "So, Mr. Chairman, do you know why I picked you?" He took a sip of his drink and looked at Ben over the rim of his glass. "Lots of people vied for your job. My political guys were against you because you advised my opponent during the primaries."

"He was my college roommate," Ben said.

The President waved away Ben's objection. "In politics, if you're explaining it means you're losing. I never said that Milquetoast Michael didn't have good taste in the people he surrounded himself with. That had nothing to do with it. The man just didn't have the temperament for the job. A president has got to be tough."

Ben couldn't argue with the sobriquet that Turner had used to great effect in the primaries. Michael St. Louis *was* a bit of a wimp. Nice guy. Very smart. And he was actually pretty tough emotionally. It just didn't come through in the campaign where visual imagery was key. Most interpersonal communication is nonverbal, and Mike sent the wrong cues.

"Ben, dozens of people come through my door every day of the week. I've come to appreciate that each and every one of them thinks they are supposed to tell me what they think I want to hear. It's always, 'Yes, Mr. President,' 'You're so right about that, Mr. President,' 'That was a great point, Mr. President.' Nothing ever seems to go wrong on my watch—at least not that they want to tell me about.

"We've met maybe a dozen times—when I interviewed you and in the four months you've been on the job. You've never flattered me once. Never been rude either. It's always been the facts, and you never sugar-coat those. Nearly everyone calls you a pessimist because you always seem to bring bad news. But you invariably turn out to be spot on."

"Well, sir, it is the dismal science."

Turner turned to Ben's wife. "Tell me, how did Mr. Never Flatter Never Cheerful ever catch you? Please tell me he at least tried to prop-erly court you. His style isn't one that's going to get a girl to jump in the sack."

"Will, really." Cynthia gave the President a withering stare.

"Actually, Mr. President, he was not a shameless flatterer." Bernadette thought back to *The Music Man*. "He's quite matter-of-fact and to the point. To a fault, I might say. It's actually quite seductive after the initial shock. Women know what men are after, so they tend to discount the flattery as much as they enjoy it. When a woman instinctively knows the man is interested but doesn't get what you call 'the full court press' the gentleman suddenly becomes more interesting. The chase is no longer one way and often the lady likes that challenge. At least I did."

Bernadette gave Ben a knowing wink that signaled to both the President and the First Lady that they were still very much in love.

"Now, I am really impressed." The President signaled to the staff to bring on the main course. It was also a signal that the direction of the flattery was about to change. As dinner was presented on White House china by silent and efficient staff, Ben took in the exquisite food beautifully arranged on his plate.

"Mrs. Coleman," the President finally said, "may I call you Bernadette?"

"Of course, Mr. President."

"Bernadette, you are a most remarkable woman. I know Ben obviously thinks so and he is a very discerning man. But your reputation precedes you."

"I'm not sure what you mean, sir. I am just a simple Virginia housewife. And loving every minute of it."

"A simple Virginia housewife? You are far too modest. How many of your peers have had seven bestselling novels—Edmund Whitehall?"

Bernadette gave a modest smile. "Mr. President, you are remarkably well informed."

"It is a president's job to be well informed. Which means I know of your other alias as well. Dare I call you Red Ninja?" The President and the First Lady studied Bernadette to gauge her reaction.

Her background equipped her to keep her shock well hidden. She smiled demurely. "Mr. President, I have already agreed to have you call me 'Bernadette' instead of 'Mrs. Coleman.' Perhaps we should stick to that."

"My husband obviously lacks Ben's grace and finesse," said the First Lady. "I do hope you will forgive him. But it is a bit of a habit. Directness was the key to his success in business, and he has managed to carry that over into politics. I assure you he meant no offense."

"None taken," Bernadette said. "Each individual has his or her own interpersonal strategies." The President had used flattery on Ben, but directness with her. Bernadette found that strange but was intrigued to see where it led. She remembered Ben's synthesizing mind had warned her about what might follow and realized that Willard Turner was doing something not all that different from what Ben had done on their third date. Perhaps she had underestimated him; he was not the mono-chrome alpha male boor and bully that the media painted him out to be.

"Now that Cynthia has let the cat out of the bag regarding my style, I will be very direct." The President deliberately placed his fork on the side of his plate. "Hector Lopez briefed me thoroughly on your resume and said that, when it comes to understanding China, you are the best. Present tense. No one has come close to you in terms of skill.

"You know, I actually read *Dragon's Heart*. And I loved it—it was all so real. Then Lopez explained your little arrangement with MI6. You're still on top of things through your novels even though you technically haven't been in the business in the eight years since you left. Fortunately, our 'special arrangement' makes us privy to what you're up to."

Not everything, Bernadette thought. One piece of disinformation was aimed at sending the CIA looking in the wrong spot for who had bugged the Secretary of State's phone several decades back. MI6 correctly thought that the man was too close to some not-so-nice people in the IRA and arranged the tap. So Edmund Whitehall spilled it all out plainly in one of his books—it was the Cubans. The CIA fell for it. Discovering the truth would not have been so good for the 'special relationship' of which the President had spoken so fondly. She kept few secrets from Ben, but out of necessity that was one.

"I am so glad to be of service to the cause of freedom," Bernadette said deliberately, not differentiating between her native country or her newly adopted home.

"I'm glad you feel that way." The President was about to drive his evening's agenda through the door she had just opened. "I am sure you're aware of what your husband has been up to over the last twen-ty-four hours or so. The Chinese are going to do their best to upset the global financial system. We know that their goal is to topple the dollar from its status as the world's key currency.

"But it likely doesn't stop there. Their leadership is desperate. They have botched their economic management and the natives are getting restless. They will do anything to distract the population from what has happened to their daily lives. That includes creating an external threat around which they can rally the population to defend the status quo.

"The government of the United States would like to enlist your assistance to stop them. It is no secret that CIA has not done that good a job in anticipating the Chinese government's next moves. In fact, they have done a downright terrible job. It reminds me of their forecasts in the 1970s of how Soviet economic growth would soon overtake us. It's a real institutional failure. But of course, you are the expert on things like that.

"So I would like you to volunteer for your adopted country. I need a real team B at the Agency. Actually, you will probably be team A given their current incompetence, but it would be bad human resources policy to say that. I need to know exactly what China is planning, what their weaknesses are, and maybe even how we can exploit them.

"Ben is giving me insight on their economy, but I need reliable intel on their decision-making structure. Ultimately Li must answer to the Politburo, so I need to know what they're thinking and where their divisions are. And I need to know if war hawks plan to turn this into more than an economic battle and what I can do to stop them. Get the picture?"

Bernadette took her time to finish chewing and placed her fork on the side of her plate as deliberately as the President had. "How am I supposed to do this, Mr. President? I have been out of the business completely for eight years and was phasing out before that. I don't have access to information and the data I need. I need intel on the characters in the game. At this point I really am a Virginia housewife who writes novels."

"I'll use my presidential authority to grant you any and all clearances you need up through and including code words. You can see anything that I can see. In fact, you can see things that Ben has been excluded from, though if you accept, I will open the gates for him as well. Can't have something slipping out during pillow talk, now can we?"

Cynthia gave him a raised eyebrow.

The President ignored her nonverbal chide. "You'll work directly with Lopez and his staff. No holds barred. You won't have to report to Langley every day, only when you need to. Lopez will fill you in."

"Mr. President, I haven't said yes. I really do have to think this over."

"Of course. Lopez will call you at nine tomorrow morning for your answer. Not that we have a backup plan. You are the best there is and I intend to have the best for the sake of this country. I hate to be in this situation, but I have no bargaining power. Unfortunately, I can't pay you anything as the press would find out. But the President of the United States would be in your debt, Mrs. Coleman. When you need a favor, anytime, you need merely ask."

"I will give it thorough consideration," Bernadette said.

The President nodded and, not missing a beat, turned his attention to Ben. "Would you join me in the study for a brandy? I want to get your take on something. Ladies, you are free to join us, but maybe you two would like to get to know each other a bit better." The President pushed his chair away from the table, placed his napkin on his plate, and led Ben to another room.

Bernadette sat at the dinner table agape at what had just happened. She looked at Cynthia. "Did I hear that right? The men are going to retire to their brandies and the lady folk can go do their womanly things?"

"Don't mind Will. To be perfectly frank, I set him up to that. I knew that he would give you his usual hard sell, but I wanted to give you a fuller picture of the situation."

"What do you mean?"

The First Lady relaxed into her chair, throwing her napkin on to the table. "All relationships are different. You and Ben obviously have a very successful one. You know and respect each other's boundaries. But your relationship with Ben is different from the one he had with Ellen, his first wife.

"Remember, I'm wife number four. The first three thought their role was to look pretty and run up credit card debt to achieve that end. Combined duration of all three marriages was eleven years. I've been married to him for twice that."

"Congratulations. You have my envy."

"No need," said the First Lady. "You and me, we're very much alike in a way. We're both married to men who are visionary, perhaps at the expense of everything else. They need an anchor."

Bernadette laughed. "Tell me about it. Ben is so . . . so . . . ."

"Yes." The First Lady nodded.

"It's like that thing with Einstein not wearing socks. Once Ben gets something in his head, he's like a cat with a mouse, batting it around to the exclusion of everything else. It's like they need us to civilize them."

"Exactly. And that's probably why Will's other marriages failed. He doesn't need a bauble. He needs a manager. He is an unbridled force of nature who will go and go and go in whatever direction he is pointed in. In that sense he is unstoppable. Subtlety is not his style. He went through school on a football scholarship, the son of a truck driver and a waitress at a diner. If you've ever seen a film of him playing you would understand. If he had possession of the ball, he would push and dodge and weave for five or six yards when most men might gain one or two. He ran his business ventures the same way. And frankly, when he decided to run for office it was pure dogged determination that got him here. All the way through it has been my job to help manage and direct that raw strength.

"But now here we are, and neither of our jobs is like anything we've ever seen before. Washington is like quicksand. The harder you move, the more it sucks you down. Unlike business there is no real overall objective. It's everyone for themselves, a never-ending search for power where there is only so much to go around. The classic zero-sum game."

"A bubble," said Bernadette. "The Beltway is like the border, and once you cross it's like you're in this … well, it's a reality, but it's different from what's on the other side of the Beltway. Out there you have people working just to make the house payment and get their child braces and a college education. In here, the priorities are so different. So intense."

The First Lady nodded. "I'm glad to hear you say that. Because it's our job to provide an anchor into that reality."

"And point out the obvious," Bernadette said. "Because men never stop the car and ask for directions."

Now the First Lady laughed. "Exactly." When the laughter passed, she looked Bernadette straight in the eye. "Now I have a confession to make. I have had my eye on you ever since Ben was nominated. That's why I read all the briefs. How else am I to manage my end of the job? The President needs you and the country needs you, and maybe even the world needs you to get us through this China task. But I need you to help me do my job in guiding the President. Psychology and organizational behavior? I use those talents. I need someone like you to bounce ideas off of.

"See, most of the wives in this town are those baubles, strictly for the campaign trail. You have real substance. Real talent. And you understand that the reality of things is not all inside the Washington Beltway."

Bernadette paused to take it all in. She had heard of direct and to the point, but here was the First Lady of the United States asking her in the most direct way she could. Her tactics, the directness, could be explained by a lack of time and a lack of opportunity.

"What exactly are you asking of me?"

"I need a friend. I know how strange that sounds. Real friendship takes a long time to develop as trust builds. So I'm asking for friendship in the business sense of the word. Someone I can count on to bounce ideas off of. Someone who is willing to tell me that I'm nuts. It's the same thing Will said he saw in Ben. He was the only one who did not tell him what he wanted to hear. Do you think it's any different for me?"

"I see your point."

"So what do you say?"

Bernadette sighed. "Between you and Lopez, it sounds like there will be a lot of demands on my time."

"Think of it as joining a team. I learned that one from Will. It's how he thinks. And he is intensely loyal to anyone who has ever served on his team. That bit about the President of the United States owing you a favor. He really and truly means it. If twenty years from now you need a favor, he will deliver. That's his form of organizational behavior— intense, unending loyalty."

Bernadette realized Cynthia Turner was a woman after her own heart, an extraordinary talent who found the right niche to make the most of her talents. She was the best there ever could be at managing Willard Turner.

"Mrs. Turner," she said, "I would be honored—"

"Stop right there," said the First Lady. "I know what you've been told about protocol, about using titles no matter what, but if we're going to be confidantes, we must dispose of that once and for all. So from this moment and forever more, you must call me Cynthia."

Bernadette smiled at her. *Well,* she thought, *orders are orders. And this is coming from the top.* "All right ... *Cynthia.* I'm in."

CHAPTER SIX

BEN WAS SITTING ACROSS FROM BERNADETTE AT THEIR KITCHEN table when his mobile phone rang. It was Peggy.

"I have Governor Li on the line," she said.

Ben excused himself and walked into the living room where he picked up the old-fashioned corded phone that constituted his landline. Seemingly obsolete, landlines were still a Washington necessity—scrambled calls couldn't be transmitted any other way.

"Li Xue. What do I owe the honor?"

"Ben, per our agreement, I want you to know that the Politburo has chosen to implement the policy you and I discussed. I will be making a formal announcement before our markets open on Monday morning, tomorrow night your time. I have persuaded the Politburo to do it in a fashion that minimizes collateral damage."

"Thank you, Xue. I have thought through our response to your government's decision to sell its holdings of U.S. Treasuries. It is also designed to minimize collateral damage."

"You mean, 'large bills or small?'"

"I'm never going to live that line down, am I, Xue?" Ben was happy that the two men could inject a little humor into the conversation at such a tense moment.

"I'd rather have the large bills," Xue said.

Ben chuckled. "Thank you so much for your call. We both have a lot of work to do now, I know."

The two men hung up.

Ben immediately called Peggy. "Hope you didn't have a hot date tonight."

Peggy said, "After I took the call from Li's office, I knew that it wouldn't be possible, even if I had one lined up."

"We're going to need an emergency Federal Open Market Committee phone call tomorrow, probably around eleven o'clock. The exact timing is going to be determined by the call you have to make first, which is to get President Turner on the line. If you could give me Lopez's home number, I'll call him and Steinway myself. You'll be too busy calling the other eighteen members of the FOMC."

"I'm on it," said Peggy.

Three minutes later, she called to say, "I have President Turner's assistant on the line. She's waiting for you to pick up."

"Ben here," he said.

Immediately the President came on the line. "I doubt you have any good news for me at this hour, do you, Ben?"

"No, sir. Li gave me advance notice that the Chinese are going to proceed before their markets open on Monday, tomorrow night our time. Might I suggest, sir, that we convene again in your office some-time tomorrow afternoon? I am going to have to get the permission of the FOMC to implement our plan and am setting up a late morning telephonic meeting."

"How does eight o'clock sound," said President Turner. "We can discuss and then watch the markets open in China."

"Perfect," said Ben. After hanging up, he immediately called Peggy. "Let's set our meeting up for eleven."

¥ $ €

With the emergency FOMC conference call starting at eleven, time would be tight. The conference call was all about getting the ducks in a row for what was about to happen in the next few days. But ducks liked to quack. Ben realized that thought was a bit unfair. Their job was to quack. He was a great believer in diversity of viewpoints, and that was being offered. He just wished they could quack more succinctly and only when they had a relevant noise to make. Too many felt that they had to make noise in order to be relevant, and the situation had gotten worse since verbatim transcripts of the FOMC meetings were published. Members now felt obliged to say something, while trying to not say anything that would look controversial or foolish. So set-piece speeches replaced free and frank exchanges of views. The real purpose of a committee—to entertain a wide range of views, especially some that might be out of the box—had disappeared. The public and the politicians demanded transparency and accountability. What they got was conformity and mediocrity.

He unbuttoned his suit jacket and slid into his chair. Peggy had already placed a glass of water and a stack of paper on his desk. As he waited for the green light from Peggy letting him know that the calls were ready and waiting for him, Ben knew what he had to do.

"Ladies and gentlemen, I have bad news and I have more bad news." He could hear the chuckles; he had never been known as a font of good news. And if it wasn't bad news there wouldn't be any need for an emergency meeting. "Before I begin, I can't stress enough how extremely sensitive what we are about to discuss is. If there are any leaks from this meeting, I will not hesitate to ask the office of the Inspector General to interview everyone on this line under oath. Am I clear?" Ben paused, letting what he had said sink in. He knew that the silent voices on the other end of the phone were aware of the serious nature of an information leak, but it was his responsibility to ensure that he reiterated this fact.

He proceeded to sketch out the conversation he'd had with Governor Li the day before. He concluded the way he had with Secretary Steinway. "The markets are going to be hit with an additional $700 billion to $1.2 trillion of Treasury securities over the next six months on top of the existing supply needed to cover the deficit and maturing securities." He then added what to everyone in Washington would be obvious but might not be so outside the Beltway. "This is more than a monetary policy matter. It will be perceived in many quarters as an act of war." He paused, letting his last statement sink in.

"So let me give you the second piece of bad news. I am due to meet with the President later today. I hope to convey to him that this is more an act of desperation on the part of the Chinese than an act of war. But even if he bought that intellectually, it is not a sentiment around which he can rally the country. Make no mistake, Governor Li is not our friend. His long-term goal is to have the yuan replace the dollar as the world's reserve currency. That makes him a competitor in a game in which there can be only one winner.

"But it does not make him an enemy. Unlike some of his friends in the Politburo, he does not want to drag down the entire world economy during this competition. However, he reports to some who do view us as an enemy in the truest sense of that term and will be willing to inflict any collateral damage required to win, including collapsing the global economy."

Ben took a second, staring intently at the sweating glass on his desk. What came next had to be said carefully since there were both public and highly classified sources for the information, and he wanted to stick with the former and avoid the latter.

"The men we are facing are desperate. And desperate men take desperate measures. There were published reports that units of the People's Liberation Army had been dispersed to guard bank branches. There were also reports that a bank run got disorderly and PLA troops fired on the crowd of depositors demanding their money.

"There are reasons to believe those reports are accurate. What is not publicly known is that I was in the midst of one of those bank runs. I saw the crowds. I saw the PLA fire into the crowds, and candidly, I found myself hiding in a dumpster to avoid the bullets. It is an experience I will never forget." Ben picked up the water and took a measured sip. The pause had the intended effect. There was shocked silence on the phone.

That had softened the group up emotionally. Now for the institutional *coup de grâce* that he hoped would secure what he needed from this meeting.

"I believe that the Federal Reserve System has an obligation at this point in time to act as a stabilizing force. While politicians talk about the dual mandate of minimizing unemployment and inflation, those mandates presuppose an orderliness in markets and in global financial and economic conditions. It is maintaining that orderliness that is our real mandate.

"We are at a moment in time where the ranking of that fundamental priority should be apparent to all. This is a moment when cooler heads *must* prevail. By definition the members of this committee are the cooler heads in a world otherwise succumbing to a state of madness. It is my judgment that Governor Li and his associates at the People's Bank of China are in a similar, though not identical, circumstance and that they realize it. We must do our part to maintain that level of fundamental orderliness just as Li must do the same on his end.

"I am about to meet with the President, the Secretary of Treasury, and the Director of the CIA. I believe that my colleagues will all be representing the institutional interests of their agencies, each of which also favor orderliness. They will be advising the President to take as calm an approach as possible. I suspect that the CIA will be cautioning about how a misstep could quickly escalate into war and therefore caution is advised.

"That is not the strongest argument to make to any president. It is the President's job to show strength and resolve and the public elected him to do just that. Steinway is going to defer to us; he always does on monetary matters and in this situation, he is right to do so. It will be my job to reassure the President that everything will work out. That we hold the cards and will prevail if we play them carefully. That in risk lies opportunity. I need to convince him that America—and by implication, *he*—can win."

Ben looked up, giving everyone time to process what had been said when a voice broke in. It was Sarah Miller, who as President of the New York Fed was also Vice Chair of the Federal Open Market Committee. "Yes, Vice Chair Miller . . . ."

"Mr. Chairman, I think I understand what you are saying. I also think I can speak for this committee in wishing you good luck this afternoon. But it would also be less than appropriate if I didn't ask if you were all right. After all, not many of us can say we have ever been shot at."

"Sarah, I am fine. Thank you for asking. Got a bit of a scolding from

Bernadette for having taken some chances, but aside from those bruises, I am unharmed." He chuckled to make clear he was joking and could hear the same on the other end of the line.

He continued. "To the point, the motives of the Politburo are to make us feel the same sense of panic here that they are seeing on their own streets. Earlier I told you I was going to tell the President that things are under control and work with my colleagues to convince the President not to escalate matters. That is exactly what I am going to do. But here at the Fed, in the realm in which we operate, we are already at war, a currency war. It is one we cannot afford to lose or we will be seeing the same panicked faces on the streets of our towns and cities that I saw in Beijing."

"Mr. Chairman," said Sarah Miller, "I am glad you were so candid with us. For what it's worth, you have my complete support."

Most of the members of the FOMC had not voted for Turner in the last election. They had been appointed by his predecessor. They were not going to be in any mood to hand any of the FOMC's power over to the White House. That included Sarah Miller. But she also knew her job as Vice Chair was to support the Chairman. If she thought Ben was going too far in that direction, she would have ample opportunity to tell him so.

"What would you like us to do?"

"I wish we could discuss this in more detail, but time is short. I would like to be able to walk into the Oval with the support of this committee to tell the President that we will do whatever it takes to preserve orderly markets and assure that the People's Republic of China will not take advantage of the United States."

"That's pretty vague," interrupted Governor Avery. A former academic, Avery was no fan of the incumbent. In fact, he loathed him. Ben knew that loathing extended to him as well. Avery instinctively mistrusted anyone who had left the ivory tower of academia and entered the real world unless it was a direct move into public service. In Avery's view, going into the private sector meant giving up one's purity and objectivity. The two would never see eye to eye.

"Governor, believe me, I wish I didn't have to be vague. But honestly,

I have no idea how the meeting is going to go in the Oval. What I am asking this committee for is to give me as strong a hand as possible and the freedom to play that hand as necessary to attain our objectives. Our objectives are to save America, its people, and its economy from the Politburo's intentions and to do so in a way that preserves the independence of this institution. At this point we are at the level of strategy—at 37,000 feet. As we approach resolution, I will be much more specific about the tactics we will need to employ. After I have ascertained what the President has in mind and what his advisors are recommending, I will have the ability to provide something far more concrete than what I have done so far. It would be my hope that we could reconvene this meeting later this afternoon to do so."

"That's all well and good, but what exactly do you mean by, 'whatever it takes'?" Avery wasn't going to let go.

Ben decided to give Avery the answer in as direct a manner as possible. "I believe that 'whatever it takes' includes, but does not necessarily require, that the Federal Reserve purchase in the open market every Treasury security that the Chinese either sell or fail to rollover. The Chinese operation would thus be nothing more than a transfer of assets from one central bank balance sheet to another."

"In other words, 'large bills or small?'" By the tone of his voice, Ben knew Avery had a smile plastered across his face.

"Well, if that's what we have to do, that's what we have to do," Ben replied, with a smile as charming as the one he knew Avery was wearing. "As I committed to Governor Avery, I fully expect that we will be able to have a fuller discussion of this matter later in the week when we know more. For the moment, I would ask your consent to a statement that the Federal Reserve will do whatever it takes to maintain the current structure of interest rates and the level of liquidity in the markets." He crossed his fingers. "Are there any further questions at this time?"

"I don't like the phrase 'whatever it takes,'" said Avery.

"And I don't like emotional contagion," said Ben. "Let me frame it for you. We've all heard the stories from the Great Depression, the people leaping out of windows, bank runs, all of that. Well, here's a more recent example. You remember the initial days of the 2020 pandemic?

The panic buying? You couldn't get toilet paper or rubber gloves or disinfectant in any form for love or money. And that was when people could still go to their ATMs and get out all the cash they wanted, even though the bank lobbies were closing.

"Now, take away people's ability to get money. You can have all of the toilet paper in the world available, and if they can't get their hands on something to buy it with ... never mind food, gas, utilities. You want to see panic? Now we won't be using the military to fire into the crowds, but it's not going to be a pleasant scene. Especially for you incumbents.

"Gentlemen, this threat is very real. So you ask me if I mean it when I say 'whatever it takes,' my answer is, hell, yes."

There was silence.

"Very well then, we shall reconvene as soon as we have more information. I will make sure that all your offices have a thirty minute advance warning. Thank you all very much." Ben ended the call, stood up, gathered his paperwork, and strode purposefully to the door.

¥ $ €

The President, Hector Lopez, George Steinway, and Ben all sat in the small sitting room off the Oval Office. Ben had handed each man a copy of the statement he was to make after Li's announcement. It was the one blessed by the FOMC earlier in the day.

The President said, "Good job, Ben. You have remarkable political skills."

Ben replied, "I'm not sure what you mean, Mr. President."

Hector cleared his throat a bit too loudly.

The President's face went slightly red. After a pause, he said, "Corralling a committee of nineteen men and women cannot possibly be an easy thing to do. Especially one packed with people with far too many years of schooling." He followed that up with what he thought was a disarming chuckle.

"The members of the FOMC function as a board of directors, sir, not like a legislature," Ben said.

"And you make a remarkable chairman," said the President, a little too quickly. "As a former board chairman myself, I know that there is more than a little politics involved. But you made it happen. Like you said, whatever it takes."

"Thank you, sir." Ben's radar went up. He looked from Lopez to the President and back again. Lopez looked calm, typically unrattled. The kind of look he got from Bernadette sometimes when she wasn't entirely forthcoming. The President, on the other hand, was looking a little too innocent, like he'd almost gotten caught with his hand in the cookie jar. Ben pondered whether to press forward or to let the matter drop. Curiosity got the better of him. "I know I was asking a lot. Whatever it takes and all."

The press paid off. The President said, "Whatever it takes is pretty open ended. They must really trust you."

Now it was Ben's turn to flash a neutral look. "Sir, the statement I handed you does not contain the words 'whatever it takes.' They're implicit. But it's funny you should use them in context with the FOMC statement, sir." Ben stared straight at the President, daring him to lie.

Turner did not. "You caught me, Ben. Your conference call was not completely secure."

Hector sat forward in his chair. "Mr. President—"

"I asked Hector for a transcript."

Ben's face reddened. "Sir, that is a breach of the independence of the Federal Reserve. How do you expect me to maintain the trust of my colleagues when you do something like that? It's not exactly like you are their favorite person."

Hector intervened. "Ben, you know perfectly well that every call out of this building is monitored."

"But this is the White House," Ben said.

"The same is true with the Pentagon, Foggy Bottom, the CIA, the FBI, the NSC, and any part of official Washington that is involved in foreign affairs matters. Whether you like it or not, the Fed is now at the center of a foreign crisis."

Ben was not mollified. "Do you bug the board room as well? You know that if any information leaks that is a violation of the Federal Reserve Act and could result in fines and imprisonment." Ben knew he was stretching it just a bit. The law involved trading on leaked information.

The President realized it was time to back down for the sake of keeping the team together. "Ben, I am sorry. I made a mistake in asking Hector to do this. Please accept my apologies. I meant no disrespect. As Hector said, we are in the midst of a foreign policy crisis."

Ben sensed that this was the best he was going to get but was still annoyed. "Let's consider it water under the bridge, sir. When this is all over, I think we should all meet again and discuss appropriate protocols. I hope the tapping of the phone does not become public. It will cause trouble in the committee and we will be subject to all kinds of hearings on the Hill."

"Of course," said the President, though he knew there was an element of a bluff in Ben's statement. But as had been said, water under the bridge. At least for now.

Steinway glanced at his watch. "If I can shift gears, gentlemen, the Chinese markets are about to open. I suggest we watch."

The men turned their attention to the television. CNBC International was on the screen, the main anchor talking in front of a live video feed of a Chinese man stepping up onto a dais. The hot board at the bottom of the screen was scrolling through bond yields, stock market values, and currency exchange rates. If this had been a football game the crowds would have started to thin out around halftime. Compared to the massive swings of the previous week, this was like watching grass grow. The Shanghai composite was up three-quarters of one percent and the yuan was barely moving against the dollar. The U.S. ten-year yield had risen three basis points, or three one hundredths of a percentage point. This was not going to change the world.

The screen cut to the Beijing correspondent standing in the foreground, and behind her left shoulder Governor Li stood in the center of the dais, speaking from behind a lectern. She was listening to Li speak in Mandarin and translating—actually more like paraphrasing—for the viewing audience.

"The People's Bank of China wants to assure every citizen of China that their money is as good as gold, whether it is deposited in a bank or held in cash. Today we are beginning the liquidation of our holding of U.S Treasury securities and those of other nations. We will use the proceeds from this liquidation to purchase and maintain gold reserves enough to back every yuan now in circulation. This sell-off will be orderly to maintain the stability of the global economy. We will not reinvest the proceeds of maturing securities in new securities. No one need worry any longer about the integrity of our currency."

Ben chuckled at that. Li had the talent for massaging words that any successful bureaucratic politician would require to claw his way to the top as Li had. The word *orderly* was an unusual one to use when talking about liquidating two trillion in securities over six months. As for not worrying about the *integrity* of the yuan, Li had made one small mistake that Ben sought to exploit. Holders of the yuan could not simply walk into a bank and get gold. The gold had to stay in the government's hands. They could still buy gold in the market, but Li was trying to tell them not to bother.

The television cut back to the Hong Kong studio anchor. "Thank you, May Ling, we need to come back though. A statement by the Federal Reserve Bank of New York has just hit the wires. It says, and I'm quoting here, 'the Governor of the People's Bank of China has announced that they will cease the reinvestment of their holdings of U.S. securities as they come due. The Federal Open Market Committee stands ready to engage in whatever open market operations are needed to maintain the stance of monetary policy in this period. This includes supplying liquidity as needed to assure the Treasury securities liquidated by the People's Republic of China, up to and including the total dollar value of all securities."

"Yes," said Steinway.

"Okay," said Hector Lopez. "For the spook in the room, what just happened?"

"Confidence," Ben said. "The Fed just promised to buy up all the Treasury bonds as the Chinese sell them off. Suddenly it's a solid investment, and with any luck other market participants will swoop in and start buying whatever is needed to hold our interest rates in the same place. Saves the Fed the trouble and the dollars."

"So as long as people believe the Fed will buy enough debt to maintain interest rates, other markets do the work for us."

"Give that man a cigar," said Ben. Lopez smiled.

The hot board had been tracking the minute-to-minute movements of the 10-year U.S. Treasury bond since Li's statement. The yield had moved up three basis points—three one-hundredths of one percentage point—to 6.154 percent. Within minutes of the Federal Reserve's announcement, it had fallen to below its starting point and was trading at 6.11 points.

Lopez, now getting into the Saturday Night Football aspect of watching markets, said, "Fascinating. You guys countered Li's move and the market overshot to your side. He gained three points and you took back about four and a half."

"It's the Coleman magic," said the President. "He set up the play and executed it. And we're going to get a little more tomorrow."

Steinway cast a quizzical glance at the President. "What rabbit is Ben going to pull out of his hat tomorrow? If it's about bonds, I think I would have known about it."

Turner smiled. "This is family talent, George. Kind of like the Mannings, right? One brother quarterback for one team, the other brother calling plays for another."

Ben could see unease growing on Hector's face. "Mr. President," he said, "the other team hasn't signed a contract yet. And it won't be for quarterback. Bernadette's not going on the field. She's going to stand at the fifty-yard line with binoculars and an earpiece. The actual quarterback is going to call her in the morning to confirm."

Turner said, "She's not going to say no, is she, Ben? If she does, I'm going to have to go back to charm school to hold this job."

"Mr. President, your job is not about charm, it's about power. And you wisely didn't pull out the power play. She would have taken that as a challenge and, sir, you would have lost." Ben put on his best grin. "No, sir, you charmed Bernadette."

Hector said to Steinway, "She's the best China analyst around. She and her father are a dynasty all their own, like the Ming. I'm going to call her first thing in the morning."

"That should make for some interesting pillow talk," said the President, a little too relaxed. *In vino veritas* sometimes meant too much *veritas* on the second drink.

Hector looked away to avoid the President's gaze.

The screen showed the yield was up again, now shy of the starting point. Ben ignored the pillow talk line in favor of watching the action on the hot board.

"See, no Coleman magic," he said. "We are right back to the starting point. No harm, no foul. This is the way all currency wars should occur."

"That's the way all wars should be fought," said the President. Then he added, "Congratulations, Ben. It looks like the markets believed you. Credibility is a great thing to have. We politicians certainly don't have it. Maybe if I hang around you long enough, some will wear off."

"Thank you, Mr. President. I'd like to claim credit, but the key was Governor Li's statement that they would let their holdings of Treasuries wear off as they matured. That means that only about $30 billion or so would be dumped on the market in a given month. That is less than a third of what the Treasury is issuing to finance the deficit. No big deal."

"Speaking of the deficit," the President said, "I campaigned against it. Promised to eliminate it by the end of my second term. I should hope that the voters will forget that promise. All my predecessors have made the same promise and failed to follow through. I would like to think I'm a man of my word. The worst part of it is that we're spending over $1 trillion on interest alone. If it weren't for that we'd have something close to a balanced budget. I'm taking the political heat for a deficit that is paying for my predecessors' shenanigans."

"Sir," said Ben, "in risk there is opportunity. If this conflict with China works out the way we want, we may be able to do something about it."

"I'll hold you to that Ben," said the President, standing to indicate that the markets had become too boring to watch. "Besides, you've earned a good night's sleep. Let's chalk this one up to the home team."

¥ $ €

There was a group of men who were displeased over the American economic victory. They were government officials, the two dozen members of the Politburo of the Communist Party of the People's Republic of China, gathered to watch the events unfolding in the market.

This was where all the decisions took place in a nation that was the world's most populous, had arguably the largest economy, and was the most powerful militarily. It was the official position of the Party that there would be no argument about these latter two points within the next couple of decades. China was to be the world's sole superpower.

General Deng Wenxi was addressing the group, pointing directly at Governor Li Xue of the People's Bank. "Comrades, we have squandered an opportunity out of pure cowardice. I sat in his office as Li gave advance warning of our intentions to his American counterpart. Our enemy. But it is not too late. Here is our chance to strike a death blow. To avenge all of the humiliations we have suffered at the hands of the Americans and other Westerners over the past two centuries."

"Comrade General," Li said, "the path we are on was approved by the Politburo. We did so in order to minimize the potential damage to our own economy ...."

"Again, cowardice. And spoken like a true capitalist roader. Li, you have adopted the thinking of your profession. You have abandoned the teachings of Chairman Mao, who founded modern China. We are cowering like a bunch of old women afraid that we might lose some money! You bankers need to remember that power comes from the barrel of a gun, not a ledger book."

Chairman Ren Xi Wu, the head of the Communist Party and president of the nation, decided it was time to move on from the personal theatrics. "General Deng, you said something about it not being too late. That we could still strike a death blow."

"Comrade Chairman," said Deng, "you heard what the American banker said, that we were going to liquidate our position gradually. That allowed him to claim that they would act to stabilize their interest rates and protect their economy. Our advance notice gave them time to prepare for our attack. And this so-called attack made the classic mistake about which all of China's great military minds—from Sun Tzu to Mao—warned. When you attack you do so with overwhelming force so great that the enemy cannot resist. Let's see if the American bankers can stabilize things if we up our sales by a factor of ten or twenty. If we act now we may have an advantage. The enemy has been lulled into complacency by the weakness of our actions so far. Let us surprise them with a full force attack."

Chairman Ren looked at Li, acknowledging that it was his turn to speak. "Comrade Chairman, I know that I am not worthy to address this Politburo. I am here only to carry out your commands. But I do owe you my candid judgment. We are not in a strong position to launch a full force operation. Have you forgotten only last week troops in Beijing were forced to fire on crowds who were trying to get their money out of a bank—"

Deng interrupted. "Yes, and where are those crowds today? They got what they deserved and know not to come back for more. As I said, force, not money, is what works in this world and that is our Party's founding philosophy."

Li said, "Those bank runs can restart at any moment."

Deng would have none of it. "Comrade Li—and I use that term very loosely, for I have my suspicions about your loyalty, something that extends to your daughter."

Ren interrupted. "Comrade General, we should have no doubt about Li's patriotism."

"Comrade Chairman, that may be, but the counterrevolutionary thoughts of Li's daughter are recorded. So, might I add, are the counterrevolutionary activities of others in her generation, some of whom are children of members of this Politburo. I am in charge of the security arrangements for the PLA, so I know of what I speak. The lack of party discipline within our families is something we must confront."

Ren could sense the mood shift in the room. Deng had touched a very sensitive spot. The threat was hardly veiled at all—he would expose other members' children if he had to. Ren could not let that happen. It would tear the Party apart and lead to a full-scale bloodletting.

"General Deng," he said, "this is not an issue of patriotism or of family. Let us focus on the matter at hand. It is how to confront the Americans.

I personally see some merit in what you are proposing." Heads began nodding around the room. The consensus was clear if unspoken. Better to give Deng what he wanted than to open the families of the Politburo to disciplinary inspections.

"Governor Li," Ren continued, "from what I understand you are liquidating our Treasuries at a rate of about $30 billion per month. Do we have the capacity to sell more than that? Can we sell ten or fifteen times that amount as General Deng suggests?"

"We can sell, or try to sell, as much as you order me to. At some point there will be such an imbalance of sales that the markets will freeze up and no transactions will occur."

"What do you mean? We can't just sell everything?"

"You have to understand that every time we sell, the price of what we sell goes down. If we sell, we are supplying bonds, so the price has to fall in order to attract buyers. Comrade Chairman, we must realize that when we sell, the price for everything we still hold will drop and we may lose money."

"You are speaking of supply and demand," Deng said. "Comrade Li, you sound too much the capitalist. Perhaps you have been a banker too long. We may lose a little money, but we will gain a huge victory. We will replace America as the world's leading economic power."

"Comrade General, we are in complete agreement on our desired endgame."

"But Governor Li," said Ren, "you said we might not be able to sell as much as we want. General Deng is correct, a loss on our bonds will be a small price to pay for victory. What you are saying is that we might not get that victory because we won't be able to sell enough."

"Every time we sell something there has to be a buyer," Li explained. "When markets work well, there is always a buyer although the price may be a bit lower. But buyers must have a sense that they are buying at a price that won't go down more in a few minutes. That would be a recipe for losing money, something capitalists do not like to do, and will be wary of. If it looks like we are going to keep selling, everyone will think the price will keep falling and in fear, no one will step in to buy."

"Are you saying the market will not work?" asked Ren.

"Yes comrade. It will crash."

"So much the better," said Deng.

"Crashes cause many unintended consequences," Li said. "We could find it difficult to engage in trade, sell our production, or buy the things we need from abroad."

Ren nodded, having made his decision. "We have endured much in our long march to be the world's dominant power. A little disruption in our trade with the rest of the world seems minor in comparison. Besides, after we vanquish the Americans and their capitalist system, we will be able to set whatever terms of trade we wish as the emperors did when China was the Middle Kingdom. Please proceed, Governor Li. If we must crash the market, then crash it we will."

"Perhaps, Comrade General," Li said. "But if markets are frozen then the ability to conduct international transactions will disappear for a time. World trade will come to a halt. As we are the world's largest exporting economy, it will not be painless."

"We recognize that," said Ren. "This is the Politburo's decision, not yours. As long as you faithfully execute this strategy you will not be held responsible for any unintended results. Might I suggest you begin executing this plan right after our markets close so as not to add needless disruption here?"

"Of course," Li nodded, realizing that Ren was acting to protect the personal fortunes of the members present.

"Then we are agreed," Ren said, a statement and not a question.

As the gathering dismissed, neither Li nor Ren could help but notice the grin and the rare chuckle that could be heard coming from Deng.

CHAPTER SEVEN

"LOGAN, I CAN'T EXECUTE THE ORDER. NO BUYERS."

"Me either."

"It's like the board is frozen."

Logan managed Citi's bond desk in London. That meant until New York opened, he was solely responsible for Citi's $1.3 trillion bond portfolio. He could feel the bile rising in his stomach. In the last sixty seconds there had been no executions and the rules under which he operated were telling him that he had to liquidate as many positions as possible. If the prices on the screen were accurate, Citi was now out more than $25 billion over the last few minutes.

If this went on much longer, Citi would technically be broke. Despite that, Logan was not thinking about his career being over. A native of Canada, he liked living here with his family. Citi's offices were in Canary Wharf, an extension of the City of London that had grown exponentially. London was now the trading hub for this time zone, and it was ideal. It opened an hour before Asia closed and closed two hours before America opened. He was thinking the careers of more than half of the three hundred people on the floor were over.

Visions of people carrying personal effects out of Lehman that horrible weekend flashed through his mind. And it wasn't just going to be Citi. The same thing was happening at Morgan-Chase, at Bank of America, and all the rest.

He picked up the phone to call the head of asset allocation for the bank. He knew in his head what was supposed to happen next. The CEO would be informed. He would place a call to the president of the

New York Federal Reserve Bank. The Fed would step in as the buyer of last resort. In the end, they would make a market. It wasn't like you were going to have a real buyer and a real seller. There would be only one buyer—the Fed. And they were literally going to print the money to do the buying.

It wasn't really printing, of course. It was the electronic version. The Fed could print $1 for every $1 of bonds it had in its portfolio. They would keep buying and keep printing until the market calmed down. Then would come the unwind, which could take months or years.

Then Logan could hear a scream.

"What the fuck!"

He glanced up at the huge screen mounted above the trading desks. There was no volume—nothing being traded. The prices being quoted were five to six percent below where they had been an hour ago. It wasn't $25 billion anymore; it was more than twice that amount. Citi was about to go below its minimum capital requirement. Unless something happened, they were going to have to begin taking the first steps to unwind the bank.

The depositors would get their money back. The politicians wouldn't let Grandma lose her life savings. But she would be paid back out of freshly printed money.

¥ $ €

Ben's cell phone rang on the table next to his bed. All he could think was, *What time is it?* When he saw four-seventeen on the screen he knew there was trouble.

It was Peggy. "I have Governor Adams on the line."

"Good morning, Ben. Sorry to disturb you but we have a bit of a problem." Ben could hear the classic British understatement in John Adams's voice. As head of the Bank of England, John took his share of ribbing about being the namesake of a great American revolutionary. "Trading here in London has virtually ceased in the Treasury market, and the spillover into equities and futures is beginning."

Ben sat up. "What the hell happened?"

John replied, "Best we can tell, the Chinese started dumping everything they could after their market closed. And I mean dumping. Never seen anything like it in terms of sell orders. Markets froze up within two minutes."

"But Li said they were going to let the bonds run off."

"My hunch is he was overruled. MI6 sent me a heads up that the Politburo met most of the day in Beijing. The limos began scampering to their home bases around two Beijing time. Li probably didn't have much time to order some refined move, likely just said, 'sell' and his minions sold. The PBOC must have coordinated with the other big Chinese holders of U.S. Treasuries. It was unified. No pretense of multiple actors. If I were a military man, I would call it an attack of overwhelming force."

"Sounds like Deng," said Ben. "You heard about my little episode in Beijing last week? Soldiers firing point-blank into a crowd of people who simply wanted their money. That guy is evil, pure and simple."

"MI6 briefed me on him as well. Speaking of which, you may want to wake up the division of MI6 lying next to you. Sorry, but she is still very much missed over here. Lost to a great guy of course. I will let you get on with it." Ben could hear the click on the other end.

"Trouble in paradise," Bernadette said, stirring under the covers.

"You might say that. All hell is breaking lose. John Adams sends his regards by the way. Says you are still missed."

"I heard Deng's name. That woke me up. He is the stuff of which nightmares are made. May as well get up, too, sounds like we are both going to be on duty today. Let me get the coffee. You're going to be more pressed than I am." She gave him a kiss on the cheek, donned her robe, and headed downstairs.

Ben called Peggy back. "Call Lorianne at CNBC. Tell her I want on Squawk Box at seven sharp. I'll go straight to their D.C. studio on Massachusetts Avenue. Better book me for twenty minutes including Q&A. And do be blunt. If she can't deliver, I will go straight to Maria Baritromo. I'll start calling folks from the car."

Yes, he thought, *it was going to be one of those days.*

¥ $ €

Ben's mini motorcade pulled up promptly at six. Departure was scheduled for six-fifteen but getting there early was part of protocol. Ben knew he would get to the studios on Massachusetts Avenue by six-forty and have plenty of time for makeup.

Bernadette gave him a kiss on the cheek, a sign she was worried about him. His hormones were already flowing as the testosterone was kicking in for combat. She didn't need to add any additional stress to his system, even of the pleasurable variety.

As he got in the back seat, he sensed immediately that there was something on his driver's mind. Anthony had been driving him since he started on the job and Ben always made it a practice to befriend whoever was in the front seat. His life was dependent on the driver, not only for safe driving but in the event he might end up taking a bullet for him.

"Anthony, how are you this glorious Monday morning? Everything okay?"

"Well Mr. Chairman, I don't usually ask work questions, but I am a bit worried. Had the news on driving out here and they said something about the banks failing. Is my money safe?"

Ben said, "I guarantee it. You have nothing to worry about. And I should know, right?" Reassurance seemed like the best step. Volunteering details might only worry the man.

"Funny thing, Mr. Chairman. Here it is only five-thirty and there were two or three people at just about every ATM I passed. Don't you think it's a bit strange?"

"Those people don't have anything to worry about either." A little follow up at this point seemed harmless. "What exactly did they say on the news?"

"Something about the banks losing a lot of money overnight and that they didn't have enough left. Something about meeting capital requirements. I've heard it enough driving the last twenty years and should know what it means. Isn't it like they don't have enough money?"

Ben decided it was time for candor. "They have enough to pay everyone back, but we require them to have a little extra on top of that. Our job at the Fed is to lend them cash to cover any shortfall while they are selling what they need to sell. They're not going to run short. The Fed will make sure of that. In the unlikely event that they do run short, your deposits are guaranteed up to $250,000."

"I'm a little shy of that," Anthony said. "But maybe I'll drop by an ATM while you're in the studio to get a couple of hundred. In case."

Ben knew this response. It was the very part of human nature that drove those bank runs in Beijing. Folks wanting a little extra cash at first. When more people line up, they decide to get their money out while they can. The crowds intensify and so does the amount each depositor wants.

"God help us all," was all Ben could mutter under his breath.

"What was that, Mr. Chairman?"

Ben said, "Nothing. Just playing over the interview I'm about to have. Gotta figure out what questions they're going to ask."

"Don't know how you do it, sir."

"Sometimes," said Ben, "neither do I."

¥ $ €

General Deng was still smiling. He couldn't help it. No, he gloried in it. He felt he was presiding over the ultimate feast, a victory parade, the greatest celebration his nation had ever known.

He and his comrades were watching CCTV, the state-owned and -controlled link to the rest of the world. The screen showed chaotic trading in London with worried brokers and investors staring up at the electronic tickers. They zoomed in on some with tears in their eyes.

The screen switched to live scenes from New York, a montage of shots outside the branches of Citi, HSBC, and Morgan-Chase. The doors weren't open as it was still before seven in the morning in New York, but crowds were forming at the ATMs.

"Wait until one of those machines runs out of cash. Then the fun will really begin." His broad smile afforded the others a view of his badly stained teeth from decades of tobacco use and insufficient attention from a dentist, but he clearly didn't give a damn about it.

"Comrade General, your plan seems to be working out precisely as expected." It was one of his sycophants. Deng didn't tolerate contradictions or those who made them. He preferred not to retaliate against critics right away, but merely smiled as if he were taking it all in. But inside his head would be visions of a mangled body, preferably still alive. Watching the prolonged agony was one of the true joys of his life. Revenge was a dish best eaten cold, and Deng had no problem going back for second or third helpings.

An aide came into the room and handed Deng a note. "Chairman Coleman is about to go on television. This should be particularly entertaining. Not even his wife can help him out of this one."

Targeting Bernadette was the key. She and her father had been a pain in the side of the state since the late 1960s. Ben was an afterthought. He had become a subject of interest when he married her. Deng had personally chosen Zhang Jin from a lineup of five similar agents. Inspected them each up close. It was not out of sexual interest. His preferences ran in other directions. He wanted to see how each showed fear: the look in their eyes, the smell coming from their sweat, the sound of their breathing.

Deng knew what he was looking for. The way to Bernadette was through Ben Coleman—by creating sympathy for his minder in the American's psyche. The story of how he had landed Bernadette was well documented in the state security files. His profile was one of a hopeless romantic buried deep within his enormous intellect. Zhang Jin was perfect to appeal to his heroic American psyche. She was professional, but with a touch of genuine vulnerability. Ben would fall for her at some point. It was simply a matter of patience.

Deng congratulated himself at the brilliance of his choice. Now that the mouse was in the cat's paw it was time to savor the moment as the mouse struggled to escape.

¥ $ €

"Mr. Chairman, thank you for joining us on 'Squawk Box' this morning.

I know you're going to be having a busy day."

"Thank you for having me, Kelly." Ben had decided to get his message out first, before any questions. There were three reporters on the show and any one of them could lead him down a path he had not intended. "Yes, it is going to be a busy day. But I want to begin by assuring every American that the U.S. banking system is solid. It is our job at the Fed to make sure that is the case. We will be using our discount window as needed to guarantee liquidity. We are also going to follow through on the commitment I made last night. Whatever the People's Republic of China chooses to do with its holdings of Treasuries, the Federal Reserve will engage in open market operations to maintain the structure of interest rates."

"Mr. Chairman." It was Andrew, who doubled as a *New York Times* reporter. He was not where Ben wanted to go at the start, so he was glad he had led off with his statement. "The wire services are running stories that Citi, Morgan, and HSBC have fallen below their capital requirements on a mark-to-market basis. Doesn't this require regulatory action?"

"Andrew," he said, "those wire services are remarkably well informed. Or should I say self-informed. They seem to have made up the stories themselves. Let's start with the fact that marking to market is done *after* the business day is completed, at four this afternoon. Nine hours from now. How they could have discerned market prices that haven't occurred yet and then done the math and run that story is beyond me. As a reporter, Andrew, you should know you can't run a story about an event that hasn't happened yet."

Andrew said, "Well I'm sure they were hypothetical calculations—"

Ben stayed on him. "Andrew, central bankers do not deal in hypothetical calculations. They deal in real-time facts." He held up the palm of his hand to stop Andrew from interrupting. "And as I said, the Federal Reserve is going to engage in open market operations to maintain the structure of interest rates. That is not a statement of some limited amount of intervention. We are going to be in the market with whatever it takes to maintain the structure of interest rates."

Andrew tried again. "But how do you know—"

"We are going to do whatever it takes to maintain the structure of interest rates." Ben made sure his voice was firm, not loud. "That means at four o'clock this afternoon the yields at every point on the curve will be back to where they were when markets closed last week. That is what maintaining the structure of interest rates means. Interest rates will be coming down and bond prices will be going up, simple as that. What you are calling hypotheticals aren't that at all. They are fairy tales."

Ben knew he was hammering Andrew too hard, but this was a battle that could not be lost. Markets needed to be convinced that the Fed would return things to where they had been. The more convinced the markets would be, the less the Fed would actually have to do. Markets were self-correcting. In essence he had just said, *If you buy bonds now you will make money by the end of the day and the Fed will make sure of it.* When markets are told how to make money, they do it.

Kelly stepped in to steer away from the blood on her colleague's face. "Your point is well taken, Mr. Chairman. But what do you make of what China is trying to do?"

"That is a good question, Kelly. When Governor Li announced their intention to sell their Treasuries when the Chinese markets opened, he said it would be done in an orderly fashion. He said they were going to let their bonds run off as they matured. That was a very sensible decision. It would assure that the Chinese government would not lose any money in the process of liquidating their positions.

"However, it appears that Li's sensible approach was overridden by someone who does not understand markets or economics. It does appear that after their markets closed the Chinese began a massive selling operation in London. It has driven bond prices down. So the Chinese are now selling bonds at prices below where they bought them and at prices below where they are going to be this afternoon. If they were a U.S. company the Securities and Exchange Commission would immediately begin an investigation." Ben knew he was on a roll. Now for the *coup de grâce*.

"Frankly, as an American taxpayer, I hope that the Chinese will keep selling at these prices. We will keep on buying. We'll be getting a bargain. The Chinese are now selling our Treasuries to us at a three percent discount. That means for every billion they sell, they put $30 million in our pockets. If they sell their entire holding of $1.5 trillion, we make $45 billion. Not bad for a day's work, don't you think? So, to whomever overruled Governor Li's very sage advice I say, bring it on and thank you very much."

Andrew, Kelly, and Becky, the third anchor, could all see where Ben was going and decided to play along. Becky asked, "Why are the Chinese doing this?"

Ben felt like it was Christmas. "Becky, a very wise man once told me politicians think desperate times require desperate measures, but that central bankers know desperate times require calming measures." He hoped that Li was watching.

"The Chinese are in some very desperate times right now. When I was there last week, I found myself caught in the midst of a massive bank run. Every bank on the street had people outside it pounding on the doors to get in. Soldiers showed up and fired point-blank into the crowds. The Chinese politicians who ordered that brutal act were taking desperate measures.

"Their mass liquidation of Treasuries is another desperate measure. Desperate people who do desperate things only make their situation worse. Our intervention to preserve the structure of interest rates is a calming measure, the very opposite of shooting into a crowd or screaming 'Sell everything.'"

Andrew saw an opening and a chance to regain some stature. "Mr. Chairman, there are reports of bank runs happening right here in New York City."

"I have heard those reports," Ben said, "and we both know how misinformation gets spread at times like this, especially through social media. So let me repeat. The U.S. banking system is perfectly safe. No depositor need fear at all for the safety of their deposits."

Andrew wasn't done with him. "Are you saying it is unpatriotic to take your money out of an ATM?"

"Of course not," said Ben. "If you need some cash, go to an ATM and get some. If you don't, don't. It's up to you. There is plenty of cash to meet the demand. The Fed's cash divisions will be working full-time today to get cash to wherever it is temporarily needed. If your local branch ATM runs out, come back in a few hours or go inside and make a withdrawal the old-fashioned way. Right now, we have over $5,000 in cash printed for every man, woman, and child in America. If we need more, we'll convert some other assets into Federal Reserve notes—money. In America, your money is yours. You can do with it what you want."

Perhaps using the patriotism card had caused a twinge of guilt, or perhaps a producer talking into his earpiece was saying to get back on the right side. Whatever the case, Andrew now decided to help. "And you can't do that in China, as you saw for yourself last week. Another reason why we are proud to be Americans. Good luck today in your efforts, Mr. Chairman."

"And thank you."

As Ben walked off the set he turned on his cell phone to find a text from Steinway. *Good job. We made back half our losses during your time on set. You really built confidence.*

Confidence, Ben thought. *Yes, confidence. That was what stood behind all money. It wasn't gold or silver or even the full faith and credit of the government. It was confidence.* Ben felt himself square his shoulders. Today he was going to have to exude confidence. That was his job. It wasn't doing anything on a calculator or a spreadsheet. There were no regressions or complex economic models involved. Those might be useful another day. *Right now, it's all about confidence.*

CHAPTER EIGHT

WHEN HECTOR LOPEZ ARRIVED AT HIS OFFICE AT SEVEN-THIRTY HIS secretary had some unexpected news. "Mr. Director, Monica Jenkins and Richard Wei have requested a meeting with you at your earliest convenience. They said it was fairly urgent, came here personally. I put them in the side conference room and told them you would be here shortly."

"Thank you, Bob. Give me about three minutes and then bring them in."

Jenkins and Wei were his top China people. He had wanted to see them as well, not so much for analysis as for a bit of bureaucratic politics. They were about to be hit with a not-so-minor invasion of their turf and Lopez knew better than to leave them totally blindsided. "Anything else?"

"Sir, Secretary Steinway would like to have a word with you. But he is tied up in a meeting until six. I took the liberty of setting up a call for you at that time. This would seem to be a busy time for both of you. Also, Mrs. Lopez called but did not leave any information other than to say call when you get a chance. I hope six works for the Steinway call; if not I will arrange another time."

"No, we'll make it work. More precisely, you will make it work by interrupting me." He didn't wait for the inevitable "Yes, sir," but headed straight into his office. Bob Franks was one of his best finds. He ran his life with military precision the way quality Army staff sergeants were supposed to. Franks had worked at the Pentagon but had been commended by his superiors to Hector when he had come on board.

Even the fact that he was gay was not an issue like it had been in the past. When he came out the Army counseled him wisely: as long as you are upfront with us, we know you can't be blackmailed. Avoiding the potential for blackmail over some deep secret was one of the primary reasons for having clearances.

Jenkins and Wei arrived, and they got right down to business.

"We have analyzed the recording of the call between Chairman Coleman and Governor Li," said Monica Jenkins. "We have high confidence that there was someone else in the room with Li when the call was made. The sounds of at least one other individual were clear. Signals Intelligence says with reasonable confidence that it was Deng Wenxi. We know that General Deng made a call from the vicinity of PBOC headquarters about half an hour after Li's call was made. No other calls had been made from Deng's cell phone within half an hour on either side of the Coleman-Li call."

"Good work, Monica. Though we probably should not be surprised. Deng is the top enforcer for his faction and Li is probably perceived as being too close to outsiders. I doubt the Politburo would have allowed the call had Deng not been there to supervise. Any thoughts on the call, Richard?"

"Sir, I found it odd that Governor Li would tip his hand like that to Chairman Coleman. It would seem that he was giving up the element of surprise."

"Surprise can lead to miscalculation of the deadliest sort," said Hector. "This is a huge gamble by China and Li knows it. Transparency, at least in small quantities, can be quite helpful. That was the whole idea behind establishing the Hot Line between the White House and the Kremlin back in the sixties. What would you say is your division's degree of confidence about what is motivating the Chinese at this particular point in time?"

"Sir, I would say that we have as strong an analytic team as possible," said Jenkins. "Our on-the-ground intelligence is as good as possible in an authoritarian state. Our signal intelligence is excellent."

"Then why did we not see this latest move by the Chinese coming? The first we heard of it was the call from Li to Coleman. I haven't seen a paper across my desk saying that the Chinese were about to risk a currency war at this point in time." Hector realized he was being a bit too harsh and vowed to switch to his kinder and gentler tone.

But it was too late. Jenkins's hackles were up, ready to defend her turf. "Sir, our emphasis has always been on the military and strategic threats China poses. We do not profess to be experts on global monetary policy."

"Of course, Monica. We tend to defer to the Federal Reserve and the Treasury on those matters. We do have an economics branch, but they are more bean counters estimating GDP growth and things like that, not policy analysts. So I think it is time to bring in some outside help." There it was; explosion about to happen.

"What do you mean, sir?"

"The President has decided that some very close interagency coordination at the very highest levels is essential if we are to deal with the current threat from China. We will be adding someone to the team who will have the President's ear as well as that of the chairman of the Federal Reserve."

"A new member of our division," said Richard Wei.

"Not exactly. An independent agent."

"But there is no time for the clearance process," Wei said.

"Not an issue. The President himself signed the waiver for full code word clearance."

Monica and Richard stared at each other, dumbfounded. Finally Monica said, "I'm not sure anything like that has ever been done before. We will have to look up the proper protocols."

"No need. We will be setting the protocols as we go. And we will be doing so beginning at ten o'clock this morning. By the way, clear your schedules. Mandatory meeting for your division. Ten o'clock. Conference room." Hector could feel stares of silent protest from his subordinates. "It's a done deal. Presidential orders. Oh, by the way, our new asset doesn't know the full details about her involvement. She is about to find out. So this is definitely not to leak—understood?"

"Yes, sir, of course. We will see you at ten with perhaps half a dozen of our top people if that's okay?"

"Done." And as he escorted them out of the room he said to Bob, "Get Mrs. Lopez on the line."

¥ $ €

The call to the Coleman household came in at nine o'clock as scheduled. "Mrs. Coleman, I have Director Lopez for you." Bernadette could tell by the delay in the response time that the signal was being scrambled.

"Bernadette, how nice of you to take my call."

"I don't believe I had a choice, Mr. Director."

"Okay, forget the pleasantries. Neither of us really has time for them, now do we? I will skip right to the point. What is your answer to the President's question?"

"Why, Mr. Director, did you have the residence bugged?" She said it in jest but then realized it just might be true.

"Who told you?" said Hector. "No, let me guess. Was it Turner?" Lopez's reaction was to be disarming, intended to make light of the whole issue. Whether it was true or not, he certainly wasn't going to let on.

Bernadette said nothing.

"Damn him. I need to have a private word with that man. That's twice in two days he's burned me. What do you two have on him?"

"You wish," Bernadette said. "Meantime, back to the President's question. I thought for sure you would ask me all on your own."

"Touché. Let's say this has been hardwired."

"Well then, Mr. Director, you already know my answer is yes."

"I suspected it might be. A car will be there to pick you up in ten minutes. He is actually waiting down the street."

"Now, Mr. Director. You are a married man. You should know that a woman can't possibly be ready in ten minutes."

"I've read your brief, Mrs. Coleman. You are already ready. In fact, I suspect you have been ready for over half an hour. The Red Ninja is never unprepared."

Bernadette grimaced. Of course, she was a known quantity. And she was about to go back into a world in which she was known inside and out—a world where people had files on her that reflected everything that was even remotely public about her behavior and had been analyzed and reanalyzed into a compartmentalized format. It was a world she thought she had left behind when she married Ben and moved to America. Whatever twinge of sympathy she had had for Ben and the day he would face had vanished. She was going to have a much rougher day.

She checked herself in the mirror one last time, said a silent prayer, and left the house. The car was an added twist. Lopez did not want to take chances. It would not be wise for her personal car to be seen pulling up at Langley. It was much harder for the curious to track where all the agency cars went about town. She would not be recognized. But she was also somewhat captive under this arrangement. It was subtle, and it would be a card he would never play, but Lopez controlled her transportation home.

¥ $ €

"Don't let this go to my head."

The driver of the limousine looked at Bernadette through his rear-view mirror. "Ma'am?"

"Webb. That's your name, right? I'm sorry. I used to be so good with names, but that was practically a lifetime ago now. It used to be critical to what I was doing, but now it's like a muscle I don't use that much."

"You're fine, ma'am," Webb said. "I like to say, 'My name is Webb, but I've been called everything but that.'" He smiled as Bernadette laughed.

"Thank you, Webb. And promise me you won't let this go to my head."

"Ma'am?"

She looked out the window of the limo. "I live in a place where people show their status by the vehicle they drive. Mercedes, Lexuses, Beemers. And yet—" She shook her head as they passed a van the color of Florida coastal water. "The ultimate status symbol around here is the Aqua Blue service vehicle. What better way to show the neighbors you have a pool in your back yard?"

"Pools are no big shakes," Webb said. "Most everyone around here has one."

Bernadette nodded. "And to my point. With this little parade I'm riding grand marshall in, I think I've got most folks in this neighborhood trumped. Except for maybe my husband."

"This is small by comparison," Webb said. "To some."

"That's where you promise to not let this go to my head. In ancient Rome, the emperors would come home from war and throw a big party."

"A victory parade," Webb said. "Showing off animals from captured lands, treasures, lines of defeated people who were now slaves."

"I knew I liked you," Bernadette said. "And the most important thing. A slave riding in the chariot with the emperor. His sole duty—" She waited on him.

"To stand behind him and whisper over and over into the emperor's ear, 'You are mortal. You are mortal.'"

"Exactly."

"You don't seem the type to be prone to that," Webb said. "But I promise I'll do my best. So when does Aqua Blue come around to your place?"

"We don't have a pool."

"Well, then. You're mortal after all."

"Thank you, Webb," Bernadette said, thinking that perhaps the twinge of nerves she'd been feeling were just first day jitters, and that today would be a great day after all.

¥ $ €

The identification check at the gate was rather perfunctory—at least by modern standards—and the car drove right into the garage, sparing her having to walk across the outdoor lot if she had driven herself. An advantage of being a guest of the Director. She was dropped off at the VIP elevator and instructed to push the button for the eighth floor. There she was greeted by an unenthusiastic suit with a manufactured smile and escorted straight to the Director's office.

"Bernadette." Hector Lopez smiled. "It is so wonderful to have you on board." He seemed genuine enough about his sentiments for now.

"Thank you, sir. I hope you can assure me that all of your staff will be as happy about my arrival."

"Point taken. We are team players here. Perhaps too much so. How strange it is that we recruit for the capacity for independent thought and action. After a few years the bureaucratic instinct tends to vanquish any real independence. I'm sure MI6 was a hotbed of deviant thinking, unlike us here."

"Fair enough," Bernadette said. "I suppose I was cut more slack than most because of my father. But the pressure to conform was still there. Ultimately, it came down to the individual's willingness to tell his or her employer to go fuck themselves. Not an easy thing to do, is it? I was ready. I had acted all along that I could do it, and the act was largely believed. It was what a poker player would call a semi-bluff. But it was Ben who actually provided me the opportunity to do it."

"That is why our current arrangement might work well. Between Ben and your novels, you have financial independence. But your relationship with the First Lady is what gives you real independence and power."

Bernadette raised an eyebrow.

Hector handed her a printout. "This was added to the *Drudge Report* about half an hour ago. It was designed to look like a scoop, but it was actually a leak intended to send a signal."

Bernadette read the headline. "What's Up Between the Colemans and the Turners?" The story went on. "Fed Chair Ben Coleman and his wife Bernadette (a/k/a bestselling author Edmund Whitehall) had dinner last night in the residence portion of the White House with President and Mrs. Turner. The arrangement was highly unusual as the residence is usually reserved only for family and their closest friends. Word has it that the First Lady and Bernadette Coleman have become very close. That would make it the ultimate power friendship in Washington."

"Straight from the First Lady's office," Hector said. "She wants the world to know that you are not to be messed with. Don't expect a lot of outright hostility to manifest itself. That snippet has already made the rounds here." He paused to chuckle. "Funny how the world works, isn't it? All news is manufactured, produced in a way to make it seem spontaneous and unearthed by the hard work of the fourth estate. That narrative serves everyone, source and reporter. Shall we go into the lion's den?"

Bernadette and Hector entered the conference room at precisely ten o'clock. Everyone stood as the Director entered. He signaled Bernadette to take the chair at the front end of the table and the room sat as she did. Hector remained standing to make introductions.

"Ladies and gentlemen it is my pleasure to introduce Mrs. Bernadette Coleman. She is probably better known to you over the years as the Red Ninja of MI6 fame, and to some of you as author Edmund Whitehall, author of such novels as *Dragon Heart* and *Dragon Rising*. She has graciously agreed to provide her insights on China at this delicate moment. I have other matters to attend to so I will leave you to get acquainted." And with that he exited, leaving her to face the lions on her own.

¥ $ €

As Lopez strode back into his office, Bob Franks stood at a civilian version of attention—sort of a cross between a rigid body and at ease. Lopez knew the signal. Franks had something to tell him. "What is it, Bob?"

"Sir, I could not help overhearing Dr. Jenkins and Mr. Wei discussing General Deng."

Lopez was taken aback. Then realized there must be import behind this or Franks would not have stood the way he did. He decided to encourage Franks to be as candid and open as any person could be to the director of the CIA.

"Real creep, don't you think? Sure hope they broke the mold when they made that one." Then to underscore the point in a military way that would leave no doubt, "Permission to speak freely."

"Yes, sir. It's funny you should refer to General Deng as a creep. I may have some intelligence you could find useful in that regard."

"Speak."

"The man is a real pervert. Among certain members of, shall we say, my community, sexual tourism is a thing. Cambodia, Thailand, Indonesia, some other places where you can ... get what you want. I mean, straight people go, too, usually underage girls, but—"

"Tell you what, let's skip the political correctness. It's getting in the way of this conversation."

"Yes, sir." He seemed to relax at this. "Like any community, there's talk, advice, places to go, what to avoid. Especially important to have an information network if you're in the military—"

"To the point, Bob."

"Sir, it has come to my attention that General Deng is a regular at a certain place in Laos. See, a bunch of us ex-military intel types hang out together every Thursday. Started as kind of a support group as we transitioned out. We're like any of those cliques in this town that share just enough to get things to move. Deng's picture had been in the paper for some reason and one of my buds said, 'Hey, I saw that guy last time I was on vacation in Laos.' He goes to one of the resorts in the Golden Triangle for a week or so every year. His favorite is the King's Roman. Right across the street from the Mekong—literally where Laos, Myanmar, and Thailand come together. Wild place."

"Always has been," Lopez said. "Too far away from the capital for any of them to care. Forty years ago it was the opium capital of the world, before Afghanistan took over."

"Yes, sir, and sex tourism is now the dominant industry. China runs the whole area, as it does most of Laos. But this is like a lawless extension of Yunnan province. Laotian nationals aren't even allowed to buy land there. Only Chinese, and only those very well connected with the PLA. Perfect place for a guy like Deng to go to, uh, unwind."

"And how does Deng prefer to unwind? Anything we can use?"

"I believe so. He loves whipping teenage boys. It's his thing. Bloody shirt kind of stuff. Has a special belt with a steel inner shaft just for the job. Sometimes he does two or three boys at the same time."

"Yes, perfect ...." Lopez muttered, his mind in fast forward, thinking how best to deploy this new intel.

"His aide pays them off," Bob continued. "A kid can feed his family a month for a few hours of rough play. Maybe it's a way of getting some repeats or maybe he hopes they will tell their friends. Seems to be an open secret around the area. Doesn't seem to be a shortage of kids willing to put themselves through it. Deng can go through a dozen in a weekend."

"Who else knows about this, Bob?"

"Here at the agency? Nobody."

"Over there?"

"Like I said, an open secret. Everybody knows. Nobody talks."

Lopez thought about this. "You have any documentation of this?"

"Nothing that could be lifted out of a trash can, sir. Deng plays pretty clean over there, has his assistant do all the dirty work, acting as a firewall, keeping away anything that might taint the General's reputation. I'm sorry I don't have more. I thought this might be the kind of thing you want to keep in your back pocket. In case."

"In case," Hector said. "Yes, indeed. It's nice to have a card up one's sleeve when the game gets tense, even better when it's an ace. And that, Mr. Franks, is one hell of an ace."

¥ $ €

As if on some prearranged cue, the meeting continued as if Lopez hadn't been there at all. The woman to Bernadette's left began.

"Mrs. Coleman, I am Monica Jenkins, head of the Agency's China Division."

"I recognized you from your file," Bernadette said, then caught herself. "I'm sorry. I'm falling back into my old habits. Didn't think it would happen so easily. Please, call me Bernadette. I think the American custom of starting off with first names is the right way to go. So Monica, I think that your report on the passing of the Red Guard generation a few years back was absolutely brilliant.' She could see the faintest hint of a smile on Monica's face. Bernadette knew she was being a classic politician, and maybe this hardened group of professionals knew it too. But although flattery might not get you everything, as the saying claimed, it was a good place to start. The tension in the room began to dissipate noticeably. This was Organizational Behavior 101.

The man to Monica's left then spoke. "I'm Richard Wei, deputy director of the China Division."

The conversation then went around the table with each person identifying themselves. When it came around to Bernadette, she said, "I am here to learn. So if you would be kind enough to give me your standard briefing and how you see the situation. I will do my best to be a fast learner."

At around eleven-fifteen Wei went to the coffee machine and brought Bernadette a cup of dark roast along with packets of half-and-half and sugar. He whispered, "Agency policy is I bring you the first cup. After that you're on your own." Bernadette rewarded him with her best smile.

By twelve-thirty sandwiches arrived along with sides. People helped themselves when there was a lull in the action. By one-thirty the group had gone through the entire standard briefing—who the players were, how they interacted, where the decision nodes were in the bureaucracy. *Both very thorough and very conventional,* Bernadette thought.

As division head, Monica made the break. "So you've heard our analysis. What do you think? I've got to tell you that your reputation precedes you. All of us want to know what Red Ninja's assessment of the situation is." The words were spoken genuinely enough, but Bernadette knew that this was the trickiest part of the transition. To be effective they really had to stop thinking of one another as competing teams and work on the cross-fertilization of ideas.

"You've given me a lot to think about," Bernadette said. "And I am going to need a few days to come up with a real assessment. But let me try out a few initial thoughts and see what you think. First and foremost, I think we need to be careful about our classification system—hawks and doves, hardliners and moderates. Factionalism tends to be overdone everywhere, even here. We talk about Republicans and Democrats but there are really one hundred separate parties in the Senate and 435 in the House. Politicians at this level here and in China didn't get where they are by blending into the crowd.

"What intrigued me most in your analysis was the perceived tradeoff between external cohesion and internal paranoia. I have my own prejudices on that score, but I will admit they might be a bit out of line. Monica, could you give me your thought process on that?"

And so it continued for the entire afternoon. Around five fifteen Director Lopez came back to be greeted by an intense discussion. "So how's it going?" The question was rhetorical; it was obvious that his team and Bernadette had bonded. "May I join you?" He pulled up a chair. Bernadette moved slightly to her right to make room and Hector sat directly between her and Monica.

Bernadette motioned to Monica to do the honors.

"Well, sir," Monica said, "we are at the strategizing stage, gaming out different responses on the part of the Chinese. Bernadette has pointed out something that may be an even more fatal flaw than what we had thought. The question to ask is, 'Who is going to take the bullet if something goes wrong?' Does that person know it? Will everyone else in the group let that happen to save their own skin?

"We think we have a consensus. The scapegoat is going to be Governor Li. It is his area of operations. He is, by the nature of his job, more outwardly focused than everyone else. He is also to some extent isolated at the central bank, with no obvious allies. He must understand his situation. Any look at his resume shows that he's a man who understands office politics quite well. He's been in the lynch mob himself a number of times, but never the guest of honor. He understands the dynamics quite well. He is the perfect candidate.

"He therefore becomes our weak link in the decision tree. In an ideal world we should simultaneously stoke his paranoia and give him an out. And I mean that last one in the literal sense."

"You mean asylum?" Hector couldn't help himself. It would be an almost impossible stunt to pull off.

Bernadette decided it was time to come in on the side of the newly forged consensus. "Hector, it would only be a last resort. Asylum wouldn't necessarily be the best outcome, which would be for us to somehow make him look like the hero who saved China from a tough situation that others had gotten the country into. He would save face and maybe his life, and would actually gain face in the process. He would also know that we did that for him. As a way to produce smooth economic relations with the People's Republic that would be, as you Americans say it, a home run."

This inspired a number of conversations to break out around the table. Bernadette decided to take advantage of the break and reached for her cell phone.

"Sorry," said Hector. "That won't work in here. No phone, no text, and no email, at least on that device. I suspect you intended to call Ben. We've already let him know you're running late, so don't worry." To help Bernadette recover from her embarrassment, he went on. "Ben is working late too. We all have the same problem. No, let's call it an opportunity. The President is giving a nationally televised address to the nation on Tuesday night."

The pained expressions were on every face around the table. The last thing anyone in the bureaucracy wanted was for the President to be out there winging it. It would complicate their lives, their planning, and inevitably limit their options. There was a constant tension in Washington between who was the boss in theory, constitutionally, and who actually thought that they were in charge.

"I did say opportunity, didn't I?" Hector said. "Speechwriters have it now. First draft will be around tomorrow. We are on the distribution list. So is Chairman Coleman. And so, I understand, is the First Lady." Hector looked briefly at Bernadette who was doing her best to maintain a poker face.

"Input to the speechwriters?" Monica asked.

"Secretary Steinway has asked me, Ben Coleman, and Secretary Reynolds to put together something preliminary for tonight. Recommendations?"

With that began two hours of give and take. Bernadette thought about being back in the joys of life in the civil service. Her first day was going to run 11 hours. *But then again, to be honest with myself,* she thought, *it's really great being back in the fight.*

CHAPTER NINE

"MY FELLOW AMERICANS. TONIGHT I COME BEFORE YOU AT A TIME OF grave peril for our nation."

"No, Mr. President, I don't think we can use the term 'grave.'" It was the Secretary of State, Dianne Reynolds. Her job was to advocate for maximum calm in the world stage. "It means deadly. Too bellicose and scary. How about 'a time of challenge'?"

"When have we not been challenged?" This was Roger Lombardi, the President's chief of staff. It was his job to protect the President's interests, and he felt that Secretary Reynolds was tarnishing the President's reputation as a tough man who tackled tough challenges. A president needed someone who could say things that a president could not and get it right about ninety-five percent of the time. Everyone needed to assume that when the chief of staff spoke, he was carrying the authority of the president. If he stepped out of line the president would tell him so, but privately. "The President cannot sound namby-pamby about this. With all due respect, Madam Secretary."

"Dianne," said the President, "I think Roger has a point. But folks, this is only the first line. I've got a speech to give in just over twenty-four hours. I can't have you bickering over each and every word."

"Mr. President, perhaps we could balance the risks with something more upbeat," said Lombardi. "At a time of genuine peril, but also one that offers great opportunity."

"I like it."

The boss had spoken, and no one wanted to challenge him. Besides, President Turner had been right. They did have to put a speech together before they went to bed tonight in order for it to be circulated tomorrow morning. Then in the afternoon would come the background stories. The press secretary would call carefully selected journalists and leak some of the contents of the speech. In return for the scoop, the coverage would be generally fair and balanced. But more important for the White House, the stuff that was leaked would be the main message the President wanted to send. It was a way of massaging the media to shape the story the way the President wanted.

On and on it went. Six hours of constant back and forth. Finally the President said, "Lombardi, I think it's yours. Put it together and ship a copy up to the residence to read over. I'm headed there for a drink."

Everyone stood as the President rose. He turned to his secretary of state.

"Dianne, I know you didn't get everything you wanted. But the speech is far short of a declaration of war, don't you think? I know that's what you were afraid of."

"Yes, Mr. President." An effective member of the president's team knew when to stop the argument. She could push her view as far as possible, but when the give and take was over, you fell in line. That way you could fight as hard the next time and everyone knew that in the end, you would be a team player.

"You're carrying the ball tomorrow on the talk shows. I'm counting on you."

"You can count on me, Mr. President."

"I know I can." The President had completed the ritual. Dianne would play for the team and would be rewarded for it with a permanent place at the President's ear. In the unspoken world of signals at the top, Turner had reiterated the implicit terms of the contract. To drive home the point that a deal had been struck, the President shook her hand as she moved to the door.

"George, Dianne says war won't break out. Can markets handle it? I'd rather not have Wall Street give me a Bronx cheer for what I'm going to say."

"Sir, markets will do what markets will do. You signaled resolve and hinted at good ideas to come. After the initial shock, the markets are due for a bounce. They just need a reason. I think you'll give it to them."

"That was pretty one-handed for a two-handed economist."

"Remember, I'm not really an economist." George smiled, the President chuckled, and they shook hands.

"And Roger. When you're done could you also messenger a copy out to Coleman at his residence and Lopez at his?"

"Will do, Mr. President," Lombardi said, and turned to his task.

¥ $ €

Roger Lombardi left the Oval into Alice's office. He was muttering to himself. As chief of staff, he had to keep a lot of personalities appeased. He and Alice were the two who managed the President the most—at least officially.

"I think the First Lady will want a lot of changes, so this is going to be a long day."

Alice was nonplussed. "We won't know until she talks to Bernadette Coleman. The President told me to send one copy to their residence. I put two in the package to make things a bit more efficient."

Lombardi chuckled. "That piece on *Drudge* sure made the rounds, didn't it? And you want to know the best part? That leak came straight out of the First Lady's office. Had the menu and everything."

Alice laughed. "Nothing like a little color to establish the strength of an article. I think the word they taught me back in college was *verisimilitude*."

"Wonder what she's up to." Lombardi shook his head. "Won't tell me, of course. Views me as a rival. She and I are the only ones who have absolute claim to the President's ear."

"You better add Bernadette Coleman to that list," Alice reminded him. "Talk about the ultimate Washington power couple. Chairman of the Fed and the new BFF of the First Lady. This is a hot story. It'll make the mainstream for sure."

"You think? How long?"

"My money's on Sunday. Time for the President's speech to cool.

Perfect follow-up, perfect Sunday news show fodder for that matter. Perhaps even *The Washington Post* magazine section. A little too inside baseball for *The New York Times*, although they might like the financial angle."

"Alice, there's more, believe it or not. But at the moment it's classified."

"I hate it when you do that."

"You know the drill. Can you keep a secret?"

"Yes. Of course."

"Well so can I. Besides, I would probably have to shoot you if I told you or the President would skin me alive."

"Then," Alice said, "we'd both be in hell. You for shooting me and me for having conspired with you for so long."

"You know," Lombardi said, "you and I make a great team. Too bad we didn't meet in a less stressful life."

"You wish," Alice said.

With a chuckle, Lombardi gave her a respectful nod and headed down to his office.

¥ $ €

The car pulled up at the Coleman's at 9:37 p.m. The Secret Service agent brought the package to the door. "For you, sir. The chief of staff ordered me to get it here ASAP."

"Thank you." Ben took the package with both hands and closed the door. He then ripped it open. "Hey, sweetie," he yelled into the living room, "they sent two copies."

"That was thoughtful. That way there's one for you." Bernadette was going to use her new volunteer work at the agency for maximum leverage at home, at least in the teasing department. "It was very thoughtful of the First Lady to make sure you were included."

She's in rare form tonight, Ben thought. *Guess I would be if I were in her shoes.*

"Actually, you were the thoughtful one for suggesting that I be included. It is a pleasure to be on your team, madam." He gave her a kiss on the back of her neck as he handed her one of the copies.

"How might I return the favor? Would you care for some espresso? Decaf perhaps?"

"Given the hour and the kind of week it's been I think a bottle of Margaux makes more sense. This is a task best approached while a little more relaxed."

Ben gave her another kiss on the back of the neck, and then slowly began moving his lips forward, giving her small pecks. When he reached her cheekbone, he knew that he had sent the signal that some extended relaxation would be in order later tonight. "Your wish is my command, my lady. Is there anything else you might require?"

"I am sure there will be. But work before pleasure." That was the deal that made a two-career relationship possible, just so long as the pleasure followed.

Ben moved toward her with two glasses in hand. "Lombardi was sending us a signal by giving us two copies. It was his way of saying, 'We're on to you.' It was an acknowledgment of our power, but one saying, 'Don't push that power too far, please.'"

"This came out at nine-thirty tonight. The President and his senior staff have been working on it all day. Lots of really delicate compromises involved. Dianne Reynolds was there. So was Lombardi. So the doves and the hawks came together on something they could both agree on. Perhaps it is best not to rock the boat too much. Unless it really needs to be rocked."

Bernadette took one of the glasses and gave him a kiss on the cheek. "You are so smart. Have you ever considered a second career in intelligence? I am sure CIA could use someone of your qualifications and insight." Back to teasing. Then switching back, "Thank you, partner. I didn't think of it that way. Should have perhaps. But it is all so overwhelming. Never quite done it at this level." She held up her glass to his and gently clinked it. "Cheers, love."

They settled in and read the document, each on one end of their living room couch. When they had finished, they exchanged a knowing glance.

"Well, the world is safe," said Bernadette. "So is the West Wing.

You were right, of course. This really was a compromise document. Work's over."

"Almost," Ben said. "I am going to give Roger a one-minute heads up. The guy deserves a good night's sleep. And maybe a little thank you. If Mrs. Turner is going to get involved tomorrow, he will want to know we didn't put her up to it."

"Yes, Cynthia will call in the morning, I am sure," Bernadette said. "She really doesn't like Roger very much. I think it's the competition. I pity him. I really do."

"Pity? The guy is secure in his job. Will Turner is not the kind of person to leave only one way to access him." He reached back to rub at his shoulder.

"Your war wound bothering you?" Bernadette teased.

"Stitches," Ben said. "They should come out; I just haven't had time to make an appointment."

She kissed him, the taste of wine on her lips. "I could take them out for you."

"Your MI6 medical training?"

She kissed him again. "Field craft and improvisational skills."

"What about the pain?"

"I'm not worried. I know you'll do anything to get me to stop."

"You're on," said Ben, returning her kisses.

¥ $ €

At 9:00 p.m. Eastern Daylight Time the next day, President Willard Turner looked straight at the teleprompter positioned atop the camera. He had become expert at using this setup. Done right, each and every American sitting in their living room would feel that the president of the United States was there with them, talking to them and them alone. It was a powerful tool. His black suit, white shirt, and red tie conveyed the solemnity of the moment. Cynthia Turner had picked it out.

"It's the uniform of the alpha male. And tonight, that is who you are."

With that signal from his wife, the President addressed the American people as the most confident man in the world.

"My fellow Americans. I come to you tonight at a time of great peril for our nation. But it also offers great opportunity. An opportunity to come together. An opportunity to put our party differences aside. An opportunity to fix some of our own problems before we face the kind of desperation that the leaders of the People's Republic of China now face. And, perhaps most importantly, to prove once again that we are the greatest nation on Earth and that our founding principles of freedom and opportunity provide a shining beacon for all mankind.

"When you elected me a year and a half ago, I promised that I would be straight with you. That I would not mince words. And tonight, I am going to carry out that promise. In our system, you, the American people, are the boss. And as a man who spent his life in business, I know that the boss wants and needs the whole, unvarnished truth.

"As you doubtless know, last week the government of China unleashed what could only be described as an act of aggression. With their actions, they set in motion a set of events that could destabilize our markets, undermine the U.S. dollar, and drastically reduce our standard of living.

"We met that challenge. You need to know that your government stood strong. We withstood the greatest act of economic and financial warfare ever unleashed by one nation against another. Our economy remains intact. The dollar continues as the world's reserve currency. And our bonds continue to be the safest of safe havens for money from all around the world.

"But while we demonstrated our strength, the leadership of China was demonstrating their weakness. They unleashed a torrent of financial instability to destabilize us and cover their own economic mismanagement.

"My friends, China is broke, plain and simple. The government knows it. The people know it. As a result, their own people have been lined up outside their government run banks for weeks now, trying desperately to get their money out. Shocking as it may seem, at one point the authorities opened fire on a crowd of people whose only crime was to want the hard-earned money that they had saved over the course of their lives.

"Tonight, our sympathies go out to the people of China. They have suffered mightily from decades of economic mismanagement. Theirs is a country where the government thought that it knew best. Their government directed the hard-earned money of their people into investments that brought prestige to the authorities rather than prosperity to their people. What happened in China is living proof that although our free enterprise system is not perfect, it represents by far and away the best path to prosperity.

"Nearly four decades ago, the Berlin Wall fell for a reason. State run economies cannot compete with free ones. The government knew they could no longer afford their military. The people knew it and clamored to escape to the West.

"China only learned part of that lesson. They adopted parts of the free market system. Whole sectors of the economy came to be driven by private enterprise and those sectors prospered. But the Chinese government continued to control what they thought of as the 'commanding heights' of the economy. State-owned enterprises dominated heavy industries such as steel and energy. Most important, state-run banks dominated their financial system. These banks lent money to failing enterprises simply because they were owned by the government and that government could not let them fail.

"The only problem is that when banks lend money to prop up failing businesses and not profitable ones, they never get their money back. So the banks failed. And everyone knew it. That is why the people of China want their money back. But the money isn't there. It has been wasted on projects owned, operated, and managed by their government.

"As I said, our sympathies go out to the people of China. They are the victims here. And it is because of our sympathy for their plight that we are using maximum caution and forbearance in the face of the actions of the Chinese government. The actions they took were not primarily directed against us but in support of their own desperate position. Make no mistake: those actions were misguided. They will likely fail just as their government continuously failed through years of bad investment.

"But let them fail on their own. We do not need to give them an excuse to blame us for their own failings. We are blameless. The policy of the United States of America was to hope that China succeeded in raising the living standards of its people. We showed maximum forbearance over their trade policies and over their currency manipulation. We did so not because they were right, but because we Americans believe in prosperity for all.

"And yes, we did pay a price for our generosity. But prosperity for the people of China also meant that we did not have 1.4 billion desperate and potentially starving people pushing a government to take military action against its neighbors and the world. Prosperity is the best alternative to war. When people have something to lose, they are less desperate to take risks.

"I want to be clear. We hope that China succeeds in righting its economy. We hope that they will follow our lead in recognizing the limits of state power and give more power to their people. We hope that China and the United States can work together for our mutual benefit. Yes, there are lots of things we hope for because we want the best for all the people of the world.

"But hope alone is not a policy for success. We can and indeed we must simultaneously hope for the best and prepare for the worst. So tonight, I will lay out our principles for action to prepare for what may lay ahead. This is where I must be most direct to you, the American people, the ultimate boss of what goes on in Washington.

"Our first principle must be to protect the American people and the American economy from whatever actions the Chinese might take. We have done this thus far. The Federal Reserve met the challenge posed by the actions of the People's Bank of China head on. They will continue to do so. This battle is being fought out in the markets and we will not allow an attack on our prosperity through Chinese actions to destabilize our markets.

"Our second principle is to do this as a unified nation. Secretary Steinway and Chairman Coleman have already met with the bipartisan leadership of the Congress. Yes, that's right. Both parties. Together. In the same room. I know that is not how Washington has worked in the past, but it is how Washington is going to work from now on. We are going to view our friends on the other side of the aisle as our partners.

America is a country in which the majority party ultimately prevails, but in which the minority party's views are taken into account. Most important from my point of view, both parties must be fully briefed. I believe that if we share the facts as broadly as national security permits that the chances of any misunderstanding are kept to a minimum.

"I am therefore asking the Majority and Minority leaders of both houses to designate three members of their own party from their chamber to, along with the speaker of the House and the president pro tempore of the Senate, form a joint intelligence task force to receive regular briefings, on at least a weekly basis, from both CIA and the Federal Reserve on what is happening.

"Our third principle must be to learn from the mistakes of China. We are not in the desperate straits that China is in. Our country is strong. Our economy is strong. The full faith and credit of the United States is respected around the world. But it is no secret that this country has too much debt. And if we continue on our present course of promising more than we can deliver, we could end up facing the same problems China faces. As I said at the outset, we can hope for the best, but we must prepare for the worst.

"So I am also asking the bipartisan leadership of both houses to appoint members from the budgetary and appropriation committees to join with Secretary George Steinway and the Office of Management and Budget Director Victoria Potter in hammering out an agreement to bring our fiscal house in order.

"My administration has already proposed legislation to save and secure our Social Security system, to reform and coordinate the myriad transfer programs that comprise our safety net, and to reform our tax system. These ideas are sound, farsighted, and principled. But I also recognize that it cannot be 'my way or the highway.' I hope and expect that these ideas will form the basis for substantive reform. And I welcome the bipartisan leadership of Congress to advance their own ideas in these, and particularly in other areas, to put America's budgetary house in order.

"Finally, I plan to act on another lesson that the Chinese have taught us. That government does not necessarily know best even though it thinks it does. That the free-market system offers the best path to prosperity. Government rules and regulations of every facet of American life have simply exploded over the past few decades. Many, indeed, most, of these regulations are well intended. But as the saying goes, the road to hell is paved with good intentions.

"Washington has created too many building blocks for that road. So I have directed my chief of staff, Roger Lombardi, to assemble a competitiveness council to review all government regulations. The council will be comprised of my senior economic advisers and the members of the Cabinet whose departments are responsible for those regulations. Each and every rule needs to be examined to make sure it passes a rigorous cost-benefit analysis.

"Washington must no longer make rules for the sake of making them or because the bureaucracy needs something to do. Each and every rule we promulgate must have a purpose, and that purpose must assure that the American economy is the best in the world.

"My fellow Americans. Thank you for inviting me into your homes tonight to discuss the events of the last week. I want you to know that we have responded successfully to the challenges that have been thrown at us so far. We will continue to respond to make sure that your livelihoods are safe. And that we will prepare for the future to make sure that the United States of America remains the world leader that it has become.

"We do this not just for ourselves, but for our children and grandchildren, and indeed for all the people of the world. Freedom and prosperity are what all the people of the world strive for and America offers the best hope for all mankind to achieve those noble goals. Thank you. Good night. And God bless the United States of America."

CHAPTER TEN

"Hey there, beautiful. Here's your coffee." Ben handed Bernadette the black mug emblazoned on one side with *I'm the Boss*. It wasn't randomly picked.

Bernadette sat up and stretched, a huge grin on her face. Memories of the night before went through her head. "How are you feeling this morning, Mr. Stud? Enjoying the freedom from your stitches?"

"Yes. And I'm looking forward to a rematch. Unfortunately, this stud still has to get to work. My car gets here in forty-five minutes."

"Forty-five minutes? What time is it?" She noted it was six fifteen. "My ride will be here then too."

"Still have to one up me, huh?"

"Blame it on Hector. He decided it's easiest if they position the Company's car in with your motorcade and be part of it until we get to an Agency exit. No one will notice one more car in with the Chairman's procession."

"Spycraft." Ben rolled his eyes. "Listen, if that's the case, why can't we ride in together? We could drop you off."

"Sweetheart, that would be fun, but having your entourage pull through security at Langley wouldn't exactly keep things a secret."

"Well, our motto at the Fed is 'transparency.' Guess you guys haven't gotten on board."

"Well, there are some agencies where transparency works and others, not so much." Bernadette finished her coffee and put the cup down. "I'm not sure what you've gotten me into with your new friend the President but having a day job now is going to put a crimp in my life as a novelist."

Ben gave her a look. "Don't give me that. You love the idea of being back in the game."

"I got out at the right time, and I don't regret it."

"But I have at times. Usually when your latest book comes out. All I have to do is read it to see how much you miss your old life. Besides, when I read your books, I realize that you never really left the game, did you? At least not the part where you have a desk in a corner office."

Bernadette's eyes narrowed. "What makes you think that?"

He smiled. "You're not the only one around here who knows things." He gave her a kiss on the cheek. "Enjoy your day at work, my dear."

¥　$　€

Both Coleman cars in the motorcade were stocked with the same news-papers: *The Washington Post*, *The New York Times*, *The Wall Street Journal*, and *USA Today*. The front-page stories were all about the President's speech. But what really mattered were the editorials. They would be shaping journalistic opinion all day long, particularly for the nightly news shows.

Although their work was in separate realms, knowing what America was thinking and hearing was key to their strategy. Bernadette knew that intelligence did not exist for its own sake, but to inform politicians. Politics was the art of the possible. No point in providing intelligence that was only useful in some theoretical Neverland.

Ben's challenge was more direct. He and George Steinway had been crafting a reform that the President did not mention: a currency and financial reform that would be the biggest since the passage of the Federal Reserve Act in 1913. So Ben was checking the papers with the same objective—to see what the art of the possible really meant.

Although in separate cars, out of habit both reached for the same paper first: *The Washington Post*. Washington was a company town, and the *Post* was the company billboard. The *Post* not only shaped other jour-nalists, it shaped what the bureaucracy thought. And of course, as the lead newspaper in the city of government, it leaned toward the idea that what was good for the government was good for its readers. This meant leaning left on domestic issues. The more money that flowed through Washington-run programs and employed bureaucrats, the better. But it also meant leaning center or slightly right on foreign policy. A strong and assertive foreign policy was good for Washington too.

Today there was only one editorial. It took up the whole editorial space, two columns wide, top to bottom. The headline was encouraging: "Turner Steers toward the Middle." In the *Post's* worldview, the middle is where you wanted to be. Of course, their middle wasn't really the middle. It was to the left on domestic spending and assertive on foreign policy. In the press, words such as *moderate* and *middle* went back to *what is good for Washington.*

Each of them read quickly, slowing to absorb the highlights.

President Turner pledged national unity as the best way of confronting the destabilizing actions of the Chinese …

Perhaps as important, he steered clear of the bellicose language he has sometimes been associated with, pledging that America hopes for prosperity for the people of China …

He also made clear that hope was not, by itself, a foreign policy …

Turner made some proposals that reflected his ideology: budget cuts, tax reform, and deregulation. But he also promised to move forward on these in a bipartisan fashion. For now, at least, we and all of Washington should not only take him at his word, but hold him to it.

It left them both with the same opinion: *Not bad for a paper that endorsed Turner's opponent.* They would be opposing him on those items that reflected his ideology because budget cuts, tax reform, and deregulation meant a smaller Washington. That was not *moderate.* It was *ideological.* Still, it was as good as Turner was going to get from them.

They split on their next read. Ben went for the *Journal*, Bernadette for the *Times.* The two could not be more distant ideologically on their editorial pages. Ever since the days of Bob Bartley in the 1970s, *The Wall Street Journal* editorial page has been the focal point of conservative and free market opinion. Sometimes it was a lone voice in a media establishment that overwhelmingly tilted left. Again, a single editorial covered the entire editorial space. The headline read, "The Return of the Reagan Cowboy—Finally Someone Talks Sense."

While we have had our doubts in the past about President Turner's commitment to the principles that made our country great, last night's speech laid those to rest.

It started off discussing initial doubts about Turner's commitment to basic principles of leadership, but the remainder of the editorial was downright glowing. It praised his demands for economic reform, concluding that Turner was a refreshing cure for Washington's decidedly immoderate ways: greedy, officious, perhaps a bit dangerous.

One would hardly know that *The New York Times* editorial board was a little over three miles from where their compatriots at *The Wall Street Journal* sat. Both were describing the same speech given on the same night, but it didn't sound that way. The title of the *Times* editorial was "Turner Wraps His Ideology in the Flag." It accused the President of trying to roll back social reforms and protection for American workers and the environment by beating the drum against a supposed Chinese menace. Ultimately it played the moral equivalence card by drawing a line between China's government induced financial woes and the times when U.S. financial institutions defrauded citizens or bilked shareholders with their fraudulent policies.

Ben blanched at that. Turner was calling for reforms, but Ben knew that there would have to be even more far-reaching ones in the monetary realm. This was a period to wait, watch, and prepare. His preparation would be a lot of hard work at persuading. If Turner was running into this kind of flack, what would he face? Had he misjudged the mood of the country?

Finally, Ben flipped to *USA Today*. Its editorials were intellectually slimmed down versions of the *Post's*—targeted to the middle. But their middle was different from the *Post's*. It wasn't Washington who read *USA Today*, but the business traveler—a key part of Middle America. It was the safe, easy-to-digest way to get news while away from home. One really didn't want to read the local paper in a strange city. Too much of the content was simply irrelevant. *USA Today* delivered headlines you would have gotten from your local paper less the local content. So the paper geared its editorials to reflect this broad and inherently centrist readership.

The editorial title was, "Turner Tells It Straight: Compromise to Build Consensus." It praised Turner for striking the right tone in the time of a new kind of warfare, and for acknowledging the nation's chronic spending problem. It called for unity of purpose in facing the new challenge and affirmed the President's resolute strength as conveyed in the speech.

Ben wanted to stop by the *USA Today* building on his way into work and give them a big kiss. Best to wait. But maybe their editorial board, looked down upon by their more upscale peers, would be a good place to start to sell the financial reform package once he got it through the administration.

As they made their way down the parkway past Spout Run, his media strategy began to gel in his head. His instincts were that the *Post* would be helpful if it were sold in an institutional way. The Fed was one of the premier members of the Washington establishment, so it would have to be, 'This is good for the Fed and good for Washington—therefore it is good for the country.' The *Journal* would be an easy sell. They had been calling for changes for decades. The *Times* would have to be influenced through its readership. Then he realized how much he was jumping ahead. Unless he made a mistake, or something leaked, the press would not catch wind of what he was up to for another month. Best to focus on today's challenge.

¥ $ €

Bernadette's car pulled up to the elevators at seven thirty-five. She proceeded to the same conference room on the eighth floor and was not surprised to see it more than half-full even though the Director would not be there until 8 a.m. People were standing around chatting in hushed tones and enjoying the coffee and donuts on the sideboard.

The Director entered and motioned everyone to take their seats. As if by magic they were in exactly the same seats they had occupied at Bernadette's first meeting.

Hector got straight to the point. "Okay, folks, how are the Chinese going to interpret what the President said last night?" He turned to Monica Jenkins and indicated that she should lead off.

"Mr. Director, the Chinese aren't going to know what to think. They won't like it, of course, but in their hearts, they know it is true. And some of them know it in their heads as well and have been advancing that argument for quite some time. In the short run those elements, who for the sake of brevity we will call 'Reformers,' will have to keep quiet lest they be called traitors and running dogs of America. But in the long run it will strengthen their hand.

"No reaction from the public at large since their media blocked out the speech, but it will still circulate around the internet. But they're going to be the natural ally of the Reformers.

"The military are going to be holding their breath. Most of their leadership does not want an outright war with America. They know they might lose. They also know that even if they won, the cost would be dear. Now there is a faction within the People's Liberation Army that wants war for all the usual reasons, but they're in the minority.

"My bet on the Politburo is that they're confused and arguing among themselves. That's a good thing. It is exactly where we want them to be. An adversary who is uncertain is not one who is going to take precipitous action. We are not ready to respond to precipitous action, so our stance is to watch, wait, and prepare. It was brilliant. And as everyone here knows, I am not necessarily one to give that kind of praise, particularly when it has anything to do with President Turner."

"Mr. Director," Bernadette said, "I agree with Monica. Tactically it was a brilliant speech. And not just from our perspective *vis a vis* China. It was brilliant from a domestic perspective as well. We've all read the morning papers. With the exception of the *Times*, reaction was quite positive.

"My suspicion is that our counterparts in Chinese intelligence will see Turner as feeling he needs to unify his country. I suspect they will read the media reaction as him having largely succeeded in that effort, at least for now. That is decidedly not good news for them if that unity persists. The right response from their perspective is to figure out how to create fissures in the American political scene."

"What's your take on how they would go about doing that?" asked Lopez.

"The speech left two obvious avenues to do this," Bernadette said. "The first was on the domestic front, and that was apparent from the *Times* editorial. Make Turner look like a right-wing ideologue on domestic policy. Trouble for them is there really isn't an elegant way to do so. Any direct attack on this score will be read by most of the public, and most of Washington, that Turner is right. And the Chinese leadership has too much on its plate now to worry about getting involved in America's domestic social policy.

"The other natural fissure is between hawks and doves. Although America is far more united on foreign policy than on the domestic front, that is where they have the most leverage to manipulate our opinion. So if I were them, I would start a combination of a charm offensive on people they think they can influence and a not-so-subtle message that they view Turner as being far too bellicose.

"That latter point will be an extension of views that are already held, even though the speech last night largely papered them over. The goal will be to get that portion of elite opinion that they can influence to force the President to backpedal on his comments on China. Of course, if they succeed in forcing us to retreat on the foreign policy front, then they will have scored a major victory that will help them regionally and also on the home front."

"And what do you feel is the position we should take in this situation?" Lopez said.

"The position of the Agency should be to advise consumers of our analysis to take care and make sure that doesn't happen. Let the domestic political battles go on. The President opened the door to letting domestic disagreements be the safety valve for dissent. His language on compromise not only invited that but also provided a means to contain it and channel it constructively.

"But with that safety valve, the country can come together more easily across the political spectrum on the need to take a firm line with China. Monica was absolutely correct. To the Chinese, the President's theme of pitying the Chinese people was highly subversive. As long as we keep advancing that line and making it clear that it is the American line and not just President Turner's, then we are going to keep the Chinese off guard."

Hector Gonzales nodded and turned to Richard Wei and asked for his analysis. Bernadette congratulated herself on her still having game, even after eight years of inactivity. For a brief moment, she let her mind wander to how her husband was doing.

At that exact moment, across the river, Ben was getting a phone call that would confirm Bernadette was indeed right about the Chinese reaction.

¥ $ €

Ben had been at his desk for about forty-five minutes, going through his emails, when he heard the phone ring in Peggy's office. They tended to keep the door open when Ben wasn't in a meeting so they could communicate directly. "Mr. Chairman, Governor Li on the phone."

"Thanks, Peggy. Would you mind closing the door?"

Of course, Ben thought. *The Chinese arrived at the office to hear the President's speech. Beijing must have been buzzing all day about what he said and what he actually meant. Li was about to give him what the Party wanted Ben to think.*

Once the door was shut, Ben picked up the phone. "Governor Li, what an unexpected surprise."

"Mr. Chairman, we are getting to know each other quite well. And remember, please call me Xue." The voice on the other end of the phone was gentle, but Ben knew he was a man that commanded authority in a quiet way.

"Very well, Xue. And please remember to call me Ben." He could tell this was the start of a charm offensive. Nothing wrong with a bit of charm. It made communication more pleasant, as long as one knew that one was being charmed.

"Thank you, Ben. Please, may I be frank?"

"Of course. Central bankers should always be frank with one another, even if we are not always so frank with others." Given that what Li Xue was about to say was scripted, it would be anything but frank. Ben pictured Li sitting at his desk with his prepared conversation.

"Didn't you find your president's speech last night a bit warlike? He openly criticized the internal affairs of my country. Why would someone do such a thing? We can't have a shouting match between the two sides. We need to reinforce the dignity of each other if we are going to maintain a dignified relationship."

"Xue," Ben said, making sure to use his first name, "I am all for a dignified relationship. I didn't think the President shouted last night."

"He was very undignified about the things he said about China. He basically accused my colleagues in government of stealing from the people!"

"He didn't actually say that. He said that your nation's savings had been mismanaged because decision-making on capital allocation had been driven by politics, not by economics. Tell me, do you as a central banker consider that to be untrue?"

There was a long silence on the other end. Finally Li said, "Surely you are not asserting that China is unique in that regard?" Ben recognized that phrase. It was from *The New York Times* editorial. Li was phrasing what he had seen in the American press as the best way to approach him.

"Xue, America has long had a capital allocation decision making process that is far too political. And we have paid a big price for that. The President admitted that last night. That is why he called for us to make reforms. At least he indirectly thanked your country for having shown what can happen when politics has too much power over markets. We definitely do not want to walk in your footsteps." Ben knew that he was pushing back hard, but his gut told him it was the right thing to do. Li Xue would now have to consider another line of attack, one that would carry more risks for Li personally as it would depart from the Party line.

"We are going to have to disagree about that," Li said. "But you and I must be facing a similar dynamic. There are those in both our countries who would like to see our current disagreement spill out from being merely a conflict that takes place in markets. You have your war hawks, we have ours. You and I have a similar challenge. We must keep this conflict contained. Neither of us, and neither of our nations, will benefit from things getting out of hand."

"Be assured. And tell your colleagues the President feels the same way. However you may have interpreted him, that is clearly the message he was intending to send. He hopes the best for the people of China. That is his genuine sentiment. It is certainly my sentiment as well, that of Secretary Steinway, and to my knowledge, all of the President's advisors."

"Thank you for that, Governor Coleman. I will convey that sentiment to my colleagues on this end. I must tell you, however, that most of them will probably not believe you. They were very concerned, as I was, about the approach that your president took. It is not that I disbelieve you. It is just that your president was so crude, so warlike, in his tone that it is hard to read what he said in any other way."

So the charm offensive was over. Li was back to the party line. He had signaled it quite plainly and in a way Ben would pick up on, switching to the more formal method of address. That was for the benefit of everyone listening on his end. His conversation would be recorded and reported throughout the Politburo. Ben was also not so naïve as to believe that the conversation had also not been recorded on this end. But it would not be circulated. It would be kept private, used only as a source of intelligence.

Li had played his role. He had likely been ordered to try a charm offensive and attempt to drive a wedge between Turner and his subordinates. That had failed. He then tried to play the hawks and doves game, trying to establish a rapport with Ben that labeled them both as doves against the hawks who would drive the world to war. That, too, had failed, so he had no choice but to revert back to the original script and signal to his minders that he was only playing his part, not actually agreeing with the Americans.

Ben decided to help Li out. "Governor, I am sorry you feel that way. I can only assure you that America wants a friendly, peaceful, and mutually beneficial relationship with the People's Republic. One point on which we do agree is that we central bankers need to keep this avenue of open and frank conversation going. I do hope that you will feel free to call me with your concerns at any time." Bernadette had told him that Li might be running into trouble and that he should be prepared to help his counterpart when asked. He could only hope that he had sent that signal.

After a set of formal goodbyes, Ben called George Steinway. He wanted to convey the conversation with Li and hear the Secretary's thoughts about the speech and what the President's mood was. He got them, along with some marching orders.

"Ben, that speech gave us some breathing room. Now we wait, watch, and prepare. Prepare is your job. I think we need to get on the President's schedule to discuss your thoughts about financial and monetary reform. And soon. I will try and set that up. This is not to leak. Not to Congress. Not even to the FOMC until the President has signed off. I am going to try for Friday or Saturday. Will you be ready?"

"Of course."

"I know you will be. You have been since our dinner at the Metropolitan Club. That is what convinced me to recommend you for the job. We both know something has to be done and your idea is the most straightforward and elegant around."

"Thank you, George, that means a lot. Give the word and I'll be there."

CHAPTER ELEVEN

"GOOD MORNING, LADIES AND GENTLEMEN."

The President stood from behind his desk, placed his coffee down and moved toward Ben, George Steinway, and Dianne Reynolds as they entered the Oval. "I understand that we have some preparing to do today." He motioned for each of them to sit on one of the couches that flanked his chair.

Today indeed, thought Ben. Since his phone call with Steinway on Wednesday, he knew he'd have to dust off his thoughts from the plan he'd presented two years ago at the Metropolitan Club. And when George had called back ninety minutes later to let him know the meeting with POTUS would be Friday morning, he barricaded himself in his office and got on his computer. He went through the notes he had made in the intervening time, updating, adjusting for the various changes the economy and the times had introduced. He had laughed to himself, remembering how he had so studiously kept the plan current, dreaming of the time when he would be standing before "Someone Who Mattered" in the hopes of making it a reality. Now the moment was upon him, and he realized that the last time he felt these rising nerves was as he waited for Bernadette Murphy to walk down an aisle to meet him and a priest in front of an altar. As he took his seat, he found himself wishing he could have a shot or three of something strong before starting.

The President took his seat. "I'd like to preface this by saying that half an hour ago I got off the phone with Cheryl Atkins at General Motors. She couldn't stop singing Ben's praises. That appearance on

'Squawk Box' as well. Sounded to me like they are thinking of introducing a new car line: the GM Coleman. You're not thinking of chal-
lenging me in the primaries next time around?"

Ben knew the President was trying to build him up in front of
Dianne, who had been a doubter about his appointment as Chairman,
but also knew that he'd better do a formal rejection. "Sir, to quote General
Sherman, if nominated I will not accept, if elected I will not serve."

"Oh, Ben that is such bullshit. If Bernadette and Cynthia decide to
replace me on the ticket with you neither one of us will have any choice
in the matter. And if the two of them say you will serve, then God help
you if you don't." The President let out a belly laugh, not a frequent
event, but memorable when he did.

"I don't think either of us have much to worry about Mr. President.
Bernadette adores you."

"Is that why she gives me such a hard time?"

"Do you think I get away scot-free at home? Sir, she actually does
what you tell her. I get the push back and then she does what she wants,
which may or may not have anything to do with what I suggested." Ben
glanced over at Dianne Reynolds, who had a bemused look on her face.

"Well, I know why she and Cynthia get along so well," the President
said. "But seriously, Ben, it wasn't just Atkins who said you're taking the
pressure off and giving them some pricing power. At least a dozen of
my old business friends have told me the same thing over the last few
days. They're all happy about it. But to me that sounds like inflation.
And while I used to *love* being able to raise my own prices, I never much
cared for it when everyone else could as well. I don't think the voters will
like it much either."

George Steinway cut in. "Mr. President, believe it or not, Ben and I
discussed this very issue before you were elected. I think he has a great
plan that will put us on the side of the angels and restore trust in the
integrity of the dollar. The Chinese won't stand a chance."

Secretary Reynolds said, "Before you gentlemen build up Ben's ego
to the point where we can't all fit in this room, I want you to know
that some of our embassies are getting complaints about an intentional
devaluation of the dollar. So your actions are far from being universally

applauded. Cheryl Atkins and I were at Harvard at the same time. Great person. Hope you reminded her, Mr. President, that GM sells twice as many cars in China as it does in the U.S. It is no longer true that what is good for General Motors is good for the country. At least just this country."

"I stand corrected, Dianne," said the President. "Like most Americans I never knew that was the case. I will be sure to use it next time she asks a favor—which she does about every six weeks or so. But are you saying what Ben has been doing is a mistake?"

"Not at all, Mr. President. I just want to remind all of us that there is no free lunch. Isn't that the phrase, Ben?"

Ben decided that straight and businesslike was the only way to proceed with the conversation. "Madame Secretary, you're right. There is no free lunch. We policymakers have been acting like there is for quite some time. The Chinese were calling us on that fact. They have been playing the free lunch game as well, even more so, only they thought they would be immune because their view is that power grows out of the barrel of a gun, not the ballot box.

"Properly used, the ability to print money is an incredibly powerful tool. Abused, it can lead to ruin in less than a generation. Dianne, you were spot-on about the ego issue and central bankers, and dare I say, finance ministers. We love to be glorified as masters of the universe. Probably the high point came in early 1999 when the Chairman of the Fed, the secretary of the Treasury, and the deputy secretary were on the cover of *TIME* magazine with the headline "The Committee to Save the World." And I'm sorry to say, all three probably believed the headline, at least to some degree.

"So there is a natural tendency for central bankers and finance ministers to want to print, to push the envelope on what is sound policy. I believe they—should I say 'we'—must be checked. But taking away all discretion regarding money creates problems as well. That is why we must strike the right balance."

"And from what you've been telling me these last couple of weeks," the President said, "simply using gold doesn't work either. Remind me why."

"Two problems, Mr. President. First, gold can be too rigid. In theory, when there isn't enough gold, the price rises, and there's incentive to go out and dig it. To put it simply, at the current rate the supply of gold is going up only one and a half percent a year. But the world economy is growing between three and a half to four without any inflation. In the long run, you would need prices to fall two percent a year to finance three and a half percent more economic activity with one and a half percent more gold.

"So we'd go from an inflationary economy to a deflationary economy. And periods of sustained falling prices discourage people from investing in, say, a new machine, because the price of the output that comes out of the machine is dropping two percent a year. That means I don't want to pay full price now to produce things that go on sale next year and every year after that.

"The second problem is supply. The U.S. has the single biggest gold reserve in the world—a bit over 8,000 tons, or nearly 300 million ounces. Now the Federal Reserve has a balance sheet—think of it as roughly the total money supply—of about $4.5 trillion. That means for gold to cover the whole money supply, it would have to run $15,000 an ounce."

The President said, "So whoever has gold is going to get rich if we went on the gold standard because there isn't enough of it."

"That's why FDR confiscated all the gold before he revalued it," Ben said.

"And that's not just true within the country," Dianne Reynolds said. "It's true between countries as well. If we've got more gold, relative to our economy, than everyone else, the U.S. would gain enormous prestige and power."

Ben continued. "I wish it were that easy. Other countries might decide not to go on a gold standard. Their currencies would drop sharply. Their people would be a lot poorer internationally, but the goods they exported would also be a lot more competitive."

Dianne finished the thought. "That would cause problems for our manufacturers."

"So this would all work more smoothly if everyone did it together," said Ben. "Gold is kind of a tyrant that way."

The Secretary of State immediately went to the logic of where her job would take her. "But that would require a huge international conference. Getting everyone on the same page would take years. And we can't force anyone to do what they don't want to do."

"But we can lead by example," Ben said, "and let them figure it out for themselves. The Chinese already have. They've been acquiring gold worldwide for over a decade. In 2019 they had less than a quarter as much gold as we had, and that was after having bought some on the market and keeping their own gold production to themselves. Today they have three-quarters as much as we do, and that number is growing all the time."

"Are you saying that in ten years or so they would be well ahead of us?" the President said.

"That's what they were planning," Dianne said. "For industrial and military world domination as well."

"The good news is that their leadership moved too quickly," Ben said. "They saw a chance to disrupt our markets and drive us down that way. I know that Governor Li urged them to be patient, but they weren't."

The President said, "So you plan to exploit that?"

"Well, yes," said Ben. "But I want to do it by disrupting things as little as possible. Remember that $15,000 per ounce figure? That's at least twice what it is today, and you've already heard the talk about speculators making all the money. Do you want to run next time as the guy who let the speculators double down again?" Ben could see the President grimace and wondered if he had gone too far.

"And I assume you have a way around that," said the President.

"An idea hit me in the aftermath of witnessing that bank run in Beijing. I think we want to establish the concept that gold is 'the people's money,' while cash and checks are 'the banks' money.' So what's going to happen is that President Will Turner will bring the people's money to America."

"Now you're sounding like a politician," the President said. "But if it's going to be me, you'd better give me more details."

Ben continued. "Money serves two functions. It is a medium of exchange, a thing we use to facilitate transactions. It is also a store of value. It is a way of holding everything you've saved your entire life so that if times get tough, you have a reserve. The people weren't rioting outside the banks to get money to go grocery shopping. They had that in their wallets. They were rioting to get their life savings. They wanted their hard-earned share of the store of value money represents, not the medium of exchange.

"So we create and circulate gold coins that can be 'People's Money.' They don't have to put it in the bank, unless it's in a safe deposit box. More likely it is going to be tucked away someplace as secret and safe as possible within their homes. It is their money in a place that they control.

"The banks are great for the money that is needed as a medium of exchange. They provide cash services, checking services, wire transfers, credit cards, debit cards, business loans, car loans, mortgages, the whole nine yards. That is the bank's version of money. Gold won't get in the way of that. No one is going to take a stack of gold coins down to the showroom to buy a new car."

"Why don't gold coins and things like Bitcoin do that now?" asked the President.

"Because they have no guaranteed value in terms of being a medium of exchange. The holder has to sell it and has no idea what price he or she is going to get. People's Money is going to have a guaranteed value that President Turner is going to give it.

"Under this plan, we are going to put out gold coins with guaranteed values that are close to the value of their gold content. They won't be $50 coins. More likely $5,000. The number will be stamped right on them. And under the Turner Monetary Reform Act—or whatever you choose to call it—those coins will be legal tender. A bank or the government must turn over fifty crisp $100 bills in return for one of those $5,000 coins anytime the holder wants. You can't do that with Bitcoin."

"And if the gold in the coin is worth more than $5,000?"

"Then the holder would be foolish to turn it in. The coin is worth at least $5,000, it could be worth more."

"And it only costs $5,000 at your local bank?"

"Yes. To start with there would be less than $5,000 worth of gold in it. But the buyer could always turn it in for $5,000. If gold goes up—or the dollar goes down—the buyer makes a profit."

The President said, "Sounds like quite a deal."

"That's why it's People's Money. People will hold the coins as a store of wealth. Regular money and bank deposits will be used for transactions, like now. If gold rises in value, then there's a signal to us at the Fed to start tightening monetary conditions. If we don't, folks will be lining up to buy our coins and we will start to run out."

"Hold it," said the President. "What do you mean by *our* coins and *we* will start to run out?"

"The coins are Federal Reserve coins just like the paper in your wallet is a Federal Reserve Note. The Federal Reserve stands behind both. What stands behind the coins is our solemn commitment to buy your coin from you for the specified amount. What stands behind the notes is the assets of the Fed. Right now, that is government debt. But in the future, it will include a lot of gold. Our goal is to be able to tell the American people that the dollar—their money—is as good as gold whether it is in the bank or in their wallet or in a safe place at home.

"This is the second part of the plan, Mr. President. Right now, the government has about $2 trillion in gold. What I am proposing is that the Fed buy it from you, giving you the highest-yielding bonds we hold as payment. The U.S. national debt goes down by $2 trillion and the currency of the United States is now at least forty percent backed by gold. And the holders of the paper money can get it in real gold anytime they want by buying one of our coins with paper money. It would make the U.S. dollar untouchable in terms of credibility."

Secretary of State Reynolds said, "That's what's going to give us leverage over the Chinese, right?"

"Yes," Ben said.

"What about Europe?"

"The Europeans are in a heck of a mess, as you know. But they have enough gold, roughly as much as we do, and about the same amount of money out there. They can either pool it and back the euro or they can go back to their own currencies, which seems to be where they are headed anyway. Even the Italians have enough gold to credibly back a lira, about fifty percent more gold per unit of currency as we have. They will need it, since Italian state finances are not exactly trustworthy.

"As for China, it depends how they play it. They have about thirty percent more 'money' out there than we do and it is in trouble, thanks to the bank runs. They have only seventy-five percent as much gold. So they have less gold backing for their currency than we do. And because their currency already lacks credibility, they are going to need a whole lot more than we will to build confidence. Their bank runs are likely to get worse. Or we could arrange a deal."

"What kind of deal?" Reynolds said.

Ben smiled. "That would be for you and the President to decide."

"I'm sure you'd be happy to help if we asked," the President said.

"Sir, the only person who can pull this off is the president of the United States. People's Money—as credible as it comes and backed by gold—will be the legacy of President Will Turner. Not me. Prevailing over China in the currency war they started will be your legacy too. You brought me in to get the best advice I could give, not run the show." He paused for effect. "Sir, the decision is entirely yours. It's a big step. But in my opinion, it is the best chance we have to come out of this ahead of the game."

"Let's make sure I get this straight. The government—I assume you mean the Treasury—swaps $2 trillion in gold for $2 trillion in our debt, which is like paying off that debt. Then you issue gold coins that people can buy with dollars that they can always cash in for the purchase price. But if gold goes up in value, they are ahead of the game. This puts a check on you, the Fed, from printing too much money. That builds confidence in the dollar and promises that inflation won't be a problem in the future. Do I have that right?"

Ben nodded.

"Steinway, I assume you're okay with all this?"

The Treasury Secretary said, "That's why I recommended Mr. Coleman as Fed Chairman."

"Dianne?"

"I'm not one to rock the apple cart, and this plan certainly does that. But the apple cart has already been rocked by the Chinese. There's a lot to take in here. But it makes sense to me. Ben, I assume

I can give you a call tomorrow with any questions?"

"Absolutely, Madame Secretary."

The President pressed a button on the table on the right side of his chair. The door opened on the southwest corner of the room that led to his study and a butler walked in with four glasses and an ice bucket. Each glass was about half full.

The butler said, "I have taken the liberty—"

"Yes," said the President. "Thank you. Everyone is going to have their usual. That is an order. But first, a toast. 'May God bless this country and give us the wisdom to see this plan through.'"

George Steinway raised his glass and chimed in. "To the Metropolitan Plan."

This was followed by a round of "Hear, hear!" and each took a sip. One could sense the relief in the room. At least now there was a plan.

There was a moment of idle chatter as the men sipped at, then ultimately drained their glasses. Dianne took a couple of demure sips.

"Forgive me," she said, setting her glass down. "I've got one of those rubber chicken banquets at noon. There will be wine."

"There'll be more when we get this thing pushed through," said the President. He gave a nod to indicate they were through and Dianne picked up her briefcase. "For the time being, let's keep this between the four of us until we can get our ducks in a row for garnering support." He looked at Ben. "To that end, I hope you and Bernadette will join my wife and me for dinner tonight. Seven-thirty sharp."

"Of course." Ben gathered up his briefcase, said goodbye to the others, and headed out to where his limo was waiting. He was pleased with himself. He didn't think he'd oversold it, hadn't included any extraneous details that could be covered later, and Turner had liked it. In his excited state he thought about calling Bernadette to give her an update, but knew she'd be unavailable.

He was whistling "Seventy-Six Trombones" from *The Music Man* when he walked into his office. But hearing the jaunty tune did nothing to wipe the stern look from his secretary's face.

"What's wrong, Peggy?"

"You'd better turn on the television," she said.

¥ $ €

Christopher Avery was a governor, a title given a member of the FOMC. As he wasn't its chairman, he ranked neither the time slot nor the time allocation that Ben Coleman had enjoyed due to the media pecking order.

But Avery was not deterred. He had been trained in academic politics so using backhanded and sometimes underhanded techniques in a battle was not exactly out of his ken. Right after the President's speech he made sure one of his old colleagues got an op-ed prominently placed in *The New York Times*. He also gave a background briefing to a *Washington Post* reporter. The rules of backgrounding were that one could use the information but not the name of the source. Avery had appeared in the reporter's story as a 'well-placed official at the Federal Reserve.' It offered plausible deniability but was clearly a signal that the quotes came from him.

With both the op-ed and the story running Friday morning, Avery became a hot enough commodity that he could get a six-minute slot on the "Power Lunch" show.

Joanne Chilton, the female reporter in the tag-team that ran "Power Lunch," introduced him and then started the conversation. 'Governor Avery, your old colleague, Professor Louis Greenstein at Harvard, ran an op-ed today that warned of serious domestic repercussions from the President's China policies. They echo criticisms you have made in the past. What is it that has you worried?"

"First, Joanne, let me assure you that everyone supports the President's goal of blocking China's attempts to undermine the American economy.

"My concern is that there is an agenda being added to those efforts that will transform American economic policy in ways that have nothing to do with China. The President has already mentioned budget and regulatory reform. No doubt these will roll back the protections of workers and the environment that have been put in place over the years.

"But there is another part of the agenda that I think is quietly being advanced by my colleague Ben Coleman."

Joanne interjected, "You mean the FOMC Chairman?" Even she

was surprised to hear Ben described as Avery's colleague. She hardly thought of them as equals.

"Yes, Ben Coleman and I have an extremely collegial relationship." Avery wasn't going to give an inch in making himself Ben's equal. "We respect each other's intellect. In fact, it is because he is such a clever fellow that I am a bit suspicious of his plans for changing monetary policy. America is blessed to have a monetary policy that the appointees of the president, confirmed by the president, have control over the nation's money. They can expand or contract the money supply in order to assure maximum employment with stable prices. That is our mandate at the Federal Open Market Committee.

"But Ben Coleman has long been critical of this democratic control of our money. He wants to go back to the old way of doing things— using gold or silver for our money or some variant thereof. The period of the gold standard in America is notorious for bank runs and bank failures, for the impoverishment of the nation's farmers, and the rise of the robber barons.

"Coleman isn't a bad man. I don't mean that. He just has very little faith in the rule of the people, by the people. When you rely on gold and silver, once you get rich, you stay rich. He's someone who thinks that the country is better off when the rich and the privileged control the money and the people, indirectly through a Federal Reserve that is democratically accountable, are not in charge."

"That's quite a charge, Governor Avery," said Joanne. "How do you know this? Neither Coleman nor the President has ever said anything like this."

"They will," said Avery. "I've known the man too long and know how he thinks. I am here today to blow the warning whistle about what's ahead. I hope that Congress, the Senate, and the people of the country who think like I do will make their voices heard."

¥ $ €

Across town on Constitution Avenue a shout rang through the office.

"Son of a *bitch!*"

Peggy called into her boss's office. "Bad news, Mr. Chairman?"

"How did he know?" He said it loudly, without picking up the phone.

"Know what, Mr. Chairman?"

Ben pulled himself together. "Nothing. Sorry I mentioned it."

Peggy nodded. It was one of those moments, she knew, where she couldn't ask, and if she did, Ben couldn't tell her. And when he was like this, it was best to leave him alone to settle.

Inside his office, Ben went into a deep reverie. *Avery had more than a hunch. But, how?* He had a distrust of password-protected or encrypted files, instead relying on paper and pen, using DaVinci's coding technique of writing in a mirror image. It was remarkably incomprehensible to the untrained eye, but not that hard to do with a little practice. A bit like driving on the left-hand side of the road, as in Britain, rather than on the right, as in America. Once you realized that everything was reversed, including the stick shift, it all made sense.

So it wasn't notes that had been left around. It couldn't have been the President, or Steinway or Reynolds. They wouldn't leak. Besides, there wasn't enough time between his meeting with the President yesterday and Avery's appearance. He wished he had Bernadette's sense of spycraft.

Well, he thought, *this will certainly be a topic for conversation on the ride into dinner tonight.*

¥ $ €

The Friday papers all had poll results on the President's handling of the China crisis. Gallup had asked, "Do you think that the President's response to China was 'too tough,' 'not tough enough,' or 'about right'?" 'About right' won the day with fifty-one percent. Thirty-one percent said, 'not tough enough,' and fifteen percent said, 'too tough.' Only three percent were 'undecided.'

Even though it was not technically CIA business, the Chinese had made the poll the Agency's business. Richard Wei gave the briefing.

"What the papers don't say is that the Chinese embassy commissioned the poll," he said. "And they paid handsomely to triple the usual sample size to get demographics with small margins of error and to ask some more detailed questions that were not in the papers. We, of course, got the details through a cable intercept by NSA. It was appended to an analysis by Ambassador Fan. I will tell you that the folks at NSA think the ambassador wanted us to get what he sent. He used a code we think they know we have broken.

"We know the ambassador's position institutionally and as an individual. He is a great believer in improving ties with America, so this is definitely not an easy time for him. His analysis was quite clear. Do not push America too hard. It may be a weak and decadent place, and may appear divided, but it tends to pull together quickly when attacked. He even cited Pearl Harbor as an example and noted what a tactical mistake that was.

"One of the internals in the poll that was not released publicly was the question, 'Do you think that China's actions were primarily motivated by legitimate internal needs or by an effort to gain advantage on the United States?' Wasn't even close. Only twenty-nine percent said legitimate internal needs while sixty-four percent said gain advantage. That was referenced right after the Pearl Harbor reminder.

"Something the ambassador did not mention in his analysis but was in the data was that the only groups who were even vaguely dovish were the elites. 'Legitimate internal needs' got a plurality only among people making over $200,000 and those with advanced degrees. They were also the only two groups where the 'too tough' response got to thirty percent."

"So the doves have the Upper East Side and the Upper West Side," said Hector Lopez, "plus San Francisco, Beverly Hills, and Cambridge. Richard, if the Chinese do that breakdown they will reach the conclusion that the elites are their natural allies and will move to gain a footing there. They probably overestimate the extent to which elites dominate political thinking here. They use their own domestic perspective on these things and still can't quite fathom how Will Turner got elected. Remember, they had the same problem with Trump."

Wei nodded. "Mr. Director, I think you are right on both counts. The political interpretation that is likely to take hold in Beijing is to go after both the capitalists and the intellectuals. They know how to massage the capitalists; start dangling lucrative contract deals in the air. Boeing aircraft, agricultural imports for the farm belt on the purchase side. Some of the big box stores that sell Chinese products on the export side. The latter group will like the devaluation of the yuan that is going on. It makes the Chinese goods cheaper.

"As to the intellectuals, the Chinese will tend to use surrogates, what some might call the usual suspects. The common rallying cry will be the same one that has worked for sixty years, 'America is the belligerent power.' The cultural and intellectual elite has never really liked our way of doing things.

"Power is much flatter here. The elites have far more power overseas, and so they are more naturally attracted to elite-based societies. They view the mass marketing of goods here as tasteless, wasteful, and bad for the environment. Obviously, they feel the same way about defense spending.

"But appealing to our elites will only be half of the response. The other response, advanced by their hawks, is that America is getting ready for war. They will cite the 'not tough enough' group as evidence. And in a funny way, they will turn the ambassador's Pearl Harbor example on its head. It will be proof that America will ultimately respond in a more belligerent way and so China must be strong in order to resist our supposed aggression.

"It's still early days, but we seem to be headed back to the Cold War strategy the Soviets employed. A military buildup at home coupled with a propaganda campaign aimed at our chattering classes. They will bet that the President will not have the ability to carry on a sustained struggle. Currency wars don't carry the same punch as real ones when it comes to mobilizing the country. At least that will be their operating principle."

Lopez frowned. "So what advice do I give to the President? 'Sir, the Chinese don't believe you have the staying power for this.' I know how he'll react to that one. We're supposed to be in the business of minimizing the chances of mistakes happening. You do not challenge someone's manhood unless you want the testosterone to really start flowing." A long silence followed as everyone awaited the Director's next thought.

Bernadette broke the silence. "Hector, you identified the next move earlier. The Chinese are going to overplay their hand. There is little we can do about that. So let them. Some of our intellectuals are going to overplay their hand as well. Let them. Some good 'America is a warmonger' commentary will soon start to appear. Both will drive up the 'not tough enough' side in the polls because most Americans resent that. If the President is told to expect this response and advised to be patient and let them get way out over their skis, he will understand the strategy. Patience now gives him more freedom to maneuver later."

"Perhaps," Lopez said. "But I don't have any better plan. You're telling us to let the inevitable happen. Always sage advice. And I will take your word for it that the President will go along. But somehow that doesn't sound like a stable equilibrium to me. In the absence of any better ideas—" Hector let a pregnant pause follow. "We'll go with it. But mark my words, this is the type of thing that generals complain about. 'No battle plan survives first contact with the enemy.'"

A wicked grin crossed Bernadette's face. "So we ensure that if the equilibrium tilts, it tilts in our favor. We've just discussed how the Chinese are going to try and curry favor among those here who are naturally sympathetic to their cause."

"One problem," said Hector. "If someone over there shows sympathy toward our cause, they disappear in disgrace."

"Granted," said Bernadette. "But as the Chinese try to undermine our position by currying favor, we must undermine their position in the best way we know how."

Wei smiled. "Spycraft."

"That's a dangerous game," Hector said.

"You think they wouldn't do it to us if they had the chance?" Bernadette said. "They're probably doing it anyway; we just haven't kenned to it yet."

"What do you propose?" said Hector.

That wicked smile came back. "One thing communism does extraordinarily well is produce corruption. Not merely among the leadership. It's pandemic right down to the street level."

Wei said, "I don't think our network of assets over there is in a place to start throwing bribes around. And time is an issue if we were to develop more."

Now Hector Lopez smiled. "I don't think she's talking about bribing." He turned to look at Bernadette. "Are you?"

"This is why I love working here," she said. Then, to Wei, "We don't have to undermine them with our money. We let them undermine themselves. By exposing corruption. Not to the world, but within the party, and at such a level that they start chasing their own tail. Infighting. An internal power struggle."

"An operation like that would still take time I don't think we have," said Wei.

"Maybe," said Hector, "we don't need to undermine the entire infrastructure. When Samson destroyed the Philistine temple, he only had to push down two pillars. We might not need to bring the whole house down. One rotten beam might provide enough weakness in the overall structure to give us needed leverage."

Bernadette narrowed her eyes at him. "You have something in mind."

"I might," said Hector Lopez.

¥ $ €

At eleven-thirty Bernadette walked out of the CIA briefing to see Bob Franks waiting with a handful of pink phone message slips. He handed two to Richard Wei, and as she walked past, he said, "Mrs. Coleman. For you." She took it, thinking Ben was calling to touch base, and saw Franks try to hand the remainder of the slips to Lopez. But Lopez didn't seem interested in the messages. He put his hand on Franks's shoulder and led him into the conference room.

She looked down at the message and saw that the box beside *Call Back ASAP* was checked and that the phone number was one she didn't recognize. She took it with her outside to a place where her cell phone worked and dialed the number.

"White House operator. How may I direct your call?"

The breath caught in her throat. "Uh—this is Bernadette Coleman. I was asked to return a call—"

The voice brightened from being businesslike to friendly. "Yes, Mrs. Coleman. Thank you for calling back. The First Lady would like to speak with you. Please hold and I will connect you."

The telephone clicked. "Bernadette, this is Cynthia. I know this is short notice, but do you think that you and Ben could join Will and me for dinner tonight at seven-thirty?"

"Of course, Mrs. Turner."

"Don't you dare *Mrs. Turner* me. Remember, I'm desperate for real friends, not the toadies who dominate this town. I said it was 'Cynthia' from now on, and I mean it."

"Of course, Cynthia. Ben and I would be delighted to join you. Can we bring the wine? You and the President are always hosting, and we would at least like to do a small part."

"To tell you the truth, Will set this up, God love him. Our dinner went so well last weekend that he is using it as the model for how to run an administration. We make it social to camouflage the real purpose. We'll handle everything. We're always hosting because we are who we are. If we were to come to your house, they would have to close half the roads in northern Virginia and we can't have that, can we? You know how much Will hates inconveniencing hundreds of thousands of people, especially at rush hour."

Bernadette realized Cynthia had not given the real reason they couldn't meet at the Coleman's. Was it possible the President hadn't told her? "Cynthia, Ben has a bottle from a vineyard a friend of his owns. Would you mind if he brought it along?"

"If it helps with getting him to dinner, then of course." The short notice defined the conversation topic. *Better tell Ben we have plans for tonight.*

Peggy helped her locate him. He was in front of the computer reading the Bloomberg website.

"Don't tell me," he said, picking up. "Dinner with the Turners, right? Say tonight at seven-thirty?"

"Well done, you," said Bernadette. "How'd you do it?"

"I have my sources," Ben said. "I'm trying hard to catch up with you."

"Well, Mr. Chairman, you seem to be well informed. Have you been spying? Truth be told, Cynthia invited me and suggested that you might come along if I wanted your company."

"Do you?"

"Only if you promise to behave."

"In truth, the President invited me and figured Cynthia would be inviting you. So he asked me to come along and make sure that he'd behave and promised to keep an eye on me as well. If I can get out of here early, do you suppose we'd have time to misbehave before we go? Get it out of my system so I can be on my best behavior."

"What did you have in mind?" Bernadette let a smile come to her lips. "If you leave now, you'll be home by three. I already know which dress I want to wear, so that'll give us a chance to get everything done. I have a long list of chores for you."

"A long list, huh? Well, if you put it that way, I'd better get in my car right away."

"By the way, this does not include carrying me up the stairs. I know you can, but your war wound needs a little more healing time. Besides, I want you at full strength for your other chores."

"An offer I can't refuse."

"You'd better not," she said. "Come straight upstairs. I'll be waiting."

CHAPTER TWELVE

"Shut the door," said Hector Lopez. "I'll try and make this quick."

Bob Franks pushed the door to the meeting room until it clicked shut. "What can I do for you, sir?"

"You talked about the proclivities of a certain general who is behaving in an unfriendly fashion toward our country," said Hector.

"Yes."

"You wouldn't happen to have any photos of Deng in action, would you?"

"My friend does. On his phone. Well, not exactly. Not *in flagrante delicto*, anyway. There are some of him outside the hotel and a couple in the lobby. He used the fake selfie method. You know, someone at a bar you think is cute, want to get a picture without them knowing. So you take a selfie but the focus is on them in the background. A nice ruse.

"Anyway, anything more explicit would have been problematic. Deng's aide does all the soliciting, but Deng sits in the lobby inspecting the merchandise. But the way a spy would. No one would notice unless they had the right training. I can have what my friend has for you tomorrow, such as they are."

"That probably won't be enough," Hector said. "What about something that would carry more weight?"

"Sir, you're the one who would know what assets we have deployed in the area. I'd be happy to do the research if you give me permission."

"I've already checked. No usable assets in the area, and this is not something that can be outsourced. The Agency has to have full control. I guess we're going to be shit out of luck."

"Sir, I hope you don't think this is out of line. You do have an outsourcing option that would still be totally under Agency control."

"What would that be? Sounds like an oxymoron."

"Me and my friend Tom."

"What are you suggesting?"

"Sir, Tom and I are very motivated. We hate everything about what Deng is doing. We're a few years out of the army and have been keeping fit enough to qualify for field work. Tom's been there and knows the area. We'd travel together. Might need some help with expenses though."

"Expenses are not the issue, we've got plenty of dark pools. What did you have in mind?"

"Well, sir, I'm thinking on the fly, but whatever it takes. We'd probably have to decide when we get there. But once there we'd be all in to get the most compromising stuff on Deng we could. Pictures of victims, for example."

"Bob, I can't ask you to do that. Deng is well protected. You might end up being victims yourselves and get tossed into the Mekong."

A light went on in Bob's head. "Sir, if you give us *carte blanche* to run our own operation I think that we might be able to get you something quite usable."

Lopez said, "And what would that be?"

"Sir, I just asked for *carte blanche* to run our own operation on the ground. And if something bad should happen you would need plausible deniability. All you did was give me some much-needed time off. And the money for the trip, of course, but that wouldn't come from you directly, now would it?"

Lopez came back, "I can see your mind at work. You've got an idea and you're probably right that I don't want to know. This all sounds a bit like *Mission Impossible*. Should anything happen to you or your team the Secretary—that's me, by the way—would disavow any knowledge of your activities.

"Still, even under *Mission Impossible*"rules I can arrange a little assistance for you on the ground to get you in and out; that's it. Otherwise, you call the shots. And we will keep our ears open to get a sense of when Deng might be looking for some R&R. I will put Monica on it right away."

A huge smile crossed Bob's face. He loved his job, but he'd been behind a desk too long and wanted something that tested him physically. He had just turned twenty-nine and the dreaded three-oh was constantly on his mind. "Sir, thank you for giving me this opportunity along with your trust. It means a lot."

Lopez said, "Bob, what I am about to say is critically important. I want you to know that you should feel free to back out at any time. There is no obligation for you to do this in your current job. This is strictly volunteer. And it is almost certain to be dangerous. I will not think any less highly of you if you tell me you want out at any time. You also need to know that this has to be as operationally clean as possible but done as safely as possible. There'll never be any public glory or parades in your honor.

"You know those stars down in the lobby? The medals those men got never left this building. They were presented, then locked away. The agent and their family can come view them by appointment. That's it. That's how little public recognition you will get for taking on this kind of job."

"Sir, I understand," said Franks. "Let me double-check with my buddy, but consider me in. I'd love to get that bastard for a lot of reasons."

"Once this is over, I'll make sure you get some comp time off the books. If this goes well, you'll have more than earned it. It's the least I can do."

"And if it doesn't?"

Hector shook his head. "We never talk about that. It's the number one rule of my job."

¥ $ €

The Colemans arrived at the East Executive entrance. They breezed through security and were met at the door by one of the Secret Service detail.

"Mr. and Mrs. Coleman, would you follow me."

It really wasn't a question but an order, delivered politely. This time they skipped the staircase to the state floor and continued on to the elevator to the family quarters just before the covered walkway to the West Wing.

The agent motioned them. "The President and First Lady are expecting you." He pressed the button for the family level and stood outside the elevator, looking quite stoic as the door closed.

The Turners were standing at the elevator. Cynthia spoke first.

"Bernadette, Ben, so glad you could come on such short notice. I see Bernadette decided to let you accompany her this evening." She gave a knowing smile coupled with a wink.

"Mrs. Turner, my wife is always quite generous in this regard. Lord knows she dragged me to most of London's high society back in her days as a wedding planner. I think she likes me as an escort. It gives her cover."

"Well, Cynthia," Bernadette said, "he is rather distinguished looking, don't you think? Don't think any of the escort services around town could provide anything comparable unless I wanted to be a complete cougar."

The President decided to join in. "Ben, from what I read in my daily intelligence briefings, those young studs they use to prance around with older women don't have anything on you. Everything I read says that the term 'Chairman Stud' is there for a reason. Chinese intelligence would not simply make something like that up."

"Mr. President, I—I don't understand."

Bernadette's eyes widened. Lopez hadn't told her that part. But it was obvious now. The Chinese were listening in on her and Ben, but the Agency had tapped into the Chinese bugs and was listening in as well. Everything they intercepted made its way full circle back to the agency. "Cynthia, I think these men are going to get into some salty man talk. Perhaps we ladies should excuse ourselves—"

"No," Ben said. "I want you and the First Lady to stay for this. We're all friends here. Apparently, the President has some information that goes beyond what friends normally share with friends, at least in my circle. Mrs. Turner, I assure you that the President and I have never discussed the intimate details of either your relationship or my relationship with Bernadette. Besides, the President just said something about Chinese intelligence and his daily security briefing."

Cynthia sensed there was trouble brewing and guessed that Will had again put his foot in his mouth. "Ben, it's obvious to both of us that you and Bernadette are madly in love. More power to you."

Bernadette realized there was not going to be any soft pedaling about this with Ben. "Mr. President, you are remarkably well informed. I didn't realize the turnaround from Chinese intelligence to Beijing gave our team time to intercept and write it down in time for your morning briefing memo—let alone in such detail. The way the Agency works, it would seem you have some alternate intelligence gathering capacity in real time."

"Mrs. Coleman, I thought that Lopez had briefed you. Apparently, I am being indiscreet and downright rude. We are on the same frequency as the Chinese bugs. The agency decided we needed to know in real-time what the Chinese were hearing in order to coordinate our actions."

In as controlled a voice as he could manage, Ben said, "If you'll pardon my French, would somebody care to explain what the fuck is going on? I seem to be the only one here in the dark, and I don't appreciate not being in on the joke. I believe I am owed an explanation."

Bernadette glanced at her husband. His face was crimson. He was beyond embarrassment and angrier than she had ever seen him. She slipped her arm through his and grabbed his hand.

The President said, "Ben, I am truly sorry. My comment was absolutely out of line. I meant well, but obviously it seems this has gone too far. Please accept my most humble and sincere apology."

Before Ben could answer, he continued. "I owe you the truth. Bernadette is now going high profile as a Western intelligence asset, higher even than when she was at MI6. She is now a back channel to the Chinese." He held up his hand to make sure Ben didn't interrupt. "I had to explain that to Dianne. She said, 'Isn't that my job as Secretary of State?' and I explained what I meant by back channel. In her position, Bernadette can say things to the Chinese that I can't, that Dianne can't.

Your wife is the ultimate speaker of truth in this case. After all, they know she's the Red Ninja.

"See, the Chinese know we have hired her for this mission. Now they know, thanks to *Drudge*, that she is tight with the First Lady. So they assume that there's a free-flowing conduit of information among the three of us. When we need to send a signal to them, there are two very credible people to do so.

"You, Ben, are the other one. The Chinese know it and that is why Li is talking to you. Since you're both from the money end of things the rest of the government—theirs and ours both—think you're out of the loop on the foreign policy and therefore don't have an ulterior motive. And they're kind of right. Obviously, through Bernadette you become a back channel as well."

Ben drew a slow breath, trying to rein his temper back and show respect for the office of the man in whose house he now stood. "It's all James Bond stuff, sure, and I'm just a money guy. But what's with this 'Chairman Stud' bullshit?"

"I was getting to that," said the President. "As I said, the primary channel to the Chinese is your lovely wife. We can use her covertly or overtly. So if the Chinese, say, put a bug on her and we know about it, we can arrange for her to give them misinformation." The President took another long pause, allowing Ben to absorb it all.

"Sir, am I to understand that the Chinese have bugged our home and that through the Agency, you knew about it? That you listened in on their communication? And if I can put in the rest of the pieces you've neglected to give, they have bugged most of our home, including our bedroom?"

"Yes."

"And how far was my privacy invaded? Were the recordings video or just audio?"

"Just audio. Yes, it included the bedroom. They entered your house on Monday, when you were both at work." Ben started to speak but the President knew what was coming. "They got past your home security pretty easily. Set up four mics. No cameras we could find. We found them Wednesday. That's the real reason I asked whether you had discussed your plan with Bernadette during our Oval Office meeting. If you had, the Chinese would have heard. I'm sorry to say—they heard plenty of other stuff.

"Ben, I was wrong for not having brought you into the loop. I am genuinely embarrassed and deeply sorry. This may not be the right thing to say, but I wanted to lay it on the table. I hope you will take it the right way. And I hope it's the kind of thing you'll be able to laugh at someday."

"You're more the optimist than I," Ben said. "Sir." He said "sir" in a way that non-coms use to show nominal respect to their immediate superior while making it clear they disagree with what was said.

"Ben, do try and lighten up a bit. There is some humor to be found in the situation. I mentioned some unusual phrases that allowed us to put things together? Our codebreaking didn't know quite what to do with them, which is why they were flagged so quickly. Ben, you now have a code name in Chinese intelligence. Chairman Stud."

Ben's faced flushed instantly. "They put in the bug on Monday?" Memories returned. How they'd said that their weekend of abandon hadn't quite been enough—

"There are worse code names," the President said. "Hell, if it were mine, I'd be damn proud." Cynthia shot him a withering look. Realizing he may have erred in bringing out the humor too soon, the President turned and signaled to the butler to bring another round of drinks.

Ben turned to Bernadette. "Did I hear correctly that you were informed of this on Thursday morning at your meeting at the agency? So this afternoon's summons from the damsel in distress was to deliver a message to Beijing? And you accused *me* of treating work like a mistress! That little bauble, as you described, it wasn't for me. It was for the Chinese."

Ben set his glass down and walked toward the living area at the west end of the residence. He pretended to be staring at the view of the West Wing and the Executive Office building. Inwardly he was raging.

Cynthia gave Bernadette a deep look of sympathy. But Bernadette was still in business mode. As a wife she knew Ben would get over it. Her focus was on the moment. *This guy actually does have a conscience*, she thought about the President. *He genuinely seems sorry for what he did to*

Ben. Maybe, like a lot of Americans, she underestimated the character of Will Turner. For some reason Ben seemed to appreciate Turner early on. So this must be completely devastating in more ways than mere embarrassment about the code name. *He thinks Will betrayed him and he thinks I betrayed him.* She looked away from Ben and over to Cynthia, who nodded sympathetically.

Then Cynthia Turner moved down the hall to Ben and put her arm in his. "She's a great woman, Ben Coleman." She could see tears in his eyes. "But even great women make mistakes. You know she didn't mean to hurt you."

All Ben could muster was a whisper. "I know."

"You, Bernadette, Will, and I are in this together. I know that sounds corny, but it is true. Our fates are one. We're going to have to stick together."

Ben was silent.

"Between you and me, Will was an asshole for bringing it up without having checked the background first. He's a good man. Good men make mistakes too."

"When did you know?"

Cynthia knew he was testing this new relationship they had. This was going to hurt. "Thursday, when Will found out. He asked me what I thought about our sex life. I fibbed a bit as some wives do. And Will said, 'This Coleman, he has it all. Looks, brains, stamina.' I asked if he was jealous and all he could say was, 'Wouldn't you be?' Truth be told, he wasn't jealous. He was proud, the way a father or an uncle would be. Trust me. He would never do anything to deliberately hurt you any more than Bernadette would."

Ben remained silent but let the First Lady gently lead him back to join the President and Bernadette. They arrived in time to hear Bernadette say, "Thank you, Mr. President. That was most generous."

Turner approached Ben. "I was telling your lovely bride that this nation is going to owe the two of you an enormous debt of gratitude. I know what a sacrifice this is for you—admittedly more than I realized fifteen minutes ago. These are the kinds of debts that will never be known to the public at large. But I want you both to know that if you ever need a favor from the President of the United States—or far in the future an ex-president—you need only ask."

Ben mumbled a less than convincing, "Thank you, sir."

Cynthia Turner decided it was time to intervene lest the real business of the night slip through the cracks. "All this talk and we haven't even had drinks yet. Will isn't the only one who has forgotten his manners. Ben, I noticed you had brought a little bag with you. I assume that is for dinner? Let me have that decanted."

As if on cue, a butler appeared from around the corner with a tray carrying four martini glasses.

"I took the liberty of selecting the cocktail for the first round since you selected the wine," Cynthia said. "I figured we might need a strong one tonight. In retrospect I should have ordered a triple. Bernadette, it's vodka, not gin. I wasn't sure."

Bernadette gave a polite nod as they took their glasses. "Cynthia, you remembered James Bond's drink was a vodka martini, shaken not stirred."

"Of course," said the First Lady. "We should expect nothing less from the Red Ninja. Cheers, everyone, and thank you so much for coming." She motioned them to the sitting room on the far west side of the family quarters where Ben had retreated.

Will Turner took charge. "I'm sure you saw Chris Avery's little bit of grandstanding on "Power Lunch" this morning. Not sure I'll be able to count on his vote for my reelection campaign. That's not an announcement, so don't tell the Federal Election Commission. They'd have me tied up in red tape faster than you could bat an eyelash.

"As you can imagine, the White House switchboard lit up more than the national Christmas tree. Folks are angry about the impact that China's little ploy is starting to have. Our insta-polling from Thursday night showed 'not tough enough on China' gained four points, all at the expense of 'just right.' The eggheads and fellow travelers who think we're being too easy haven't been moved. It's those guys in the middle whom I care about and Avery hasn't budged them. Maybe even made them angrier by seeming to divide the nation.

"The direction of the movement in the polls is clear. I'd say we have three weeks, tops, before the pressure becomes too great and I will have to announce something more drastic."

Noticing that the butler had discreetly returned to the doorway of the sitting room, Cynthia Turner motioned for them to move to the dining room table. "It's the drastic part that worries me," she said. "We don't want to end up with a divided country over this. I think the sooner we respond, the more we can hold things together. To me its three weeks, tops."

"You see who the real power behind the throne is." The President smiled broadly to show that he meant it.

As they sat down, Bernadette said, "Mr. President, we are willing to help in any way we can."

Ben shot her a warning glance that said, *You two aren't out of the woods yet, so don't be rushing to offer any more than we already have.*

The President seemed to read Ben's mind and decided to extend an olive branch. *Hell,* he thought, *it might take the whole damn olive tree.* "I thought you'd say that, so I've come prepared. I've given a lot of thought to Ben's idea, the Metropolitan Plan? At least that's what George Steinway calls it.

"Ben, it is absolutely the right way to go. It appeals to my Midwestern instincts about how a country should work. So, policy-wise, you're in charge. And you're also right about me being the sales guy. A president has to do this, not the Fed chair, even though he's the brains behind the whole thing. So think of yourself as the ventriloquist and me as your puppet on a string."

Bernadette had never imagined a national leader saying that to anyone. Yes, it was largely spoken as a peace offering, and yes, the President obviously knew that this was the best—perhaps the only— way to get to Ben. But it was still a magnanimous thing to say and gave every appearance to have been said genuinely.

The President continued, "It looks like we'll have to move on it before the three weeks is up. We'll have to prepare the congressional leadership first. Start with the bipartisan leadership and the ranking members of both foreign relations and banking. They will gradually disseminate the ideas among their colleagues.

"I wish I could say that this was going to be a cakewalk, but there are bound to be some snags. Some of the hawks have already been in touch with me and are talking about slapping on tariffs while we polish our bayonets. I wish that folks remembered that Trump's tariffs were hardly a painless act in terms of domestic support. That might have worked for Trump when he faced down Xi, but it pissed off a lot of people in the process."

"That was a trade war," Ben said. "Different animal from what we've got now. This is an economic struggle." Talking shop made him feel more comfortable despite the anger still inside him. And it was sinking in that he had won the President over on the Metropolitan Plan.

"We're also going to have to keep an eye on Chris Avery," said the President. "I don't think he's the type to put the knife in, but I wouldn't put it past him to be eyeing your job, Ben, at least after I leave office. He's positioning himself to be the choice of whoever leads the other party. A party man through and through, but one who can disguise it with high sounding phrases."

"Good read on him, Mr. President," Ben said. "He's not a fan of my work, but I think he'll come around to our side if we can make it attractive enough. But you're right. He does need to be watched during all of this. He's a living example of the Ten-Dollar Bill Rule."

The others looked at him.

"Supposedly," Ben explained, "it comes from a grizzled veteran Army drill sergeant. 'You line up a hundred guys and start handing them ten-dollar bills, and there's going to be one son-of-a-bitch who asks you for two fives.'"

They all laughed, feeling the air in the room lighten as they did.

"All right," the President said. "At some point after the congressional briefing I am going to make another formal address to the nation. Best for that to come from the East Room, though they might let me address a joint session of Congress. That should be two weeks from this coming Monday. I figure that will give us next week to get our operational ducks in a row and the following week to start the briefing process.

"That kind of timing, coupled with a full court press, ought to get the bill through committee before the Fourth of July recess. Then they come back for three weeks before leaving for the August break. We can pass the legislation then. Total elapsed time from now is just under three months." He looked right at Ben. "Your thoughts?"

"That sounds doable, Mr. President," Ben said, "at least from my end. The FOMC meets the week after next, Tuesday and Wednesday. Technically the district banks that the presidents head own all the bonds in the System Open Market Account, which we call SOMA. The plan we have in mind is going to radically change the content of the SOMA and the operations of the Fed in implementing our policy. We will need a vote of the committee to formally agree to the plan."

"Can we get that?" asked Turner.

"It'll pass," said Ben, "but there will be a lot of explaining to do, especially now that Avery is campaigning against it. I'd love to know how he found out about our plan."

"I've got people on it," said Turner.

Ben said, "I hope they'll be very discreet. If Avery thinks he's being investigated, it will fire him up and you and I will both be attacked as trying to set up a police state."

"Discrete it is," said the President.

Bernadette interrupted. "Gentlemen, there's an old saying from spycraft. 'Don't ask a spy to hunt down the answer to a question you might not like the answer to.'"

"Meaning?" asked the President.

"Let's do some elimination. Ben, do you think Avery broke into your office at night and rummaged through your desk to find notes?" She saw Ben shake his head. "Not to bring up a difficult subject, but it couldn't have come from the Chinese because Ben and I never shared any information about it. That leaves four people as sources—you two gentlemen, George, and Dianne—the only people in the meeting. So do you want an investigation begun that will end up naming any of the four people who were in on the discussion?"

After a moment of taking it all in the President said, "Ben how did you find such a smart lady?"

"The same way you found yours, Mr. President. But remember, I started as just an escort, and sometimes returned to that status like I was at the start of this evening."

Bernadette said, "Don't you believe a word of this nonsense. He set a very elaborate trap worthy of a spy master. There was no escape."

Ben decided to make a joke of what had happened tonight and spread some of his embarrassment around. "As I recall the only struggling you were doing that weekend was to get out of bed. Imagine if the Chinese had bugged your apartment back then? What would your nickname have been? I've got it—Queen Bee. Doesn't she require a whole army."

Cynthia decided her friend had suffered enough and started laughing hysterically. Between guffaws she managed to get out "Ben Coleman, you are too much! I do not want you hanging around Will anymore. It will take his language back to his football days and I have worked so hard to get him to grow up. You two really must have an extraordinary relationship."

"We do, Cynthia," Bernadette said. "And you've gotten a taste of why."

"Sir," said Ben, "my apologies for the distraction. But back to business. When we do the briefing of the Federal Open Market Committee and even the Congressional leadership, it would help if George Steinway and Hector Lopez could hold a briefing at the start of the meeting. Lopez will put the fear of God into them. Steinway will represent you and the administration's willingness to go along. I will have to give a few key members a heads up, probably over the previous weekend. And if you need me to go to the Hill, I can do it the Thursday and Friday after the FOMC."

Cynthia Turner said, "Bernadette, while the men are doing the arm-twisting in private, you and I are going to do the kinder and gentler work of uniting the country. You're a famous novelist and a knockout speaker, so you have standing in your own right.

"As I see it, our job is to keep the country as calm as possible and build a national consensus. Let me start with one thing I am particularly worried about—the reaction of the public at large to Chinese Americans. Remember how, after 9-11, Bush went out of his way to reassure America that Muslim Americans were not a threat? Obama took that even further by not even using the phrase 'Islamic extremist' to describe the enemy.

"I thought to myself, what do all Americans think positively about what's related to China? The answer is their local Chinese restaurant. So I propose that you and I have lunch at that fantastic place out in Seven Corners. They have the best dim sum.

"From there we go to some of the larger Chinese chamber of commerce groups and fraternal organizations. I think you should go on the morning shows and stress how we are all in this together. Your novels are high drama spy thrillers, so a theme like 'Yes, we are at something like a cold war and it's one we will win if Americans stick together,' and then give a human side. Something about Ben and what it's like living with a man under stress twenty-four seven. You could do that on the money channels as well.

"Ben's input would be crucial about what to say and what not to say. That's something for the two of you to discuss. But the personal side is surely going to help ratings. The morning shows are typically watched by women and the money channels are always interested in an inside look at the personalities of the Fed chairmen. That'll be a real human-interest story and maybe even engender some sympathy."

Bernadette said, "Of course," and then noted that Ben sat passively during the First Lady's pitch. Cynthia's plan was really about him, even though Bernadette herself would be doing it. He'd had a rather distant stare through it all. *This night isn't over for us yet*, she thought.

The ladies carried ninety percent of the conversation through dinner with President Turner interjecting at key moments. By nine-fifteen it was time to leave. Missions had been assigned. Everyone knew it would be a rough few weeks, though most had no idea just how rough they would be.

¥ $ €

The Salamander Resort was a great place for a weekend getaway or a private conference. Excellent food, a first-class spa, and golf. Best of all, it was far enough outside the Beltway that there would be no media, and that was the organizers' intent.

In the main conference hall a banner hung behind the moderators' table at the front of the room. *Enough Is Enough. Stop China Now.* The first part of the phrase was sufficiently vague. Enough of what? Well, enough of lots of things. That is what brought these people together. Each represented an organization that had its own grievance.

By the standards of a K Street lobbying shop, those assembled represented a veritable dog's breakfast of disparate interest groups. There were representatives of various manufacturer trade associations who had seen their businesses hollowed out by Chinese competition. They were joined by some of the smaller craft unions whose members had been hurt in the same fashion. Environmental groups were also present, notably the umbrella group GWC, the Global Warming Coalition—China was the largest emitter of carbon dioxide on the planet by a large margin.

Various human rights causes normally associated with the left were present, such as Human Rights Watch. The LGBTQ community had representatives angry about the persecution and murder of gays in China. The Free Tibet movement was there as was one of Hong Kong's dissident legislators. Both would be delighted to join any organization that would weaken Beijing's grip.

Groups normally associated with the right were there as well. Right to life groups were present to denounce the massive number of forced abortions that had been performed by the state to enforce its now-abandoned One Child policy. The Liberty Lobby was represented, a group that opposed big government both here and abroad. Finally, one could see remnants of the old Taiwan lobby present. Indeed, three of the former benefactors of that lobby, all right-leaning billionaires, were picking up the bill for the room. They had each also contributed $10 million to a fund to run the campaign.

Altogether about eighty delegates filled the room representing some five dozen organizations. But a professional lobbyist would notice one other fact about the group aside from the diversity of their interests: none of the big-name organizations was there. The AFL-CIO and the national Chamber of Commerce were not in attendance. Nor was the national right to life group. These larger organizations were quite bureaucratic. The gathering at the Salamander was for the lean and hungry, the entrepreneurial, and the second-tier groups who sensed a chance for an opening to the big leagues by hooking their wagons to the anti-China train and seeing where it would take them.

The organizers knew this. It was the hunger of those in attendance that they hoped to harness to carry their banner. Mark Swift and Renee DeAngeles had been retained by the Taiwan Interest Office. He had earned his spurs in the 2016 crusade of Bernie Sanders. She was a consultant for Ted Cruz the same year. They had both worked for the Number Two and they understood the drive and passion of the runner-up who'd almost derailed the leader but fell short. They were now going to take on the ultimate foreign power, the People's Republic of China. And they knew that the big special interests had already cut deals with the PRC. They were older now, but the 2016 campaign had made them both hungry for victory. Though they came from opposite ends of the political spectrum, their passion to win had drawn them together.

Renee and Mark had also learned a lesson from Trump's trade war with China: it helps to have a united country if you really want to win. Trump had made some progress, but too many in Congress and in official Washington were more interested in punishing him than punishing China. China had exploited that to the fullest. It had united big business to oppose the tariffs as economically dangerous in a way that played into the more general "Trump is dangerous" narrative. Fortunately for their current movement, Will Turner did not stir the kind of emotions that Trump had.

Renee led off. "Thank you very much for coming. I know many of us do not agree on many issues. But we are all united by one. China must be stopped!" Applause broke out in the room. "Thanks to their economic aggression against America we have an opportunity to remake the American political landscape like never before. The public is on our side. But they don't know how to act to make change happen. We are gathered together to force change. And united, we will do exactly that."

The lights dimmed and all eyes focused on the two large screens on either side of the speaker's podium. A scene of factories belching color-enhanced black smoke took center stage. A male voice intoned, "China has made itself the world's major industrial power."

This switched to a series of pictures showing a crowd of factory workers headed to work in what appeared to be bitterly cold weather. Each was garbed in the quilted jacket so reminiscent of Chinese winter garb since the 1960s. In fact, it was unclear when exactly the footage was taken.

"It has done so on the backs of people who earn an average of just $300 per month."

Now there was a montage of footage. The filthy air of a Beijing winter when the visibility was less than half a mile. Pipes gushing who-knows-what into the air. A stack of grim thirty-story apartment houses built one next to the other. The clothes draped over every balcony bespoke people who made washers and dryers for others, but who had no access to one for themselves.

"They breathe foul air, drink polluted water, and are forced to live in nightmarish conditions. A whole family is packed into a three-room apartment that measures just 450 square feet."

Another cut to impoverished children playing with the most rudimentary toys in a concrete space between the apartments.

"Meanwhile the ruling elite live in the lap of luxury."

Now a giant state banquet, followed by an upscale mall lined with Gucci, Hermès, and Chanel shops.

"This is the image that the Chinese want us to see. But this great wealth comes at a price."

A headline appeared reading, "Worker Strike Broken Up by Militia Firing Point Blank." A scene of panic—from a source that was not credited—followed by a scene of the street with a dozen dead bodies.

"But the Chinese elites can't squeeze their people anymore. Now they have decided to squeeze us."

A new headline: "China Dumps U.S. Securities." Followed by a scene of the New York Stock Exchange in pandemonium. Given that electronic trading now made the floor of the exchange appear more like a movie set, the footage was dated. But it gave the right impression.

"Goods produced by workers paid slave wages. A rigged currency to let them steal our markets. Now this. China must be stopped. We cannot let them do to us what they have done to their own people. Join us."

A shot of a diverse group of Americans arranged in a crowd. Not a tight shot—the contrast was between the individuality on which America prides itself and the Chinese. To drive home the point, the screen split with the diverse individual Americans contrasted to a scene of Chinese workers packing themselves on a bus with a crowd still waiting to get on.

"The time has come for us to tell the Chinese government that "Enough Is Enough." And we need to do it the only way that they care about—money."

More Americans on the screen, again quite diverse, picketing a large big box store. Each carried a sign: *Enough Is Enough. Stop China Now.*

"Join us in boycotting Chinese-made goods. Do it until they stop their attacks on our economy and on their own people. Stop China now."

The lights raised. The total elapsed time was just sixty seconds. Applause broke out throughout the conference room. There was action in it for everyone. Labor got its message through with the appalling working conditions. Business liked the market-stealing narrative. The environmental groups, the smokestacks belching black smoke, and the human rights groups, the dead bodies in the street. This is how one built a coalition of diverse groups.

Mark Swift took the stage. "We have a $3 million buy for this ad to run on all the cable news networks across the spectrum. Fox News, CNN, MSNBC, CNBC, Bloomberg, and Fox Business. The buy is aimed at policymakers. The money shows are aimed at corporate America. We want them quaking in their boots if they are importing cheap goods from China.

"But to drive home this message, we need you to bring two big things to the table. Your social media outreach to your members and your activist members. We need to spread the message. We are prepared to help each group assembled here prepare its own message targeted at its members.

"Many of you have your own resources and we will help only to the extent you want us to. For those groups without a media center, use ours. You write the script. We will pull the visuals together. The target is your own membership stressing the issues they care about. The ending will be, 'Tell Senator so-and-so that Enough Is Enough. Stop China Now.' This should be followed by a link that tells them how to email or phone them.

"But the real impact is to turn the last scene in the ad into a reality across the country. We need your members to start picketing the big box stores that deal with China. Walmart, Target, Home Depot, and Loews. We will help you attract local media to the protest. As scenes flood in on the networks' local affiliates, the national news shows will pick them up and carry them. It won't take long before the Chinese get the message.

"Questions?"

Hands went up. The questions were all technical and logistical. That meant Renee and Mark had made their sale. No skepticism. It was all, "We'll do it. Tell us how."

When the last delegate left forty minutes later, Mark and Renee high-fived each other. The train had left the station and there was no turning back.

PART TWO

THE DANGEROUS GAME

CHAPTER THIRTEEN

IT WAS A LONG RIDE HOME FROM THE WHITE HOUSE TO THE COLEMAN residence in Great Falls. It wasn't just the seventeen miles, and at this hour there was no rush hour traffic. Total time door to door was just under half an hour.

Ben was staring out the window from the back seat on the driver's side. Silent. Bernadette put a hand on his arm but got no response. No movement at all.

"I'm getting to really like Cynthia," she said. "She has a head for this business but remains a real person."

Ben did not respond.

Bernadette sensed trouble brewing. Ben wasn't this way very often. In fact, she could count on one hand the number of times he hadn't been communicative in their eight years of marriage. She decided maybe she should let him be. He would eventually come around. But she left her hand on his arm nonetheless. No point in retreating or withdrawing. At this point that would be the wrong approach. She needed to signal that she was there.

When they got home, she stood at the base of the stairs and said, "I'm going to bed."

No response.

"Want to join me?"

That produced the functional equivalent of a grunt. One word, "Work." Then he headed off to his study.

She knew he was exhausted and wouldn't be working long. Nor was it clear he would be any more talkative later. She decided to go to sleep.

When she awoke at her usual weekend time of seven-thirty she noted that, indeed, Ben had come to bed. His side remained rumpled although the covers had been pulled back toward the pillow. She slipped into her Saturday homebound attire and headed down the stairs.

. She noted Ben was again in his study staring at his computer. "Good morning, dear. Still working?"

"Your coffee's in the kitchen," was the only response.

She got her coffee and came back to the study and stood there, waiting for him to say something. But all she got was silence and Ben didn't take his eyes off the computer. She could feel anger boiling up inside of her. She raised her voice to just below a shout.

"Ben, you're more than happy to fuck me, but not to talk to me."

"At this point I'm really not much interested in fucking you either."

"What," she said, "are you still mad at—"

He cut her off. "Enough," he said. "Our marriage is based on trust and us sharing with each other. Yet you didn't trust me with the most basic thing. That is not a marriage." Ben stood up from his computer and Bernadette noticed that he was in his gym outfit. He announced, "I'm going for a walk."

"Can I join you?"

The response was cold. "It's a free country. I can't stop you." Then he made motion with his jaw, pointing with his entire head at the chandelier. He stormed out of the room and out the front door, slamming it shut behind him.

She quickly found her jogging shoes and headed out after him. Once outside she noted that Ben was a block away, moving at a saunter, then slowing to a stop near one of the ubiquitous Aqua Blue vans backed into a neighbor's driveway.

He really didn't want the rest of the conversation heard by the entire world. So he was not acting for personal reasons, but for national security as well. He had set her up to have a frank conversation out of earshot, their first such talk since the bugs were planted. Better make the most of it.

"Are you still mad at the President for his wise crack?" she said as she caught up. "He more than apologized."

"I'm not mad at him." Ben started walking at his usual brisk pace. "I'm mad at you for betraying me."

"I don't understand. I had no idea. To think, our own country was spying on us, and why? To make sure you didn't unintentionally slip me some intel?"

"The hell you didn't." Now Ben's voice was as loud as hers. "Not only listening but giving the President and God knows who else the details of our sex lives. The great Red Ninja didn't know the most basic thing about spycraft! How the fuck do you expect me to believe that?"

"Hector never told me."

"Ah, but Hector knew. And how many other people? Lombardi? Chief of staff must get the intel. So must Steinway and Reynolds. So there I am, working day after day with people who are quietly laughing at me.

" 'Chairman Stud.' Do you know how professionally demeaning that is? At best it makes me some kind of well-endowed racehorse. And likely one who is past his prime." Ben turned away. "By the way, that list probably included your new BFF Cynthia Turner. What did she say? 'Will, why can't you perform like that?' Please spare me the 'I didn't know' bullshit."

"But I didn't, at least not until Hector told me on Thursday."

"Oh, and you didn't guess on your own? Come on, Bernadette, I'm not that naïve."

"Just a damn minute here, Ben. You're forgetting one thing. I was spied on too."

"But it's your trade to be spied on."

"Not in the bedroom. Not like this. I was violated too. I said other things besides calling you a stud, you think I want that lover's talk to be part of someone's water cooler conversation?"

"You don't have people calling you 'Chairman Stud' behind your back."

"No. They call me Red Ninja to my face. Red? How original. Ninja? Not even Chinese. Aren't you the one who compared your confirmation hearing to a colonoscopy without the drugs? Suck it up, Ben. You're in bed with politicians. What the hell did you expect?"

Ben's expression melted into one of utter shock.

"I'm sorry," she said. "I got caught up in the moment. I apologize for that. And I should have known about the bugs. I didn't, but I should have, and for that I am sorry as well."

"I had no idea," he said. "You never told me—"

"Of course I didn't. It's that damned MI6 mindset." She tried to smile but it didn't go over.

"And there it is," Ben said, face stiffening.

"What's that supposed to mean?"

"It's that same CIA, MI6, KGB bullshit that's been happening for decades. You're sorry you got caught. You're sorry that you fucked up. Nothing more, nothing less."

Bernadette shrugged. "Well, you think you know all there is to know about the situation, then. What more can I say?"

"Probably nothing. Maybe I am realizing that I am not the person I thought I was. Not as tough. And a lot more naïve. I was genuinely surprised and angered last night. Now if I were a typical male, I should take it all in stride. But that is a stereotype. Adult men do not share every detail of their sex lives with their buddies. At least, not this one. That's always been sacrosanct, between you and me.

"But now it's all over Washington, no doubt. 'Ben Coleman is so good in bed that the president of the United States is commenting on it.' Maybe *The Washington Post* could write a column on it. For the style section. Yes, that's it! 'Ben Coleman, the guy everyone wants to be like.' And then *Cosmopolitan* will be calling you. 'The Ten Things Ben Coleman Does in Bed That Drive Me Wild.'

"So, yes. I am pissed. And I feel betrayed. But it wasn't me who was betrayed, it was the person I thought I was, still naïvely believing what I learned as a kid.

"I can get over the Chinese doing it. In the simple world of the old Ben Coleman, they are the bad guys and bad guys do bad things. Well, it turns out the good guys aren't all that different than the bad guys, are they? Or at least their governments aren't.

"And here I am, in what many consider one of the most powerful jobs in America. Does that make me a bad guy too? Part of a bad system? You're part of that system, too, remember. You should have known, and you should have told me. Maybe you take things like this for granted so the sense of violation I feel doesn't make any sense. And I don't understand why you don't feel violated too. Everything I have believed since I was a boy, everything I assumed Colemans have believed for generations about what is right and wrong is being turned on its head."

Bernadette listened. He was venting, true, but these were legitimate and deeply held feelings. Her psych training said that it was good to let them out. He did have a strong sense of right and wrong, and she loved him for it. Finally, she put her hand in his and stopped him, mid-angry stride and gave him a kiss on the cheek. "I love you."

"Am I off my rocker? You're the one trained in psychology. Shouldn't I feel this way? Or am I living some fantasy that was drilled into me in childhood about the way things are supposed to work?

"Worse, I am upset, downright angry, frustrated, and mad at a time when I need every bit of me to do my job and do what's best for my country. And that despite feeling that my country has let me down."

"Darling—"

"Do you think Governor Li is going through something like this too? I've read his brief. Decent guy. Not really a believer in Marx or Mao, but a real believer in China. But he can't be happy with all that is happening. You once told me that one day he would need a favor from me. I have always assumed it was because at some point the system he lives in would be out to get him. They play for keeps and he doesn't have the luxury I have of being naïve. But he still is in a way. He believes in China the way I believe in America."

"Ben," she said, "you wanted complete honesty, right? That there would never be any secrets between us? You know that is not part of my profession."

Ben nodded and looked straight at her.

"We have to set him up."

"What the hell are you talking about?"

"Li," said Bernadette. "Part of the Agency's strategy is to sow discord and distrust among the Chinese leadership. He's part of the team of those who have been Westernized and who want to make China a normal country. The other team, mostly in the military, believe that they must 'Make China Great Again.' And their way is through the use of force.

"Sure, the force guys realize that a strong economy is good for building up the military, and the economy guys know that a strong military is a part of a strong China. It's mostly a matter of degree. But we want it to be more than that. We want them to be so divided that they cannot work together."

Ben took it in. "So you want the new, decidedly *not*-improved Ben to put that into an operational plan? We are going to use the bugs to send some disinformation to the guys on the other end that Li may be disloyal and working with us?"

"Not exactly. But you're getting the idea."

"So it's not enough that I feel betrayed by you and by my country, I now have to betray someone else. Not exactly a close friend, but certainly a professional colleague. In case you didn't know, the way the world economy sticks together is that central bankers don't betray one another. We may argue, but we don't set the other guy up, ever. How can your colleagues trust you in a future crisis when you have a reputation for doing things like that to your colleagues?"

"I know, my dear. We will do it in a way without your fingerprints."

"Just my grunts and cries of pleasure."

"Ouch. Glad you haven't lost your sense of humor."

"You're confusing sarcasm with humor," Ben said. "When exactly were you going to tell me this? Tonight in bed? Oh no, I forgot, the whole world would know then."

"I'm telling you now."

Ben began to shout, something he rarely did. "So now you've moved from not telling me anything to telling me on a walk far from our home that no one gets to hear. And for good measure, it was a walk I set up so that we could have a private conversation about us!"

Bernadette put a hand on each of his shoulders. "Ben, calm down. Look at me. I was told to use you as someone to talk to and not involve you when I dropped news to the microphone. I could have done that. I didn't do that. It would be, as you said, treating you like an escort.

"And you're right. This is shitty. The whole thing is shitty. Statecraft is shitty. It's a shitty business. But it is what it is. And you said it your-self, they play for real. There is a difference between the two sides in this struggle, not as much a one as we might hope, but there is a difference. Here, if you're on the losing side you get to write your memoirs. There, you're lucky to live and luckier if they let your family live.

"You know in China, a family is billed for the bullet that the State puts through their loved one's head? We aren't perfect, but we sure are better than the alternative. This is a battle we have to win."

"So why do I have to put a colleague's life on the line? Is it because we are just enough better than they are that I should be grateful for being given the opportunity?"

"You're right again. Forget it. I never said it. I will call Lopez right now and tell him to get those god-damned bugs out of the house this instant. We won't have that conversation and Li will never be set up, or at least not set up by you and me. We'll let someone else do it.

"Only then you and I won't have any control of the situation. So if it is Li who ends up on the losing side and if he comes to us, it won't be you and me who have any leverage on how to deal with him. It'll be someone else. Because it was they who did the hard part and planted the seed of doubt that led to the whole thing."

"God, you're good."

Bernadette smiled. "I'm the fucking best there is."

"All right. Let's hear the whole sales pitch now that I've been snagged. Tell me more about this so-called leverage we might earn. So far I have exactly none. Maybe it's my ego, but I really don't like being a helpless pawn. Especially when the ones actually moving me around the board are about to make a play that ruins my professional reputation. Exactly what kind of deal are you suggesting?"

"I'm not in a position to make a deal. That's what you money guys do. Sorry. I shouldn't have said that. You are the one with the conscience here. I'm just an operative, a pawn to use your phrase, and I always have been."

" 'Operator' would be a much better word," Ben said. "Think about the strings you are able to pull. The one thing you are not is the suburban housewife who writes novels to ease the boredom. I can't think of a one who has the CIA Director sending a car to fetch you and the First Lady treating you as her new best friend."

Bernadette felt her face redden. Ben was right. She had been trained to serve. Duty, honor, king, country. All her life. She really had viewed herself as a pawn, just like one of the characters in her novels. True, a James Bond could bend the rules at the edges. But M always had a firm hand on the leash. It was strange to think of herself as off the leash. But she was. And Ben had let her slip the knot.

"Okay," she said. "I will go to Lopez. For that matter, to Cynthia if it comes to that. The deal will be that if Li gets into any trouble, we will grant him and his family asylum. Kind of overdoing it by the standards of my profession, but you're right. It's time that we give ourselves a little responsibility for trying to clean up the mess we helped make."

"And when do we get those god-damned mics removed from the house?"

"The plan was for Monday, when we are at work."

"What is this?" Ben said. "Some kind of union deal where the Agency folks can't work on weekends? Or do you have to pay them time and a half and somehow the black budget doesn't cover those kinds of expenses?"

"The one thing we can't have is the other side thinking that we knew their mics were there, so they have to do it when we are not home. Waiting until Monday gives us more leverage because we can agree to send a couple more messages in the meantime."

"I'll give you one," said Ben. "One more message, and it'd better be good."

"Fair enough," Bernadette said.

"When?"

"The ideal time is when Washington power couples, of which we are one, have their quality time together. During the Sunday morning talk shows."

"And what are you going to say?"

She thought about this. It was a little too long for Ben's taste.

"Well?"

"You're going to have to trust me on this," she said.

"Depends. What's the plant?"

"It's not in the what," said Bernadette, "it's in the how. We're in bed. There's foreplay. Then I stop and say, 'What's wrong, it's like you're not here.' And you say something like, 'Those damn Chinese, I wish to hell I knew what they were going to do next.' Only you can make it sound more convincing than that.

"Then I'll say, 'It's all right. We'll get that for you soon enough. We have a mole.' You go, 'A military insider isn't going to do me any good.' And I say, 'The mole isn't in the military.' You say, 'Baby, you're brilliant,' and we slowly start fooling around again."

"Do I have to say you're brilliant?"

"Yes. And after that you damn well better ravage me because I want to give all those fucking voyeurs a memorable parting send-off. Something that will have them chattering long after they can no longer listen."

"And then we get rid of those god-damned bugs?"

"Then we get rid of those god-damned bugs."

Ben smiled and looked deep into her eyes. "All right," he said. Then he took her in his arms. "I love you, and more importantly in this moment, I trust you."

"I love you too, Ben Coleman. And I trust you too."

¥ $ €

Monday evening found Ben and Bernadette flipping between Fox, One America News, CNN, and MSNBC.

"Did you notice," said Bernadette, "that Fox and CNN ran the same lead story about Enough Is Enough and how their campaign might lead to protests? How often does that happen?"

Ben replied, "Once in a blue moon. But in the electronic age even blue moons can be manufactured."

"This one certainly was," Bernadette said. "It's only been forty-eight hours since the start of their ad campaign and now talk is everywhere about people hitting the streets. The NSA told us Enough Is Enough mobilized more than a dozen single-issue groups to follow up with their own social media releases and website videos. It's like their plan from the beginning was to start the picketing after the issue had been primed by national cable buys."

"Those media buys gave the channels incentive to carry stories supporting what those who bought the time were saying," Ben said. "In a way, it's theater."

"Our guys up on the Hill told us that the effect was immediate," Bernadette said. "By tomorrow afternoon nervous nellies in Congress will be on the floor to demand that the president do something. You can almost smell the jet fumes as they catch the red-eyes back from their home districts."

"Whoever put this together is smart," Bernadette said. "I hear it is two media guys from losing presidential campaigns, one from each side of the aisle. It's hard to get used to how important entrepreneurship is here. Back home the BBC calls the shots, and the papers are too proud to be bought off so easily in what they cover. Here it's like the news is for sale."

"Wait until Sunday," said Ben. "Thursday's the day for final decisions about who will appear on the Sunday talk shows. Senators with strong anti-China positions are aiming to put themselves at the top of the list. The more memorable—or outrageous—the floor speech, the more likely they are to make the cut."

"It's like they're getting free advertising," Bernadette said.

"The most valuable kind," said Ben. "Voters back home are tuned in and all of a state's media take a cue when one of their own is on. Editorial coverage back home creates an echo chamber." He paused to watch the screen, then added, "I don't mean to be too cynical, but for a senator, the real advantage is national coverage. They needed the exposure. There's a saying in Washington, 'The most dangerous place in town to stand is between Chuck Schumer and a bank of television cameras.'"

Bernadette laughed.

"See, most senators view themselves as future presidents and every member of the House looks at himself in the mirror and sees a potential senator."

"Ambition, I get," said Bernadette, "and politicians are the same everywhere. But here it's all about building name recognition in the public at large. In a parliamentary system like Britain's, your audience is your fellow politicians. They expect you to be wise and thoughtful and not to have a toothy grin and get coverage by being outrageous."

They flipped to CNN. It was a report on conditions in China and one could tell, even with the sound off, that it was a negative report as Beijing's smog was the backdrop. More than half the pedestrians were wearing surgical masks. Some person in a mask was interviewed and the English translation was a complaint about conditions. Then the reporter turned to his unnamed sources and talked about the latest round of protests.

"Let's try MSNBC."

The screen went to stock footage of port facilities filled with piles of container boxes ready to be loaded onto ships. Then it flashed to numbers detailing China's trade surplus and its impact on American jobs. Next were people standing in unemployment lines. They returned to their Washington newsroom and their waiting anchor.

Next they went to Fox. On the screen was a suburban Walmart.

"That's the one in Falls Church!" said Bernadette.

"It is, I'm sure. Do you think these guys travel far? The reason all the scenes are in New York, Washington, or Los Angeles is because that's where are all the reporters are."

The Walmart segment was predictable, foreshadowing the picketing at big box stores that sold goods labeled "Made in China" and employees unhappy about having to report to work in spite of potential protesters.

Ben shook his head. "They always leave out how those goods were cheaper and that the greatest part of that savings was passed on to consumers, particularly with basic goods. It once took a median income worker about seventeen minutes of work to buy a package of men's underwear back in 1960. Now it takes less than three minutes."

Bernadette grinned at him. "Only you would know a fact like that."

Next up was The Home Depot headquarters outside Atlanta. To make up for a lack of comment from the business's higher ups, Fox cut to a bearded man in his late forties with a bookshelf brimming with academic journals. A caption associated him with a local school of business as he discussed how the chain bought nearly a quarter of its merchandise, except for wood products, from China. "But the money made on those products make up about a third of its total profits," he said.

Bernadette sat up. "I thought Fox was supposed to be conservative and pro-business. That was a double whammy. They implied Home Depot is dependent on China and uses cut-rate prices to gouge consumers."

"Well, we know where the polls are going," Ben said. "The President is going to have to become more hawkish at some point."

"That takes care of the instructions Lopez is going to give at the next team meeting," Bernadette said. She sat up and patted her husband on the knee. "Forgive me, my darling, but I've got to turn in for the night. I have a suspicion the First Lady is going to be on the phone tomorrow. I'm getting a headache just thinking about it."

CHAPTER FOURTEEN

BEN KNEW EXACTLY WHAT PEGGY'S FIRST WORDS WOULD BE AS HE walked into his office. With the bugs gone there had been a blissful week of peace on the home front along with the usual celebration when the making up was done. But peace at home meant trouble among his colleagues and the week's worth of silence was too good to be true. Something had to give, and Ben figured it was to happen within the next forty-eight hours.

"Mr. Chairman, Governor Li asks that you call him as soon as possible." It took no more than a nod from Ben to set Peggy's fingers flying on the secure phone.

Ben settled into his chair and put on the speaker phone, waiting for the call to be connected. When his Chinese counterpart uttered a greeting, he was ready.

"Governor Li," he said. "It is an honor to hear from you this morning."

"Mr. Chairman, it is always a pleasure," Li said. "And very good for the world that we are still on speaking terms. I hope that can continue."

Ben caught the double entendre in Li's comment. Conflict between the two countries meant relations were strained. The conflict that Bernadette had planted within the upper ranks of the Chinese government also meant that Li might not be around too long.

"I am sure that it can for many years. The current unpleasantness is sure to pass." Ben knew that was a lie. In fact, he was planning how to bring the Chinese to their knees and force them to stop destabilizing the American financial markets. More importantly, Li knew it as well. And given the tone in Li's voice, Ben was sure that others were listening.

Worse, he had just done something that likely would shorten Li's tenure and maybe even his life.

Li said, "I certainly hope you are correct. But these are interesting times."

"The old Chinese curse," Ben said. " 'May you live in interesting times.'"

"I am glad we understand each other," Li said. "In the interest of further good relations, I was wondering if we could meet in London this coming weekend. I know the FOMC is meeting next week, but a private side conversation between us might indeed prove useful in addressing some of the differences we have. I have spoken to Governor Adams at the Bank of England and he would love to host a meeting that might ease tensions."

Private side conversation meant that Li was being listened to on his end. Ben's secure phone was only secure up to the point of Li's office. So Chinese state security was indeed listening. The rest of the conversation was going to be in code.

Ben proceeded with caution. "I always enjoy getting together with you and this would normally be a difficult time, but I am going to have to check my schedule. I might be able to juggle things. I assume that this is a matter of some urgency?" Thinking, *Okay, Li, the ball is now in your court.*

It was a delaying tactic and both men knew it. Li's comment left many questions unanswered about the true purpose of the conversation. Ben was not naïve enough to believe that Li was speaking out of a heartfelt desire for better relations. If he was being put up to it by others in the government, the Chinese were almost certainly hoping both to gather intelligence and attempt to confuse the American side with separate messages.

But Li might not have been put up to it and was acting freelance. Maybe the agency was right about Li turning and becoming a source. Ben doubted that. Li was always a forceful advocate for China, if not always for a system that had created a real mess for its economy. Then there was Bernadette's view that Li would approach him for a personal favor, at which point Ben would know he had won. Or worse, that Li's enemies such as General Deng had won, at least in the internal Chinese battles over policy. So many possibilities. Ben was intrigued and decided to be a little more forward leaning.

"This is a very perilous time, Mr. Chairman," Li said. "The word *urgent* is a fair one. Perhaps the always fascinating and charming Mrs. Coleman could join us."

That was an unexpected twist. Why would Li want Bernadette there? Was he trying to send a message to CIA as well? "I am sure she would love it, and we both would love the chance to get away. It is a great suggestion. But of course, I am going to have to check with her. She is so very busy these days."

"Is she writing another novel?" Li said. "Perhaps you could remind her that London makes a great setting for any kind of spy novel. So many things happen there. And besides, authors have more flexibility in their schedules than we government officials do."

Ben almost fell off his chair. Li may as well as called Bernadette the Red Ninja. Even calling her an author had been part of the same coded message. It was a clear reference to her not-so-secret background at MI6. *Sure sounds like he wants CIA in on it.* Ben decided to make sure. "Will Mrs. Li be accompanying you to Europe? I am sure the ladies would love to do some shopping while we chatted."

"No. Sadly, Baozhai must remain at home to look after our daughter. She really has no opportunity for travel when I am out of the country."

Ben recalled that Li's daughter was old enough to be starting graduate school, which meant that she certainly didn't need a babysitter. Perhaps Li was in some trouble if his wife could not leave the country with him. But it also meant that having Bernadette come was not a matter of socializing. This was an important phone call and a meeting was urgent. Ben decided to grab the chance. "I have to be in D.C. through Thursday. Perhaps I could take the overnight and be in London on Friday morning. Could we plan on an afternoon meeting Friday at the Bank of England? If need be, we can continue our conversation on Saturday. That way we both can take Sunday flights home. I will have to check with Bernadette, though."

"Mr. Chairman, you have a reputation for moving the logistics of heaven and earth when you want to get something done. I now know that it is fully deserved."

While it was true that Ben was obsessive-compulsive about logistics, that was not Li's meaning. He was acknowledging that Ben had figured out the code and therefore understood the urgency. Ben decided they were fully on the same page and that everything else needing to be said should be a private side conversation. "I do so look forward to seeing you in London for dinner on Friday. Thank you for your suggestion that we speak."

"Thank you, Mr. Chairman. Please notify me when your plans are set in stone."

"Of course."

Ben punched a button on the phone. "Peggy, get me Bernadette, then check on flight availability for London, departing Thursday night, returning Sunday. Two tickets please." When he explained everything, he felt confident that Bernadette wouldn't pass this one up and it wouldn't be because she wanted to do research on some new book.

"Of course, Mr. Chairman. You should know that the President's chief of staff called while you were on with Governor Li. I will get him on the line now."

Lombardi skipped the pleasantries. "Ben, turn on your television—any cable news. Not the one you market junkies watch, the kind the rest of us do."

Ben's set automatically went to CNBC, but what Roger wanted him to see was important for market junkies too. The female reporter stood to the side of what looked like a mob scene, replete with a long line of police holding nightsticks.

"We are here at the Walmart in Parsippany, New Jersey, where a crowd of almost four hundred protesters are confronting police. Apparently they made an attempt to enter the store *en masse* a few minutes ago but police blocked their way. The store manager called the police when the early shift was starting but workers were unable to get in the store because of the crowd. There were a number of scuffles and at least six protesters were taken into custody."

She turned to her left and the camera panned to reveal a squat, balding man with a USA FIRST button on his lapel. "I have here Joe Napolitano, head of the SEIU local, a group that is part of the protest. Mr. Napolitano, what is going on here?"

The man spoke in a typical New Jersey accent. "We are here to exercise our First Amendment rights to protest the intolerable conditions facing Chinese workers and Walmart's support for that system. Walmart is a big importer of the goods made by people being exploited by the system. We want everyone to know that when they shop at Walmart, they are helping to oppress millions of people in China."

"Mr. Napolitano, apparently there were some arrests earlier."

"We are here assembling peacefully. We attempted to go into the store to make our feelings heard. Walmart is famous for having a greeter when you go in, but we were greeted by police carrying nightsticks! Is this America or is our government working with Walmart and other big corporations to make us more like China?"

"How long will you be protesting?"

"As long as it takes for the executives at Walmart to realize what they are doing and stop supporting an oppressive regime."

Ben hit the mute button, thinking, *Here we go again.* It was exactly what he and Bernadette had been discussing the other night as they watched television. As Lombardi had said, "Turn on any cable news channel." The story was so scripted he could have written the rest of the day's broadcast. "Roger, you didn't call me because you're a fan of Walmart. What's the story?"

"This is happening all across the country. The President is worried that we may have to accelerate the schedule. At some point he is going to have to say something."

"You can figure that part out. I don't know how I can accelerate things very much on my end. I have the FOMC meeting tomorrow and Wednesday morning. They have to be briefed. I'll be on the Hill Wednesday afternoon and Thursday briefing the leadership and relevant committee chairs. Don't think the President can say much of substance about our plans until that has happened. The law-and-order situation is another matter.

"One other thing. I just hung up with Governor Li. He requested a meeting in London this weekend and I am going to go. There are a few interesting details that make this a compelling meeting that I would like to fill you and Hector in on. Can you set something up this afternoon?"

"I'm sure you have good reasons," said Lombardi. "What do I tell the President about the effect these protests might have on the economy?"

"What? 'We respect the constitutional rights of the American people to peacefully assemble to seek redress of their grievances.' Why does the President need to comment? At this point this is a foreign policy issue. China should know that over here it is the people who are sovereign, not the party and not the government."

"Okay, no comment. But off the record, what is the effect of the protests?"

"At this point, minor," Ben said. "Insignificant. The much bigger question will be what the effect will be on the economy if our battle with China over currency and capital flows does not go our way. We are in a high stakes game, no question about it. I don't mean to sound too cynical, but the protests probably help our cause. On the other hand, they doubtless might lead to a less rational response by our adversaries. This is not something they know how to handle in a mature fashion at home or abroad. Look at their responses to protests in Tibet and Hong Kong, on their treatment of their own people during the bank run."

"Thank you. I'll arrange a time for you to talk to the President and Hector."

Ben hung up and called for Peggy. "I need someone on staff to monitor these protests very carefully," he told her. "Number. Tone. Press coverage. Also, would you ask the economics team to start doing model runs of various scenarios for an increase in the scale of protests up to and including a full boycott of Chinese products?"

"Yes, Mr. Chairman. Hope for the best, prepare for the worst. Things are backing up on the schedule for the week and this trip to London is not going to help. We will make it work, but please, please, don't add much more." Ben took the admonishment in stride. He had no intention of making his life any busier, but the world might.

¥ $ €

Deng Wenxi was pacing the floor of his office to burn off nervous energy after doing fifty pushups. It was an old military habit he had adopted at his more advanced age when the adrenalin was really flowing. The pushups had barely winded him, and they gave him a healthy way of burning off some of the excess energy along with reminding himself how fit and powerful he still was.

He was winning. That meant China was winning. He knew his plan was the right one. Chaos in the capitalists' markets was always a good sign. But the Americans were proving to be more resilient than he imagined. And he knew the reason why. The Red Ninja. He hadn't counted on her resurfacing after all this time. She had been a thorn in China's side as had her father. Now she had managed to get hired by CIA, become best friends with the wife of the American president, and was married to the chairman of the American central bank.

Deng did not believe in coincidences. She had planted herself deep inside the American government through long and careful planning, likely with some help. Like her father, she had close ties to the Spensley family and their current front organization—the Churchill Society.

The Spensleys had first come to prominence after the War of the Roses when they used their money connections in Amsterdam and Florence to help bankroll the Tudor ascendancy. They had been amply rewarded for their efforts and for nearly 600 years, someone in that family had been circling around in the center of power in London. They made out like bandits from the Opium Wars and the unequal treaties imposed on China and had been at the top of some of the enormous trading companies that had created Hong Kong. And it was in Hong Kong that Ian Murphy, the Red Ninja's father, had been most dangerous.

One thing was for certain. The Red Ninja had to be neutralized and hopefully eliminated. With her gone, the entire network driving American policy would be decapitated and collapse.

He had given much thought to this problem. There could be no Chinese fingerprints on the operation and certainly none of his. Taking out someone as highly placed as Bernadette Coleman was tantamount to an act of war. His Politburo colleagues would view him as reckless for even thinking such a thing. He would have to use his own network.

Deng picked up the phone, a scrambled one that only the disciplinary wing of military intelligence would intercept. He had limited knowledge of English, but one phrase he did know was one of his signature codewords in his global network of connections.

"I'm feeling like playing a little blackjack this weekend. Care to join me?"

There was no need for him to wait for an answer. Acceptance was automatic.

He then sent a long text in Mandarin. *Would you remind me of the odds in blackjack? I have forgotten the probabilities for 13 against a face card and 17 against a face. Also, would you calculate for me how to play against a nine, a four, and a six when I am showing anything between a 12 and an 18. And there's a side bet. If a Queen is showing on the board and I have two Queens in my hand, what are the odds the dealer pulls a Queen? A double match pays 1,000 to one and 5,000 to one if it is Queens. It is called Get the Lucky Lady.*

Deng began pacing again. This time there was a faint a smile on his lips. He had just ordered something as hard as that four Queen double match.

First, he had Li in check. He always sensed that Li was a sentimentalist and in him he had found his trump card. Second, he had played that card to gain Li's participation in his current gambit—removing Bernadette Coleman from the picture.

Even better, he would be in a remote place at the right time, so no fingers would be pointed his way. But it would also constitute a means of making the payoff for the *Get*. Priding himself on his own cleverness, Deng dropped to the ground and did fifty more pushups.

Yes, I haven't lost any of my touch, he thought as he completed his set.

¥ $ €

Renee DeAngeles and Mark Swift were huddled around a small conference table with four other senior members of the team, glued to the television. They kept the sound off, knowing from the start what the commentary would be like. The media always liked an underdog.

Mark summed it up. "So far we are having our way in the media. We can accelerate the number of protests, but that will only hold us for another forty-eight to seventy-two hours. Eventually we will become yesterday's news. If we are going to keep our momentum going, we need to do something different and more dramatic."

A man with a long gray beard and his remaining gray hair tied in a ponytail raised his hand. Everyone knew him as Captain Bob, one of the lead actors in Greenpeace. Mark acknowledged him, and he stood.

"Speaking from experience," he said, "a private blockade would do that. We could assemble a four or five boat flotilla by the end of the week. The technique is tried and true. Used it against oil tankers and the megalith transporters. Also blocked the annual seal hunt in Newfoundland. We simply find a ship loaded with Chinese goods headed for the Port of Long Beach and surround it. Make it impossible for them to move. They will send out a distress signal, but we will be just outside of territorial waters. Not much the Coast Guard can actually do.

"Only other thing we need is television coverage. We can put our pet CNN reporter on board one of our boats and use the ship's satellite connection to get the story home. The networks will send their camera crews out on helicopters. Makes for a much more dramatic picture. Full view of the blockade. We might even try some ramming and a faux attempted boarding when the copters are around. And we want to time it so it will be the talk of the Sunday shows."

Renee gave an uneasy shrug. "That image should work, yes. But it will make the folks on my side of the spectrum nervous. Your plan covers the left's flank, but the retailers and others with goods on that boat will mount a media counteroffensive. You may not like it but interfering with trade will upset a lot of folks. The word *piracy* comes to mind. We need to generate a powerful outrage against China on the right as well, in a way that won't interrupt your coverage but will create a follow-on story that will prevent any backlash against your fun and games at sea."

"What do you have in mind?" Mark said. "What does your side really care about? Besides money, I mean?" The words came with a smile showing he intended to be jocular, not serious.

"Nothing wrong with money," Renee said. "You lefties certainly like to tax it to spend on your pet causes. But you're right; it is kind of passionless. A diplomatic incident of some sort might work well. Mark, how'd you like to spend some time in a Hong Kong jail cell? You'd be out in forty-eight hours, tops. They're still very British about it. No rubber hoses, no bullets in the back of the head. A lot of sleep deprivation and some pretty in-your-face interrogation. Just enough to appease Beijing that you have been punished without going to court. And although it is a Special Administrative Region, there will be representatives of the Politburo behind the glass, watching carefully and deciding when to release you."

"Typical fascist pig," Mark said. "Always willing to sacrifice someone else to do your dirty work. Still, I'm intrigued."

"The Liberty Lobby as well as our friends in Taiwan do believe in free speech," Renee continued. "They would be prepared to come to your defense. And Fox News, *National Review*, and *The Wall Street Journal* editorial page will all make a big deal out of it.

"My idea is a mass protest at which you are the featured speaker in Central. It will be a big deal locally and certainly picked up by all the mainstream media. A little flamboyant on the rhetoric, something which is hardly out of character for you. Chinese sweatshops, worker oppression, shooting strikers. Time for folks to rise up, yadda, yadda, yadda. You won't even need a written text.

"They will make the appearance of trying to extract information from you even though they know you have none to give. Names of co-conspirators. We are all safely over here and have no travel plans to China. Resist, then when you can't take it anymore, give them whatever you need to appease them. Sponsors in Hong Kong? Hardly worth asking, the local dissident movement. Members of the legislative council will all be there, but they really can't touch them. Plans? To convince the Chinese to stop their economic war against America, the workers both in China and around the planet, the destruction of the environment, yadda, yadda, yadda."

"Not exactly my idea of a good time," Mark said. "I'm not sure."

"No, not a good time," Renee said. "But at your age, you're still young enough to withstand interrogation. It's not going to be bamboo slivers under your fingernails or waterboarding. Sleep deprivation, with a slap on the face or a bucket of water to revive you. Hong Kong authorities aren't beyond the use of psychedelic drugs. Maybe get put in a sloped room with disorienting patterns on the walls. Worst case scenario, mild to moderate PTSD, but we've got some great shrinks in our ranks who could make short work of it."

"You don't understand me," Mark said. "By 'I'm not sure' I mean, 'What's in it for me?'"

Renee frowned. "A little out of character for you, isn't it?"

"You're not the one who is going to be interrogated."

"Then let me put it this way." Renee closed in on him. "Publicity. Your name will be known in the household of everyone with a cause, the guy who went the extra mile for his clients, a guy who is connected. The kind of guy we need to know. We need on our side.

"In short, you spend a little time in hell, and when you come out, you're set. Your reputation, your business. You'll have bonafides like few others in the industry. You can write your own ticket. The kind of publicity money can't buy."

Mark thought about it. "Since you put it that way," he said, "I'm in. Anything for the cause."

¥ $ €

Bernadette sat up with a jolt as the car pulled up to the gate at the CIA. She had never heard of CIA being picketed before, at least not since the Vietnam War.

Webb hit the button to send down the privacy screens. "Sorry, ma'am, but this is going to get a bit tricky."

"You're in charge." She thought about trying to make light of the situation, but then she saw the television cameras. A gray-haired woman standing at the forefront of the mob. Spotting her attention through the rear view mirror, Webb said, "I can focus one of the car's remote mics on the gaggle of reporters if you wish, ma'am."

"Please, yes." Bernadette peered through the privacy blinds to watch even though the view was blurred.

The older woman was a pro, playing the part of a retired senior citizen quite well. Her hand gestures were too perfect.

"They took my oldest son in Vietnam. Now they're stealing my money. My retirement nest egg. You can't live on Social Security alone. My late husband and I toiled all our lives to build for our retirement and now the Chinese are out to take that away from us."

What the hell is she talking about, Bernadette thought. *She's gotten the Vietnamese confused with the Chinese. And no one is stealing her money.* Then she realized that the woman had made herself appear older than she really was. Perhaps by ten years, maybe more. No one was going to press a woman in her late seventies on her memory, let alone a sympathetic reporter.

"I had my money where my broker said I should," she ranted, again too perfectly. "He called it 'global diversified.' Last month I had almost $200,000 in it; now it is under $150,000. We all know it's the Chinese who are doing this to us. The President even said so the other night, not that I am a fan of his."

It was a great opening for a softball and the reporter grabbed it. "Mrs. Roberts, if the President were right here, what would you tell him?"

The woman furrowed her brow to make it look like she was thinking and then came out with what was obviously a prepared home run. "I would tell him man up. He's the president. It's his job to stop the Chinese from stomping all over the American people."

"Turn it off, please," Bernadette said. "I'm going to throw up." Mercifully, the gate opened, letting the car in.

In spite of the protest, she arrived early and headed straight to the Director's office. She wanted to tell him about the weekend Ben had proposed for London.

As she walked into the outer office she saw Lopez handing Bob Franks a sealed manila envelope and heard him say, "Good luck, son." Franks saluted and the psychoanalyst in her detected a bit of moisture in Lopez's eyes. She dismissed the thought but filed it away as she did so many other seemingly insignificant details.

Lopez acknowledged her arrival with a curt nod. "So, Mrs. Coleman, exactly when were you going to tell me about going to London with your husband?"

Bernadette realized the formality was to put her off guard. She decided whatever the reason was, she was going to play along, but make it clear she was not going to be pushed around.

"Mr. Director, what is Agency policy on advance notice needed for a volunteer to take a day off?"

Lopez didn't flinch. "In my office." He barked as if it were a command and motioned with his right arm to the open door.

As she passed, she caught a glimpse of Lopez giving Bob Franks a pat on the shoulder. *Another detail to file.*

When Lopez closed the door he said, "Bernadette, you are going to have to disappoint your husband. But I don't want him to cancel the ticket or change the reservations."

"Of course, sir. Might I inquire why?"

"Yes. But this whole thing is on a need-to-know basis. Let me just say I consider it a sound precaution based on some recent chatter. I will let your vast experience figure out the rest."

"Is what I just saw between you and Bob Franks need to know as well, sir?"

Lopez knew that the "sir" was intended to unnerve him. And it did, ever so slightly. He flashed back to her use of the word *volunteer* and it suddenly hit him. There was zero chance she would stop helping or even slow her efforts. The woman was hooked. But he needed to acknowledge her sacrifice as he had with Franks.

"My apologies. I was a bit out of line. You are volunteering and your service is invaluable. So let me push the envelope a bit on the need to know.

"That young man just volunteered for duty that I would call extremely hazardous. And he did so of his own volition, bringing me information and offering to act on it without me saying anything. It may have not been the right strategy, but I was in the midst of acknowledging that when you walked in. Let's call it bad timing, and no fault of yours."

Bernadette put a hand gently on his shoulder. "Hector, thank you. I caught the pride in your eyes."

"You mean the tear, don't you? Not exactly in character, is it? I'm getting too damn old and sentimental for this job."

"Actually, it is in character. It means you care about the risks people take. You don't view the people who work here as cannon fodder. I know you can't tell them that. Feelings like that are never articulated, but they are displayed subliminally. Whatever Bob Franks is doing must be extraordinary and giving up a weekend in London is nothing."

Hector decided to end the sentimentality. "Even with Chairman Stud?"

Bernadette withdrew her hand and said, "Hector, that was a low blow, but a good one."

"How's he handling the situation now?" asked Hector.

"Benjamin Augustus Coleman understands duty as well as you and I do, probably as well as Bob Franks. He tends to follow his own orders and not those of others, but his every waking breath is in the line of duty. Consider the trip off. He won't like it and will want to know why, but he will salute when I tell him need to know."

CHAPTER FIFTEEN

BERNADETTE AND HECTOR HAD AGREED THAT IF SHE WAS GOING TO meet Cynthia Turner for lunch, going in a CIA car was a non-starter. They were implementing the softer touch side of the plan that had been discussed at dinner. And the start was lunch at China Garden, a northern Virginia landmark for over six decades.

She parked in the lot of a now ancient shopping center next to the restaurant seven minutes ahead of Cynthia Turner's scheduled arrival. It would be well publicized. The motorcade would be obvious, and it would doubtless be augmented by an expanded press pool. The First Lady's office had made sure this lunch would be well covered—that was the point of it, after all.

Bernadette decided to use the time to touch up her makeup. It was then that she noticed the third car in the protection that Lopez had arranged. It hadn't been hard for her to notice the first joining her as she pulled out from the long *cul-de-sac* that formed their neighborhood.

The second had joined as they turned onto Route 7. Despite her training, the third car was new, and she realized it had been parked here all along to observe. The CIA was not allowed to operate as a law enforcement agency on U.S. soil, but that didn't mean they couldn't protect one of their key assets.

When the motorcade came into view, she got out of the car and walked up to the entrance of China Garden. It made her part of the reception committee. The proprietor would be there, too, but would stand back as the First Lady held a brief and seemingly spontaneous press conference near the entrance. No restauranteur could ask for better advertising. There were no fewer than six cameras already in position in front of the door, the words "China Garden" were prominently displayed on the entrance awning.

Cynthia stepped out of her limousine as soon as the accompanying Secret Service agents had given the signal. Then, as choreographed, she and Bernadette came together in front of the sticks, as the mics accompanying the camera crews were called. They gave each other pecks on both cheeks, part of your typical Tuesday lunch out with the girls—or so the casual viewer of the television news would believe.

The First Lady stepped before the two dozen reporters crowding in with the cameras. "It is so good to get out and join my good friend Bernadette Coleman for lunch. I love the White House, but a little fresh air is good for the soul." No one would consider the air in Seven Corners as fresh—not with forty thousand cars driving past every single day. But as with all news, this was theater.

"To tell the truth, Mrs. Coleman and I are here because we want to emphasize the deep contribution that Chinese culture has made to American society. Chinese Americans, like people from all of the other parts of the world, have long been part of the history of this great nation of immigrants that we call America. And today, Bernadette and I are here to enjoy some fabulous dim sum."

Cynthia turned as if to walk in for lunch, allowing enough time for the reporters to shout questions.

"Mrs. Turner, do you anticipate deepening hostilities between America and China?"

"You'd have to ask my husband. Bernadette and I are here to catch up. It's not part of our world. But I do know that the President is committed to making sure that our differences do not boil over." She had given the administration's answer while denying that she was here to do any such thing.

"Mrs. Turner, what do you make of the protests now breaking out across America against the import of Chinese goods?"

"It's a free country and people are allowed to express their ideas peacefully in any way they wish. We are lucky that in America citizens can spontaneously organize to express their feelings. In many countries that is not allowed. It is the government that organizes the demonstrations. This is clearly not the case here." *Message delivered to Beijing.*

"Ma'am, what do you think of the boycott of Chinese goods now being called for?"

"Folks can do what they want, shop where they like, buy whatever suits their fancy. I really never look at labels. If I like the look of something or if it gets good reviews, I buy it. But that's me." Another signal sent. *Housewives of America, spend your hard-earned dollars the way you want.* Of course, the bit about labels was a bit of a stretch. Cynthia was wearing a Christian Dior dress, accented by pumps from Tory Burch and a Zac Posen handbag.

"Mrs. Turner—"

"Folks, I appreciate you all very much," she said, "but I am really here to have lunch with a friend. And frankly, I am getting hungry." With that she turned and made it clear she was through.

The proprietor greeted them both at the door with the press snapping photos in the back. He knew he would have lots of photo souvenirs to collect from them.

Once inside Bernadette took command. She spoke to the owner in Cantonese, the CIA and Secret Service having already researched his background. "Bring us an assortment of your best dim sum. I haven't been here before, but your reputation precedes you."

A handsome young man in his late twenties served tea and then placed the pot on a warming plate on a nearby table. "May I get you ladies anything else right now?"

The accent was perfect, too perfect in fact, as was his posture. Very polished and rigid. No sign of having grown up as a couch potato playing video games. He clearly had not grown up in Arlington. From his age and paler skin tone she guessed he was from northern China, quite possibly Beijing.

Bernadette decided to try her Mandarin. "No thank you. By the way, would you mind telling me where you grew up?"

The young man responded with enthusiasm. "Oh, you are familiar with Mandarin! Your accent is perfect, madam. It is a particular pleasure to serve you today. I grew up in Beijing. With all apologies, I am the nephew of the owner's wife. My parents sent me here to polish up my English."

Switching back to English, Bernadette replied, "Well, in that case, let's do our bit to help you. That way my friend can participate in the conversation."

The young man bowed ever so slightly, but his expression was blank. Surely he knew who Cynthia was, but gave no indication of it. "Thank you. You are most kind to help me." Something in the way he said it suggested his English really didn't need much polishing. The formality of the structure of his sentence seemed a bit put on.

Once he left, Cynthia began the conversation. "It's great to see you outside of that gilded cage they have us living in. I never realized how much of a prison it really is. All that security! It is supposed to be protecting us, and I suppose it is, but it also keeps us locked in. But even here it is a bit strange. There are no real customers in here! Just a couple of agents. Don't you think the Secret Service is overdoing things a bit?"

"I'm not sure it was just them," Bernadette said. "Although they certainly didn't object. Technically they can't force the place to close down, just sweep it and all customers who might enter."

"Hadn't thought of it that way. Yes, it is a blessing. But do tell me, how are you and Ben getting along? He seemed, shall we say, distracted at dinner the other night. I hope it wasn't Will's lapse of tact. I assure you I scolded him mercilessly. Sometimes the wide receiver in him keeps cropping to the surface."

"No worries. The President was most apologetic. Ben and I talked it through."

"Bernadette, you don't have to spare my feelings. You and I have spent a lifetime reading men. It is in our DNA, and we wouldn't be where we are today if we weren't good at it. Ben was angry, and he had every right to be."

"I certainly won't dispute you." Bernadette pondered how candid to be, but something in her said this was not the time nor the place. She was saved from her quandary by the arrival of the first course served by the same handsome young man.

"Ladies, these are shrimp dumplings. May I recommend that you try them with our sweet chili sauce?" He placed a small bowl of it between them, along with another bowl containing a darker substance. "Some people prefer the standard dipping sauce. This is a mixture of soy and rice wine with a touch of rice wine vinegar. Enjoy." Again the young man left with a slight bow. Bernadette made note of how he exited with exacting precision.

"I thought you gave some great answers out there," Bernadette said, pivoting to current events. "I am not a practiced politician, but you certainly are. Three messages, each delivered. Dear public, we are not headed to war. Dear Beijing, the U.S. government is not behind these protests. Dear Wall Street, bet on stability. You left the media thinking you answered their questions. In fact, you said what you had planned to say and not a word more."

The women wolfed down the dumplings until Bernadette was stabbing at the last one with her chopsticks. As if on cue, the waiter returned.

"My uncle's own creation. A pork-and-vegetable mixture combined with bean threads and wrapped in an ultra-thin rice noodle wrap. It is then very lightly fried. I suggest some hot mustard, but this is good with any of the sauces." He placed a small bowl of mustard on the table and then refilled their teacups from the pot on the warmer.

"This is good," Cynthia said. "I stuck to my half grapefruit for breakfast, so I am famished. But if I don't slow down, I will be heading for a nap." She paused, then returned to the subject at hand. "Thanks for the compliment. Strange what a campaign will do. You run the same basic thing day after day and the media calls it a stump speech. They stop covering it and try to force you off point by creating some irrelevant issue or scandal and asking you only about that. The discipline is to use the new stock answer then pivot back to the core message you want delivered and make it seem as seamless as possible."

"You've certainly mastered it," Bernadette said. "As well as when and how to end the conference. That was brilliant. And I suppose it had the added advantage of being true. We were both hungry." Bernadette saw Cynthia nibbling on the pork wrap and decided to let her eat. "You know, in my profession the key is to stick to the truth as closely as possible, whether on a mission or if interrogated. The key to success is always omission, not commission."

"Bernadette," the First Lady smiled, "you didn't even catch your own little Freudian slip. You said, 'my profession.' I thought your profession was a bored suburban housewife who took to writing to add interest to her days." She gave a huge grin to show that the ribbing was good natured. What she didn't know was that it exposed a small piece of vegetable stuck to one of her teeth.

"Cynthia—" Bernadette made a move to scrape to the mirror image of the tooth in her own mouth, knowing that the First Lady would subconsciously follow. She did, and they both laughed. They now had a reason to be slightly embarrassed, enjoying the fact that they were developing an actual friendship.

"You love what you're doing, don't you?" Cynthia asked. "Getting back into the action. Everyone says you are the best. And I need not remind you, it is not that you once were the best. It is that you *are* the best. It is hard to stray far from the gift that you were given, and you do have a gift. Even in your writing you were playing it out. Fiction can be a real release, can't it?"

The waiter returned. Oddly though, the two Secret Service agents were quietly coming up to the table behind him. "I hope you enjoyed the pork. This is your classic lettuce wrap, a dish for sharing."

One of the agents put a finger to his lips. Then lifted the warmer under the tea pot to reveal a small microphone.

The waiter saw Bernadette's gaze go over his shoulder and turned in time to see the agent with the warmer in his hand and the other agent pulling handcuffs out from his belt. The waiter bolted toward the table and sunk his hand under his shirt.

"*GUN!*"

Bernadette reacted instantly. With one hand she lifted the edge of the table and pushed it into the waiter, then came out of her chair and leapt at the First Lady, pushing her out of her chair and landing on top of her, cradling the top of her head with one hand.

"Don't move—"

There was a clatter and a loud thud, followed by the reassuring click of a pair of handcuffs.

"It's all right, ladies."

Bernadette raised up from on top of Cynthia Turner. "Well, this is awkward."

"Nonsense," said the First Lady. "Thank you."

Bernadette helped her to her feet and brushed off her dress before starting on her own.

"False alarm," said one of the agents. He held a small tube of lip balm between two fingers.

Bernadette held out her hand. "May I?" The agent handed it to her. She pulled off the cap and studied the balm. "Chapped lips?" she said in Mandarin.

The waiter nodded.

"It's open but hasn't been used." She rolled the balm out of the tube and scratched at the waxy substance. The waiter strained against his captors as she did. She rubbed the balm between her fingers until it revealed a small object the size of a pea. "Potassium cyanide," she said. "A popular item in the intelligence community since the Second World War."

One of the agents shook the waiter. "You little bastard—"

"Not for the First Lady," said Bernadette. "For himself." She turned to the waiter. "You have some explaining to do."

The agent holding the waiter said, "Somebody does." Then he turned his head toward the kitchen and in almost a shout called out, "Mr. Shu, would you come out here please?"

The proprietor stepped out of the kitchen and the color dropped from his face when he saw the overturned table, the disheveled women, and his nephew in handcuffs. He hurried over to the table.

"How long have you known this man?" It was the agent who had revealed the microphone.

Shu stumbled a bit. "He is my wife's nephew; his parents asked us to take him in while he studied English. Is there a problem?"

Bernadette took over and addressed Shu in vulgar Cantonese. "You little lump of dog shit. You are lying to us. He is not your nephew or your wife's nephew and he's not fucking here to work on his English."

Shu turned bright red.

The interrogation continued in Cantonese. "So you tried to poison the First Lady of the United States. Do you know that carries a minimum sentence of life in prison? Want to know when your pathetic little ass is going to see your comrades again? Never. And you're not going to be a martyr with three hots and a cot, either. Your fellow inmates are going to fucking hate you for what you mean to this country and will devote themselves to making your life a living hell, day after day."

The restauranteur stammered out in Cantonese, "But there was no poisoning."

"But the cameras outside won't know that, will they? They are going to see the First Lady being hustled into her limo and speeding away. Then I will go before the cameras and say that she felt sick and had thrown up. Nobody will ever come to eat in this little dung hole again. I can see the headlines now and the nightly news. And that little sign on your awning, China Garden, will be front and center as I tell the world your food smelled of cow shit and the tea tasted like dog piss."

The waiter in cuffs glowered at Shu and in Cantonese said, "Remember your wife's family." Then the agent holding him yanked his shackled arm to silence him.

Bernadette continued, this time in English. "Mr. Shu, all you have to do now is tell us who this man really is. The First Lady and I will leave here full of smiles and tell the world how fantastic the food really is. You see, this is the difference between the American way and the Chinese approach. We can play nice in English. Or we can play rough in Cantonese. Just as rough as this piece of shit you have as a waiter. Only difference is they can't play nice, can they? But remember, we can play rough too."

Shu chose to speak in English. "A man from the embassy came here and asked us to hire this man. He then showed me a picture of my wife and her brother as children. Of course, I recognized the photo. My wife came here as a student twenty years ago and her brother stayed behind. Her parents were mid-level party functionaries, which is why they were not punished for violating the one-child policy. But in China, it is the son who is the pride and joy. May-ling was lucky to be able to come here to study. There was never any reason for her to go back." The man was practically sobbing.

Bernadette softened her tone, but not her message. "Shu, do you know anything about this man? Does he behave erratically? Work odd hours? Take time off?"

Shu nodded. "He works when he wants to. Does a good job, so I really don't mind, but he usually peruses the reservation list before deciding when to come in. Always serves the tables of his choice. Told me that he was going to be serving today. Yes, I suspected something was up. How could I not? Especially when it was the embassy that approached me and in the way they did."

"This is a popular place from what I understand," Bernadette said. "Especially among people with office jobs in Washington. So I suspect this is not the first time your so-called waiter has used this particular tea set."

"Sounds like an accessory to me." It was the agent holding the waiter. The other agent took out an identical pair of cuffs.

"Thank you, Agent Donnelly," Cynthia said. "I don't mean to tell you how to do your job, but I would wager that Mr. Shu will be happy to testify in court. Nor do I think he is much of a flight risk. This restaurant was opened by his grandfather. But we have another kind of problem, one that the President has a real interest in, I assure you.

"Outside of here are a bank of cameras and a huge gaggle of reporters. We are here to try and calm the anger in the country. And if word gets out about this, things will not be so good."

Bernadette decided Cynthia had it exactly right. "Mr. Donnelly, there are three cars from CIA outside. I spotted them before I came in. Obviously they have no jurisdiction here. But their presence should confirm both the national security interest in this matter and the importance of discretion that the First Lady has pointed out. I will be happy to phone the Director and have him speak to you personally. He can assure you that we do not want this to become a public incident."

"All due respect, ma'am," said Agent Donnelly. "This place is now a crime scene. We're going to have to shut it down, do a thorough sweep of things."

Shu took one staggering step back and sat heavily into a vacant chair.

"Tell you what," Cynthia said. "Let me get the President on the line."

The two agents looked at each other.

"Gentlemen," said Bernadette, "this is what I propose. You take this scumbag—" She poked the waiter for emphasis, "and set him down in a chair over there, securely restrained. You can interrogate him or do whatever you wish. Mrs. Turner and I will straighten ourselves up and then sit here another twenty minutes to make it look like we have had a wonderful lunch together. Then we will go outside and briefly attest to that fact. The reporters will break down their equipment and be out of here within the hour. Then you can call for whatever back up you need and take this man to wherever you like, book him, and hold him in solitary. Of course, he will have to be allowed to call a lawyer from the embassy. They will know, but they are not about to blab about this to the press anyway.

"From there you call your boss, I will call my boss, and Mrs. Turner will call her boss, and the three of them can work out what to do about this tricky situation."

Now she turned her gaze to the waiter and spoke in Mandarin. "I don't know what your name is, but I suggest you tell these men as much as you can. You know that fate I described to Mr. Shu? That is now reserved for you. Your life isn't forfeit, but your future certainly is."

Bernadette knew that was unlikely to work. This guy gave every impression of being one tough cookie. Probably Chinese military intelligence. They knew that their only way out was not to break and pray that somewhere down the road there might be a prisoner exchange. That would be worthless if he spilled the beans before then.

She turned back to Agent Donnelly. "How does that sound, gentlemen? As the First Lady said, she would be happy to call the President, and I'm sure that he would be glad to speak to you and remove any doubt."

Donnelly nodded. "Mrs. Turner, Mrs. Coleman. We do have to do our job and take this man into custody. But an hour or so of on-site interrogation is certainly appropriate. Besides, we need to question Mr. Shu more carefully. As long as he is willing to cooperate fully and not demand counsel, he is obviously not a flight risk. Of course, if he chooses not to cooperate, all bets are off." Donnelly stared at Shu to make sure he got the message.

Shu nodded.

"Well, Mr. Shu," said the First Lady. "The matter seems to have been decided. Since our waiter is indisposed, perhaps you could bring us some fresh tea. And if you would be kind enough to bring us the check as well?"

Shu bowed from the waist. "Please, accept my deep apologies. Today's lunch is on the house."

"No," Cynthia said, "it will not be. It is illegal for me to receive any gift over $25 without reporting it. And it simply will not do to have this lunch reported as a gift. It can only raise questions. So you will bring me the check and I will be putting it on my American Express card.

"However, Mr. Shu, this does not mean that you are not in my debt. Even more, you are in Mrs. Coleman's debt. I am not sure what she said to you, but I know her pretty well. She is a lady of her word. And so am I. And if a word of what actually happened here today leaks out, even to your lovely wife, then these nice gentlemen will come back and take you and May-ling to wherever Mrs. Coleman said.

"And by the way, your food is excellent. Particularly that pork roll concoction that you invented yourself. It would be such a shame if the only place your culinary talents could be put to work were in a prison kitchen."

Shu scampered away to get the tea and check, and the two women smiled.

"We make a good team," the First Lady said.

"Actually," Bernadette replied, "I wish I could manage your ladylike behavior. I have never heard a better example of the iron fist buried in the velvet glove. An iron fist with inch-long spikes on the knuckles."

"The velvet glove only works if someone else shows the spikes. Not sure what you said but I am sure that it did not involve his culinary skills. I don't know the language, but the meaning was perfectly clear. One can gather a lot from context."

They toasted, and after a stop to fix mussed hair and makeup, made their way to the door, thanking both Secret Service agents on the way.

So much for dim sum diplomacy, Bernadette thought as they stepped toward the waiting press.

¥ $ €

Bob Franks and Tom Butler used the twenty-two-hour trip to northern Laos to the fullest. The Agency had outfitted them fully, even paid for business class for the Washington to Singapore leg of the trip. Gambling money. Some super-high-resolution cameras for their cell phones and miniature recording equipment. The dark pools that existed in the intelligence and defense budgets allowed the option to spare no expense.

But there was a lot to do, starting with getting to know each other. Although Tom and Bob had been in the same group for two years, they had never had a date. The purpose of the group's weekly get-togethers was professional bonding, not sex.

That didn't mean the group was celibate. Nearly all the members had dated two or three of the other guys, but early on it seemed like everyone passing one another around got in the way of the group functioning well. It was the same in most Washington social groups of people in their twenties and thirties, where networking was the goal and dating happened on the side.

Both men were driven by the specter of General Deng. He needed to be brought down. Not only was he inflicting pain on teenage kids, he was doing so from a position of power. Getting his jollies not by giving something of himself but being constantly on the take. The very fact that Deng could do it was part of his motivation. He was proving to himself that no one could stop him.

Both men were also driven by patriotism. They were ex-military and understood the challenge China posed to America. At twenty-eight and twenty-nine they were at the peak of their vigor and fitness yet staring at the inevitable decline that hit in the thirties. If someone was going to do something physically heroic this was the time to do it. This high-testosterone behavior allowed them to acknowledge the physical risks but be willing, and perhaps even eager, to accept them. And the plan they hatched was nothing if not ambitious.

¥ $ £

The abandoned warehouse wasn't much to look at. It was in a dying industrial park, a crumbling and weedy place on the outskirts of Passaic, New Jersey, that one only went to if one absolutely had to. With most of the windows broken out it could be cold at times, but a clever person could do a little rearranging and set up a draft-free office. There was lots of space to keep things that shouldn't be seen in public, and urban legend had it the place was haunted, so the locals stayed away. Mobile phones made landlines unnecessary, and one could poach electricity from the factory next door, enough to run a lamp or two, but most importantly, the transmitter.

Sean O'Malley smiled when the coded signal came through that transmitter. It would be both an honor and a pleasure to see this request through. He understood the message and from whom it arrived.

Get the Lucky Lady.

He and Deng had never met, but he had known about him since he was a small child. Deng had been a long-time supplier to the family business.

Sean's grandfather, Patrick, had served ten years in a British prison for his part in planning the attempted assassination of Margaret Thatcher by bombing her hotel. But his real skill was in arms procurement. Patrick had made deals on behalf of the IRA with the Soviets, the Libyans, and then-Colonel Deng. By the time he got out, the IRA had negotiated the Good Friday Accords and its political wing, Sinn Fein, had gone legit. There was a ceasefire, and the IRA had no need for arms. To support his family Patrick fell back on the skills he knew best.

Patrick brought Sean into the family business when he was seventeen. His father had been estranged from the entire family since Sean was young. The story in the family was that he had been killed by the British, but something in his mother's behavior told Sean that was not the whole truth. It didn't matter; Patrick was the father Sean never had.

And the business boomed. The O'Malleys weren't fussy about the politics of the buyer. A booming part of the business was in North America: various drug cartels and their downstream distributors. So among his other identities, Sean carried a forged American passport and maintained a New Jersey residence.

Unbeknownst to him, Sean shared something else with Deng other than business—an overwhelming hatred of traitors. And Bernadette Coleman, née Murphy, was a traitor, as was her father before her. They had abandoned Ireland and signed on with the British—and had risen to great heights in the British international spy operation. Bernadette herself had played a part in hunting down some of the family's friends among the last IRA holdouts.

Getting the Lucky Lady was returning a favor to a business associate. But it was a favor that Sean O'Malley would truly enjoy carrying out. Sean focused on the word *Get*. Lucky Lady played triple for matching the Queen of Spades, but the message had not mentioned that. So for now he simply had to get her. The code for "kill" might come later, but there was a lot of latitude in that order. Deng might want her alive, but that entailed a wide range of conditions.

He looked around the warehouse. There was much to be done. He could keep her here, but another abandoned site down near Harrison would be better, keep her away from all of his precious merchandise. A place for her would have to be prepared.

Then there was finding her residence, learning her routine. Getting a crew together. Only his best men would do. Finding a place for them to stay within striking distance of the D.C. area while they carried out their surveillance.

And finally, the abduction itself. He had heard some stories from Patrick about grabbing the odd British soldier or sympathetic priest, but those had been sloppy, often alcohol-fueled affairs. Bernadette Murphy Coleman had her wiles, and they would have to do all they could to keep her from using them.

Yes, he had much to do. But the results would be extremely satisfying.

CHAPTER SIXTEEN

NEVER IN ITS NEARLY NINETY-YEAR HISTORY HAD THE BOARD ROOM of the Eccles Building seen so many members of Congress packed inside. Keeping a secret in Washington is almost a contradiction in terms. But if one were going to try and keep something secret for a while, the place to do it was at the Fed.

In attendance was a who's who of D.C. leadership. Besides George Steinway, Dianne Reynolds, and Hector Lopez, the guest list included higher-ups from the board of governors and the Federal Reserve Board, leaders of the House and Senate including the majority and minority whips, and members from a multitude of congressional and Senate committees. Finally there were the grey beards—those members who actually knew the substance of the issues and were respected by their colleagues, ranging from specialists on China specialists to experts in monetary policy.

Ben opened the proceedings. "Ladies and gentlemen, distinguished leaders of the Congress, I would like to welcome you to the board room of the Federal Reserve. This is where the Federal Open Market Committee meets eight times a year to set monetary policy and where the board of governors meets, usually twice a week, to discuss economic events and decide the various regulatory issues that come before the board.

"Today we meet to brief you on one of the greatest monetary crises that not only this country, but the entire world, have ever faced. The Secretary and I have briefed the President on what we are about to discuss and now it is urgent that we discuss it with you as well. Let me begin."

Ben forced himself to take a slow pace. He had been through this material so much since this had all started, even since developing the Metropolitan Plan, and could have done it in his sleep. In fact, he was certain he had done it in his sleep a time or to, for it occasionally popped up in his dreams. But he needed to keep the pace down because most of the people in this room were hearing the details for the first time.

So he started with the state of the economy, how the federal government was carrying too much debt, so much that it would soon reach the point of no return—consuming the totality of the nation's GDP. How the Fed owned too much of that debt in the wake of the 2008–2009 recession, and how that debt was now under water—the term for being worth less than the price originally paid. How the sale of U.S. Treasury bonds kept interest rates artificially low, and how foreign markets began to see them as an attractive investment—to the point where China and Japan were the two largest investors in American debt.

"The odds are," Ben told them, "is that we are only weeks—perhaps a few months at the longest—away from a meltdown. This system was created with no plan for an endgame—no idea, no way to unwind the bond purchases and the massive money creation that went along with it. Having that much debt and that much money out there was a risky idea that might lead to a collapse in confidence, what we call an endgame. We are at that end game now and have to decide how to play it."

Ben paused for a moment to look around the table and gauge the reaction to what he had presented so far. They were with him up to this moment, he could tell. Even those who had been responsible for not addressing the status quo during their political careers had set aside their squirming. *Thank China for that*, Ben thought.

He continued, describing his conversations with Li and the uneasiness of those in the Politburo. How it saw the opportunity for an offensive play against the U.S. economy, wrecking its role as the world's preferred currency and elevating the yuan into its place.

"And if that happens," he said, "China, not America, will be the world's greatest economic power and that military and geopolitical power will soon follow.

"But it does not have to end this way. Today we have asked you

ent a plan that will address all three of these problems—too
too much paper money, and an aggressive China."

Ben paused again to draw breath. *Here we go,* he thought. *All that planning, all that refining. This is the moment.*

And then he began to describe the Metropolitan Plan, beginning with the meeting with Steinway and describing how the Fed and the government would swap debt for gold—with the Fed authorized to mint the gold into proprietary gold coins that would become a superior form of currency, with a guaranteed worth no matter the price of gold. And along with that half of the U.S. debt would be paid down.

"Now," Ben said, coming to the cautionary note, "this is not a free lunch. Not for us at the Fed, not for you guys. This system will preclude us from running an inflationary policy. If the price of gold rises too much, people will demand our face value gold coins and give us our paper money back. Remember, paper money is designed to be spent. These gold coins, not so much. So this will lower the amount of cash outstanding relative to the size of the economy and cool off any inflationary pressures. While the Fed is losing some option value, the people of this country—the ones who worry about gas prices and making the mortgage, about putting their kids through college and being bankrupted by medical bills—will now have the assurance that their currency will hold its value and not see its value washed away by some future Federal Reserve action. Ladies and gentlemen, we call that confidence, and in economics, confidence is everything."

Ben smiled. "Now the part you've been waiting to hear. For our good friends the Chinese, this system creates a bit of a problem. Remember, they are telling their people that the yuan is backed up by gold holdings. They are far short, but they still have about fifty percent gold coverage for their currency. That usually is enough to build a lot of confidence. But that is at the current record price of gold. The Metropolitan Plan is going to cause them two problems.

"First, when the Fed takes the gold, the Treasury now has and mints gold coins, we are increasing the supply of gold available to the market. Meaning all that treasury gold sitting in Fort Knox or similar depositories. As things currently stand, it never goes on the market. Now some of it *is* going to hit the market. Supply is increased. And when supply is increased the price goes down. Simple as that. When the price goes down, the Chinese ability to cover their money supply with gold is reduced.

"The second effect is potentially even bigger. We are going to be issuing a gold coin that is superior to gold in its raw form—with an option value. The holder might be able to sell it for more than he paid and will never get less in terms of dollars than the face value.

"This will leave Chinese workers and peasants with three options. They can keep their money in yuan in cash or in the bank knowing full well that the government's ability to cover it is dropping because the value of the gold they hold is dropping. Or they can, as they now do, take that money across the border to Hong Kong or Macau and trade it in for another currency. Typically this is Hong Kong dollars—which are tied to the U.S. dollar. Or they might buy U.S. dollars directly or some other currency. When things start to unravel, they will want to be in anything except yuan. So their third option will be to buy these newly created Federal Reserve-backed gold coins with a guaranteed face value that is superior both to gold and dollars.

"Note that as this process continues, the value of raw gold will continue to fall as people switch into U.S. gold coins. The longer it goes on, the worse the Chinese situation gets as the gold coverage of their currency continues to drop along with the international value of their currency. The chances of a snowball effect begin to grow. They will stop being focused on destroying the U.S. dollar and start focusing on saving themselves."

Ben stopped. The room was silent. Finally, the Speaker of the House broke the silence.

"Bravo. Couldn't happen to nicer people!"

Chuckles went up around the room which turned into outright laughter. The pall that the recent crisis had created was lifted. There was a way out. Not a costless one, but they now knew that the light at the end of the tunnel was not an oncoming train. Looking around the room, Ben saw the reaction was bipartisan. Even the ranking members of the House and Senate Financial Services Committees, both of whom were women who didn't care much for Ben, were nodding along with their colleagues.

Sensing the positive reaction, the Speaker continued. "What do you need from us?"

Secretary Steinway, speaking on behalf of the President, handled the query. "The courts are all over the map on what can and cannot be done by executive order. I know the President feels strongly that this is a time to show national unity in the face of the Chinese threat. And I must say that Chairman Coleman and I agree with that judgment. So the President would like to seek enabling legislation to accomplish this as a package. And I would like to add that this is a matter of some importance, so going into deadlock is not an option. Neither is padding out the legislation with pork. Under the circumstances, neither is acceptable.

"To your question, first the Congress is going to need to authorize the swap of the gold the Treasury owns for the bonds the Fed holds.

"This will involve a number of details. Our recommendation is that Congress authorize the price of gold for purposes of the exchange and that benchmark will be the basis for determining how much gold will ultimately be in the coins the Fed will issue. Our suggestion is that we select $400 per gram as the exchange price of gold. Note that we will not buy or sell gold to all comers at this price. It is simply for purposes of the exchange between the Treasury and the Fed and to set a benchmark for sizing the gold coins. It is a *de jure* price for this transaction only.

"The second detail will be determining the price at which the bonds in the Fed portfolio will be reacquired by the Treasury. We suggest that it be face value. Currently most of those bonds are underwater. But the Fed carries them on their books at face value and that face value supports the current money stock. Moreover, when they are reacquired by the Treasury it will reduce our debt outstanding by the face value, not market value. This seems the most logical price between the buyer and seller."

The chairman of the House Budget Committee interrupted. "Why aren't we using market values for everything? Seems to me the Treasury is losing out by paying above market for the bonds."

Ben stepped in. "That's a good question, Mr. Chairman. Like you I am a believer in market prices. But this plan has a number of objectives including minimal disruption to the U.S. economy and maximum disruption for the Chinese.

"So let's start with the price of the bonds. It is true that the Treasury is paying over market for the bonds. Remember, the reason the bonds are pricing below market is that the economy has revived since they were purchased and as a consequence interest rates have gone up. The Fed bought those bonds to support the economy and if we hold them to maturity, it will get repaid at face value. If the Fed were to sell them below face value, we would have to reduce the money supply by an amount equal to the difference because those bonds back the money we issue. There is no reason to cut the money supply at this time and if we did, it would likely harm the U.S. economy.

"The other thing that I would remind you is that this is not a market-based transaction. It is a deal between two parts of the government. The Fed and the Treasury pretend to have separate balance sheets just like two divisions of a large, diverse company might. In reality, the Fed and the Treasury are part of the same balance sheet. The United States government owns the Fed and the Congress authorizes its existence and can change that authorization at any time. The government uses the Fed as its fiscal agent, buying and selling its bonds. So think of this as a deal between two divisions of the same company.

"In effect, the Fed is paying well over market value for the gold. We will carry that gold on our books at the contract price. This will help our monetary operations. But more important, the power of what we are going to be doing is enhanced by maximizing the difference between the face value of the coins we issue and market price of gold. We have agreed on $400 per gram, or about $11,200 per ounce even though the current market price is just $300 per gram.

"The coins we are offering have an option value in case the price of gold goes up and a guaranteed value if the price of gold goes down. So it makes sense that the market valuation of the gold be less than the face value of our coins. Right now the market value of the gold is about seventy-five percent of the face value of the coin. We think that is a fair option value.

"But the bigger this differential, the more trouble the Chinese will have in trying to wreck our currency. As investors rush to hold our coins with a minimum face value, they will sell their raw gold. More gold on the market will drive the price of raw gold down and increase the value on our coins, a sign of confidence in the U.S. dollar. The Chinese, who lack public confidence, will therefore be seeing the value of their holdings drop along with their ability to support their currency.

"This is not an arms-length transaction. It is between two people on the same side—the Treasury and the Fed. They can pick any price they want for a deal. We are picking a price that protects America the most and hurts the Chinese the most."

Steinway took up the narrative. "The second piece of legislation we will need from Congress authorizes the Federal Reserve to issue gold coins at a given face value. It comes straight from the Article I grant of enumerated powers to the Congress to 'coin money and regulate the value thereof.' So the value of the gold in the coins will be determined by Congress.

"We will be embedding a special security chip in the coin to prevent counterfeiting. Obviously if the market value of the gold in the coin is less than the face value of the coin there is money to be made turning gold into coins. But only the United States government by the actions of the Federal Reserve can do that. Our security agencies say that the technology behind the embedded chip will not be able to be replicated for at least twenty years, but we will be updating as we go along."

The Senate Minority Leader asked, "How fast does this have to happen? We are a deliberative body after all. We will need to hold hearings, get committee approval, pass resolutions on the floors of both the House and the Senate, then go to conference and get the conference committee's legislation through both houses. Nothing is done quickly."

The Speaker of the House was quick to respond. "We recognize the truth in what the distinguished leader from the other body says. But we would remind him and his colleagues that Congress can act very quickly when it needs to. Declarations of war, for example, have been passed by both houses in a single day. I don't see why the leaders in both parties in both houses can't sit down and iron out things privately with the help of the administration and move the legislation expeditiously. I don't think the analogy to a declaration of war is all that far-fetched."

Ben decided to underscore the point. "Mr. Leader, Mr. Speaker. I recognize that the structure of the Congress was created by the Founding Fathers to be deliberate. And I support the value of deliberation. But as I said earlier, we are on the precipice and have months—perhaps only weeks—before we will be in the midst of a financial crisis. We have an adversary who is provoking the crisis in order to gain power, so I agree with the Speaker that this is not unlike a declaration of war. I can assure you that when the Chinese find out about it, they will view it that way."

The Minority Leader decided to push back. "Chairman Coleman, I recognize that you are an authority on monetary policy, and I will admit that I do find merit in your plan. But I am less certain that your background qualifies you to be an expert on Chinese politics. So let me raise a very delicate question within the confines of this room. My distinguished colleagues on the Intelligence Committee have learned that your wife has been spending a lot of time over at the CIA. I thought she was a housewife who wrote good action novels. She is certainly not recorded as an employee of CIA. Is she going there to get some background for her next book? I think not.

"Congress has not been briefed on this matter and I think it is untoward for the spouse of the Chair of the Federal Reserve to be consorting with our foreign intelligence agency at a time of national crisis. There are lines of demarcation of responsibility that must be adhered to. Let me be blunt. Is she your personal mole at CIA and are you and Director Lopez in cahoots to force certain policy choices on the country?"

Hector Lopez spoke. "Mr. Leader. Let me say that I fully appreciate the concerns that lie behind that question. But in order to answer it, I would have to divulge some highly classified information that is ranked above Top Secret as it involves human intelligence. In a normal Committee hearing I would leave it at that and not answer the question.

"But because of the special nature of this meeting and the urgency of action, I am going to divulge some information on a need-to-know basis to the people in this room and to them only. If any of what I say leaks I will ask the FBI to do a full-scale investigation of the source of the leak and will prosecute the violator to the full extent of the law regardless of whom he or she might be. Am I clear?"

Sensing that heads were nodding around the table, Hector continued. "Bernadette Coleman, Chairman Coleman's wife, had a long and very distinguished career in the intelligence community before she got married. She was the top analyst of Far Eastern and Near Eastern affairs for MI6. Her father was also an MI6 operative who ran British intelligence interests in Hong Kong during a very delicate period. She gained her knowledge of Mandarin at that time and went on to study the patterns of organizational behavior within the People's Republic.

"I will spare you the details, but she was widely considered not only the best in MI6 but probably the best in the world at what she does, and despite her retirement from that world when she married Ben, is still considered the best.

"When the current crisis broke out, I asked Bernadette to assist us at the Agency. She is not an employee. She is doing this as a volunteer, and, may I add, as a patriot. I consider her services to be invaluable. She is not the Fed's mole at the Agency, and she is not the Agency's mole at the Fed. As a professional she is very well versed in the lines across which information should and should not pass."

The Minority Leader wasn't pacified. "That's all well and good, Director Lopez," he said, "and I am not questioning her motives or yours. But it is highly irregular. And what is more irregular, you permitted a foreign intelligence service to bug the home of an American citizen and did nothing to prevent it. What should have happened is that our domestic agencies, not you, should have gotten involved. There was no report of this to the Congress or to the Intelligence Committee. Moreover, we understand that the bugs in the Coleman house were numerous and included their bedroom." A slight smile came over the leader's lips, his way of warning them that he would be prepared to spill the beans if he was not satisfied.

"Mr. Leader," Ben said, "I want to thank you for the concern you expressed in defense of the privacy of the American people, including mine. From your comments I can tell that you are very well informed, so I will be blunt. When this crisis began to develop, I had no idea how deeply I would become involved. And when I learned of the matter you are referring to, I will admit to being shocked.

"But I had a choice to make. Frankly, the country is at risk and our way of life is at risk. If I was going to do my duty to everything that I believe in, I was going to have to play the role of good solider and put up with things that would not ordinarily meet with my approval. So, sir, you are right on all counts. Like me, you are going to have to weigh the values of privacy and liberty that you hold dear against other highly valued goals such as our nation's security and our way of life."

He paused as he worded the *coup de grâce* in his head. "The reason I consented to having the Chinese maintain listening devices in my home was that it provided a way of providing disinformation to them. That is why CIA wanted them there and my wife handled the information flow beautifully. Her background left her far more able to compartmentalize the issues of our private lives and national security than I could."

The minority leaded nodded. "Thank you, Mr. Chairman, for your honesty and candor. I must say that I am aware of recent revelations about your reputation and will spare this room the details. But you appear to be a man of many accomplishments."

Ben felt himself blush.

"One of those accomplishments," the Minority Leader continued, "appears to be a deep and abiding faith in what you are proposing to do. There are many on my side of the aisle who would look quite skeptically at all that is going on here. Invasion of privacy, secretive meetings, failures to properly inform Congress. And I cannot assure you that whatever legislation the President might send up will get the acquiescence of even a majority of my caucus. But I can assure you that as Minority Leader, I will not use my various powers to obstruct that legislation and will actually vote for it.

"The reason is simple. You, sir, have done what most people in Washington never do. You have not only talked the talk, you have walked the walk. You have made real personal sacrifices to advance the cause which you bring before us today. I value that. It is a rare commodity in today's world.

"But let me make it clear to the Secretary and the Director that I do not countenance their actions. And if this flagrant violation of America's values is ever repeated, I will use my full power to expose the culprits."

"Thank you, sir. That is most generous." It was all Ben could manage.

The Speaker took over. "Ladies and Gentlemen, thank you very much for your time and your candor at briefing the leaders of the Legislative Branch. I share the distinguished Senate Minority Leader's view that this is a very unusual set of circumstances. At this point, we need to discuss these matters privately among ourselves. We also look forward to the legislation that the President will send up and will do our best to act on it as expeditiously as possible."

Secretary Steinway spoke for the hosts. "At present the President is planning a televised speech to the nation next Wednesday. Formal legislation will arrive that afternoon. Chairman Coleman will be briefing the Federal Open Market Committee in full at their meeting the previous day. I want to thank you all for being here. May this day mark a new milestone in co-operation in doing what is best for our country.

"And let me reiterate this. Cooperation in this matter is of utmost importance. There is no room for grandstanding. The President will not tolerate that, nor will he tolerate addenda. I speak for him personally when I say that he doesn't want to resort to strong arm tactics on this matter, but if need be he can and will take the gloves off. It's that important."

Then, with a curt nod, Steinway rose and shook hands around the table as he headed for the door. There was nothing more to say.

CHAPTER SEVENTEEN

GRAHAM AND EDITH SPENSLEY WELCOMED BEN INTO THEIR HOME as if he had seen them only last week. That was the thing about old friends. He and Bernadette always dropped by whenever they came to London, but only imposed as house guests when Edith insisted. And this time she had insisted that Ben stay with them. It made things so much easier. Ben was here relatively incognito and a meeting with Governor Li at the Spensley's home would not attract a gaggle of reporters.

After the requisite kisses on each cheek, Edith said, "Ben, I know you have to grab a nap and a shower. Those overnight flights are so tiring. And the jet lag is horrendous, especially flying east. Your room is at the top of the stairs on the right, as usual. I do insist that you make yourself right at home."

"Edith, I can't thank you enough. And you were most generous in hosting Governor Li for tea this afternoon. And of course, Bernadette sends her love."

"Yes, I know. A pity she couldn't make it, but I know how frustrating it is when illness changes your plans." Edith knew better. Being Lord Covington's daughter let her sniff out a ruse in an instant. But that same pedigree meant she would stay quite discreet about it. "Tell me, Ben, I do hope she is not working too hard. These are very curious times. I did see in the papers that she and the First Lady are now the best of friends and that you and the Turners dine regularly together. That must be a good source of information for her novel."

"Edith, how can I carry on a conversation with you? You know everything already."

"Well, almost everything. You know one of my proudest achievements is introducing you and Bernadette? Oh, but do listen to me go on. You must be exhausted. I'll leave you to your nap. We won't bother you until two. I believe a Bank of England car is picking you up at three-thirty, though there is more to it than that. Dinner is planned for eight."

Actually, a Bank of England car was driving, but it contained Governor Li. The same car would then depart from the Spensley's garage and return to BOE. Governor Li had arranged it all. This was to be a truly personal meeting between Coleman and Li, who would be coming to the Spensley's for dinner.

¥ $ €

Li Xue, Governor of the People's Bank of China, arrived at the Spensleys at three-thirty. Edith was at the door to greet her guest, who entered through the pantry from the garage. "Governor Li, so wonderful to see you."

"It is my pleasure, Mrs. Spensley," Li said. "Your hospitality is much appreciated. A venue for a discreet and candid conversation is hard to come by." He bowed slightly.

Edith hid her surprise. That was a remarkably direct comment with no diplomatic niceties. He might as well have said, "Let's get on with the meeting."

Ever the good hostess, she obliged and led him to the library where Graham and Ben were seated. After pleasantries Graham and Edith gave their apologies and left the two men alone.

Li began by punctuating the urgency of the meeting. "Thank you for accommodating me, Ben. I asked you here in part for personal reasons, for which I must apologize. But I also hope that we can have a free and frank exchange on what is going on within our two governments."

"Certainly," said Ben. "You know that I value candor when it comes to our profession."

Li smiled in understanding. "And may I express my regrets that your lovely wife was not able to make the trip with you."

"She sends her regrets as well," Ben said. "Unfortunately, viruses have no respect for friendships or personal schedules."

"Well," Li said, acknowledging the lie, "please send my wishes for her recovery."

"I most certainly will."

"Let me now begin with a personal request as it will help you understand the gravity of what is happening. My daughter, Jun, has applied to a number of major universities in the United States for graduate studies. She is following in my footsteps and hopes to be an economist. Her original intent was to work in one of the Western financial companies that are opening in Beijing. But events have caused her to change her plans.

"The situation in our government has become quite fragile. A group you Americans call "hardliners" is ascendant. They sense the current uneasiness in global markets as an opportunity not only for economic gains but for military ones as well.

"I know that there are hardliners in every government, yours included. We central bankers tend not to be among them. Our profession is first geared toward maximization of economic well-being. The goal of hardliners tends to be maximization of national power. Those are not totally incompatible, but we tend to believe that national power stems from economic power, or, as Adam Smith noted, the wealth of the nation. The hardliners believe the reverse.

"As central bankers, we also understand risk. It is part of our professional training. Hardliners tend to be ideological and believe that history is on their side. Again, we are both patriots who believe in our nations. So I am speaking very generally."

He paused, waiting so long that Ben thought for a moment he had missed a cue to reply. But then he could see it in the man's eyes. This next part was going to be difficult, and he was composing himself.

"I fear," Li finally continued, "that current events are getting out of hand. The level of risk being undertaken by both sides is far too great. This can only end badly. It may be one side or the other that bears most of the loss, but neither side will escape unscathed. And it very well could be that both sides will lose disastrously."

Li paused again, this time to gauge Ben's reaction. The look he saw was sympathetic, but not one that indicated that a sale had been made.

"This brings me to my personal request. I mentioned that my wife could not travel with me. I am sure you surmised why. The hardliners do not want both of us out of the country at the same time. They feel themselves ascendant. And I fear that I share that assessment. You see, if China were to win this conflict, they will be in a position to claim the credit. And if China should lose, then the reason will be given that we technocrats are too Western in our thinking and that a purge may be in order.

"Which brings me to my daughter. I would like her safely out of the country as soon as possible to study in America. Whatever happens to me and my wife, she is all we have. Our one child policy was very much still in force when we were in our childbearing years. Jun is all we leave to posterity."

Li sat forward, his eyes staring straight into Ben's. "I know you have connections, particularly at Yale. I was wondering if you could arrange a special letter from one of the senior professors asking her to come over and begin some kind of internship before entering the formal program in September. I know what I am asking is highly unusual. And I am a bit embarrassed to be in this situation. But I am sure you can appreciate the predicament I am in."

Ben remembered Bernadette saying this day would come. That Li Xue would ask for a favor and that how Ben responded might determine the course of events. Ben decided to proceed in a slow and careful way to obtain what he needed the most—information about Chinese thinking.

"Xue, thank you for being so honest and candid with me. As I am sure you know that is how we Americans like, or at least claim to like, to do business. I am sure Jun will be an excellent economist and has a remarkable pedigree. She will be an asset to any graduate program she will enter. I will be happy to make inquiries and to recommend her.

"But if I may be equally direct, the timing you are talking about does raise some interesting questions. Why so sudden? Are events moving so quickly that she cannot simply come over in August or September when the academic year begins?"

"Ben, you can see what is going on in global markets. Gold is rising more than $100 on some days. The yuan is dropping by nearly two percent per day. These are hardly normal times."

"No," Ben said. "They are not. Markets are moving quickly, and we should discuss that. But that is not what I meant. Is your personal situation and that of your family deteriorating that quickly? This trip to London happened very suddenly. And your daughter's need to leave the country so quickly? The urgency seems extraordinary."

"Ben, I envy your closeness to the President. I also envy your lovely wife's closeness to the First Lady. That story about the Chinese restaurant made news in our country as well. Not the part about the spy, but the honor the two ladies bestowed on China by lunching at a Chinese restaurant. All news is manufactured in both our countries. That snippet, properly edited, appeased the hardliners as a bow to the Middle Kingdom and us modernizers as an olive branch for peace.

"I carry no such closeness. I was a compromise choice. Supposedly safe. A technocrat. But I argued against the sale of Treasuries from the start. I warned that it would wake the sleeping dragon. A bit like General Yamashita opposing Pearl Harbor, I suppose. China has made tremendous gains under reform and America has been very tolerant. I know the history. Washington and Tokyo decided that the surest path to peace was to allow us to get rich. And we did.

"As I said, we central bankers appreciate risk. Risk has propelled us from a poor nation, maybe twelfth in GDP, to number one or two depending on how you count it. We are now your economic equal. In another twenty years we will completely dwarf you.

"Perhaps I stated my opposition to the Treasury sale a bit too vehemently. It made me a marked man. Then last weekend our intelligence agency sent a memo to the Politburo that I might be disloyal. There was nothing definitive, no actual charges, no real evidence. But the sort of whisper campaign that goes on constantly. The same thing happens in Washington. But the stakes are higher in Beijing."

Ben felt a lump in his throat. He had agreed to the deal with Bernadette. Now he was having tea with the man he helped to condemn.

"Xue," he said, trying to sound settled, "you have never been anything but a total patriot to your country. Your advice was always sound and on the international stage you were a formidable spokesman for China. I can't believe this is happening." Except for the last line, it was all true. Ben hoped that the truth in what he said helped camouflage his deception.

"Thank you. But when has truth ever governed the course of politics?"

Ben chuckled. In this context Xue's comment was a bit of gallows humor. He knew at that point that he would have to actually make the offer that he and Bernadette had established in return for the forbearance on removing the bugs. But first he needed a bit more information. "I will see what I can do. I have learned that in this kind of political situation targeting the right person is always the best policy. Would it happen that the man who was advancing those charges of disloyalty be linked to your military intelligence operation? I believe his name is Deng?"

Ben could see his counterpart's Adam's apple move in what was obviously a hard swallow. Li Xue need say nothing more.

¥ $ €

Bob and Tom were met at the Chiang Mai airport by Boonsri, a gorgeous woman with the affectation of a tour guide. But in spite of her beauty and the way she carried herself, both men knew she was Lopez's way of keeping an eye out for them.

"Welcome to Thailand," she said. "It's about a two-and-a-half-hour drive to Golden Triangle Park and the bridge to Laos. Customs formalities should be pretty straightforward."

She put them in a van with a *Let It Happen to You in Laos* logo. It was an old advertising slogan, but suitably appropriate for the modern version of the area's tourism.

Safely in the van, Boonsri continued, "Good news, gentlemen. Our information has it that your friend is arriving tomorrow for a little stress-reducing R&R. I am told you have a free hand tactically and I will not interfere. But I do know that you may well need extraction from the situation. I will be here for you. There are closer airports, but none with regular commercial service. If an emergency departure is required, we will do it from there."

The two men nodded. Then Tom Butler spoke. "Any chance you know of a past victim of our friend? I've seen one young man being helped out of the hotel, so I have a sense of things. I'd love to show Bob the sort of stuff we're getting into. It will be both cautionary and motivating. It would be even better if we could get some pictures."

"Thought that might be something you wanted," Boonsri said. "I have arranged for three young men to meet you at one of their homes about ten minutes outside of town. It isn't pretty, but then, you're not here for the scenery."

Minutes after crossing the bridge they pulled onto a side road that led them up a hill lined with small houses made from a combination of whatever was available. Most had roofs of corrugated metal, some were covered with thatch. Small children ran everywhere. Sanitary facilities were generally out back and the town showed no sign of open sewers.

"What do these people do?" asked Bob.

"Work in the fields. Most families used to own their own plot of land but the government took it. They called it "collectivization." Now the land is owned by Chinese. Native Laotians are not allowed to buy. The landlords live in Ton Pheung. Zhao Wei and his wife Su Guiqin were granted a ninety-nine-year lease on most of this land—10,000 hectares in all. A Laotian family could support itself on one hectare of rice fields. So you get the size of how much they took."

Bob Franks did the mental math. "That's almost forty square miles. And a single Chinese couple owns the whole thing? That's outrageous. How do the people stand for it?"

"Welcome to Laos," Boonsri said. "The government in Vientiane is bought and paid for by China. Did you notice the patrol boats in the Mekong when we crossed the bridge? Those are owned and manned by the People's Liberation Army. The casino itself is not the only revenue source. This is also a center for the smuggling of endangered species.

"And opium has not exactly disappeared. It is just out of sight, mostly farmed in small patches in the jungle. The locals do it to support themselves. God help them, though, if they are caught farming on Zhao's land. They are usually pressed into indentured servitude."

"Virtual slaves," said Tom. "That's why the boys sell themselves. It helps support the family. I can't imagine being in such need that you could submit to that for a month's worth of groceries."

They stopped the van in front of one of the houses along the dirt road and got out slowly, not exactly looking forward to seeing their enemy's handiwork.

¥ $ €

Edith Spensley knocked on the door to the study where the two men were meeting. She was carrying a multilayered rack of plates that contained everything needed for an English afternoon tea. There were scones with strawberry jelly, a sweetened whipped cream that had just turned to butter, and little sandwiches made of cucumber, tuna salad, and rolled asparagus, each with a heavy dose of mayonnaise. In general, it was an understatement that the British were not particularly good in the culinary arts, but Ben had always thought an exception to that rule had to be made for tea.

"I hope I am not interrupting," she said.

Spotting the tray, Ben waved her to enter. "Edith, you are a mind reader. Xue, you're probably familiar with the tradition of an English tea, but I'm not sure you've seen one at the level that our gracious hostess has presented."

Xue said, "I have had the pleasure whenever I have been in London. But I doubt I have seen an array as tempting as this."

Edith simply smiled in acknowledgment. "Do let me know if I can get you anything else," she said.

"Thank you," Xue said.

"It's my pleasure," Edith said, and made her exit.

Ben looked at Xue. "Edith can arrange just about anything. Do you think she could pull off inserting some common sense into the heads of politicians?"

Xue laughed. "Sometimes I would settle for competence at math."

Ben realized that since pressing personal matters were finished, this was the time for the business part of the meeting.

"Xue, you are right. The one thing politics can't change are the laws of math. I've done them. And I am sure that you have too. I don't think you have enough reserves to get to your target. You are not going to be able to truthfully tell your people that the yuan is gold-backed. I calculate you are even going to miss the fifty percent gold-backed threshold that is needed even for plausibility." It was a dangerous gambit, almost a fishing expedition. But if Xue confirmed it, he would know that the Metropolitan Plan would succeed beyond all expectations.

"Ben, you must be using a Japanese-made calculator, not one of our finer products made in China."

"Actually, I used a Hewlett-Packard."

"HP manufacturers its chips in Taiwan. An integral part of China but one still run by a bunch of renegade bandits."

Ben frowned. Then he sat back in his seat signaling a withdrawal from the personal rapport the two men had established. It was a ploy, but it worked.

"Ben, what is interesting is that some calculators made in China, which makes the finest calculators in the world, sometimes come up with different answers. For example, I have an imported calculator, I think it may even be an HP, that comes up with the answer you have suggested. I also have a very fine Chinese calculator that tells me that fifty percent is within reach.

"But there is a third type of calculator, one specially programmed to give the user the answer that he or she wants to hear. Our Politburo has some of those. I believe they exist in Washington as well. They are what your government uses for their long-term budget calculations."

Ben chuckled and again leaned forward, signaling Xue that he got the message.

"Those calculators are very common in the world," Xue said. "You use them for budget projections, we use them for five-year plans. But no user ever complains when the answer does not meet reality. Complaining would mean they would have to use another calculator, and no one ever wants to switch from one that always gives the politically correct answer.

"By the way, the Politburo's calculators, and even my HP, give an identical answer to another question that has been put to them. What is the outcome of a trade war between our two countries? The answer is quite clear. No matter how many times we do the calculation, the answer is always negative. It is negative for us. It is negative for you. We learned that in the Trump era, but as things turned out they were more negative for us. Fortunately, though, you have regular elections.

"So both the Politburo and our illustrious staff at the People's Bank of China are very concerned about the antics of a group in your country called Enough Is Enough. They are trying to provoke a trade war. They are picketing various retail stores that sell goods imported from China."

"I am aware of the group," Ben said. "Your word *antics* is quite appropriate."

"Our intelligence services indicate that those so-called antics are about to escalate later today in the eastern Pacific. We understand a flotilla of boats intends to surround one of our container ships bound for the port at Long Beach. They will make it impossible for it to proceed.

"I will tell you that our military and our Politburo will consider this an act of war. There is very little understanding in China of what a civil society actually means. I may know that Enough Is Enough is completely independent of your government. But it doesn't seem that way to most Chinese government officials, and it certainly will not look that way on Chinese television. The demands for war will rise."

"Xue, you are a remarkably well-informed individual. I am quite certain that our domestic intelligence services are unaware of that." He checked his watch. It was five here in London, noon in Washington, nine in the morning on the West Coast. There was a chance he had gotten this information in time to get the word to the States. But for Li's sake, he needed to stay, finish playing this out, and pray for time.

"Xue," he continued, "I apologize. But I want for a moment to return to your original question you asked. I will, of course, do all I can to get your daughter into Yale, but I am concerned about your whole family. Is there some way your wife can accompany your daughter to New Haven to help get her set up at school?"

"Perhaps, once I return to China. I'm the man they really want there."

"Of course," Ben said. "And you shall return with a diplomatic success of sorts. You will have single-handedly arranged for the American Navy to terminate the blockade of the cargo ship and head off a war. That may not make those itching for a war happy, but it should cover any questions about your loyalty to China.

"I also firmly believe that future negotiations along similar lines will occur in the future. You will be the natural individual to lead negotiations over the subject. Those negotiations might be timed with a meeting of central bankers to defuse the economic situation."

"You are very prescient, Ben. Though I am not sure that I would be the choice to attend such meetings. But I understand the possibilities. We can only see what transpires. Thank you for your understanding. We will doubtless meet again soon."

As the two rose to shake hands, Ben could tell that his counterpart was not fully convinced another meeting would ever happen. But, nonetheless, he left with more than he hoped. Odds were good that both Li's wife and his daughter would be safe.

¥ $ €

Deng Wenxi landed at one of the small airports that Zhao and Su had installed to cater to the higher-end traffic from China. It was only a two-hour ride from the Chinese border and tour buses catered to those of lesser means.

He was dressed in an expensive business suit with no sign of his military rank. Here he was simply known as Mr. Yam. The plane belonged to one of his companions, who referred to himself here as Chen, a wealthy businessman who shared the same tastes as Deng. Theirs was a symbiotic relationship. Deng provided the legal cover and protection, and, in return, he enjoyed these outings whenever he could arrange them.

The two men entered the hotel with three younger men in cheap suits who served the role of bodyguards. The entire entourage was treated like royalty and were greeted by the manager himself.

"The usual arrangements, gentlemen?"

They were shown to two suites on the top floor, at the end of the hall and across from each other. The three guards tripled up in an adjacent room. Security was not going to be an issue.

"Business meeting downtown over lunch," said Chen. "Care to join me? I will introduce you as another potential investor in the area. Then some recreation tonight."

Deng said, "Strangely, I do want to play some blackjack first. Need to clear my head."

Chen said, "I know how busy you have been in your official capacity. The Americans are beginning to sweat, or so it seems. You have them on the run." But he did not believe the last part. He was too good a businessman to ignore that markets had stabilized and that was not a good sign. On the other hand, he valued the protection Deng offered and would not even consider offending the man.

Deng merely grunted as they headed off to a business lunch.

¥ $ €

As soon as he had given his formal goodbyes to Li Xue, Ben immediately searched out Edith.

"Ben," she said urgently, "you need to—"

"Edith, I'm sorry, but this is urgent. Do you still have a secure phone from the days when your father resided here?" Ben knew that they did, and it had nothing to do with Edith's father. These people were as thick as thieves with British intelligence.

"Of course. Yes." She led him to a back room and left him behind a closed door.

His call was to Bernadette. He told her first about the blockade of the Chinese cargo vessel. If the administration wanted to stop a war, it would either have to intercept the boats before they surrounded the cargo ship or somehow scare them away. It would be a bad news story either way.

Then he told her that CIA and State would have to keep up their end of the bargain on Li's family. The call was short and sweet, with Bernadette promising to deliver the intel as soon as she got off the phone with him.

When he was finished, he made his way out and wandered the house until he found the Spensleys in their media room, staring at the screen that took up one wall. Across the bottom of the image was a red banner with white lettering: BREAKING NEWS.

"Edith," Ben said. "I'm so sorry for being abrupt. What were you trying to tell me?"

She took his arm and led him to an overstuffed chair. "You need to see this, I think."

On the screen, the BBC was broadcasting a scene off the California coast. U.S. Coast Guard helicopters were circling a freighter loaded with cargo boxes. Around the freighter was an array of boats. Most surprising was that a Warriors for the Planet flag was flying from the freighter. The voice was reporting that U.S. naval forces were headed to join the mission.

"American citizens and members of the environmental group Warriors for the Planet have successfully boarded a Chinese merchant freighter and seem to have control of the vessel. Any potential for war between the U.S. and China has been greatly enhanced as a result of this action and there is little room for miscalculation.

"The ships are outside of U.S territorial water, but Beijing has called this a case of high seas piracy. Apparently the U.S helicopters arrived just minutes after the boarding. There appears to be a standoff. The White House issued a statement that the President and his top advisers are monitoring the situation closely."

"When did this happen?" Ben said.

"It came on as you were seeing Mr. Li to the door," said Graham.

On the screen, a scruffy man in torn jeans and a man bun walked up and down the deck of the cargo ship, waving a protest sign and a middle finger for the benefit of the news helicopters.

"Shit," said Ben Coleman. "I was too late."

"You knew about this," Edith said.

"Li just told me. That's why I had to use the phone. I thought I could get the info back home to stop this. Damn it."

"Sometimes things are beyond your reach, no matter what you do," Graham said.

Ben knew that Graham and Edith both could tell stories about that and was about to sit and watch coverage of the piracy when the Spensley butler entered and whispered into Edith's ear. She looked up at Ben.

"This may not be your night. You have a phone call. On our secure line."

Following protocol, Ben followed the butler back to the study. The handset was laying on the table waiting for him to pick it up.

"Ben Coleman," he said.

"Ben, Hector Lopez here. We're sending a private jet for you. The first commercial departure won't get you here until midafternoon tomorrow, and we're having an all-hands-on-deck meeting tomorrow at the White House. This ship hijacking has got everyone's tights in a bunch, and the President wants you there to give your take on things, given your meeting with Li today.

"The plane will arrive at Luton around four your time and is prepared for a fast turnaround. Should get you back to Dulles by seven Saturday morning. One of our cars will fetch you, take you home to freshen up, then straight to the White House."

"The Warriors for the Planet move has thrown gas on the fire, hasn't it?"

"Unfortunately. That was piracy. At least that is how we at the Agency see it. The Chinese are right on that one. How do we expel American citizen pirates from a vessel they control in full view of the media?"

"Damned if I know," said Ben. "Guess I've got a transatlantic flight to think about it."

"There will be an embassy car to take you to Luton, pick you up around three. No traffic at that hour, that's for sure. Don't stop for any more bank runs and get here in one piece."

"Will do."

As he walked back into the dining room, Ben thought about how to break the news that he was leaving early. He suspected they'd understand, but still. A mere twenty hours in London. They'd want to offer him consolation in the form of wine, but he didn't dare. It might turn his jet lag into whiplash if he weren't careful. Lunesta would be a better choice for the flight home.

CHAPTER EIGHTEEN

THE YOUNG MEN THAT BOONSRI ASSEMBLED ROSE AS BOB AND TOM
entered the room. She had given each $100 as advance payment and
promised a like amount after the meeting. That was about the rate
Deng paid and this was a lot less painful. The three appeared to be
about sixteen to seventeen, slight and undernourished as most Laotians
looked to Westerners, but still solidly built. Boonsri acted as translator.

"Thank you for seeing us," said Bob. "We'd like to ask you some
questions. There is no need to be embarrassed."

Without translating Boonsri said, "They won't be embarrassed.
Bob. It is not as culturally taboo as it might be in the States. And it is
not taboo at all since they were supporting their families. But they are
scared that the authorities will find out."

Bob got the point. "We are not here with the police and we are not
here with the Chinese. We just want to hear your stories."

Tom added, "The man who hurt you is evil. If you help us, you may
never have to go see him again. But we are going to need your help."

Boonsri translated and doubtless expanded on their meaning. The
boys removed their shirts. "They told me earlier that this happened a
month ago, when Deng was last in town. The black and blue marks have
disappeared, but you can still see the effects."

Each young man had permanent souvenirs from their ordeal. The
welts had covered over, some completely so there was only the smallest
sign remaining. But a number had ripped deeper into each boy's flesh.
They had gotten some rudimentary topical treatments, but it would not
be enough. The scarring would be permanent.

Then the words poured out of each boy's mouth. "They did it to all three of us at once. Made us take off our clothes and stand against the wall. Our arms were extended up against the wall and our legs spread. It was like we were under arrest.

"Then they began to touch us. It was more like a police search than anything involving passion. They fondled our private parts." Boonsri had chosen a delicate translation of what the boys had likely said. "But then they turned us around and made us do it to ourselves while they watched.

"When they thought we were not doing it to their satisfaction one of the men would use his belt and hit us across the butt or the back, wherever he felt like. This continued until we were finished. It really hurt and sometimes you would have to stop when he hit you. But you learned not to because if you did stop, he would hit you again and again."

Bob asked, "Did they ever sodomize you?," not knowing exactly how that would be translated by Boonsri.

Boonsri translated and came back with a surprising set of answers.

"He didn't. He never even lowered his pants."

"After touching us he let us do all the work."

"We never had to touch him."

"I'm not sure if he could."

"Me neither. That's why he beat us I think."

"Some of the men handcuffed us to the bedposts and put gags in our mouths. Then Yam began to beat us on our shoulders and our butt. His friend joined in, each taking turns and going from one of us to the other. After they had their fun with one it was on to the other. Six to eight lashes at a time before moving on."

"How long did this go on?" asked Bob.

The boys looked at one another quizzically and then spoke to Boonsri, all three taking turns. You could see tears in their eyes as they told the story.

"They really don't know," she said, then began translating once more. "Maybe two hours at the most. They guessed they each got fifty to sixty lashes. The pain was intense, and they began to become delirious. When the men saw that, they stopped the beatings and removed the handcuffs.

They were allowed to get dressed. It hurt too much to put their tee shirts on but the men made them cover up. Then they were led down the back stairs and driven back to the village. They were warned that if they ever told anyone what happened they would be back for more, and it might not stop."

Bob took out his wallet. "Ask them if we can take pictures of their backs. They can leave their pants on. The backs are enough." He used the cell phone the Agency had given him to take some pictures and handed them each $200 on top of the money Boonsri had given them.

As they walked out Bob put his arm on Tom's shoulder and said, "Let's get the bastard. I am all in."

Tom's rejoinder was the same. "All in, it is."

¥ $ €

Ben and Bernadette entered the Oval together. Ben suddenly realized that although she had been in the residence, she had never before been here.

And there was an etiquette issue. Should they sit together or separately? The President solved that by putting the economic side on one couch, Ben first, then Steinway. The foreign policy staff was on the other couch—Lopez first, then Dianne Reynolds, then Bernadette. Attorney General Eric Flynn sat next to Steinway.

"Thank you all for coming," said the President. "Eric, why don't you start off by briefing us on the legal situation regarding the ship?"

Flynn began, "Piracy statutes apply to those who boarded the ship. In addition, we have conspiracy and racketeering charges that should stick to the leadership of Enough Is Enough. The same might apply to Greenpeace, although that one is tenuous. The flotilla did carry their flag, but it is far from clear that Greenpeace leadership authorized it. My instinct is to stick to the cases we can win outright. There might be too much blowback if we stretch.

"Then there's the not-insignificant matter of taking the ship back without bloodshed. Maybe we can get the co-conspirators to talk them down in return for a lesser charge."

Dianne Reynolds added, "The Chinese will want the pirates prosecuted. Doing so can be both a signal of good faith and a bargaining chip."

"Let's not forget our other bargaining chip," Lopez said. "Bernadette's instincts were right about the waiter. He does have an uncle, just not one who is a restauranteur. The so-called Uncle Zhou happens to be head of Chinese military intelligence, none other than General Deng Wenxi. As things turn out, the young man is one of his favorites, one being groomed for big things."

The President smiled. "Well, right now the nephew is being groomed for life in a seventy-one-square-foot prison cell."

"Sir," Hector said, "our prisoner realizes full well that he is more valuable as a bargaining chip than as a prison inmate. No chance of making him talk. He has a career ahead of him, though it will be in Beijing as an analyst, not in America."

"He will be arraigned on Tuesday, Mr. President," the Attorney General added.

"Well, our hand just got stronger," the President said, "both here at home and with the Chinese. Ben, you had an interesting conversation with Governor Li I understand, and by the way, I made sure that Yale will cooperate."

Ben nodded. "Thank you, sir. May I say that gives us another bargaining chip as well? I think that Li will be very helpful in defusing the situation when the time comes to do that. But we have to keep him alive and well in the meantime. Although he would never be so indiscreet as to say so directly, he knows that China has blundered by selling the Treasuries. So when the powers that be realize that as well, he would be a natural negotiator for them.

"And he was the one who tipped us off to the takeover of the Chinese freighter. Although it was not in time to save the ship, it did give us enough time to stop more boats from joining the blockade. I think that should be made public so the Chinese know that we know. It will give him face back home, especially once we free the freighter. If I might volunteer, since the Chinese know that we met, although they think it was at the Bank of England, I could give a hot tip to one of my favorite reporters. And I could add it as a matter of fact without it being an intelligence issue."

"I like it." By saying so the President sealed the deal. No one wanted to litigate the point. There was too much to discuss. "Okay, Bernadette. What do you make of all this? Can we use this nephew as a bargaining chip to diffuse the heat that's going to come from this pirated ship?"

"Sir," she said, "bargaining chips are best used when you are playing an aggressive game and have your opponent where you want him. The purpose is to provide a way for them to back down rather than push into a full-blown crisis.

"Naturally, Attorney General will have to impound both the ship and the cargo as evidence, and some company, probably either state-owned or invested in by someone high ranking, will have some money on the line. How we prosecute and the extent to which we freeze domestic troublemakers will also be an important signal to the Chinese.

"We have made a lot out of how the boycott is a matter of individual choice, so the Chinese think we are weak. They will respect us more if they know we have cards to play at home and are willing to play them. If I may be so bold, they will respect you more if you play tough on this.

"Finally, our waiter friend should be held as long as possible and not even mentioned. Let Deng think that we intend to hold him forever. You need to increase the pressure on him. And the fact that it was the First Lady and that her life may have been endangered gives you a rationale.

"Politics in China are very much a family business. By showing that they can't mess with your family and that we are prepared to punish those who do very severely, you will only be gaining respect. Perhaps Mr. Flynn could put an attempted murder charge alongside the espionage charge on Tuesday?"

The Attorney General look puzzled, "But we have no evidence. The capsule in the lip balm was clearly intended for him to take his own life."

"What if you told him that the First Lady had taken ill after drinking some of their tea, and that the lab results came back positive for toxins?"

"Are you suggesting perjury? By you, the First Lady, the FBI—"

"Nonsense," said Bernadette. "But I've seen enough of your cop shows to know that they're allowed to bluff and outright lie to get confessions, and pile on charges to make the perpetrator's situation look dire. When it comes down to brass tacks, bargain off the charges they can't make to look like the perpetrator is getting a deal, only prosecuting the ones with the best case."

Out of the corner of her eye she could see Hector covering his mouth to suppress a smile.

The Attorney General noticed it as well. "You spies like to spin tangled webs, don't you?"

Hector said, "Only if they catch flies."

"Enough," said the President. "If it makes our hand look stronger, so be it. But we have to be careful how long we push the bluff." He turned his attention to Ben. "We just heard from our best analyst on organizational behavior that bargaining chips should be played when you have your opponent where you want him. How close are we to having our opponent there?"

"Let's move backward though the steps along the decision tree," Ben said. "The key is when the people of China start lining up at their banks again to take their money out. And it must be happening in Beijing and Shanghai, not just in the provincial cities, so everyone notices. That will happen when the price of gold reverses and starts to look like it is never coming back anytime soon.

"We should open on Monday very close to the Chinese target— somewhere between eight and nine thousand. My bet is that they use some bellicose language about the piracy to drive it up. It will start rising in Asian trading, the Europeans will follow through, and then we will jump on the bandwagon. There will doubtless be some follow through on Tuesday. This sets up what market technicians call a climax top."

"Leading up to my speech on Wednesday night," the President said.

"Precisely. We will announce an emergency FOMC conference call the next day, which will be highly unusual since we just had a formal meeting on Tuesday and Wednesday. All the chatter will be about how we are going to stop it. The rise in gold is a vote against the dollar as well as the yuan. The speculation will be that we will have to hike rates."

"Is there a way to push back against that?" said Bernadette.

"Yes," Ben said. "Mr. President, my suggestion is that you move your address to a time when the market is still open. Ideally around noon. You lay out the Metropolitan Plan. You have the bipartisan Congressional leadership ready to announce that they will move on it very quickly. This will create enormous volatility. At first gold might actually rise further as some will think that we are pegging the dollar at $400 a gram. In fact, we are not. We are merely offering an alternative medium of exchange at that price. When it dawns that we will be dumping gold on the market, the price will start down.

"To eliminate any confusion I can have an impromptu press conference around 2 p.m. after your speech. We will let it run on until the case is made. Fed staff will be monitoring the markets throughout and will signal me how it's going. I might even have a live quote device on the table with me. It will help me know where emphasis might be needed. By the end of the day, the goal will be to have gold between seven to eight thousand."

"What will that do?" asked Lopez.

"There'll be tremendous volatility for the rest of the week. The thing to watch will be how sentiment moves over the weekend in China. If lines start forming at the banks by the next Monday morning, we will know we have won."

"So you are telling me," said the President, "that this will all be over ten days from now?"

"No, sir. I am telling you that will be the crisis point. Then comes the fun part—getting the Chinese to back down in a way that doesn't wreck the world economy or start a military conflict. Meantime, how they try to wriggle free will be up to them."

"Okay, folks. Who wants to tell me how they are going to try to wriggle free?"

The President's question was met with silence.

"Come on. You're the experts. That's why you are in the jobs you're in. You're supposed to tell me."

"Mr. President," Bernadette said, "that is something we don't know. It is one of those random nodes on the decision tree. But we can anticipate the kinds of directions they might move in.

"They need two types of responses, an internal one and an external. On the internal side, one should expect them to make it as difficult as possible to have a bank run. I would think that a bank holiday would be in order. Just close them down. When riots break out, they will have to be more heavy-handed, but that will likely not be the primary response. I will leave it to the experts on the other couch as to how long they can function with the banks closed. The political response will be chaos—and who comes out on top is the real random event as the crisis rolls out. If we can neutralize Deng, the hardliners will be lacking a real leader.

"The other part of the response is with foreign policy. That will depend on the ultimate outcome of the political struggle. But in the midst of the chaos, one should expect each player to use the avenues open to them. The military will go on high alert and may even begin to saber-rattle with Taiwan and Japan. They will do this regardless of Deng. He is just part of the overall structure and the military will collectively view this as an existential threat. They will do anything to give us pause, and they know that we know that this is their strongest suit. An outright military conflict is at best a coin flip from our perspective.

"On the diplomatic side I suspect that their entire foreign policy apparatus will be active. No movement at the summit level, but at the foreign ministry and ambassadorial level. Naturally, their economic team will be motivated. I suspect Li will be on the phone with Ben constantly beginning Wednesday afternoon."

"And the ultimate outcome of the political chaos?" asked the President.

"Sir, after Churchill lost office in 1945, Stalin supposedly said, 'the trouble with free elections is that you never know who is going to win.' The upcoming chaos will not be a free election but a series of coups and counter coups. That is as unpredictable as any election.

"But we do know that the status quo is unlikely to survive. Most likely, this all ends with a *de facto* military coup, with the military replacing the Party as the key governing structure. Sounds bad for us, but the military will be suddenly become inwardly focused as they take on new responsibilities. They really won't want to be in a conflict with their own population near revolt and their economy is in chaos.

"Or a hardliner could take over, possibly in alliance with the military. Call this the Return of Mao scenario. A hardline dictatorship

can produce order, at least temporarily. But the pri̇ [...]
collapse."

"Is the Chinese political system really that fragile?" He [...]

Bernadette chimed in. "Mao's Great Leap Forward and hi̇ [...]
Revolution were both economic disasters that led to widesprea [...]
vation. If real socialism actually worked, the Berlin Wall still [...]
up, or worse, the Germans and the French would be speaking Russian.

"And remember," Ben said, "that the Chinese people are becoming
unsettled over the instability of the economy. These bank runs are symp-
toms of a bigger cancer at play."

"Why wouldn't the powers that be keep putting them down?" said
the President. "Like what you saw. Remember Tienanmen Square."

"Tienanmen Square was a localized uprising," Bernadette said, "relatively speaking."

"Exactly," said Ben. "From what we've been able to piece together,
these runs are a widespread thing. China might have the world's largest
army, but two-plus-million soldiers can only do so much when facing a
billion-and-a-half people. It won't be a simple matter of taking control
in population centers. There are others in the political system who are
watching this and understand that some problems don't go away if you
prod them with a bayonet."

"Reformists," said the President.

"Exactly," Ben said. "The last scenario. The reformists could prevail.
This might also involve a very complex calculation by the military. They
might realize that an economic renaissance is a prerequisite for their
ambitions. One thing about the Chinese, they can be very patient when
they want to be. At the margin the military has been getting ten to
fifteen percent of the expansion of their GDP.

"Remember, they are now spending close to two-thirds of what
we are spending, and they are getting a lot of things for free—such as
manpower. So there are lots of new toys to play with. That makes them
a real stakeholder in prosperity. The tough sell will be that even more
economic freedom is the path to prosperity even though it might look
like freedom has led to chaos."

"And the odds?"

ernadette said. "Call it fifty-thirty-
dds in each scenario are against a
[hat might not be the case in the

269

ne said. "I would be a bit less opti-
:ely peaceful outcome, though. A
of the strategy. Use patriotism as a
ckdown."

Dianne.

"I'm with Hector. And quite worried. Remember, ever since the Wall came, down we have been a promoter of Chinese prosperity as a force for geopolitical stability. Our bet was that rich people don't go to war. We are reversing that process."

"George?"

"With all respect to the Secretary of State, it is not *we* who are reversing that process. The Chinese have dug themselves a deep hole with their own inept economic management. They used a very aggressive economic strategy that targeted us. We are simply responding to protect our own economy in the best way available to us. No one gets rich without American prosperity. So please don't blame us."

The President decided to stop war from breaking out in the Oval. "I am quite sure Dianne was not blaming us. But I do share her concern about the use of foreign entanglement as a domestic political ploy.

"So, Dianne, I want you pre-positioned in their time zone and able to go to Beijing on a moment's notice. I suggest you fly to Tokyo with arrival Thursday morning their time, as markets open in Asia after my speech. The news will break overnight on Wednesday in Asia and you should pre-schedule meetings with the Foreign Minister and hopefully the Prime Minister. They are going to be nervous as hell.

"Eric, I want that ship retaken no later than midnight Tuesday morning East Coast time. Serve the RICO warrants tomorrow if you have to on all of the leadership of Enough Is Enough. You can offer them what you want in terms of jail time. But we want them shut down financially without me seeming like a dictator, so getting that ship back without a shot being fired is worth a pardon in my book. Besides, I want this to be yesterday's news when I get up to introduce this plan to the American people.

"As to the actual boarders, they are going to serve time and you are to make sure of it. And the more I think about it, I want Uncle Deng to sweat a little regarding his nephew. We have a lot of chips on the military side, so let's use the ones we have to the maximum.

"Ben, I like the timing of moving the speech to noon on Wednesday because I won't have to answer any questions. Make your part short and sweet. Fifteen minutes maximum. And we will need the bipartisan leadership wired to go. They seemed quite amenable. Of course, if it goes south, they will announce they had tried to talk me out of it and it is all my fault, that they went along out of a sense of patriotism. Hector, I want you and Ben to bang out a draft by tomorrow night.

"So Ben, you've got the ball. And, by the way, if those distinguished members of the legislative branch are after my hide you can count on me to toss you their way first." The President chuckled to show he was kidding. "But there is one part of the Metropolitan Plan you never told me about—how to pick up the pieces.

"If it's the military or the New Mao, we really don't care. But having a plan to help out should the reformers win ought to be in the offing. It is the best chance I can see of altering the odds that Bernadette gave."

"I have been thinking about that," Ben said. "We have a couple of things to do. But frankly, it is going to depend on the next moves by the Chinese. And I need a little more time to think things through."

"Okay, folks," the President concluded. "We have our jobs to do. Busy week ahead. Dianne, you're headed to Asia. Ben, I expect you to stay in this time zone and not go gallivanting all over the world. Not sure when you would have the time, but don't do it. Sending a plane to fetch you in London practically broke the bank, though you'll be buying the bonds to finance it. Regardless, Bernadette, it is your job to keep him in line."

"Yes, sir, I will do my best. But as you know, Ben is a tough fellow to manage."

"Oh, you'll find a way." Then he realized that Cynthia would almost surely scold him if she had heard that one.

¥ $ €

Like most casinos, there was a special area for the high rollers. All the
bets were denominated in dollars. Bets in the high roller area started at
$100 but most of the tables had $200 and $500 minimums.

At first Bob Franks thought it was strange that dollars were the
denomination of the chips instead of yuan as most of the customers
were Chinese. Then he realized this was a great spot for money laundering. Customers bring in their yuan and convert them to dollars. The
dollars stay behind in a safe deposit box or are deposited in an international bank of which he had counted at least six. Then the customers go
back home having "lost" all their money in the casino.

Bob and Tom Butler took their seats at a $10 table and each
pulled $1,000 out of their wallets to buy chips. They had positioned
themselves to keep an eye on the raised tables in the high limit
area but to not be too obtrusive. Their positioning was rewarded.
Eventually, Deng and his companion appeared. They were greeted
by the pit boss in the high limit area and got a bow as greeting. They
were given seats of honor where they could survey the action in the
part of the casino reserved for table games. Their younger associates were positioned behind them, eyes alert. Bob and Tom made
sure they never made eye contact and seldom even looked in Deng's
direction.

"Time for some advertising," said Tom. He proceeded to get up and
look around for the men's room. He made sure his search took him past
the high limit area twice as he deliberately headed in the wrong direction on the first pass.

Both Tom and Bob were ex-military and had endured six years of
daily physical training. They each had made sure to visit the gym four
times a week and regularly did road work. With desk jobs they knew
they had to. They were solid but not overbuilt and enjoyed advertising
their fitness back home.

Here in Laos that meant tight but not quite form-fitting tee-shirts and shorts that ended a good five inches above their knees to expose solidly built thighs and calves. They wanted to look like a couple of very fit tourists, but not the kind who would look like they were stalking the hotel for customers.

Bob watched Tom and kept his eye on Deng and his companion. The companion had mumbled something to Deng on Tom's first pass by their table and Deng was definitely watching as Tom returned. Both men became engrossed in a detailed conversation. Then the companion asked the pit boss to call the casino manager over. Within minutes of Tom's return there was a dealer change and one from the high limit room moved to their table.

Suddenly both Bob and Tom were getting the cards. They would split nines and win on both hands, then go against the odds and split sevens, winning both times. Blackjack managed to hit about twenty percent of the time even though the odds of that happening were only seven percent.

Bob knew that they were being played. They were decisively winning, but not so much that it was obvious. Within a couple of hours they had nearly tripled their starting $1,000 chip piles. Throughout, their dealer was always one of two men who rotated in and out of the high roller area.

People began standing around them to watch them play. The older middle-aged women would come up and touch them gently as if to suck in their luck and say in probably the only English they knew, "You Lucky." The cocktail waitresses doted on them, regularly bringing them drinks and being sure to touch them in a sensual way. The waitresses were rewarded with tips of $2 to $5. One of them managed to balance her tray on one arm and slip the other arm down on Tom's upper thigh. He shook his head and put his arm around Bob's shoulder. It was correctly taken by the waitress that though they loved the attention, she wasn't going to get much more.

Finally, the manager approached them. In respectable and only slightly accented English he said, "You gentlemen. This is your lucky day. Perhaps you should try our high limit table and carry your luck over there. Drinks are free and we can comp your room and meals."

Tom looked at Bob and both men played the innocent young

tourists. "You mean our room is free if we play over there?" said Bob.

Tom asked the manager, "Is that offer still good tomorrow? We just arrived and I am dead tired. Jet lag." And then to make good on his intentions he said, "What time does the high limit area open?"

The manager said, "Noon, usually. We run all night, though. But if you gentlemen come by and ask for me or whoever is the manager at the time, they will be sure to open it for you." He then ordered the dealer to cash up their chips. As if he had not done enough already, he handed each man a $1,000 voucher good for matching play at the high limit tables.

They went to the casino's restaurant that served Thai and Laotian food. "So now we wait," Bob said. "But it won't be long. Not long at all."

Tom said, "He couldn't be more obvious, could he?"

Bob replied, "It was those broad shoulders of yours that we can thank. You should have seen Deng ogle you as you walked past. He was making plans."

Tom said, "You're not so bad yourself. Those killer pecs and squatter's thighs and all."

Both men knew they were starting to flirt and said simultaneously, "Not tonight." Both had a big day tomorrow and they would need all their wits.

CHAPTER NINETEEN

AS HE GOT THE COFFEE FOR HIMSELF AND HIS BRIDE, BEN REFLECTED on yesterday's meeting in the Oval and all that was going to happen today. He started with the basic premise that if you hear a conspiracy theory about Washington you should dismiss it out of hand. *Government was just too incompetent to pull it off.* But every now and then, things did function with ruthless efficiency. *When everyone comes to believe that the nation is threatened*, he thought, *this town pulls together. At least for a time. Like after 9-11.* And today the Chinese currency and bond move was viewed in Washington as a financial 9-11, thanks in large part to himself.

Eric Flynn's men were ready to execute their warrants just before dawn that morning. Federal judges in the D.C. circuit can get as caught up in the moment of unity as anyone else and were happy to help the wheels of justice spin a bit quicker than usual.

Renee De Angeles was served at her home and taken into custody. Mark Swift was nabbed at the airport, and when CIA later heard there was a ticket to Hong Kong in the pocket of his suit coat, they realized they'd dodged another bullet.

Once incarcerated, their homes were methodically searched for evidence and boxes of files and notes were confiscated along with their desktops and laptops. The offices of Enough Is Enough were raided and the bank accounts frozen.

Mark and Renee were both experienced in the ways of Washington crises, though neither had ever experienced anything like this. Both had sensed on Friday that the seizure of the ship could only mean eventual trouble. Captain Bob had gone off book, taken the ship instead of bringing it to a standstill. But there was little they could do.

Now, as they stood before the Honorable Patricia Jackson, they were being confronted with an offer they couldn't refuse. Get Captain Bob and his pirates to surrender the ship peacefully and the government would be forgiving—to a point. Enough Is Enough was out of business and its bank accounts would stay frozen. Captain Bob would have to do jail time, but the rest of the men and women on board could plead out to a misdemeanor.

Swift and De Angeles would be held in custody until the ship was under the government's control. They would be afforded all necessary communication devices to contact the ship and every other reasonable request to help them accomplish the task. Then they would be released on their own recognizance after surrendering their passports. The final deal would be pleading guilty to a single felony count of conspiracy, paying a manageable fine, and having their prison term commuted by the President.

The boat was retaken thirteen hours before the President's deadline.

An hour before, Ben opened the regular Monday meeting of the Board of Governors of the Federal Reserve System. It was just the seven of them. Ben proceeded with regular order, though he knew that not a person in the room was focused on the review. He was waiting for Avery to grow impatient.

He was rewarded when Avery finally blurted, "Mr. Chairman. I believe this board has more monumental things to discuss than how many initial claims for unemployment insurance were filed last week and how many building permits were issued.

"We are on the cusp of a major change in the way monetary policy is conducted. If we adopt your so-called Metropolitan Plan, this board will soon be irrelevant and monetary policy will be driven by the trades of millionaires and billionaires in the market and not by a board consti-tuted with the consent of the governed."

Ben wanted to say, *That's precisely the point. Look what a mess we are in when the monetary authority is set up to please the politicians without anything restraining it.* Ultimately, he decided it was unwise to pick a fight.

"Governor Avery," he said, "I appreciate your concerns. But I must stress that what you are worried about is highly theoretical. At four hundred dollars a gram, we will be minting coins at one-third above the current market price. And that price is likely to fall. So it would be a long time before any future FOMC would be confronted with some form of binding constraint on its actions. And should that occur, we'll have an important litmus test for it."

"That being?" Avery said.

"If the public perceives a move by the Fed to be inflationary, they're going to make the decision to convert dollars into gold. It would only happen under these circumstances, so an expansion of the money supply to finance real growth would not be hampered at all."

"You sound confident, Mr. Coleman."

"Confidence is exactly the word, Mr. Avery. This option for the public could be a valuable signal to the FOMC on how its actions were being perceived, a test of their confidence in the dollar. The gold coin would actually be a much broader based signal than futures markets now provide, and much less susceptible to manipulation."

The Greek chorus of the other board members followed suit to corral Avery as soon as Ben stopped. But Avery was not to be mollified. When the committee broke for coffee Ben invited him for a private chat in the Chairman's office off the boardroom.

"Chris," Ben said, "I understand your concerns. I really do. And I understand that it would be against your deeply held views about the proper role of monetary policy to return to any tie to gold, even if it is only indirect.

"For almost two generations many economists have been preaching that gold is a barbarous relic. That a gold standard has no place in a modern economy. I get it. But, as I've been saying, this isn't your father's gold standard. I doubt you could even call it that. So I am going to ask a big favor of you. Would you be willing to abstain on the vote authorizing this plan? This is a national security moment and I do not want the FOMC to even indirectly hint to the Chinese that there is division within America's ranks."

Avery gave him a hard look. "So, Ben, tell me how we are different from the Politburo? Over there things are discussed and debated but then everyone falls in line in public to affirm the dictatorship of the Communist Party. I know I won't face a firing squad if I don't play nice, but this is a strong-arm tactic, and I resent it."

Ben decided to gamble and share a piece of information that would become publicly available twenty-four hours from now. He knew at heart Avery was a patriot and could be trusted.

"I wouldn't go there if I were you. It is not public yet, but I met with Li Xue on Friday in London. And when you say things like 'firing squad' you are coming painfully close to the truth. We actually touched on that issue and the risks involved. So I will be blunt. You go there and you will soon find yourself *way* over the line."

"Sorry, Ben. I was being metaphorical."

"Chris, the real world has a finality to it that metaphors do not. And that real world is what I am asking you to think about right now. This is the closest we've come to a potentially cataclysmic global war since the Cuban Missile Crisis. And there are real people's lives on the line as well as trillions of dollars of global GDP.

"Setting Li aside, there are people who are going to starve in what we euphemistically call developing economies if this goes south. That is much more important than some hypothetical constraint on a future FOMC decades from now."

"Ben, it's incumbent upon me to express my reservations. I can't go back to academia having betrayed everything I've taught and written over my entire career. Frankly, you couldn't either. It would be a betrayal of everything I've always believed about America and how it should run."

That statement was a showstopper for Ben Coleman. His mind wandered back to that walk with Bernadette where he explained how he thought the CIA spying at his home had betrayed everything he had believed about his country. The betrayal had been so bad that it had caused probably the biggest fight of their marriage. Only he couldn't patch this one up the same way he had with Bernadette. However, he had always believed that candor worked. That was something that he had used with Bernadette, and it might work here as well.

"Tell you what, Chris. Someday when we are both out of this cesspool on the Potomac, I will hop the Acela up to Boston, you and I will get shitfaced over a great wine, and I will tell you how much I truly empathize. Let me assure you that this crisis has caused me to wrestle with my conscience more than anything I ever have had to do. I just hope that on Judgment Day the Lord will understand and tell me that I did the best I could. I have always been an idealist, a strange thing for an economist and financier to say. Didn't even know that I was until the last month or so. I was so naïve."

Ben stared out of the window. There was a melancholy wistfulness in his demeanor that was so strong that it escaped him and began to pervade the room. Some cynic might chalk it down to role playing to gain sympathy, but Avery knew Ben well enough to understand that this was no act. Both men were searching for a way to reach a consensus. To Ben's surprise it was Avery, the consummate academic, who came out with the solution.

"Okay. You will have my abstention. But we are going to have to change the rules a wee bit. Usually, dissenting reasons are only provided for those who actually vote no. This time there will be a few sentences in the FOMC statement giving the reasons for my abstention."

"And those are?" Ben could sense that a deal might be in hand. *Thank God we are both economists*, he thought. *We all believe in equilibria and do our damndest to get there.*

"I will go easy on you, in return for which I am going to cash in on that offer to get shitfaced. And by the way, you will be paying. You have a few more zeros on your net worth than I do. So how does this sound? 'Governor Avery abstained because of technical concerns about the long-term implementation of this proposal.'"

"It's a deal. Thank you, Chris. And you did make this easy. Yes, the rendezvous is on my tab. And in all seriousness, the world is going to be a little bit safer place thanks to your willingness to compromise on this. I owe you and so does the country."

It was at that moment that it dawned on Ben exactly how to thank Avery in real time. Presidents usually have no relationship with people appointed by a predecessor from the other party. But Turner had said those magic words—*if you ever need a favor* ....

Well, Turner owed Avery for this as much as he did. *Might as well make him pay part of the tab.*

¥ $ €

Bob and Tom decided to get in some pool time since they were technically here on vacation and finally hit the high-end blackjack table around two-thirty. There was a dealer rotation within minutes and one of the dealers from the previous evening was back. He high-fived them. A small breach of protocol, but one very suited for the occasion. In passable English the dealer said, "Lucky streak continue? Yes?"

"We hope," said Bob. Both men placed the minimum $100 bets. Lo and behold, their luck continued, but at a somewhat slower pace than the previous night. This went on for a good twenty minutes. At $100 per bet instead of $10 the money piled up significantly faster. Once again they got special attention from the cocktail waitresses. This time it was a rub on the back rather than the thighs. The cocktails themselves posed a challenge and both ordered bottles of water with each drink. They needed to keep their wits about them.

"I'm going up to $200 with this kind of luck," said Bob.

Tom gave him a cautious glance. "You can blow through a lot of money that way. Maybe we should quit while we're ahead and go back to the $10 table." Tom continued with $100.

Bob would hear none of it. Three hands later his luck began to change. He lost four hands in a row. He was still solidly up. Had given the casino back only about twenty percent of what the two of them had won. "Bad streaks can't continue. I'm gonna get this back and then I'll go back to $100, I promise." Bob proceeded to put down $500 bets.

Bob was counting carefully. He knew the score in a dishonest casino. They wanted to keep the fish on the hook. He won the first one at the new higher level. Then lost two. Winning the fourth and the fifth. Psychologically, the optimal way would be to let the player win thirty-five to forty percent of the time. And things became more streaky.

The dealer was watching Bob carefully to judge his mood. Bob even caught the cheating on a few occasions. Card up the sleeve that magically gave the dealer blackjack whenever Bob had a twenty. Sometimes it was dealing from the bottom of the deck. By the end of the first hour Bob had given back all their winnings plus a little bit. Bob's stack was low, and he pulled out another $1,000.

Tom declared, "I'm quitting," but stayed at the table. Deng's companion had entered the casino and spoke to the manager. Deng himself was not in sight. Through careful use of idle chatter, Tom was able to discover the companion's name was Chen. *Probably a lie, like all the other names around here*, he thought, *but at least a point of reference.*

Playing the role of someone with the gambler's curse, Bob placed all his chips, including his last thousand, on a single deal. He drew pocket eights, a guaranteed split according to the most basic rules of blackjack, but he lacked the money to do so. He asked Tom to front him the $1,200 he needed to match the split. Tom was reluctant, but out came nearly all the money in his wallet. As luck—or the dealer's skill—would have it, Bob drew a six and then a face card on the first eight and then another eight on the second eight. Another split.

"Shit," said Bob, "I'm out of money." It was clear that Tom was out of money as well. They didn't have the cash to split the eights again.

The manager came over to Bob and said, "We can give you a chit for $5,000. Just sign here. It's been preapproved." Bob signed. *This wasn't gambling*, he thought. *This was the smart thing to do given the eights.* The first eight drew a five and a four, giving him seventeen and he decided to hold. The second eight gave him a three and then a face card. Twenty-one. A wave of relief flooded over him. The dealer matched the face card that was showing. Bob had won one of the three hands.

He could pay the $5,000 back and each of them would leave down $2,200, their original thousand plus the extra $1,200 they had just laid down. Had either man been in Vegas or at the MGM National Harbor outside Washington, that is exactly what they would have done. That was the smart thing to do. But it was not part of the plan.

"I'm leaving," said Tom. "You're an idiot if you stick around." When Bob showed no sign of getting up, he said, "See you at the bar."

From then on everything went according to the plan of both the casino and the operatives. The first $5,000 voucher turned into a second and a third. Bob played the role of fish on a hook carefully and even pretended to be a bit drunk. When the last bit of money on the cuff was blown, he got up from the table and, staggering ever so slightly, made his way to see Tom at the bar.

Tom got up after hearing the news and said loudly, "You fucking idiot. We took our credit cards up to the limit to take this vacation and you blow fifteen grand! What the fuck are we going to do?" With that Tom gave Bob a good shove, one that given his solid frame would have floored most men. Bob staggered back but recovered and proceeded to shove Tom back.

The two men got into a grappling match each trying to take the other down. Basic training had given them all the instincts they needed, and they knew how to make it look like they were really hurting each other without doing any real damage. Tom landed two solid punches to Bob's gut. Bob then got Tom in an arm lock around the neck. They both landed on the floor wrestling.

A crowd quickly formed around the two men. They were starting to begin to cheer and then money came out and bets were being made. The odds were running about two to one in Tom's favor, but it was far from clear what the betting was on and how the payoff would be made. Was the crowd expecting a knockout or for one of them to tap out? Tom and Bob hadn't worked that out. They expected something else to happen.

And it did. Both men found themselves grabbed by two security men, handcuffed, and taken to the hotel manager's office. Out of the sides of their eyes they caught Chen standing a few yards away from where the fight took place. Then they passed Deng sitting on one of the couches in the lobby. He pretended to be talking with one of the personal guards, but the smile on his face was unmistakable.

¥ $ €

On Wednesday at noon, the networks interrupted their regularly scheduled programming for the President's address from the Oval Office.

Turner began with the usual formal introduction, than[k]
for watching and giving a brief recap of the challenge pos[.]
He followed this by repeating his pledge that America would prevail,
then spoke at length about how the dollar was not just the economic
symbol of the United States, but, was used by people throughout
the world.

He then revealed the work between Congress and the Federal
Reserve to issue a new series of gold coins, enough to cover every
existing dollar currently in circulation. He framed the new coins not
as pocket currency—paper money would still be viable, the preferred
way of conducting commerce—but as an investment, a way to securely
protect the value of one's money.

After giving a simplified version of the math—how the coins would
be bought with debt, the way the price would be protected, and how
it would keep the nation's spending reined in—time came for the full
court press.

"So what does this have to do with China," he said. "Remember, they
are trying to undermine our currency. They are trying to drive down the
value of the dollar and in so doing make their own currency—which
they call renminbi, or 'the people's money'—the world's dominant
currency.

Turner made a significant pause. Then, "Unfortunately, they got two
things wrong. First, they aren't going to drive down the value of the
dollar. This new currency will make the dollar as good as gold. And it
will be that way forever because we are putting the gold in your hands
if you want to hold it instead of holding cash.

"Second, the truth is that the U.S. dollar is the true people's money.
You will have the right to hold these special gold coins, or not, depending
on your choice. They aren't doing that. Over in China they are keeping
the gold in the hands of the government, not letting it out into the
hands of the people. They are saying to the people 'trust us,' 'trust the
government.' So the renminbi really isn't the people's money. It is the
government's money. And some people are saying that it is not even the
government's money, but the Chinese government's Ponzi scheme.

"So today we are telling the Chinese government that we are trusting our people with the choice of holding dollars in gold coins or in currency and you aren't. What does that say about who has the better currency?

"The difference between our currencies is like the difference between our governments. We trust the people to elect who runs the government and we trust the people to decide on how to hold their money. In China they do neither of these things. Those in power keep themselves in power, and they keep the gold all to themselves. Political freedom and economic freedom go hand in hand. So do political and economic dictatorships.

"Freedom is the sign of strength. A faith in people running their own lives. Dictatorship is a sign of weakness. A sign of fear of what people may do if given the choice. They don't trust the people with that choice because they are right to fear what the people will do—demand freedom for themselves and for their families.

"So, my fellow Americans, I have always told you that we will prevail. And the reason is that we are a free people and freedom is a sign of strength, a beacon of hope, and a promise of prosperity.

"Thank you again for inviting me into your homes this afternoon, and thank you for joining me in standing tall for our country and the cause of freedom."

¥ $ €

The two men had their handcuffs removed in the manager's office and were seated on chairs in front of his desk. The manager said, "Gentlemen, we simply cannot have fighting in this hotel. If the local police become involved, you will be charged with disturbing the peace and disorderly conduct. You will be spending the rest of your vacation in our local jail, which I assure you has no amenities whatsoever and a prison population more than happy to give you all the fights you desire. None of us wants that, now do we?"

Bob and Tom lowered their heads showing they were ashamed and said, "No, sir." Showing respect in these situations almost always worked. Besides, the odds that the hotel manager would actually bring the police in were exceedingly small. A police presence was bad for business—and the hotel was involved in a variety of business lines that would be impacted should such an intervention take place.

The manager continued. "Then there is the matter of the chits that the casino gave you. You were overheard saying that you were out of money and your credit cards were maxed out. How were you planning on redeeming the chits and paying your hotel bill when you left?"

Both men remembered the promise of a comped room when their winning streak started, but they let it go. This was part of the game the casino was playing. They kept their heads lowered in shame.

"The husband and wife who own this casino and all the land you see do not take very kindly to deadbeats. You will not be allowed to leave Laos until you pay. Under local law you will be allowed to work off your debts via indenture. But I suspect that would take several years given the amount you owe."

A look of fear crossed Bob and Tom's faces. Bob said, "We have jobs to go back to that pay good salaries. We could pay the casino off in six months, tops."

"Gentlemen, there is no surety that this casino could collect from you once you were back in the United States. Payments from America to this casino are very carefully monitored, so that would be impossible. However, we do have an option that would let you pay your debts and even leave some money in your pocket. If you choose, you could even stay at the hotel for the duration of your reservation."

Bob and Tom looked up, paying rapt attention.

"Our guests come here seeking many different types of enjoyment. We have two particular guests, both Chinese businessmen, who have some tastes that are a bit out of the ordinary. Usually they arrange to do things with local boys, generally younger than yourselves. Americans are fairly rare here and the few that are rarely find themselves in your particular situation."

"Let me guess, these guys enjoy gay sex, right?" asked Tom.

"Not exactly. They enjoy rough sex. Really rough. I believe it would be described as BDSM in America."

The men looked at each other. A clear look of fear and apprehension showed on their faces. That would make for a better negotiation.

Sadistic bullies such as Deng enjoyed watching their subjects exhibit fear. They had noticed one of the casino's ubiquitous cameras above the manager's desk. They suspected Deng was watching. Bob said, "We are not really into that."

Tom followed by saying to Bob, "You got us here, you bastard. It sounds like that or being indentured for years or maybe a visit to a jail where we might get knifed to death." Tom then said to the manager, "What exactly does your guest have in mind?"

"He envisions himself as an old-style military officer meting out old-fashioned sorts of military punishments. He will inspect you closely. He's not really into sodomy, though he will make you pleasure your-selves in front of him and the other men around him to humiliate you. Then he will beat you with his belt. I won't mislead you. It is going to hurt like hell. But there is a limit. The hotel has an agreement with him and his colleague. He will stop before you lose consciousness. The rule is you must be able to leave standing, with assistance perhaps, but no stretchers. Very bad for business."

Both men grimaced.

"What are we talking about?" asked Tom. "And how do we know he will stop?"

Bob said, "How much money are we talking about? And how can we be assured we will be paid?"

The manager said, "All good questions. It will stop. It always does. Mr. Chen and Mr. Yam know the rules and they want to keep coming back. If it makes you feel any better, I can be in the room to make sure and also to act as a translator. Most of the people he uses are local teenage boys and they usually get around sixty to seventy lashes. They get tired after that. You two are solidly built and can probably handle that easily.

"Since you seem to be Anglo-Saxon in origin, Mr. Yam will doubt-less remind you how the Royal Navy regularly meted out one hundred lashes and that was with a cat-of-nine-tails made of tarred rope. His belt is comparatively gentle. I will be honest—it may be easier than what they used 150 years ago, but gentle it is not. Still, you will walk out of there. Sore, but alive."

Bob repeated, "And how much?"

"That is negotiable. The local boys only get about $300. Enough to feed their family for a month. But the two of you are different. Mr. Yam in particular seemed anxious to be able to do his thing with some Americans. He has already provided the means to cover your debts and promised to add more if you are willing. I will go speak with him. Please excuse my directness, but he may want to inspect the merchandise. You see the camera. He is watching. If you two gentlemen might remove your shirts and do so in a way that might excite him, you could probably drive up the price."

The manager left, locking the door behind him. Bob and Tom did their best slow strip and then proceeded to flex showing off their backs, chest, arms, and shoulders to the fullest.

Bob whispered to Tom, "Never imagined that taking off my shirt would cause me to feel so squeamish. And I hate to say, it but proving to myself that I can take it in the name of a good cause seems important too."

He saw Tom nod his head in agreement. "All in is all in."

The manager returned. "Mr. Yam has agreed to cover your chits with the casino and give you three thousand each. He even mentioned that it looks like the two of you will have good stamina."

Bob was willing to jump on the offer, but Tom decided to hold out for a better deal.

"If I understand the rules," he said, "good stamina means more of a beating. We need three things. Make it five each, not three. A limit of sixty lashes each. And I want a souvenir. The belt." He nodded at Bob. "I want to be able to show this moron something tangible to remind him what we went through because of his recklessness."

"That's quite a set of demands. I will have to ask." This time the manager picked up the phone and spoke in Mandarin. Both men still had their shirts off and did some more flexing in a not-so-obvious way.

The manager continued, "Mr. Yam says that is a tough offer. He will hate to part with his belt but understands why you want it. He likes the idea of wrongdoers facing the prospect of more discipline. But in return he wants to do some of the job himself. The sixty lash limit is fine for you, but for the man who got you in this trouble he demands eighty.

With that condition you will get the belt and the extra money."

Bob suddenly understood why Tom had wanted the belt. He did not hesitate. "Deal. And by the way, I deserve the extra lashes for getting us into trouble. And if I ever do something so stupid again, Tom, that belt will be a great reminder." Bob bowed his head ever so slightly to Tom to appear to show submission. They agreed to show up in Deng's suite at 9 p.m., about two hours hence. That meant two hours of waiting and worrying about what lay ahead.

¥ $ €

Anyone charged with deploying camera crews and reporters had to know that something was up had they spent the time to consider what was about to happen. The press had been forewarned that the congressional leadership would be commenting. They always did. But the coordination among these fiercely independent individuals was stunning. Those responsible for logistics in the media were too grateful for the heads-up to have really given much thought to the conspiracy that drove it. The news anchors had a grand total of four minutes to give their own summaries and then segue to Capitol Hill. Since those anchors were the only ones not in on the coordination, no one wanted to give them too much time too gum up the works.

Out of courtesy and to make everyone copacetic with the plan, the individual with the least power, the House Minority Leader, was given the first chance. She was caught by a gaggle of reporters outside her office as she appeared to be headed to the floor. Actually, the idea of catching her was part of the plot. The anchors would have to cut to their reporters immediately and cut themselves short or else risk losing out on the Minority Leader's comments.

"While I do not approve of most of this president's economic agenda," she said, "this attack on us by the Chinese must be met by a strong response. The President has kept us briefed on developments as he should, so I was aware of what he was going to propose."

No one could miss the obvious air of self-importance that went with the comment. And like any politician, the trick was to put oneself in a win-win situation regardless of the outcome of the plan.

"Our caucus will not be taking a position, leaving how they will vote up to each member's conscience. I have not yet decided how I will vote, though out of deference to the President I am inclined not to oppose him. I will, however, be carefully monitoring the success of his plan and if it does not pay off for ordinary Americans, I intend to hold him accountable."

"Madam Leader, how quickly do you expect congressional action on what the President is proposing?"

"That is up to the Speaker and the majority. We will not be obstructing them, however. Ladies and gentlemen, I really have to go to the floor, excuse me."

Actually, she had to go offstage so her colleague on the Senate side could have his turn. The cameras had been pre-positioned in the lobby right outside the Senate chamber. The Senate Minority Leader walked up to the bank of microphones.

"The President has asked this country to stand together. Many of us disagree with some of his policies, but there is a time when our opposition must not become obstruction. We will not make use of the full extent of Senate rules to delay the legislation the President has called for. Our members on this side may support it or oppose it, but we believe that the President should have the opportunity to implement the strategy he laid out."

The Minority Leader was then joined by the Majority Leader, who said, "I would like to thank my distinguished colleague from the great State of Maine. His very generous and patriotic words regarding the process in the Senate are most welcome. I can assure him that any deeply felt concerns that he may have will be accommodated as we move forward."

A reporter blurted out, almost incredulous, "Does this mean that you two are going to work together to pass the legislation the President called for?"

"Whether or not I vote for it," said the Minority Leader, "or my colleagues do, what I committed to was to give him the opportunity to implement his strategy. We may not work to pass his legislation, but we will not obstruct its passage."

The Majority Leader piled on in what he hoped would be a bipartisan civics lesson to rebuild confidence in Washington's institutions.

"Again, I would like to thank the distinguished Minority Leader. The American people need to understand that Republicans and Democrats can work together when action is needed. We are all agreed that America faces a genuine threat. We must respond to that threat. We may disagree on precisely the right strategy to pursue, but we do know that we must pursue a strategy. Right now the President has laid forth a plausible strategy. It is only natural that at this point in time we let him pursue that strategy. If things should go awry, there is always plenty of time to refine and re-examine the approach we are taking. But right now, action is needed."

"How soon do you expect the Senate to act?" It was the reporter from CBS.

"With the consent of my distinguished colleague, I would hope that we would be taking up the legislation as soon as the House sends us a bill. By prior arrangement, both sides of the aisle will have six hours of debate time. We have also agreed to postpone our weekend recess so legislation can be adopted. This, of course, requires that the members of the other body act as expeditiously as they can. If the House does so, we may well have a bill here in the wee hours of Thursday night or Friday morning. The Senate will then be able to dispatch the bill, assuming we find it worthy, by sometime on Saturday morning."

The Minority Leader nodded her head. "I concur with the distinguished Majority Leader. Our goal is to have a bill to the President before the end of this coming weekend."

At this there was a shouting match among the reporters. But both pols smiled, turned, and walked together into the Senate Chamber. It was a preplanned visual to convey action, determination, and bipartisanship. This bill was going to happen.

The choreography of the day was to allow the networks to squawk about what had happened for about three minutes and then pivot to the press conference by the Speaker of the House, who would actually be announcing the schedule. Cutting to the network anchors would simply reinforce the message as there was only one—a determined show of unity. They would babble on as they usually did, using words such as 'unprecedented.' Those predisposed to disliking the President would worry whether there was a rush to judgment. But even the naysayers were effectively reinforcing Washington's message of the day: speedy and determined action.

The Speaker stepped before the microphones outside of his office. "Ladies and gentlemen. Today we are witnessing Washington at its finest. The bipartisan leadership of both houses is coming together to give the President the tools he has requested to confront this challenge to our country. We will give him those tools.

"What has made this possible is the very close cooperation and sharing of information that the President and his team have been practicing during preceding weeks. The bipartisan congressional leadership has been in regular meetings with executive branch officials. It is also a tribute to Washington that we have kept the substantive discussions in those meetings confidential. All Americans should be proud of how the people they sent to Washington have behaved during this time of economic challenge.

"The House of Representatives will move with dispatch. Legislation has been prepared by the Chairman of the Banking, Finance, and Urban Affairs Committee with input from the ranking member to grant the President the authority he needs. The House Rules Committee will take up this legislation within the hour. The suggested rule is that the bill lay over for twenty-four hours, to be followed by six hours of debate, three for each party. Tentatively a vote will be held in the House around seven-thirty tomorrow night. Assuming that the legislation is approved, it will then be sent to the Senate for action."

"Mr. Speaker? No public hearings? Isn't this unusual? It is almost like all of this was pre-wired."

"The President and the executive branch have been working with us closely throughout this crisis. This is American government working at its best when faced with a crisis. What the President has asked for in terms of enabling legislation is very straightforward. Operationally the program will be carried out by the Treasury Department and the

Federal Reserve. The heads of those agencies have also been involved in the discussion. Both the Secretary of the Treasury and the Chairman of the Federal Reserve have assured us that speed is essential. There will be plenty of time for second-guessing and recriminations, something that Washington is good at. But first we must act. That is precisely what we are going to do."

"Mr. Speaker?"

"Mr. Speaker?"

The shouts went up from across the entire row of reporters.

"Folks, expeditious means expeditious. I am headed to the meeting of the Rules Committee now to be available for any questions members might have. Besides, the Chairman of the Fed will be having his pre-scheduled press conference following the FOMC meeting in precisely thirty-eight minutes." With that he turned and walked down the hall.

The network control rooms knew what to do. Their anchors had been sitting not so patiently. They were expecting it would be their pretty faces and authoritative voices that would tell the American people what to think. They had been preempted by the elected representatives of the people. Noses were out of joint. Time to give them their day under the Klieg lights. Besides, they had to pay the bills. So at least six of the next thirty-eight minutes would be used for commercial breaks. No time to dawdle.

¥ $ €

Ben Coleman checked the market app on his iPhone as he entered the briefing room. Stocks were way up—over 400 points on the Dow. That was a sign of confidence. The dollar was up, too, almost one percent against all major currencies. Bonds and gold, however, were erratic. There was a lot of confusion about what this meant for the actual price of the gold that was not to be turned into the special coins. And the debt exchange between the Fed and the Treasury was causing confusion. He knew his job.

The statement released at two o'clock at the end of the FOMC meeting covered the very basics—the state of the economy, which was okay, but not great; the state of the financial markets, which were unsettled; and the unanimous decision by the FOMC not to change interest rates at this meeting. With everything that was going on, more change would not be a helpful thing.

There were two lines at the end of the statement that would be the center of attention. *The FOMC has authorized the Federal Reserve Bank of New York, in concert with the Board of Governors, to take whatever actions are necessary to carry out the enabling legislation, should it be enacted, to issue special gold coins of a set nominal value as part of the continuing obligation of the Federal Reserve to provide a currency that is both a medium of exchange and a reliable store of value. The vote was unanimous with Governor Avery abstaining due to concerns about the technical implementation of this program over the long term.*

Ben presumed that in the half hour between the issuance of the statement and the press conference that all the reporters present, indeed all market participants, would have read it. So he focused on providing context, answering questions, and spinning the market's understanding to achieve his and the President's objective.

He said, "In our nation's monetary history we have frequently had paper currency and coinage made from gold and silver circulating at the same time. That was true during the first and second banks of the United States, during the Civil War and its immediate aftermath, and after the creation of the Federal Reserve in 1913 up through 1933 when gold coins were removed from circulation. Assuming the legislation that the President has proposed and that the Banking Committee of the House of Representatives will be sending to the floor tomorrow is approved, we will be returning to that practice.

"But there will be one difference this time. The President stressed in his speech to the country that we are putting our trust in the people, not in the government. That is exactly right. It will be up to the people whether they want to hold cash, coins, or melt down the coins they do have.

"Governments have always had an incentive to print money to pay their bills and in so doing force down the value of that money. Some have claimed that the Federal Reserve was created to facilitate that process. No more. If the Federal Reserve prints too much money and drives down its value, people will be free to convert their Federal Reserve Notes—what we call cash—freely into these special gold coins. And as a stopgap measure, if the Fed were to continue to print too much money and drive the value of that cash down further, then the public would be free to melt down the gold coins and get a return for them that is more than their nominal face value.

"So today is an important day in monetary history, not only for the United States, but for the people of the world. We, the monetary authority of the United States, are in effect tying our own hands. We will not be able to endlessly print money because if we do, then the people of America, and the people of the world, now have a means to stop us. They can convert the paper money into gold coins with no downside risk in their value and, if we persist, can melt down those coins at a profit. This truly is, as the President said, the people's money.

"And because of this option the people have, we at the Federal Reserve must be careful to avoid excessive money creation. That makes the United States dollar the strongest currency in the world. It is the only currency that the people themselves can limit the creation of. This makes the dollar the currency in which everyone can have the utmost confidence. Moreover, the debt issued by the United States government, which is denominated in those dollars, is now the most solid debt there is. As I said, this is an amazing chapter in the history of mankind and our relation to money.

"Soon the countries that have liquidated the U.S. Treasury holdings will come to regret their decision. Moreover, by holding plain gold and not our special gold coins, those countries are holding an inferior asset, one that has no floor on its value. The laws of supply and demand suggest that the value of that raw gold will decline. After all, we will be supplying approximately 140 million troy ounces on the market in the form of special gold coins, the equivalent of roughly five years of new supply. And we will be issuing the coins with a price protection that makes them superior to holding gold in its raw form.

"We are carrying out this policy not out of malice, but in defense against those who sought to malign us. We hope those countries that have taken actions against us will see the error of their ways and join us in trying to forge a new path toward prosperity for all the people of the world. I will now take your questions."

"Chairman Coleman, does this mean that you are not pegging the price of gold?"

"That is correct. The value of gold in its raw form, that is, gold that is not turned into these special gold coins, will be allowed to move as the market sees fit. Only the gold we are now exchanging with the Treasury in return for their bonds will be turned into those coins. And that gold, and those coins, are the only things that are pegged in value."

"So the value of gold and the value of the gold in the coins will be different?"

"Most likely, and as long as we do our job, the value of the gold in the special coins will be higher. That value is guaranteed by the United States—and the value will be printed right on the coin, five thousand or ten thousand dollars, as the case may be. Gold that does not have a U.S. government guaranteed price, meaning that gold not in the coins, will not have a floor and so should fall in value."

"Mr. Chairman, have you discussed this with Governor Li of the People's Bank of China?"

"No, I have not. Governor Li and I did meet last Friday in London at a special meeting arranged by the Bank of England. We had a meeting in which we were both committed to resolving the difficulties between our two countries in a peaceful way. And let me commend Li Xue for the very constructive role he played by informing us of the likelihood of the piracy that occurred off the California coast. Thanks to his candor the United States was able to minimize the disruption and resolve the situation with no loss of life. Governor Li proved himself to be a tremendous asset both to his country and to the cause of world peace."

"But some of your words today were a bit harsh regarding the behavior of the People's Bank and the Chinese government. How do you reconcile that with that very generous assessment you just gave of our enemy?"

"Governor Li is not our enemy," Ben said, "and the People's Republic of China is not our enemy. We are competitors. Governor Li is doing his very best for his team, as I am trying to do for ours. One can respect a talented and honorable competitor. And I have enormous respect for Governor Li even though he is doing everything he can to have China emerge from this crisis as the winner. But at the same time, I am going to do everything in my power to make sure that the United States wins.

"The Chinese government made a very foolish decision when it decided to try and undermine the U.S. dollar. It did so primarily out of concern for its own financial system, which is in desperate shape. I sympathize with the Chinese people who must suffer for the mistakes and errors in judgment made by their government in the past. But we cannot and we will not allow ourselves to be dragged down by their past malfeasance.

"We think the Chinese will soon see the error of their ways and the wisdom of our approach. If and when they do, I hope that I will be able to work with Governor Li in order to get the global economy back on track."

Ben looked down at his iPhone and noticed that the market had continued to rise, bond yields had begun to fall, the dollar rise, and spot gold drop to just below $8,000, down more than six percent from its high earlier in the day. He had sent the desired signal. Now the challenge was to get out while he was ahead.

He had preselected the first two questions. Now, in case the jealous reporters decided to compare notes, he had better throw the next question out to the assembled gaggle. "I have time for one more question."

He hadn't bargained on what followed. It was a reporter from one of the web-based sites that were gaining popularity. Ben did not recognize him, but he would never make that mistake again.

"Mr. Coleman, we have learned that Mrs. Coleman is employed by CIA as a Chinese analyst. To what extent can you assure us that the compartmentalization of information that is required by law—both on the CIA end and on the Federal Reserve end—is being strictly complied with? In fact, there are even reports around that your bedroom has been bugged."

"I didn't catch your name."

"Who I am is immaterial. What the American people need to know is whether you and Mrs. Coleman are respecting the laws of this country in your joint capacities. For the record, my name is Peter Robinson, OpenSource News."

Ben could feel a rising instinctual need to defend his wife. But rather than go on the attack, he decided to use weasel words laced with humor.

"Mr. Robinson, you seem to be a better-informed man than I am. As far as I can tell from our monthly bank statement, we are a one-earner family. That is, of course, excepting the royalty checks my wife gets as an author. They are far larger than my salary, I must say. So large in fact, that I strongly doubt that Mrs. Coleman would see any need in seeking other employment.

"As to bugging our bedroom—maybe some kind of perverted voyeur would find that entertaining. But I am a very private man about things like that. If your story turns out to be true, and your notion of Mrs. Coleman being employed does not auger well for its validity, and I happen to find that person who is snooping on our private life, they will get a what-for from me the like of which would be most unbecoming of a central banker. I hope I have made myself clear. Thank you all very much."

Ben's stomach was churning but he thought that he had threaded the needle. Every word from his mouth had been truthful. There was no paycheck, and the voyeurs had gotten what for from him. But he also sensed that there was a leak somewhere. It was not his job to plug it, but he had no doubt that people watching this news conference would be on it right away.

CHAPTER TWENTY

The two operatives showed up at Deng's suite at 9 p.m. to find the manager there to act as guarantor and interpreter. Deng and Chen were seated in two large chairs and their three guards standing behind them. All three were casually dressed. Bob and Tom were directed to stand in front of the group.

Deng spoke through the interpreter. "You two have violated all the codes of basic discipline. Showed lack of restraint and placed yourselves in jeopardy. For this you will pay the price that this court martial decides."

He was right about the role playing, Bob thought.

Both men were ordered to strip to their undershorts and Deng came over to perform his inspection. Each muscle was tested, and Deng frequently grunted in approval. He stuck his hand down their shorts to check out their equipment. Average or a little better for a Caucasian but more ample than what Deng was used to. Another grunt of approval. He then nodded for Chen to come over and do the same, which he did, but in a perfunctory manner. Then the two men returned to their chairs.

The manager continued to translate. "First the two of you will drop down and give me pushups. Sixty for Tom. Eighty for Bob. This is to remind you of what lies ahead."

The two men complied. Their morning rituals involved pushups, but not so many and Bob could feel his biceps tire toward the end.

Deng spoke again and the manager translated. "A little humility for both of you. When I give the signal, you will strip and begin to masturbate. I will time how long it takes. My men here will give you one punch in the gut for every minute you take."

Tom thought, *This wasn't exactly part of the deal*, but there was no reason to object given they had gotten this far.

Despite their tight abdominals the punches were enough to make them double over slightly and the purpose of the sex act was humiliation pure and simple. Both men were reeling after the ordeal, knowing the worst was to come. But neither had let out any plea for mercy or scream of pain louder than a grunt when the blows hit.

The guards hand cuffed each man to a hook at the top of each bedpost, their backs and shoulders fully stretched and butts and thighs still vulnerable. Deng took his belt off and started with Bob Franks. When the first blow landed Bob felt his whole body tense in response. He had felt worse pain, but not very often. He likened it to having his teeth drilled before the novocain had a chance to kick in.

Then came the second, and the third, and he could feel his arms start to involuntarily struggle in their binds. He realized that part of the punishment was the feeling of helplessness for the person receiving the beating. He was unprepared for that and his body kept trying to free itself despite his mind telling him to stop. He focused on not crying out, in part because it gave his mind something to focus on that he might control. But the main reason is that he knew Deng would simply get pleasure out of it and he was determined to prevent that.

After fifteen blows Deng stopped and turned his attention to Tom. Then he offered the belt to Chen who took a turn, but only landed six blows on each man. Deng resumed with another round. Chen declined another opportunity but each of the guards had their chance.

After forty minutes both men had gotten sixty lashes. Tom was released from his shackles. He felt his knees buckle as the full force of his body was now on his legs. He dropped to the floor on his knees. The manager handed him a cup of water.

Bob's ordeal continued. Deng slowed down his pace, making it worse since Bob never quite knew when the next blow would land. Usually Deng made him wait thirty to forty seconds to get another. Tom looked up from his kneeling position and could see Deng was clearly enjoying this. He reminded himself why they were doing this and kept repeating, *All in is all in.*

Finally it was over. Bob also dropped to his knees and then found himself starting to drop to the floor. Tom came over to steady him and had to put his hand against the wall to keep himself upright. He was lightheaded from the pain and his stomach was rolling over, wanting to empty itself. Both men breathed heavily, sucking in air through their mouths in an effort to keep their brains from shutting down.

With great effort they put on their underwear and cut-off shorts but putting their tee shirts back on was well near impossible. There were small welts all over their shoulders and backs and a few spots where the skin was completely broken and blood was coming out. Still, none of the cuts was so deep that it would not heal with the passage of time.

The manager could not have men going through the hotel corridors looking like this and had come prepared. Each man was given a loose-fitting cover like a karate uniform top with a cloth tie to keep it closed.

Deng motioned to one of his guards to hand each man a stack of hundreds, then put his belt in a small bag and gave it to Tom. He motioned to the belt as the manager translated.

"I doubt your friend will cause trouble again. But if he does, you know what to do."

Both men were unsteady enough that the three guards and the manager split up two-and-two and the arms of each man around their shoulders. It wasn't enough pressure that they had to carry them, but it did take some weight off their legs.

Back in their room, Bob and Tom swallowed some Advil, knowing that the next dose would follow well before the time on the label. They took off their tops and grabbed the three cans of Solarcaine they had purchased in the lobby gift store, taking turns spraying it on each other's backs. It was intended to relieve sunburn, but the topical anesthetic was as good as one could get over the counter. The pain lessened some, but both knew they were going to be hurting for a couple of days.

Finally, they got up the energy to high-five. They grabbed some of the vodka from the mini bar, poured themselves a double, and toasted.

"We did it," said Tom. "All in! And we hit the jackpot!"

Bob said, "Asking for the belt was a brilliant move."

"You were the one who paid for it. I'm sorry for that."

"Don't be," said Bob. "Whatever it takes. We got the bastard."

And they touched glasses in another toast.

¥ $ €

In the wake of President Turner's announcement, the Oval Office had become a war room. This morning was no exception as staff and advisers assembled to review the world's reaction to the speech. The only missing face was Dianne Reynolds, who was still in Tokyo. In her place sat Cynthia Turner.

"I have invited the First Lady to join us this morning," said the President, "and have given her special security clearance using my authorization so none of you need feel any reason to hold back. I trust no one has any objections."

No one did, but in the unlikely event they existed, they would not be expressed.

"Cynthia was an accomplished businesswoman before she was First Lady. And she reminded me last night that we had launched a product with big fanfare but had no follow through in terms of a marketing campaign. Now there I go, committing the cardinal sin any husband can make, putting words in his wife's mouth."

Cynthia smiled. "That's okay, Mr. President. You were doing a perfectly adequate job."

It was a sign of how well the group got along that a chuckle went across the room. One of the things the Turners did well together was play a tag team routine that made everyone feel comfortable.

"This is not a criticism of you men," Cynthia said, "but women make most of the shopping and investment decisions in America. Although men think they are more skilled at it, they rarely want to devote the time. So let me begin with the obvious—a five- or ten-thousand-dollar item is not exactly what one would call an impulse purchase.

"So who is our target? There might be some well-to-do grandparents leave a special something for their grandchildren. One

that high worth individuals and families would be naturals,

vestment advisers and brokers won't make any money on these purchases. So we can't count on them to help.

"It won't be the banks, as the coins will shrink their deposit base. Other intermediaries like hedge funds don't have the time horizon to sit on an asset that pays no interest. Now I am just parachuting into this, but who is it that we expect to buy these coins and how do we incentivize them? We need to come up with a marketing strategy."

Ben stared down at the floor. Both Bernadette and Cynthia caught it. Cynthia wondered if she had embarrassed him for not having thought through this detail. Bernadette knew better. It was a different sort of embarrassment. Ben had the answer but was afraid to contradict someone who was both his wife's friend and the First Lady of the United States.

Bernadette decided to continue using the Turner's tag team routine. "Mr. Chairman, I've known you long enough to know you've already solved this one. You may as well spit it out. Cynthia won't mind. Both she and I know that men sometimes do have good ideas. Kind of like a stopped clock—it's right twice a day."

There was another round of laughter around the room. Ben visibly reddened.

"All right, Ben," the President said, "out with it. You've got to show that the male half of the human species can earn their keep. I am counting on you to speak up."

Ben decided that a little respectful formality might be the best approach to finesse the situation.

"Mr. President, Mrs. Turner is absolutely correct. We do not have a marketing strategy to sell this to the American public at large. Her analysis of the situation and consumer attitudes is one hundred percent correct. Our target market, at least initially, are people for whom money grows on trees. Our initial set of buyers are the world's central banks.

"Let me spare you the logic for now and cut straight to the bottom line. Governor Nakaso of the Bank of Japan called me yesterday. Secretary Reynolds has been doing an amazing job in Asia. She has persuaded the Ministry of Finance and the Bank of Japan to buy $5 billion worth of our special coins. Their plan is to liquidate some of their ordinary gold to pay for it in the next few days. They want to make the announcement before the opening of trading in Tokyo on Monday, Sunday night our time.

"Dianne is a very good salesperson. She and Nakaso have been on the phones. He, by the way, is an outstanding man and very supportive of the relationship we have with Tokyo. As a result of their actions, we are also expecting orders from Taiwan and Singapore. The Philippines and Vietnam are likely to follow suit with minor purchases. It is foreign policy as well as the nature of our product that is making the sale.

"You might have noticed that the price of gold slipped a bit after your speech. Actually, the market action has been much bigger than the three percent drop might imply. As each of these Asian countries sold some of their gold with the intent to buy our gold coins, the Chinese have been forced to use their foreign exchange reserves to keep the price from falling even more.

"We actually are hoping for some follow-through later next week from others. The Reserve Bank of India has a variety of motives to follow suit as does the Saudi Arabian Monetary Authority. This is really going to get the market rolling. Although we are talking about a potential stock of $1.7 trillion in new gold coins, a one-week turnover of $25 billion is quite enough to move the market. In this case, the price of raw gold goes down, while the value of our coins stays the same."

He paused to give it a moment to sink in. Then, "Remember, our main purpose here is not to sell coins, but to drive the price of raw gold down, diminishing the value of Chinese gold reserves. That will put a crimp in their plans to shore up their banking system with the promise of gold-backing and crash their plans to dump the dollar and replace it with the yuan."

There was silence throughout the Oval Office until the President broke it with, "Well done, Ben."

"The real credit should go to Dianne Reynolds for helping make the sale," Ben said, hoping that they could leave this gender gap joke behind.

The First Lady took the cue. "All kidding aside, this proves that men and women do work well together and bring different and varied talents to the table. To togetherness ...." She raised her coffee cup in the gesture of making a toast.

The President turned to the director of the CIA. "Speaking of togetherness, what have we learned about that piece OpenSource News ran about Ben and Bernadette?"

"OpenSource is funded by a consortium of Chinese investors," Hector said. "Nominally it's private sector, but that means well connected to the guys in the Politburo. The leak didn't come from our side. It was a plant by the Chinese to embarrass Chairman and Mrs. Coleman, plain and simple. They know that we are messing with their internal cohesion and decided to get revenge. Let me say we only know that from our surveillance of foreign sources, not domestic ones." The CIA Director was taking no chances given that CIA had been surveilling the surveillance.

"Any suggestions?"

"Frankly, sir, we can't shut them down. So we may as well use them. I think that, if he is willing to reenter my world, Ben might do a follow up meeting with Mr. Peter Robinson, who is the front for the Chinese and heads the organization. Confidential. Background only. Have him let loose about how shabbily he was treated. Talk about deep divisions within the administration. That sort of thing. Now is probably not the right moment, but there will come a time."

"Hector," Ben said, "I need to do a gut check. I haven't heard from Governor Li since the announcement. He's an asset we can't afford to lose. And to be honest, I committed to ensure the safety of his family—"

"We have the situation in hand," Hector said. "It's a matter of waiting. That's all I'm able to say at this time."

"It's not just the Li situation," said the President. "We seem to know nothing at all about how the Chinese are responding to our gambit."

"The truth," said Hector, "is we at the Agency don't know much either. Radio silence both externally and internally. No communication through official channels or even those unofficial ones that we keep track of. Bernadette, what is your read?"

"The Director is right about radio silence," she said. "Nothing in the usual party and government organs. It was as if nothing had happened, at least within the borders of China. The usual internet sites have been censored.

"Some news is getting through and there have been some indications of public nervousness, but nothing dramatic yet. That may all change when their neighbors all start buying our gold coins. They will have to respond to what they will perceive as a collective action against them.

"But that begs the question: why the silence? The simplest explanation is probably the best. They're trying to figure it all out. My bet is that no side is yet completely dominant. They are still in a bit of shock, and therefore slow on the uptake. Li and what we sometimes call the moderates would normally be able to say, 'I told you so,' but can't until they see how it all plays out. The hardliners are probably itching to deliver a response, but their advantages are military, not economic, and there was not even a hint of the military at play.

"So they are probably pondering how to respond. And they too are nervous about being on the losing side domestically." She stopped and gave a shrug. "Please forgive me, Mr. President. I am starting to sound like an economist."

"There are worse fates, Mrs. Coleman," responded the President. "Let's meet again at ten o'clock Monday morning," the President said. "Ben, I expect a full briefing on whether our customers are lining up outside the door to buy our new product."

"Believe me, Mr. President, nobody is going to be watching it closer than I."

As the attendees filed out of the office door that faced the Roosevelt Room, Cynthia Turned asked the Colemans to join them for dinner on Sunday night. CNBC World and Bloomberg would be covering the opening of the Tokyo market, and she wanted a running commentary from Ben on what was happening. Everyone agreed and they said their farewells and parted, each anxious about what kinds of reactions the Asian markets would bring.

¥ $ €

In their hotel room, Bob and Tom had finally found the right combination of vodka, Advil, and topical anesthesia for a small level of comfort to set in. They were on their beds, stomach down, watching the silent images of an Asian game show they had no desire to understand when there was an urgent knock at the door.

"It's Boonsri," she said without prompting. "Please let me in. It is urgent." Once inside she said, "We've got to hurry. The boys we visited? One of their neighbors ratted us out. They reported that some white people had been in the neighborhood. The police are bringing a mug book of all Caucasians known to be in the area. It won't take long until you're identified. Once Deng finds out he will almost certainly make the connection as to why you're really here."

It was only then that Boonsri noticed their backs. "Son of a bitch! He really gave it to you guys. Good thing you're well built. You weren't lying, saying you were all in. Get any photos?"

"Something better," Tom said, carefully opening the bag with the belt.

"Fingerprints!" said Boonsri. "All the more reason to get out of here."

She told them to leave most of their clothes along with a little money tucked away somewhere easy to find but still out of sight. It might signal that the men were going to return and throw their trackers off course. The men each grabbed a backpack and put a minimal amount of clothes, all but $500 of their money, passports, and the belt inside, then followed Boonsri down the fire escape stairs. They moved pretty well, their regimen of self-medication giving the situation something of a dreamlike state.

Boonsri motioned them into an unmarked Land Rover. When Bob realized they were headed north out of town and not south toward the bridge they had entered from, he began to panic, the beating and the amount of vodka he had consumed having broken down his trust. "What the hell are we doing? You're taking us farther from the bridge."

"They'll have the news out by the time we get there," Boonsri said. "There is no way they would let us cross. I have a small boat waiting for us just out of town on the Mekong and someone to take the Land Rover. It's the safest route by far." She glanced in the rearview mirror and noted headlights in the distance. "We've got company. This is going to be close."

A minute later she pulled off the main road and cut through a highly rutted path that led through the jungle to the Mekong. The reason for the Land Rover became even more apparent. She hoped that they had not been spotted making the turn.

As they got to the small boat, they could see the headlights headed down the rutted road. For a moment a wave of panic rushed through the group. Then the headlights stopped, and they heard shots ring out. The police vehicle was not meant for a road this rutted and the men had emptied from the vehicle and started to pursue on foot.

The trio ditched the Land Rover and its would-be driver climbed into the boat with them. As they pushed off from shore, they could see the first bullets start to hit the water around them. The police were still too far to have any real aim.

They were about forty yards offshore by the time the police reached the water's edge. Fortunately, it was pitch black and the bullets landed well shy of their mark.

"Keep your heads down," said Boonsri. Their luck did not hold up. They heard one of the men start the Land Rover, then it turned so the headlights projected onto the river.

"Shit," said Boonsri. She had left the keys behind, thinking that their colleague was going to drive the car back. There hadn't been the time to reassess as all four of them had climbed into the boat.

They were about out of range of the headlights when some of the bullets started finding their mark. Several hit the boat just above the waterline. Then worse news arrived. Downriver another set of lights appeared. It was a Chinese PLA river patrol boat. Its presence was illegal under international law, but the Laotian government was bought and paid for and turned a blind eye. They could see the searchlight from the boat crisscrossing the water. They knew exactly what they were looking for.

"I don't think they'd dare shoot into Thailand," said Boonsri. "It would create a big international incident. All we have to do is make it to shore."

Suddenly, there was a loud crack and a large plume of water shot skyward about thirty yards behind them. The boat was shooting its main gun in their direction. The light beam was not quite on them and the men on the boat were firing blind.

Another shell landed, this time to their starboard. Then one about ten yards upriver from their position. Boonsri noted they were about twenty yards from shore.

"Hope you guys can swim! Watch out for the crocs. You'll be putting blood into the water, so get to shore fast. Jump!" She needed no follow-up order as a shell landed close enough to drench them in water.

When the three men were overboard, she turned the boat ninety degrees and sent it north, parallel from shore. She then jumped as well and met them on shore. The patrol boat continued to follow their boat upstream firing shots the whole way. Safely on shore, the foursome watched as one of the mortars hit its target and the gas tank on the small boat exploded.

The patrol boat crept past their hiding spot, its lights scanning the water, looking for bodies. They could hear the captain shout to the men and automatic weapons began to strafe the river. Some were headed toward the Thai shore.

Boonsri kept them moving and eventually the shooting stopped. Finally, another Land Rover came into view, lights on. Bob and Tom felt a wave of relief. Both were thoroughly exhausted, and the Advil was wearing off. They could use another coating of Solarcaine as well. When they got to the car, they took both out of their backpacks. They downed the Advil with a bottle of water that was in the car and began to remove their wet tops.

Boonsri took another look at their backs and turned deadly serious. "You both are going to need medical attention, better than we can provide for you here." She pulled a small bag from the car, withdrew two needles, and gave each man a shot in the arm before they could react. "The Mekong carries just about every bad germ and parasite you can think of. This should hold off the infection for now."

She grabbed the Solarcaine and began spraying each man's back, checking carefully for any serious cuts that might need something more.

She grabbed some salve and a few bandages. "This is going to hurt, but I have to apply this by touch, not by spray." Each man winced a bit as she applied the ointment.

"Look, I care about the two of you too. Let's think of you as one big package. You still have to get the evidence into the right hands. We have a small jet with good range a few miles from here. It may not have been on your itinerary, but you two are headed Down Under."

"Australia," Bob said, putting it all together. "Five Eyes. Secure communications. Something better than Advil and Solarcaine. The whole thing. We're really and truly out. Thank you, Boonsri."

"We're all doing our jobs, right," she said. "That's what the Agency trains us to believe. But the non-agent in me wants to thank you both for what you did for people. That bastard hurt a lot of people. You two know how much. So I am going to give you a non-agent thank you." She hugged them both, putting her hands on their backs very gingerly, then gave them a kiss on both cheeks. "You are true heroes."

¥ $ €

The private jet carrying Bob and Tom landed at the Five Eyes intelligence base about one hundred miles north of Brisbane. There were stretchers waiting for them at the bottom of the ramp, but both men waved them off. The Solarcaine they carried on the plane had been used generously and they had switched from Advil to vodka. They weren't feeling much pain.

Their bag was carried straight to the commander's office along with their cell phones. They had snapped a few pictures on the plane while applying Solarcaine and those were added to the ones of Deng in the casino. Meanwhile the men were taken straight to the medical unit. About halfway across the tarmac Tom grabbed the shoulder of one of the medics and Bob followed suit. They told themselves it was the vodka, but in truth they had each lost about half a pint of blood as well.

More pictures were taken. They were given a shot for everything that might be carried in the Mekong: tetanus, diphtheria, giardia, malaria, and smallpox, with penicillin for good measure. Boonsri had called ahead and reported their swim for shore as well as their overall medical condition. Then came military grade topical anesthetic and antibiotics, which had to be administered as a cream as their backs were bandaged up.

"On top of being heroes, you guys are damn lucky," the doctor told them. "Orders from above, you're going to be staying with us for about five days for observation."

"Is that really necessary?" asked Bob. "I want to get back to work."

The doctor keyed a number into the phone in the corner of the infirmary. "Tell your boss that."

Lopez came on over the speaker phone. "Bob, Tom. I am relieved to hear you're safe. You have done your country an enormous service. The photos just arrived here. What you went through is unimaginable. But getting that belt was genius. Outstanding fieldcraft, both of you."

"Sir, thank you, sir."

"I told you that you wouldn't get any parades, or even a story in the newspaper. We don't want to tip off the gentleman to whom the belt belongs." Lopez let out a loud laugh. "That god-damned bastard. A bullet to the head with the bill for the bullet sent to his family would be too good for him. But when I tell the President what you did, he's going to want to personally shake your hands.

"So a photo op with the President in the Oval Office will have to suffice for your ticker-tape parade. By the way, I heard that line about you wanting to get back to work. You are on the clock as of right now. Your job is to make a complete recovery. We can't have you bleeding all over the carpet in the Oval Office now, can we?"

Bob and Tom exchanged glances, then said in unison, "Sir, no, sir."

¥ $ €

When Ben and Bernadette arrived at the White House, they were surprised to see Hector Lopez had gotten there just ahead of them, briefcase in tow.

"Hector," said Bernadette. "Are you and your wife joining our little party tonight?"

He shook his head. "I'm in and out, in an official capacity. Glad you're here, though. It'll save me a trip."

"Do tell," Bernadette said. "Can you give me a hint?"

Hector shook his head. "As much as I would love to repeat this over and over, it'll be best if I only have to say it once."

The Turners were waiting for them at the elevator to the second floor. Uncharacteristically, the President stepped over to shake Lopez's hand before greeting the Colemans.

"I understand you have some news for me," he said. "I hope it's good. As you see, I'm entertaining guests this evening."

"Particularly good news," Hector said. "It is in regard to Governor Li's position with General Deng."

He pulled manila folders out of his briefcase and passed one to the President and one each to Ben and Bernadette. Inside was a set of glossy photographs. One was of General Deng at the blackjack table with Bob at the side of the picture. There was a picture of the belt. Fingerprints were shown in the lower right-hand corner of the picture. Then were two pictures of Bob and Tom's backs. Cynthia Turner covered her mouth and looked away.

"Good Lord," said Bernadette, "isn't that Bob Franks? Is this the mission they volunteered for that you couldn't discuss?"

The President had a look of revulsion on his face. "Hector, you told me you had something going inside China that would give us an edge in this little war we're having with them. Would you care to explain to me what the hell this is?" He waved one of the photos for emphasis.

Lopez explained the identities of the two wounded men and the reason for the mission that had taken them into Laos.

"So they set themselves up to get this on Deng?" asked Cynthia Turner.

"Yes, ma'am," said Lopez. "The pictures came from Five Eyes base in Queensland right after we got the men there. They are safe. We are keeping them there for a few days for medical observation and let things heal a bit. The belt was Deng's tool of choice. We have confirmed that those fingerprints are his. The Chinese regime is really quite puritanical, and this would ruin Deng if the pictures ever got out."

The President shook one of the photos. "Let's see that it happens! I will hand-deliver these to the Politburo myself!"

"Sir," said Hector, "as much as I would like to see Deng and his nephew share a prison cell with some really special prisoners, I think there's a better purpose for these.

"The plan is to get these photos to Governor Li. He can hold them over Deng's head. We have already wired copies to our embassy in Beijing. Monday morning the Fed's attaché there is going to request a meeting with Li, ostensibly to provide documents related to Li and Ben's discussion at the Bank of England. Deng can't stop that meeting from happening, but he can insist on seeing the documents. We will be delivering two sets, one for Deng to hold as a keepsake and one for Li. It will be obvious to Deng that we have the evidence and are simply letting Li use them as he sees fit."

The President chuckled. "Looks like my little call to Yale will doubtless be met with a prompt acceptance by all concerned, won't it?"

"Even better," Ben said, "Li will be able to cripple Deng's ability to oppose him on currency and monetary issues."

The President said, "Hector, these young men have done a great service for our country. I'd like to meet them."

"Yes, sir. And if I can be candid, I already promised them a handshake and a photo op."

"That's not enough. I'd like to do something special for them. Can you come up with something appropriate, given the nature and security level of what they have done?"

Hector smiled. "It would be my pleasure, sir."

They shook hands all around and Hector Lopez turned to exit. The elevator door opened, and as the two couples boarded, the President turned to Ben.

"Meantime, I have a bone to pick with you, Mr. Chairman."

"Sir?"

"I thought you handled the press masterfully after my speech, but didn't you go off script a bit?"

Ben knew what was coming, but to be on the safe side, he feigned ignorance. "Sir?"

" 'Citizens will have the option to melt down the coins if the value of gold goes above face value.' Damn it, we don't want to turn the Fed into the source of a new gold rush. Isn't the idea to keep the coins in play?"

"Sir, I called an audible when I said that," Ben said. "I told the press that the coins could be melted down because I don't want the coins to be melted down."

The elevator door opened and the quartet stepped out.

"Is this more economic speak?" said the President. "I told them to melt the coins because I don't want the coins melted? Or is it reverse psychology?"

"It's to keep us honest," Ben said. "If we get too excited about printing money again, that's going to send the price of gold up. When that happens, the coins will be worth more than face value, inspiring people to melt them down for the metal. If we don't want that to happen, then we damn well better be careful about taking measures like that, otherwise the coins will become rare collector's items and we'll blow up our debt again."

Turner laughed and clapped Ben on the back. "Okay. You're forgiven. Just let me know if you decide to go off script again."

"If there's time," Ben said.

The President turned to his wife. "See? This is why I keep him around."

The second-floor residence portion of the White House had become old hat for the Colemans. But Bernadette had never been in the family room with the television and Ben had only once their first time here. If it were part of the tour, ordinary Americans might be shocked that it looked just like the family living room in their own house. A couple of couches and La-Z-Boy recliners scattered around a coffee table. Each seat focused on the large-screen television in the center.

The only real difference was the complexity of the television. It had split screen capability, up to nine separate boxes. Lyndon Johnson, who liked to watch all of the nightly news shows, had had three separate televisions installed. With the modern proliferation of news sources, this new setup made much more sense.

Tonight they had two screens on, one tuned to CNBC World,

reporting from Singapore, the other Bloomberg, which ran with the sound off. Bloomberg had better live quotes than CNBC running on a hot board at the bottom of the screen, Ben explained.

The Japanese Ministry of Finance made its announcement just before the market opened. The result was predictable. The dollar caught a bid against most major currencies, but the real action was in dollar/ yuan. In this case it was only the offshore yuan that was trading. The domestic yuan exchange rate was controlled by interventions by the Bank of China and would not trade until Chinese markets opened in an hour. A chart of the minute-by-minute trading was put on screen by both networks. The yuan was skidding downward. It had closed at 14.8 to the dollar on Friday and was now running about 15.75.

Ben played his expected role as commentator. "Yuan down six percent. The authorities in Beijing are going to have to take some action. Wouldn't surprise me if there wasn't another crash in the Shanghai exchange server before the open. They really don't want trading.

"The best news is that dollar/yen is stable even as the dollar trades up against both the euro and pound sterling. That means that the switch to our gold coins by the Japanese is viewed as a positive by the currency markets. I am certain the other Asian central banks have taken notice. Should help us with both the Reserve Bank of India and the Saudis.

"The Nikkei is opening off a touch. No big surprise. A relatively stronger yen and a decidedly weaker yuan is bad news for Japanese exporters."

Cynthia turned to Bernadette, "Is he like this all the time?"

Bernadette chuckled softly. "I could tell you stories—"

"What the hell," said Will Turner.

They turned back to the TV to see a headline flashing across the screen: *China Suffers Nationwide Internet Outage.*

"Now we know what the Chinese reaction is," Ben said.

"But nationwide?" asked the President. "That is overdoing it a bit, isn't it?"

"Sir, I think they don't want the public to know what just happened. Best way for them to limit the news flow is to shut it down. I think this goes back to our hypothesis of the situation. The authorities don't know what to do and are scrambling for time. With no internet, the ATMs are going to be down at the banks, the stock market can't open, and the public won't hear about the purchase of U.S. gold coins by the Asian central banks. At a minimum it buys time."

"Bernadette, if that is the minimum, what is the maximum?"

"We will know soon enough. My guess is that if the hardliners have gained the upper hand the outage will be blamed on sabotage and the saboteurs will be alleged to be American agents. This creates a patriotic pretext for a nonfinancial strike at us in response."

"Nonfinancial, meaning?"

"Military is a possibility, but my suspicion is that it will be tit-for-tat. A cyberattack, probably more limited in scope, may just be a threat. Even the hardliners will want to dial this one up slowly, gauge our response. Too big a move by them might cause a massive escalation by us, and they really don't want to take that risk.

"Besides, Chinese military doctrine is that America is far more vulnerable to cyber warfare as our society is more dependent on the internet than theirs. Logically, any kind of measured response would be targeted. Not nationwide. Perhaps just Washington or New York."

"*Just* Washington? *Just* New York?" The President picked up the phone and called a meeting of the China Crisis group for nine the next morning. "Let us hope the response is minimal."

Both Ben's and Bernadette's cell phones vibrated. The text regarding the meeting had gone out. Even though both knew what the message said, they were both so conditioned to checking their cell phones they reached to check them anyway. "Absolutely Pavlovian," Ben muttered when he realized what he'd done.

The television screen flashed another set of hot boards, this time indicating the open of the markets in the China region. Shanghai was closed, but Hong Kong was down nearly six percent. Singapore and Taiwan were also trading down, by two and three percent respectively.

Cynthia surveyed the faces on the others. "Is a drink in order? Something stronger than wine, perhaps?"

"My usual may be in order, thanks." The President was not known for declining a drink at times like these, at least as long as a decision was not imminent.

"A splash of what he's having," Bernadette said.

Cynthia turned to Ben. "Can our commentator handle the analysis and something stronger?"

Ben was staring intently at the screen and the comment simply flew by him.

Bernadette spoke for him. "Give him what you give the President. This one goes into never-never land when it comes to analyzing numbers. It's some form of nerd heaven. He listens to numbers the way most people listen to music." She patted his hand.

Ben momentarily snapped out of his study. "Oh, sorry. Yes, Cynthia, I will have something. Sorry to be rude, I really did hear the question, just a bit focused." He said all of this without taking his eyes from the television screen.

"And what do those numbers tell you?"

"The Hong Kong market reaction was to be expected. They are pegged to the U.S. dollar, which is rising sharply against the yuan. But a good portion of their revenue comes from mainland visitors, who now are decidedly poorer. Worse, the price of Hong Kong real estate is bound to drop since mainlanders can now afford to pay less for their *pied-à-terre*.

"The boys at HKMA are tough, though. They know they will be out of business if they break the peg with the dollar. They have to differentiate their product from the yuan somehow and this would do it. If it were not for Beijing's reaction, I would bet they would love to buy some of our gold coins.

"As to Taiwan and Singapore, they have not made their announcement regarding coin purchases. My sense is that may be deliberate. They are going to face the same kind of choice Tokyo faced. Send a geopolitical signal or help their economy by letting their currencies fall. Bernadette will have the better answer to that one.

"My instinct is that they go with geopolitics. Dianne Reynold's presence in the region was a very important signal, Mr. President. Some presidents talked about a pivot to Asia, but her sustained presence in

Tokyo while this crisis was developing was a real pivot. The economic equivalent of sending the fleet."

"I am sure the Chairman is correct," said Bernadette. "I would hesitate to intrude in his area of expertise, but if I were playing their hand, I would wait for the inevitable market sell-off to run its course and then step in with my announcement on coin purchases. The market will have hit a bottom and so it would appear that a rally was developing on the decision. If memory serves me correctly, the opening move usually takes about half an hour."

As if on cue, CNBC cut to the press briefing room at the Monetary Authority of Singapore. The spokesman read a prepared statement announcing the intended purchase of $1.5 billion of the gold coins. A partial sale of the Authority's gold stock would pay for half of the coins, other foreign currency holdings would pay for the other half. There would be no questions.

Ben reached over and gently grabbed Bernadette's hand. "Did I ever tell you that you have a career waiting for you at a trading desk in case you get bored doing what you're doing now?"

He then leaned over and gave her a kiss on the cheek. She responded by giving him one on the lips, though aware of where they were sitting, she made sure she held back a bit.

"You two lovebirds are certainly welcome to spend the night in the Lincoln bedroom if you wish," Turner said.

"Thank you, sir," said Ben. "Under different circumstances it would be a real honor. But I think it is going to be an early morning if I read my text message correctly."

Cynthia added, "Of course you are welcome, and an invitation will come, but I think a little advance notice would be in order. Besides, I suspect the gossip columnists would have a field day if you were spotted leaving here at dawn, especially if your stay was not on the official schedule."

The President took his wife's cue and decided to call it an evening. "Very well then. We will all be seeing each other in a bit over ten hours in the Oval. It is going to be an interesting week."

PART THREE

THE ENDGAME

CHAPTER TWENTY-ONE

Li Xue opened the package and briefly glanced at the contents. There were two folders, labeled in Mandarin. One said, 'Governor Li,' the other, 'General Deng.'

There was also a cover note from Ben Coleman saying, *In furtherance of our conversation in London, please consider the idea of us meeting again soon, pending the approval of the Politburo for you to make another trip.*

It had been less than two minutes since the attaché from the Fed had left his office. And it hadn't been easy for him to receive the foreign visitor. There had been a negotiation between Li and Deng just to hold the meeting. The agreement was that Deng would wait in an adjacent office and once the package was delivered, Li would show it to Deng.

Li knew he didn't have much time. Deng would know when the attaché left and would show up if he didn't call him in soon. Nonetheless, he opened the file with his name on it. He hesitated at first when he saw the contents, then quickly leafed through them, his head spinning.

Overwhelmed by what he had seen, he took a deep breath. Then he picked up his phone and told his assistant, "Please tell General Deng that the attaché has left and he is most welcome to examine the proposal Chairman Coleman sent."

Deng appeared in his office in a matter of seconds, plopping himself on the chair opposite Li. "So?"

"Chairman Coleman concluded that you might want to see his proposal and sent a second copy just for you." Li put on his most pleasant smile.

Deng was shocked to see his name in Mandarin on the outside of the manila envelope. But not as shocked as when he opened it to see photos of his belt, the fingerprints, and his handiwork on the backs of the two Americans, each one with a date and time stamp and geolocation codes embedded across the bottom.

"Treason!" he shouted. "This is proof that you have been consorting with our enemy! I will have you arrested immediately!" Deng grabbed his cell.

Li's expression did not change. "Comrade General, you might pause a moment to reconsider. It is not I who exposed myself to the enemy in a clear violation of state security. I am fairly certain that these are not the only two copies of these photos. In fact, I think the originals, including the belt with the fingerprints on it, are in possession of the CIA.

"I have not seen these until a moment ago. There is no way I could have known about these documents before the Federal Reserve's attaché at the American Embassy hand-delivered them. You have all of my phone conversations at your disposal as well as my email. I am sure there is no indication that I had any foreknowledge. I was as shocked as you are now when I first opened the package. I was not even aware that you had been out of town."

Deng scowled. "Your words will do you no good. They will fall on deaf ears. No. In truth, they will fall on no ears at all."

"As you wish, Comrade General. But imagine the surprise of the Chairman and your colleagues on the Politburo when they each receive a copy of these documents. I imagine that if Chairman Coleman does not hear from me in a reasonable amount of time, the Americans will arrange such a delivery."

Deng rose and began pacing. It took him a good minute to regain enough composure to speak. "Li, if you take me down you will be signing your own death warrant. Plus one for your wife and daughter."

Li drew breath, working to maintain his composure. "Comrade General, who said anything about me bringing you down? Your capabilities as a general are renowned and your sense of duty is unquestioned. I thought this might be an opportunity for us to cooperate. I believe the phrase in English is 'turn over a new leaf.'"

"The West has even contaminated your speech. You are far too close to the enemy, Comrade Li."

Li noted the use of the word comrade. It was a clear sign that Deng was willing to cooperate. "Comrade General, we both love China deeply and with our eyes wide open we can see that things are not good. No point in blinding ourselves with ideology when our nation is in crisis."

"Spoken like a true capitalistic banker," said Deng. But every nonverbal cue suggested that he was all ears.

"America has its troubles too," Li said. "If we persist on our current path America will doubtless slip into a recession and take most of the world with it. Meanwhile, we will have full-blown economic chaos. The people will demand change just as they have before. If we force the world over a cliff, we will be the first into the abyss.

"I believe Chairman Coleman understands this as well, but more importantly, he is preoccupied with avoiding an American recession and a collapse of the world economy. It may not make sense to you, but he is willing to let the Chinese economy return to prosperity if it means saving the world from an economic crash."

"That is proof that he is weak," said Deng.

"You may be right, Comrade General. And if you are, we will have another opportunity to prevail. Only to do so we must live to fight another day. Remember, Americans plan for tomorrow. We plan for 2049."

Deng found Li's logic inescapable but still hesitated. "And who will lead China to this victory in the future? You?"

"Not at all, Comrade General. I am not skilled like you in the art of battle. I am sure you will be leading the charge. I have no such desire, though I will be cheering your victory just the same."

"So what is your plan, Comrade Governor?" Deng said.

Li noticed that comrade was now joined to his title. *We are getting somewhere*, he thought, *now he realizes that I must retain my position for him to retain his.*

"You will support me in the Politburo. I plan to ask for permission to travel for a second round of talks with Chairman Coleman. Like him or not, he is a very clever man. My hunch is that he has already figured out how we can all extricate ourselves from this situation. When I return, I will expect your support to help get it passed. I can assure you, I can no more countenance a surrender by China than you. You will have to trust me on that score.

"Also, my daughter will go to Yale to accept her internship and my wife will accompany her. They will depart this weekend."

Deng thundered, "You expect me to let your family out of the country while you travel as well?"

Li had anticipated this. "Comrade General, your reach is long. You have already noted that if I betray you, I will be signing three death warrants. Do you doubt your own capabilities?"

Deng took a moment to contemplate Li's observation. Then he smiled. "Since we are talking about family, I have a demand as well. My nephew has been imprisoned by the Americans on some trumped-up charges. If your wife and daughter can go to America, then my nephew can come home to China."

"General, you exaggerate my sway. You can simply sign a paper and let my family depart. I am up against the entire U.S. government. Not even Chairman Coleman could arrange what you ask.

"Besides, from my understanding, your nephew actually made a heroic attempt on the lives of the First Lady and Mrs. Coleman. He is a very talented young man. Proving his innocence would be impossible. That said, I do promise to put in a good word for him with Chairman Coleman."

"Governor Li, as you said, I must trust you. Remember, my reach is long. And if my nephew is not ultimately returned to China, I can make no assurances for the safety of your family."

Li said, "I understand General Deng. Now we simply must convince the Politburo. Together."

¥ $ €

Ben's mind was reeling. It worked. It must have. Li was coming to the U.S. with his wife and daughter in tow. He must have Deng in the corner with the photos. There could be no other reason.

He turned to his speaker phone. "Li Xue, I would be very happy to meet you here. And congratulations to your daughter. As you may know, I taught part-time at Yale. It is a very fine school. In fact, we still own a house less than an hour from New Haven. Perhaps Bernadette and I could entertain you and your wife while you are settling your daughter in."

"I would dearly love to meet the very famous Bernadette Coleman. Perhaps we could accept your offer at another time. Both Baozhai and Jun have a wonderful opportunity to see your country. Our embassy will be sending guides to show them all the best sites: Yellowstone Park, the giant redwoods, and, of course, Disneyworld. So while they have fun I will have to work."

Ben knew the translation of this—Li's wife and daughter were going to be chaperoned by Chinese agents. There was winning and there was winning. Trust only went so far. Besides, Li Xue would not be on the winning side all by himself. He obviously had allies.

"Tell me when you are free, Xue, and I will make arrangements on this end."

"As I said, this is an opportunity, and not a certainty. I think the prospect for a candid conversation would carry a good chance for success. But my colleagues here in Beijing are worried about the management of my duties while I am away. They need some certainty that your side is going to act in good faith."

"What do you have in mind?" Ben asked.

"You may be aware of a young man named Deng Fei. His uncle is a good friend of mine."

"I'm sorry, the name doesn't ring a bell."

"Apologies. I was being presumptuous. Mrs. Coleman knows him, or at least of him, and I thought that perhaps she had shared his name with you."

"I'm sorry, she didn't."

"It turns out that young Mr. Deng got himself in a most unfortunate misunderstanding with Mrs. Coleman and Mrs. Turner."

Bells went off in Ben's head. "Oh, that's who Deng Fei is. As I recall his uncle is head of military intelligence. Yes, I heard about the incident but not the name."

"Ben, as I said, it was all a terrible misunderstanding. Deng had no intention of doing any harm to Mrs. Coleman or the First Lady."

"Perhaps not. But he was recording their conversation. Over here we take that very seriously as an assault on our privacy. Espionage is a serious crime. The authorities are contemplating some very serious charges."

"So is piracy. As I understand it, the ringleader of the pirates will be receiving a prison sentence. The papers said five to seven years. The rest of the pirates plead guilty in return for each paying a $20,000 fine. You have a very lenient court system. In most of the world piracy is subject to the death penalty. What Deng did was far from commandeering a ship, yet you are letting pirates go with a fine."

"So, Xue, perhaps you could be more precise in what you are asking. Of course, I am a mere central banker. This is a matter for the law enforcement authorities. But I can convey your thoughts."

"My friend, I would personally be very grateful if you could secure Deng Fei's release so that he can be reunited with his family. As I mentioned, his uncle is a close friend. I believe that his uncle and other members of the Chinese government would see this as a sign that you hold no animus toward our country or our people. It would be a sign of good faith that would then lead to some face-to-face talks between us in order to iron out the current situation. And in your system, it is not just the law enforcement authorities who are involved. Your president has the unlimited power to issue pardons."

This time Ben caught it. Li had said, *His uncle is a close friend of mine*, but what he really meant was General Deng was a close friend—well, perhaps now an ally—of his. Or maybe it was all made up and carrying the water for Deng to get his nephew released was part of the price of whatever deal they had made.

Ben hated the thought of asking Will Turner to pardon a man who had posed a threat to his wife and his nation. But there was more at stake here and he had to try. "I understand your position. I will raise the issue with the authorities over here and see what can be worked out. What day do your wife and daughter depart for Yale?"

"Next Tuesday. I hope that I could have your answer before Friday so I might book tickets with them. They will be in New York with me for a couple of days before traveling around the country. Perhaps that would be the time to take an hour or two for some preliminary discussions. When they depart we could sit down and discuss things in more detail. Is New York a suitable place for you to meet me?"

"Of course." There was far more at stake than convenience for a family traveling together. Both men knew that a way had to be found to deescalate the crisis quite soon or it would get out of hand.

As he disconnected the call Ben glanced at his watch. "Peggy, please call Director Lopez and tell him that, with apologies, I am heading straight to the Oval. Tell him that Governor Li called, and our conversation was far reaching and extensive and as a result went on far longer than expected." All true, and besides, Hector would read between the lines. As an afterthought he said, "And call Alice and suggest that Attorney General Flynn be invited to join us."

¥ $ €

Deng paced back and forth in front of his desk. Then he followed his usual regimen for getting control of his emotions. He dropped to the floor and did a hundred pushups. As a recruit more than three decades earlier he was one of the few in his company who actually enjoyed that part of universal military training. It cleared the mind and gave an outlet for the adrenaline and cortisol pumping through his system.

The workout had the desired effect. His head cleared and he realized that, yes, they had won the battle. But this would be a long war.

What had Li said? *Comrade General, your reach is long.* Indeed, it was, and would continue to be even if he was temporarily trapped into working with Li.

That reach was so long, in fact, that odds didn't matter—specifically, the odds of getting the Lucky Queen. That plan was still very much in motion. Soon the world would learn about his long reach. And his trap would be every bit as elegant as the one those American boys had laid with his belt.

Only this time it would be the Americans left reeling. And Li would pay a price too. His credibility at the negotiation table would be sorely undermined. Perhaps the whole deal would blow up. If it did, then Li's days were numbered. China would turn back to military might, not bourgeois tricks, for its salvation.

Yes, Li was right. Central bankers would never lead China to victory over America; they didn't have it in them. Their bourgeois mindset stops them. They lack martial discipline. Instead, Li and his kind would be watching from the sidelines, being forced to cheer as China returned to its rightful place as the Middle Kingdom.

Yes, Li Xue, my reach is long. And it goes forward in time as well. You will soon learn that lesson.

¥ $ €

In the Oval, the principals arrayed themselves on the couches in their usual positions, a sign of how frequently these meetings had taken place. The President suggested that Eric Flynn pull up one of the chairs from the side of the room and join the circle.

"Welcome to our little crisis management group, Mr. Attorney General. Technically I invited you here, but it really was Chairman Coleman who made the suggestion. In fact, it will be Chairman Coleman who will be leading most of the discussion from what I understand. Ben, the floor is yours."

Ben opened by recounting the conversation with Li. He lacked a photographic memory, but the essence of the conversation was fairly and completely relayed.

"You did have a long conversation with him, Ben," the President said. "Didn't realize that you economists could make deals so fast."

"No deal was struck, Mr. President. I merely said that I would check with you and my other colleagues in the government. As to speed, though, we economists do know where the equilibrium between supply and demand is likely to be and like to get there without a lot of fuss."

"Let's see what your colleagues think, then. Hector?"

"Mr. President, this conversation is all new to me. To give a proper CIA opinion, I would have to consult with my staff."

"But a good part of your staff is sitting right here. It is a bit strange that a superpower's policymaking comes down to what in effect is a family conversation, but perhaps it is the best way around the time-consuming bureaucratic process when decisions have to be made quickly. Bernadette?"

"Mr. President, all I can give you is a snap judgment. I do think that a final decision should await Director Lopez checking with CIA. But, as a matter of snap judgment, I think it is fair to say that we learned a lot from the conversation about the state of play on the Chinese side."

She waited for a slight nod from the President, then went on. "First, we know that the game is still in play even though Li has run up the score quite a bit against Deng.

"In short, if Li can't produce a face-saving way out for China, Deng's allies could still blow everything up. True, Deng would have some problems with the pictures, but the hardliners could decide he is expendable despite his enormous value as head of military intelligence. It is also possible that Deng could worm his way out of his bind if Li falls into disgrace."

The President nodded. "Is the state of the Chinese economy going to affect this?"

"We probably can surmise that the economic situation in China is in a state of steady decay," Bernadette said. "The lack of an internet connection limits our ability to get information out of China as much as it prevents information from getting in. So we don't have any real facts about what is going on. The very fact that they took down their internet means they are scared.

"The Chinese are very sophisticated about these things. My suspicion is that a lot of people in their financial industry can figure out why the internet went down and reach the same conclusion we did. Your plan is working as expected, sowing doubts about the Chinese banking system. My bet is that bank lines are forming and the fact that ATMs are down along with the internet will only make people more desperate."

"And their internal political situation?"

"So we now have a reasonable sketch about where the fault lines are forming within the leadership. Essentially it is party versus military. Most of the military, with the exception of Deng, continues to be against escalation. It would appear that Governor Li has aligned himself with them, or perhaps they have aligned themselves with him. If Li has Deng in the corner, and we think he does, then the military is now aligned against escalation."

"So where is their military going to come down in this situation?" asked the President.

"From the point of view of the military, Li does represent expertise in economic matters and was on the right, if losing, side in cautioning against this escapade. So he has their respect. They know that the Party was gambling in an effort to get world dominance while they were still in office.

"If the military is going to move against the Party and its apparatchiks, they will need expertise and a large portion of the senior bureaucracy to help them manage. The act of good faith in the release of young Mr. Deng is really a way of cementing the alliance between Li and the military."

The President nodded and pondered this for a moment. Then, "Your point of view, then, how does this play out?"

"Sir," Bernadette said, "I think this is a take-it-or-leave it offer regarding negotiating a truce. If I might ask Chairman Coleman whether Li offered a specific plan or is he expecting our side to offer something that is face-saving? Whether it is fully deserved or not, Li has enormous faith in the Chairman. Remember, he credits Coleman with asking that his wife and daughter be released."

"I deserve no credit," said Ben. "The success in getting the goods on Deng was entirely thanks to CIA. It was Director Lopez's assistant who was key. We are all grateful for him for having volunteered on his own initiative."

The President nodded. "We are all grateful for the CIA's involvement in this, but what of Mrs. Coleman's question? Who is coming up with the deal? Before you answer, let me say that I believe that my faith in you is fully warranted."

"Based on our call this morning," Ben said, "I believe Li assumes the ball is in my court. He gave an effusive if backhanded compliment to your plan, sir."

The President said, "It was *your* plan Ben, and Li knows it. If I may finish your thought. He assumes that you have already come up with a plan and is asking you to lay your cards on the table. Do I have that right, Mrs. Coleman?"

"Sir," she said. "Your confidence in Chairman Coleman and that of Governor Li is fully justified. Although I have no direct knowledge of it, I am certain that Ben has already crafted a plan."

"And your advice?"

"Sir, Li needs Deng Fei's release to hold his side together. If he can do this, then they will prevail, and he will have all he needs to negotiate a face-saving way out of the mess. But if they cannot hold together, then the Party hardliners are going to turn this into some combination of a class struggle and a great patriotic war."

"A pretty stark choice," the President said. "I conclude from what you said, Bernadette, you would be in favor of going forward with the deal that Ben seems to be carrying to us from Li. Hector, do you have anything to add?"

"I think that Bernadette cut to the chase pretty well. I strongly suspect that after two days of painful and heavily nuanced internal debate, the CIA would come to the same position."

"Letting that bastard Deng go really sticks in my craw," the President said.

Ben nodded. "Mr. President, I concur. But compromises sometimes sting on both sides, and dammit, this one is ours."

The President looked at Eric Flynn. "Eric, what Ben said is true. And as much as I might enjoy thinking about Deng getting informal justice, I fully respect the constitutional rights we all enjoy. Still, the thought of signing a pardon for the bastard seems like an issue."

The Attorney General nodded. "Then let me give you some good news, sir. Deng Fei is a marked man on the international stage. We have his fingerprints. We have his retina scan. We have his DNA. Deng Fei's days as a covert operative are over. Director Lopez will share those identity traits with anyone who requests them, and even those who don't, so he won't be able to operate anywhere without that nation's government knowing exactly who he is and that he represents a potential high value hostage.

"So I recommend you issue a conditional pardon, the condition being that he is never able to reenter the United States for the rest of his life. If he does, he ends up back behind bars facing an espionage charge. He won't take the risk. And if he does, perhaps some future Attorney General could arrange for the Bureau of Prisons to make his stay particularly memorable."

"All right," said the President. "A conditional pardon. But give the processing some time. Li will be here next Tuesday and should have the deal done by the end of the week—if there is to be a deal. Ben can tell Li that he has provisional approval, but that it will require a settlement of all outstanding issues.

"But, Ben, all we have done so far today is agreed to a deal to let talks begin. What kind of deal are you and Li actually going to cut? What are they going to gain? What are we going to give up?"

"Apologies, Mr. President. The call with Li ended ninety minutes ago, and I have been a little busy since then."

"Well, you're the guy who talks about decision trees. I assume that you have plotted out all of the branches and what the response should be on each one."

"Sir," said Ben, "the node of the tree we are now at is actually a random one. It will depend on things that I can't control, and some things you can't control. The real issue is how much freedom does Li have to make a deal and, quite frankly, how much leeway you give me in the negotiations."

"Let's start with what I can control. What are the issues that you will need some leeway on?"

"Mr. President, I need to know the various weights to assign your objectives in this negotiation. Let's start with a peaceful outcome. Obviously, we could have a peaceful outcome, at least temporarily, if we acquiesce to everything the Chinese want. That is a non-starter, of course. There have to be substantive constraints on the outcome as well as perceptual constraints. The last is easiest.

"The world is going to perceive the end of this conflict as having a winner and a loser. Sure, our rhetoric is going to be that we are both winners, but even if that is the case, that is not how it is going to be

;ived or reported. With all due respect, my recommendation on w\._re we want to end up would be for us to be perceived the magnanimous winner."

"How do we go about doing that?" The President asked.

"With terms and conditions that not only *are* fair to China but, are *perceived* by China as being fair. Given the Chinese character, this is going nowhere if they don't perceive themselves as having saved face. And only we can help them to save their face at this point. Ideally, by doing so we—or, more precisely, you—look magnanimous. This has been America's traditional role.

"Remember the saying, 'America is the right country to lose a war to.' Germany and Japan are two shining examples. So in a very real sense, the more magnanimous we are perceived to be, the higher the esteem in which America is held, and the more you will appear to be a winner."

"So," the President said. "How do we win this thing and still come out looking like the proverbial magnanimous winner?"

"Well," said Ben, "the short version of my plan, should you approve it, would be to have the Chinese adopt a special gold coin just like ours. It would be denominated in yuan of course. From a perception point of view this fits in with the notion that imitation is the sincerest form of flattery.

"From a substantive point of view, it would constrain the Chinese from attempting another currency war. They will no longer be able to print money to try and float their economy, or to try and undermine the dollar. This is going to bite on them. But it is also going to lead to a more stable global economy and a more stable trading relationship between the United States and China."

"All right," said the President. "But what about those in our own country who are against our return to a gold standard? I don't know if you've had time to look at the polling on this, but they're out there in significant numbers."

Ben knew the phrase *significant numbers* was political speak for *could influence the outcome of the next election.* He chose his words carefully to assuage Turner's concerns. "Sir, John Maynard Keynes famously called the gold standard a barbarous relic. But he did not say the same about gold. We are technically not going on a gold standard. Both China and America are free to manage their currencies as they see fit. If we continue to hit on that fact, it should have a soothing effect. At least one that would last long enough for our economy to improve and for enough antis to shift their opinion."

The President smiled. "Anything else we should know?"

"We'll need to work out the exchange rate between our two countries. Our gold coins are denominated in dollars, theirs in yuan. But since gold coins can always be swapped, if the yuan were to suddenly get really cheap relative to the dollar, people would sell yuan-based gold coins and buy the dollar-based version.

"For the initial pegging they are going to have to pick an exchange rate that is lower than the one we now have, which is about fifteen to one. I haven't done the math yet, but my suspicion is that Li is going to want twenty to one so that they can cover a bigger fraction of their currency and their banking problem. The cheap yuan will give them a temporary trade advantage. My instinct is to split the difference—say seventeen-and-a-half to one. This will make the gold coin value 7,000 yuan to the gram.

"They could therefore issue 100,000-yuan coins that weigh about half an ounce. You will take some criticism from firms that compete with Chinese imports for letting them devalue. But they always have the choice of revaluation. Moreover, I think the result is going to be inflation in China, pushing their costs of production up, so any trade advantage is going to be short lived."

"Ben, you've given me another reason not to question you. You just spit out a mouthful for me to ponder."

"Sorry, sir."

"No worries. You did exactly what I asked you to do. I get where you're headed. And I think you have the essential trade-offs about right.

"So let's start with the optics. America has to come out of this a winner; we need that perception. I like your construct of magnanimous winner. That was the America I grew up in and we were the envy of the world.

"As to the precise details on the currency, I will leave that to your judgment and your negotiating skill. Unless I am missing something, your freedom of movement as a central banker is also affected by the deal you cut. So I think our interests are aligned. And I trust your judgment.

"Do you have enough information from me to get your job done? If so, this meeting is adjourned. We will reconvene on Friday morning as Ben will have talked to Li the night before."

"Excellent," said Ben. "Now if you'll excuse me, I've got to prepare the team for our trip to New York. It's going to be a big day."

¥ $ €

"This is it." Bernadette handed him a travel mug filled with coffee. She intended for him to take it on the Acela, but knew he'd have it done by the time he arrived at Union Station.

He took a sip and kissed her.

"Worried at all?" she said.

"I haven't enough sense to be worried," Ben said between sips. "If you mean, am I concerned about the variables that invariably come up during negotiations, let's say it's going to take a pretty stunning twist to catch me off guard."

"You pull this off," Bernadette said with a grin, "and all those politicos over there in China will be calling you something other than Chairman Stud."

"As long as I lose the nickname, not the reputation."

"Fine with me." They kissed again. "I should be there in time for our dinner with Li Xue."

"You're sure you don't want to come now? I could get you a seat."

"Too much to do. And you might be brilliant, but when you talk numbers it bores me to tears. Besides, I've got a couple of things to go over with Hector."

"Duty calls us both," Ben said as the motorcade pulled up to his house. He picked up his briefcase and Bernadette hoisted up his overnight bag and walked with him to the limousine. She handed it to the driver and gave Ben a final kiss.

"Go up there and make some history today."

"For you? Of course."

In a moment the motorcade was headed down the street with Bernadette still waving, knowing that her husband already had his nose in a newspaper. She turned and walked back to the house, having just enough time to pour herself a coffee and load up her own briefcase before her ride arrived.

She was just putting the lid on her coffee when there was a knock at the door. It was early for anyone to stop by, but it wasn't unheard of for Ben, with his head full of numbers, to have forgotten something and sent one of the chase personnel back to grab it.

Opening the door, she saw a man in grubby overalls with a clipboard in his gloved hand. On the street was the blue Aqua Blue van, its engine rattling.

"Sorry for the early hour," the man said. "We've got a drainage problem with the pool two houses down and we're going to have to turn the water off on the block for about two hours."

"That's fine," she said. "I'm leaving in a couple of—"

But the man raised his hand, something yellow at the end of it and Bernadette thought *Why is he pointing his drill at me*, and then there was a click and she felt something snag the cloth over her belly. Then a rattling sound, one she hadn't heard since her early days of training and her body went rigid and ceased to exist, as if her mind had been exiled to a distant part of the universe.

She knew she'd been tased, just like in training all those years ago, but was unable to do anything about it, not even speak, even though she was aware of her groaning and the sound of the coffee mug hitting the floor.

The man rushed forward and grabbed her before she could fall, another man behind her, picking up her legs, hustling her back down the hall, through the house with purpose like they knew the layout of the place.

They put her down on the floor by the door into the garage.

"Close the front door," said the first man.

She heard footsteps and the front door close. She tried to speak. It came out in a pathetic grunt and the man tased her again. Then he rolled her over and pulled her arms behind her back. He looped something over her wrists and another familiar sound as the zip tie tightened and clamped her wrists together.

Make them tight, pal, she thought. *The tighter the better.*

Footsteps returned and the first man said, "Tape her." Another familiar sound, tearing, and then a strip of duct tape clamped over her mouth. Then, over her head, a pillowcase. It was clingy and rough against her skin. *Straight out of the package from Walmart.*

The door opened. They picked her up and walked her into the garage, pausing as a finger punched buttons. The light in the garage came on, and then the garage door opened. She heard the gurgling of the Aqua Blue van as it approached, the sound intensifying as it pulled inside.

They began to move again and now she heard the rear doors of the van open. They manhandled her up and dropped her on the floor, slamming doors behind her. The driver's door opened and closed, and the van began to move. The first man, now driving, said, "Get the door." Bernadette heard the garage door close and a moment later someone climbed in on the passenger side.

"Perfect," said a second voice.

"Shut up," said the first, and the van eased down the driveway, turning left into the street and moving ahead at a leisurely pace as if nothing in the world was wrong.

Now Bernadette's thoughts were spinning. She still couldn't move, hurt terribly from being tased, twice, in doses stronger than she had experienced in escape and evasion training. But her mind still worked, was clear, remembering from experience that this was the worst thing about the experience. *Tasing would be much more pleasant if you lost consciousness.*

She knew she had to turn on her internal recorder, try and time the drive between turns, estimate speed, figure out their route. And in between process. All those familiar sounds. The rattling of the taser, the ripping of the duct tape. The gurgling of the van's engine, the Aqua Blue. *Probably a target of opportunity,* she thought, *just stole it somehow, and nobody in the neighborhood would know any better.*

That and the way they carried her into the garage to load her into the van. Had backed the van in. This had all been planned to the nth degree. Professionals. The only question was who had taken her.

But for now she had to keep that recorder running, keep her head clear. This was exactly what her escape and evasion teacher, Colonel Garrett, formerly of the SAS, had told her class on the first day. "There will always come a moment after your capture when you will feel regret. You will replay everything you missed, every hint you overlooked, every clue you misread. Don't do it. You can't afford it. The surest way to avoid that feeling is to follow the first and most important principal of escape and evasion. That is, not to get caught."

Well, I got caught, she thought as the van made a turn, another left. *I just hope I have some time later for regret.*

CHAPTER TWENTY-TWO

Hector Lopez walked out of his office and said, "Is Bernadette Coleman here yet?"

The woman temping for Bob Franks said, "Sorry, sir, I haven't seen her. I thought she was going to go straight to the conference room."

"We were to have a briefing before our meeting, and it's not like her to miss that. Has her detail checked in?"

"I'll give them a call. Probably caught up in traffic. It was bad out there this morning."

Lopez thanked her and walked to the conference room where George Steinway and Dianne Reynolds waited.

"Thank you for coming," Lopez said. "Bernadette should be here momentarily, so let's get started." He checked his watch. "In about fifteen minutes Ben will begin his meeting with Li Xue. I think we're all pretty confident about how this will turn out, but I want to put some contingencies into place. Even if things go well today, there are no guarantees how the news is going to be received in Beijing, let alone the rest of the world."

The door opened and the temp stepped in. "Excuse me, Mr. Director. Ms. Coleman's detail is on the line for you."

He nodded and picked up the phone. "Lopez."

Steinway and Reynolds watched as the Director's face froze. "I see," he said. A shadow passed over his eyes then he said it again. Then, "I understand. All available personnel on this, got it? When you're certain, call the FBI in. Complete cooperation with them. Understand? Complete. We need this resolved immediately and by the book."

Steinway stood as Lopez hung up the phone. "What happened, Hector?"

Lopez drew in a deep breath. "Bernadette is missing. It's possible she's been abducted."

Steinway threw his pen down.

"What happened?" said Dianne.

Lopez shook his head. "They don't know for sure. Her detail stopped to pick her up. She usually meets them, but she never came out. They went to the door, saw a broken cup on the floor, coffee all over, and still warm.

"So security went in and searched the house. Empty. Her purse and cell phone were on the kitchen table, along with a half-full coffee urn and a carton of half-and-half. Her briefcase was on the living room couch still locked and apparently hadn't been tampered with."

"So they weren't after intel," said Steinway.

"Other than that, it looked clean. They must've grabbed her between the time Ben left and her detail arrived. Narrow window of opportunity. Planned perfectly. Obviously, pros did this."

"And if they weren't after intel ...." Dianne drifted off, not wanting to finish the thought.

"Yeah. That scares the hell out of me," said Steinway.

"They must be trying to get to Ben," said Dianne. "Unless they were after him and settled for Bernadette."

"Perhaps," Lopez said. "But I wouldn't be so sure. She is a catch in her own right, especially since it is now widely known that she is helping out here. Between the two of them she has made far more enemies than he, particularly the kind prone to kidnapping."

"Unless they're deliberately holding Bernadette to spike the negotiations," said Dianne. "That would make it a twofer."

"But who?" said Steinway.

"Want a list?" said Lopez. Grabbing the phone, he punched in a number. "This is Lopez. I need Ben Coleman's cell phone bricked, and I need it done yesterday." He told them to get the number from his assistant and hung up.

"What are you doing?" Steinway said.

"Making sure they can't get through to Ben the most obvious way."

"He needs to know," said Dianne.

"Not from whoever this might be. And not by phone or text."

"He has a right to know."

"But it might put him on tilt for the negotiations," said Steinway.

"And then, it might not. He might use it as a card to play with Li. I am sure Li would be horrified."

"Or not," said Lopez. "Depending on how this came about."

"Still," said Dianne, "Ben should decide when and how to play the card."

"When is a lack of information ever a good thing?" said Steinway, thinking like the investor he was.

"Or the meeting could simply blow up," said Lopez. "This is why we compartmentalize intel, to minimize the chances of a black swan event."

"He would want to know," Dianne said. "Otherwise, when this is all over, he would have every right to be pissed about not being told. How would you feel if your spouse had been abducted and your closest colleagues, not to mention the United States government, hadn't bothered to tell you? If you were Ben, you would never trust the rest of us again."

"If the negotiations blow up, we are going to have much worse things to worry about," said Steinway. "And those things will not simply blow over."

"I think Ben will be angry but will get over it," Lopez said, "providing we get Bernadette back."

"But," said Dianne, "if something were to happen to her . . . ."

Lopez turned to Steinway. "George, you're the one closest to Ben and you have institutional interest in being there. You need to go to New York and tell him. We will keep you in the loop and if something goes amiss, we can let you know and you can then pass it on. I'll order a chopper to get you there asap. You can leave straight from here and land at the Thirtieth Street heliport. It's a short ride to the Met club from there."

"And when the meeting breaks, I give him the word privately?"

"That's the idea."

"The President needs to be in the loop on this," Dianne said. "I'll tell him."

"Keep this mum, folks, including your top people," Lopez said to them. "This is going to be a roller coaster."

"Better a roller coaster than a global financial crisis," said Steinway.

"Besides," said Dianne, "we may have Bernadette back before then."

"From your lips to God's ears," said Steinway.

¥ $ €

Ben chose the Metropolitan Club as the place to meet with Li. New York was a short train ride from New Haven, so Li could be with his family before their guided—and supervised—tour of America.

And the club seemed like neutral ground. It could have been the Federal Reserve Bank building in lower Manhattan, but that might look too much like the loser coming to the home turf of the winner. Negotiating in America provided enough of that. And the Met Club would accommodate Chinese security needs regarding safety and the absence of electronic surveillance as well as the needs of the Secret Service. Moreover, as a private club, it could exclude the press from entering, though they would be staked outside the entrance on Sixtieth Street.

Ben also liked the historical ironies. This was J.P. Morgan's Club. It wasn't quite Jekyll Island, where Morgan invited the movers and shakers of the time to negotiate the outlines of the Federal Reserve, but it was close enough. Morgan had been the private equivalent of America's central banker, even bailing out the U.S. government at one point. Morgan would definitely have approved of what Ben was about to do.

The club accommodated, with one of the function rooms on its second floor overlooking Fifth Avenue. It was sufficiently grand to suit the occasion and quite secure. As a member, Ben could rent the room at the concessionary member's rate. The club itself would have been happy to let him have it for free given the publicity and prestige of what was happening, but government ethics rules required that Ben pay. This

Ben didn't mind. It was a way he could create the fiction that this was a private meeting, which put less of a burden on producing an outcome. It gave Li added face as well.

He felt good about the prospect of what would come from the meeting. Every preparation had been made. Everything was in order. As his wife had said, it was time to make some history.

¥ $ €

Bernadette lay on the floor of a van trying to gather her wits. She was still smarting from having been tased. It had all happened so quickly. *No, that's an excuse*, she told herself. *The truth is, you've been out of fieldwork for too long and you've gotten sloppy, lazy, and weak.*

She reminded herself this self-flagellation was no more useful than self-pity. She had to focus and find a way out of her predicament.

She had been trying to keep track of the van's movements, but it was no good. The driver seemed to be making random turns and changing speed solely to confuse her sense of location.

That's a clue. He's a professional and knows I am too.

Cars were whizzing past on the driver's side and occasionally honking. He was driving slowly on a major thoroughfare, but which one? The Beltway? I-66? The Dulles toll road? Logic told her they were going to head west. Too much risk to head straight into D.C. Knowing where they were headed could be useful in the future, but now she had a more pressing issue.

The zip ties on her wrists were the first concern. Fortunately, she had gotten out of them during escape and evasion training and would get out of these as well. It was all a matter of timing. Well, timing and pain. The escape maneuver would hurt like hell.

She didn't have her mobile phone, purse, or briefcase, all of which had things in them she could use with some improvisation to free herself.

No, professionals would leave all that behind as they might contain ways to track her whereabouts.

The van made a sudden right turn amidst widespread honking. Bernadette rolled to the left, but something long and soft kept her from hitting the side. She pushed herself against it to figure out what it might be and felt something slide under her. A familiar sensation, then horror as she understood the reason for the familiarity. Ben was a sprawler when he slept, and she would occasionally roll over in bed and on top of his arm.

Another person.

She nudged at the body with the heel of one foot to see if she could get a response. There was none. She tried again and again until her heart finally sank. Her companion was not unconscious. He or she was dead. It was likely the original driver of the van.

Before she could roll away the van slowed and then pulled to a stop. From the way the sound reverberated, they were inside another building. The two men in the front got out of the van, opened the back doors, and hauled her out.

"Any problems?" said a third voice. Bernadette strained her ears. There was something familiar in those few words.

"According to plan."

"Then we'll stick with it. Take care of the van and wait at the safe house. I'll be in touch once I get the princess secured."

A chill went down Bernadette's spine. She didn't recognize the voice, but the words had a familiar brogue that sent her racing back through the years to her time working at MI6 on various IRA spinoffs.

Then she picked up another clue. The voice with the brogue said, "The princess is secured." *This is a kidnapping, for whatever reason. And I'm being transferred up the kidnapper's chain of command.*

Her thoughts were interrupted when she was hoisted up and placed in a small, cramped area. There was a rush of air and a loud clang.

I'm in the trunk of a car. And rid of my travel companion. Good enough.

The van's engine gurgled to life and departed. Then the car's engine fired.

"Don't worry, princess," the brogue shouted from the front. "You're in good hands now." The speaker cackled and put the car in motion.

All right, girl. This is it. You're the Red Ninja. Time to come up with a plan and see it through. You've been out of the field too long. It's time to see if you can bring all those unused muscles back to life.

¥ $ €

Ben Coleman met Li Xue in the grand hall on the first floor. Morgan had spared no expense in building it. The ceiling was the equivalent of three floors up. The walls were marble accented by gold leaf. The men ascended one side of the enormous staircases that flanked the east wall of the hall.

Li bowed slightly as he shook Ben's hand. "So this is how robber barons lived?" he asked with a smile as they walked up the stairs. The hall had that effect on most visitors, and many of those with a sense of history had had that same, precise thought.

"You have studied the history of the place," Ben said. "So you know my choice was not accidental or simply based on convenience."

"No. Given Morgan's historical role this really is the Central Banker's Club. I think your selection was most appropriate."

"I agree and am glad you feel that way." Ben gestured for Li to enter the room he had reserved. There was a table in the middle with chairs on opposite sides. But Li moved to one of the large lounge chairs next to the fireplace in the room.

"Ben, I think this is a conversation and not a negotiation. And to be frank, it might actually be quite a short one."

"I'm not sure I understand."

Li could hear the disappointment in his voice. "You mistake my meaning. It is not going to be short because we don't have a lot to talk about. It is going to be short because I think we are already close to being in the same place. When you told me about your meeting with Secretary Steinway here before the presidential election, and then heard your suggestion that we meet here, I began to do some very careful research regarding your views. It didn't take much to figure out where your mind is. You are going to make the same type of suggestion to me that you made to Steinway almost two years ago."

"How do you know about my meeting with Steinway?" Much to his dismay, Ben was completely unable to hide his surprise.

"You are married to the Red Ninja. Do you think we do not have similarly talented people in our country? In many ways, my good friend

Deng is very much like your wife. I regret that his nephew is not quite as talented. Far too rigid in his thinking."

The Chairman of the Federal Reserve was rarely floored. But Li Xue was being extraordinarily candid, so much so that he had to confess to himself that the conversation was proceeding down a branch that was not on his decision tree.

He said to Li, "I have advanced your thoughts regarding Mr. Deng to the highest levels and have a preliminary approval. He will get a pardon from the President, conditioned on not ever returning to the United States. That pardon will not be signed until we have concluded our agreement. Since you will be here, he will be remanded to your custody for the trip home.

"I must tell you how important that condition is. The President almost choked on the thought of pardoning someone who violated the privacy of his wife and was spying on his country. It was also hard on me for much the same reasons. By the way, my wife was the one who persuaded the President to go ahead. I hope that will prove satisfactory."

"I wouldn't be here if it was not. General Deng told me that there would be conditions, but your signal that you would elevate the issue was, in his words, very transparent.

"Obviously you understand the power dynamics now occurring in Beijing, or at least a key part of them. It was Deng who suggested my making this a personal favor on behalf of a friend and not some formal part of the negotiations. He was trying to send a signal to your wife, Director Lopez, and possibly even your president about what was going on. He even complimented your wife's expertise, saying she would be the one to deliver on his nephew's release."

"He did?" asked Ben.

"Oh, yes. The string of expletives he used to describe her was quite lengthy, as were the adjectives regarding what she and her father had done to China over the years. He concluded by saying, 'Finally, there is something she does that will not be a pain in our backside.' His choice of words in reference to that was somewhat more colorful.

"I must admit that I thought carefully about his motives in this. In my experience those in the intelligence business prefer deception to transparency. We central bankers tend to prefer transparency. It minimizes risk.

"This is a time to minimize risk if there ever was one, don't you think? By making things so transparent the chances of either side making a mistake are reduced. It is very important that you and your side not make a mistake right now for it would have a very tragic outcome."

"On that we certainly agree," Ben said. "There is a path forward that would minimize the risks to both sides. We need both the courage and the wisdom to take it."

"Ah, wisdom," said Li. "A very Chinese concept. Confucius. Sun Tzu. Courage is far more American. The history of China has always been cautious, aimed at protecting the established order, what we have. Think of the Great Wall. It was purely defensive. America, on the other hand, was born of change. Taking on the greatest empire in the west. Hardly defensive, and a real act of courage. So what we are seeking would appear to be a real paradox. Cautious, yet courageous. Wise, yet bold. Deeply steeped in historical experience, yet seemingly novel."

"Xue, that was a very wise analysis. And your very act of being here was courageous."

"Ben, I could say the same about you. Your decision to issue gold coins was very much the same. My choice of words was very deliberate. Cautious, courageous, wise, bold, deeply historical, and seemingly novel.

"So you can see the real reason why our conversation is likely to be short. You have already made the sale simply by putting the product you want to sell on the table.

"I read your speech on the flexible gold standard given almost a decade ago. It is too bad that the piece has not had better attention. It should have been in an academic journal, perhaps, but I suppose it could not be because it was too courageous and too novel. I believe the term you use in America is 'not politically correct.' We Chinese understand that perfectly well.

"For all their self-image of being open minded, academics tend to be quite closed to new ideas. And the use of gold is decidedly politically incorrect here in America in the academic community. I suppose it makes sense. After all, if you are an academic you almost certainly think that academics can manage monetary policy for the common good.

"They forget that all human beings have a preference for good news to happen sooner and bad news to happen later. It's pretty basic, isn't it? We central bankers call it the time preference for money. It is why we have an interest rate. People want money now, not later, and so you have to pay for the privilege. But if you can print it now, and have someone else pay for it later, that is all to the better."

"Xue, you are remarkably orthodox. I am surprised."

Li raised his eyebrows. "What surprises you, Ben? Chinese can't be orthodox? Or is it that members of the Communist Party can't be orthodox? Facts are facts. Or as Deng Xiaoping said, 'Does it matter whether a cat is black or white as long as it catches mice?' America's central bankers and Britain's central bankers all at least have had the pretense of being orthodox. But that hasn't stopped them from exploiting the time value of money in terms of printing it, now, has it?

"We Chinese are the same. Your talk on a flexible gold standard even referenced our experience during the Ming Dynasty with silver. It is human nature, is it not?" Li stopped, saying nothing, creating a long, pregnant pause. Ben intuited that this was a calculated pause, one that preceded the beginning of the actual negotiation.

Finally Li said, "Very well, then. Let us get down to business."

¥ $ €

For Bernadette the first order of business was distraction.

Important in magic, critical in espionage. Make your target think you're trying to do one thing while you've done something else right under his nose.

Bernadette started kicking against the inside of the trunk, trying to yell for help through the masking tape and pillowcase.

"Knock it off, princess," came the voice from the front. Yes, definitely an Irish accent. There was so much Bernadette wanted to do with that information, but her energy was needed elsewhere.

Exaggerating her sounds of struggle, she rolled from her back onto one side and pushed with her feet until her front was pushed against one wall of the trunk. She now had enough clearance to push her arms up as far as they would go from her back. It was rough going, as tight as her captors had made the zip tie against her wrists, but that was going to work to her advantage.

She slowly inhaled and held her breath and squinted her eyes to prepare for the pain. the cramped conditions were far from ideal, but she likely only had this one chance.

Bernadette rolled slightly, stretched her arms up against the ache from being tased as far as she could, and then slammed them down as hard as she could against her butt. There was a snap and her wrists separated, followed by a burning wave of pain down her hands. She kept making noise, kicking her feet and making muffled screams, no need to fake them this time.

"Stop it," shouted the voice, "or I'll come put a bullet in your kneecap."

Bernadette yanked the pillowcase from her head and eased the duct tape off her mouth, breathing until the pain subsided, excited because she had done it. She put the tape on the left sleeve of her blouse and the pillowcase in her pocket, then inched toward the trunk lid.

Most sedans had an escape cord to pull on the inside of the trunk with a glow in the dark tab to make it easy to find. She groped to find it, staring to find the pull, but there was none. This was either an older car, or the pull had been cut off.

No matter. There were other things she could do.

Bernadette reached up to one side and clawed at the inner paneling until it gave way, filling the trunk with a red glow from the rear taillights. Her eyes welcomed the light, eerie though it was. She reached and probed with her fingers until she found wires and then worked them until they pulled loose. The trunk went dark.

Keeping her movements slow, she shifted around and did the same to the lights on the other side.

Now one of two things would happen. Without taillights, the car could be rear-ended in which case she'd have to stay toward the body of the car and stay alert. The sound of screeching brakes would give her mere seconds to brace herself.

Or the lack of lights and a turn signal would invite a traffic stop from local law enforcement. She wasn't sure which one she preferred. In either case, she needed to be ready to make as much noise as possible. Fortunately, the trunks of automobiles typically had lots of things in them that could be used as noisemakers. And in a pinch, they could be used as something else as well.

¥ $ €

Li continued. "The yuan is now fifteen to the dollar. That will not work from China's point of view. With the dollar pegged at $400 to the gram, that would mean only 6,000 yuan to the gram. We would not have enough gold to turn into coins to cover the issues in our banking system. Of course, for full coverage we would need to have something closer to 15,000 yuan to the gram. I am sure that would be unacceptable to you, and it would be very inflationary for the Chinese economy."

"No disagreement so far," Ben said, waiting to see if it would go where he predicted.

"I to propose just 8,000 yuan to the gram. That would set the implied dollar exchange rate at twenty."

Ben kept a poker face. He had called it. Simple enough for him—it was the math that led one there if one had the responsibilities that Li had. But he had responsibilities as well.

"Xue," he said, "that is a thirty-three percent depreciation against the dollar at a time when most analyses would say the yuan is already undervalued."

"Those analyses are of course severely flawed, Ben. Though of course I knew you would say that. We need that kind of coverage of our bad bank debts in order to keep our banking system afloat."

"Xue, you left out one word. Perceived. All that matters is that your public perceives that your banks will stay afloat. There are many ways of doing that. In fact, you have already made a demand that is key to the credibility of your gold coins—foreign acceptance. And you have tasked me with helping you do that.

"Surely having the Chairman of the Federal Reserve make a pitch for your gold coins would help change perceptions in China as well. Even better, If the Japanese and the Koreans and Singaporeans and others buy your coins, it would ensure the perception that your coins represent a credible defense of your banking system. I doubt very much those countries would make such a purchase as a means of financing a major depreciation of the yuan, either against the dollar or any of their currencies as well. I believe you know that."

Li Xue took a deep breath. "It would seem that we have to solve a simultaneous equation and not just pick a price. You are correct that the key is going to be credibility and that foreign purchases would help provide that credibility. The lower the exchange rate, the more foreign purchases. So how do we maximize credibility with the right mix of foreign purchases and profit generated from yuan depreciation?"

"That is the nature of any business decision," Ben said. "You have to make a stab at it, take a guess at what will work in the market. You never know for sure until you produce the product and actually try and market it. That is what we did for our gold coins. We picked a substantial markup from the prevailing market price for gold—roughly one-third. In some ways that was probably too much. But our objective function really was to maintain monetary flexibility, just as yours is to establish credibility. The greater the differential, the more room the Fed has for future monetary expansion if needed before the gold coins constrain us. Given our uncertainty with regard to the current crisis, that credibility was essential."

"Ben, you are suggesting a very low depreciation figure for us because you have already grabbed most of the ability to mark up above the gold price and there would be a limit to our ability to go further. I guess they call that 'first mover advantage.' The first currency to adopt some form of gold-backing for its currency pockets most of the advantages. Followers-on get the crumbs. And sadly, China is a follower, not a first mover.

"The problem is that if the crumbs this follower is able to grab are too few, he will not be able to sell the program back in Beijing. Then the other side wins our internal power struggle, and if we do not have a mutually agreed upon solution, it moves the battle to a field of their choosing. That would be a tragedy for the world."

Ben thought for a moment. Then it hit him.

"Xue, you said earlier that we were lucky not to go through life simply having followed the natural order of things, but to have the opportunity of changing that order? Maybe we are underestimating how much we can change things."

"I also said caution is a virtue."

"When the Medici and other Florentine families introduced the florin it revolutionized trade in Europe and made a major contribution to the continental economic expansion. The key was that the Republic of Florence did what no one else had done—they kept the size, design, and gold content of the florin stable for 180 years. When people can count on a store of value, international commerce can expand rapidly. What if we make an agreement today that does that? One that introduces some monetary stability for each of our countries, and for global trade and commerce as well?

"You said that you needed more than crumbs in order to stabilize your banking system. Devaluation would give you crumbs. But real international recognition would give you credibility. Certainly, getting Japan and the other countries of East Asia to procure some of your coins, like they did ours, would help. But what country would give your coins the greatest amount of credibility, not just globally, but even among the people of China?"

Xue paused for a moment to think about where Ben was going. "I think I know where you are headed. But I dare not speak it out loud."

¥ $ €

The car had been going straight for a while, probably on a back road judging from the apparent lack of traffic. It could have been minutes; it could have been hours. Her sense of time and direction was totally gone from the initial twists and turns she had experienced in the van.

They made a left turn. Bernadette added it to her mental inventory, but she was starting to see this as a futile game. Escape and evasion had talked about that too. No matter how futile things seemed in the moment, keep focused. Everything depended on it.

Then there was a loud *squawk* from behind and her heart leapt. It was a siren, the short burst used to let you know that an officer was behind you and wanted you to pull over.

A muffled curse from up front and then, "Keep quiet, princess, or you'll be responsible for this cop's death."

Okay, think this through. How do you want to play this? Risk the cop's life by banging on the side? You know they've called in the plate number if they're making a stop—

She could hear the car door open. "Can I help you, officer?" said the man with the Irish accent.

A woman's voice. "Back in the car, sir. This is routine."

Bernadette decided. She grabbed the tire iron she had found and reared her arm back to start banging.

"Your taillights—"

Two shots. Bernadette screamed.

A hand slammed on the trunk. "You've been a bad girl, princess."

She rolled onto her back, tucking the tire iron beneath her.

Keys rattled and the trunk popped open. Bernadette squinted against the sudden influx of light.

"Her death is your fault." A hard face looked down at her, then gave a grudging smile. "You've been busy, I see." He picked up the pillowcase. "I'm sure you learned these tricks from those British bastards back at MI6. I would have been disappointed if you'd just laid there and cried, I suppose. Your reputation and all."

The man grabbed her under one arm and hauled her out of the trunk. "Guess I should thank you. We have a nice new ride now, with police radio and lights and sirens. We're going to fly now."

Bernadette's legs wanted to give when she stood, but she pushed against the weakness and took a step. She looked around, trying to drink the scene in. A small two-lane highway surrounded by trees and scrub. Western Virginia? Maryland? The sun not that high in the sky, not as much time had passed as she thought. A black woman in a uniform was crumpled, half on the road, beside the nondescript grey sedan she had just been pulled from.

The man clamped a hand on her shoulder and pushed her toward the police car and laughed. "What? You not going to tell me how I'll never get away with this? Don't I know who you are? Because I do know who you are."

She kept her mouth shut. That kind of banter, she knew, was the stuff of the movies. While being silent might keep him talking, he wouldn't divulge whatever was on his mind. He'd sooner put a bullet into her. Real life worked that way.

He pushed her around the open driver's door of the police car and against the side of the trunk. Looked down to open the rear passenger door and as he looked back up, she had the tire iron in her left hand and was swinging it at him with all her might.

¥ $ €

"The answer," said Ben, "is the United States of America. Suppose China and America jointly create the equivalent of the florin for the 21st century? Technically there would be two versions—yours and ours—but they could be considered interchangeable because the value of the gold content and the anti-counterfeiting microchip technology would be identical. The world's two largest economies would both be on a flexible gold standard but with a common medium of exchange as an anchor that both countries would recognize.

"The key to success would be that we hold some yuan-based gold coins, and you hold some dollar-based gold coins. My suggestion is that we set the number large enough that it would be quite impressive to the world, say $100 billion worth of our gold coins held by the People's Bank of China and 1.5 trillion yuan worth of your gold coins held by the Federal Reserve System. We would design it as a swap. It would be central bank to central bank with no net money changing hands, so technically the political authorities would not be involved. But, of course, they would have to approve.

"When we go to the other countries of the world and ask them to buy and hold some of these special gold coins, we will not be asking them to do something we ourselves would not have already done. There is no more effective sales pitch than 'I do it myself.'

"It would also send a powerful geopolitical signal about the permanence of the economic relationship between the world's two largest economies. We would be asking the countries of East Asia and the Pacific Basin to participate in the cornerstone of that relationship by buying these gold coins. Once it is widely accepted as the coin of the realm by the regions' central banks, demand from the public would quickly follow."

Li nodded slowly. "Yes. That is bold. But it very well might work. And such a new foundation for international trade cooperation might stabilize the Chinese monetary system and stabilize our economy as well.

"But—," he paused for emphasis. "The one thing in your description that was noticeable was that there was no devaluation of the yuan relative to the dollar—none at all."

"I actually think that is one of the keys to success of the whole plan," said Ben. "Our pricing of the coin at $400 per gram captured the monetary policy advantage of the establishment of the coin. As we said earlier, all that are left for further devaluations are crumbs. But implicitly the fifteen to one price meant that China, as the second-largest holder of gold that now can be converted into gold coins, has also captured a major piece of that first-mover advantage for itself.

"The reason the coin trades at a premium above the price of raw gold is the imprimatur of the issuing state and the guarantee of constant value. And what protects the imprimatur is the microchip that prevents counterfeiting. Otherwise anyone could mint the coins if they had the proper die to apply the stamp. In effect, what this deal offers China is that, other than America, you will be the only party to be able to use that microchip technology.

"See, the technology is not just the chip, but the capacity to read those chips as well. And that technology will be held under very careful control. The patents and the production capacity would probably be held by a government-sponsored enterprise. The details of Chinese involvement in that enterprise could be negotiated."

Li thought about this. "Relative to what our initial discussion involved," he said, "you are modifying the concept of technology transfer, basically keeping the technology to yourself. It is America's technology, so that is not crucial. You will really need our involvement in that enterprise, however, or I assure you China will find a way of producing its own. But that is minor.

"The real issue is the fifteen to one ratio. I understand your argument and it is not without merit. It will make the deal harder to sell. I suppose that will actually make the deal easier to sell in Washington, however.

"In return, you are offering China the credibility of the United States government in support of our gold coins. Done right, that is absolutely priceless. I will have to discuss that with my colleagues in Beijing, in particular how to do it right. But one thing that will be absolutely crucial to that is your personal involvement.

"You will personally have to come to Beijing to make the sale to the people of China. You may not know this, but you are viewed very favorably in Beijing, despite having bested us with your move on the gold coins. Your very generous comments about me at your press conference and showing a lack of animus toward China helped. And your intervention on behalf of Deng Fei, despite the fact that your own wife was his one of his targets, was considered very statesmanlike. Of course, to the public at large it is the prestige that comes with your title that is most important."

"Thank you, Xue. You flatter me too much. Meantime, the next step in this plan is for us to return to our respective capitals and get approval. But before then we must go downstairs to the courtyard and make a joint statement to the assembled reporters. We should say nothing in detail, but smile, shake hands, and send the world a signal that the crisis is ebbing."

"I like that idea very much," said Li. "There are some key words I will be using that will signal my colleagues in Beijing that I think we have success. It may start the process moving there in a way that will resolve the conflict."

"Excellent," said Ben. "But now I need a personal favor of you. I'd like you to personally buy three of your own gold coins and give them to me as gifts for others. Two of those might include a personal note with each. I will explain later."

"Very well," said Li.

"One more thing," Ben said. "After our announcement, I am taking you to dinner at a restaurant with the most spectacular view in New

York—upstairs here at the Metropolitan Club. And I have a second surprise for you there. Bernadette will be there, and she has used her considerable skills to arrange for Baozhai to join us."

Xue looked shocked. "I have always wanted to meet the very famous Mrs. Coleman. She is legendary in China."

"For the sake of peace in my house, please don't tell her that," Ben said. After they laughed, he continued, rising from his chair. "Come on, Xue. Let's go downstairs and change the world."

Together they descended the stairs to video lights, camera flashes, and a chorus of questions from the gathered gaggle of reporters.

¥ $ €

She wanted to crush his nose. All those nerve endings and pain receptors, it would have blinded him with tears. But he had seen the swing coming and started to duck.

Still, the tire iron caught him in the side of the head and spun it to one side. He fell back into the car but quickly stood, his right arm reaching down and behind him.

That's where the gun is, she realized.

Now grabbing the iron with both hands, Bernadette brought it down hard on his right collarbone and felt it give when she connected. He smacked her with his left hand and her face caught fire. She took a step back. He tried to raise the gun in his right hand but he shouted in pain. His arm dropped and the gun clattered to the asphalt.

Bernadette came in with another two-handed swing and he caught the iron with his left hand and wrenched it from her grip. But he couldn't keep a grip on it and it bounced off the road and into the scrub. She balled her fist and aimed a punch at his broken collarbone, but his left hand came up for a block and then clamped around her throat.

She twisted and aimed her heel at the base of his foot but he pushed her away, fingers tightening on her neck. Both her hands came up to tear it away but it wouldn't budge. Tried kicking backwards but he matched her movement, keeping his balance.

Phosphors of light began dancing in the center of her vision. She twisted at his arm, tried to sink her nails into his skin, but her strength was fading. Tried to blink some vision back into her eyes but now her head was spinning, her strength fading. Then she was falling backwards.

It felt like she was gone for a million years, but when her vision returned, she was lying on the ground, the man standing above her, digging in his pocket with his left hand. She pushed with her hands to sit up but couldn't rise.

The hand came out of the pocket with something long. He flicked it and a long blade leapt out, glinting in the sunlight. The man's torn and bloodied face managed a smile, and he took a halting step toward her.

An explosion.

Bernadette winced, her ears ringing.

The man took another step.

Another explosion, this one seeming far away against the noise in her ears.

A burst of red appeared on the man's left thigh and the leg went out from under him. He fell backwards onto the asphalt and was still.

Bernadette managed to sit up and look around. The officer was laying on her side aiming a pistol, the muzzle trembling.

Adrenalin surged through her and she crawled over to the man. His left hand moved across on the asphalt, groping for the knife. A finger touched the blade and she knocked it out of the way.

"Who are you?" she shouted, traces of her long-suppressed Irish accent coming to the surface. "Who are you, you piece of shite?"

The man laughed. "You'll never know. I'm done."

"Like hell you are."

She grabbed his belt and undid it, him groaning pain as she pulled it from his waist. She wrapped it around his left thigh above the wound and cinched it tight, causing him to scream. When she finished, she could hear sirens in the distance.

"You lay there and suffer until they get here."

She rose, and in a wobbling gait, walked to the fallen officer, who was now lying on her back. A silver nameplate below the right shoulder said EVANS.

"Officer Evans," she said. "Thank you."

"Deputy," she said, managing a smile. "I called in. They're coming."

"That was a perfect shot," Bernadette said. "I needed that bastard alive."

The deputy tried to smile. "Wasn't aiming for his leg." She started to gasp for air, and Bernadette put a hand on the woman's chest. It came away bloody.

"They're near. What do you need?"

"I'm okay. Vest saved me."

"You're bleeding."

Deputy Evans shook her head. "Can't be."

Bernadette looked down at her hands. They were covered in blood, as was her blouse.

"Oh, my," she said.

And then the adrenaline was gone and the shock of it all caught up with her, her eyes rolled into the back of her head, and she collapsed.

¥ $ €

Ben had little use for the media once the work was done. It was part of the job. He and Li were heroes, but they could not act as such. He gave all credit to President Turner and Li. Li applauded the wisdom of the Politburo with thanks to his good friend Ben. The mob of reporters pressed forward, wanting their own opportunity for a moment of fame by asking a question up close.

Ben peered through the crowd of reporters searching for Bernadette. Her skill at being invisible was what made her cover as a wedding planner credible. More important was one of her MI6 skills—extraction. She would know how to get him the hell out of here.

Guess she's running late. I'll have to give Lopez a hard time. Then he felt a hand on his shoulder.

"George," he said, turning. "What are you doing here? Come to confer with the rabble?"

"We have to talk," said Steinway.

CHAPTER TWENTY-THREE

"So how are those unused muscles of yours?"

Bernadette looked up when she saw Ben walk through the door, a shopping bag in his hand. A smile came across her face. "They still work, but my body aches from head to toe. Shouldn't you be somewhere, darling? You know, saving the world . . . ."

"As far as I'm concerned the world isn't worth saving without you in it." Ben leaned into the hospital bed and kissed Bernadette on the cheek. She responded by moving her lips to greet his.

"If that's the case then a peck on the cheek simply won't do. But don't get too frisky."

"That wasn't even on my agenda," Ben said. "They told me you were a bloody mess when they found you."

She raised her arms to reveal bandages on both wrists. "I got cut up when I broke out of the zip ties. Didn't do it quite right. No big shakes."

"And passing out in the deputy's lap?"

"My goodness, you seem to know more about what shape I was in than I do. How did you find out?"

"Steinway told me as I was leaving the meeting with Li. Lopez was keeping him updated."

"Should have known my fellow spooks would be involved. But I was okay, really. Just the stress of everything, and I hadn't realized what a mess I was until it was all over."

"Still, I was worried sick. The President had sent Steinway up on Marine One and I hitched a ride back."

"Well, I got a helicopter ride too," she said with just a touch of sarcasm.

"And you wouldn't get in until they had the sheriff's deputy on board with you. I heard that too."

"I couldn't just leave her there. She saved my life. Getting hit with a bullet close up even with a vest on is rough stuff—can break a rib or do damage to internal organs. We were in the middle of nowhere a good hour from Charles Town. Haven't you ever heard of not leaving your wounded behind?"

Ben grimaced and reminded himself never to bring up that subject again, even in jest as had been his intent. Bernadette caught the look and decided she had gone too far. "Besides, what good is being married to the man who had just saved the world if you can't throw your weight around?"

Glad to be let off the hook, Ben took the olive branch and ran with it. "It seems I am the one who should be saying that about you. Marine One was sent because of you, not me. The President would have had me take the Acela if not for you. And when I took his call on the chopper his first words weren't, 'Thank you.' They were, 'How is Bernadette? Tell her Cynthia will be over tomorrow to check on her.' Then I got, 'Oh, by the way, nice job.'"

Bernadette propped herself up as best she could and motioned for another kiss. This one was much longer with more than a touch of passion in it. "Ben, you are my knight in shining armor who went out and slayed the dragon and saved the world in the process. Never forget that."

"Well, you're not so bad at slaying dragons yourself. That bastard who kidnapped you has a broken collarbone, a cracked femur, and a good array of bruises. His left eye is completely swollen shut. Nice work. Remind me not to piss you off ever again."

She glared at him. "Ben, as you well know when you piss me off, I use my training in psychological torture, not my martial arts skills. But I have you housebroken so you needn't worry. So what do they know about the bastard?"

"They did get a fake ID from him. So they used retinal scans to identify him. An arms runner out of Ireland. Here illegally, of course. Fake passport, too, a ton of priors under a variety of fake names. Just a very accomplished scumbag. He's not talking, but they've rounded up a number of his known associates and Lopez is pretty confident that the FBI will break one of them."

Bernadette had her doubts. As Britain had learned over three decades, IRA loyalists were almost impossible to break. Moreover, like any good operation, information was highly compartmentalized. Even if one of the underlings broke, he likely wouldn't know much. "Does this bastard have a name?"

"Sean O'Malley."

Her eyes narrowed. "That would make sense in the motive department. Back in Ireland, Father had dealings with a Patrick O'Malley and I was involved a bit. He'd brought his favorite grandson, Sean, into the business. It could be him. O'Malley is a common name, and this Sean was just a kid at the time. Patrick had him driving lorries and acting as a bag man. We took Patrick down, so this could be Sean's revenge. But he waited long enough. And why now? Unless there's something bigger at play—"

"Enough," Ben said. "You're making me exhausted just listening to you. We'll have plenty of time later for the postmortem."

"Well," Bernadette said, "there is one more thing. Something I feel I should keep from you, but I can't. Not really."

He gave her a concerned look. "Yes?"

"Edith Spensley called me a few minutes ago."

"Nice trick, since your cell is still at the house."

"She called on the land line." She gestured toward the phone on the bedside tray.

"How in hell did she find out you were here?" Ben said. "I barely knew myself."

"The woman is a legend," Bernadette said. "We forget how resourceful she is."

"So," Ben said, "she was calling with wishes for a speedy recovery?"

"Ostensibly. With a bit of gossip from that side of the pond. You remember Doris Billingsley?"

"The head of MI6?" Ben scowled. "I wish I didn't."

"Me too. Edith told me, 'that old bag'—her words, not mine—'is on her last legs.' Apparently she has alienated most of the cabinet involved in national security matters as well as many in the opposition. If the current government wins the next general election, and polling is showing it going that way, she will be out, and the job will open up."

"Well, you know how Edith likes to keep her fingers in different pies."

"The master arranger," Ben said.

Bernadette nodded. "Her latest arrangement is spreading a new mantra with her friends in MI6. 'We had the best, so why not get the best back?'"

Ben sat on the side of her bed. "Does that mean what I think it means?"

"She wants to arrange for my return to Britain."

"As the head of MI6?" He smiled. "Your dream job. Too soon for congratulations?"

Bernadette sighed. "I don't know. You've got so damn much on your plate, and this is the last thing in the world you need to think about right now."

"Things will ease up once the coins launch."

"I just don't know."

Ben shifted close and took her in his arms. "You want this, Bernadette. I can tell."

"It goes beyond want. It's like my father raised me to step into that position."

"You know I'm not going to say no to you if they make the offer."

"That's going to complicate things even more."

"Well," Ben said, "that's why God made transatlantic flights between New York and London."

Bernadette shrugged. "I'm not sure I'd be up for a long-distance marriage and frankly, I'm not sure you would be either."

"You're forgetting one thing, darling. I'm not going to be Chairman of the Fed forever. I was happy living in London once, and I'll thrive with you there."

She squeezed him, not saying anything.

"Look," he said. "There's an old saying in Washington—never turn down a job you haven't been offered. And there's a corollary. Never plan on how to take a job you haven't been offered. So much has yet to happen. You never know what the internal politics of the next cabinet is going to look like.

"This worry about something that may never come to pass is not going to help you recover at all. My advice is to let it go. Your recovery is priority one. I'm sure if it comes up, it will happen at the right time. And the right time certainly isn't now."

She held him tighter. "Thank you. You always seem to know what to say."

"Most of the time," Ben said. He loosened his hold on her and sat up, putting the shopping bag in Bernadette's lap. "You need to change for the trip home."

"This is perfect," she said, pulling clothes from the bag. "How did you know?" She smiled, then gave Ben a suspicious look. "Since when do you voluntarily set foot in Nordstrom?"

"I didn't. Peggy figured your old clothes wouldn't be fit to wear, so she called them with your sizes and color preferences and had an aide waiting to meet me when I got here."

"Since when does Peggy know my sizes and preferences?"

Ben grinned. "Since I told her part of her job was to make me look good. Now come on, get dressed. It's time to go home."

¥ $ €

Li Xue landed in Beijing fifteen hours later with two letters in hand and Deng Fei, who wore an orange jumpsuit and irons on his hands and legs. Though Fei would be turned over to Chinese security upon landing, the extreme dress was in deference to Chairman Coleman. The Chairman of the American Fed was now well thought of in China, and it wouldn't have done to let Deng Fei board the plane without looking like the criminal he was in the U.S.

Besides, the American president had hinted that he wanted to "make that son-of-a-bitch as uncomfortable as possible for as long as possible." He had wanted to hold him until Chairman Coleman came to China for the launch of the new coinage. So orange and irons it was, though Fei would keep some face—they would allow him to change into his street clothes before deplaning in Beijing.

Li ordered his driver to take him straight to Deng Wenxi's office and presented the letters to him. Li had briefed Deng already about the proposed monetary policy arrangements from the plane as well as his nephew's status. To his surprise, Deng dismissed the news of his nephew as if it were of secondary importance.

He uncharacteristically rose from his desk and walked over to shake Li's hand as soon as he walked in the door. It was a two-fisted hand-shake indicating extreme warmth and friendship. Li knew that Deng was incapable of either emotion, so something was up.

"Comrade Li. Let me congratulate you on your triumphant trip to the United States. We have scheduled a live interview with China Broadcasting for you for tomorrow. The stories of your brilliant nego-tiation have been leading the news for the last twenty-four hours. You are a national hero.

"You, who demanded and got a personal letter from the president of the United States assuring us of their goodwill. You have produced a plan to guarantee People's Money is safe in the Chinese banking system. And you got the Chairman of the Federal Reserve to come here personally and attest to the safety of our banks. You were the one who single-handedly demanded that the Americans purchase $100 billion of our new gold coins."

Even in the surreal world of politics in a one-party dictatorship, the turnaround in his status seemed more than a little bizarre to Li. "Does this mean that the Politburo has approved the plan I described?"

Deng's look changed. "That involves a related matter of some deli-cacy that we must discuss, Comrade."

"General Deng, we are past the stage of negotiation with the United States. Our new currency is written in stone."

"Not the currency," said Deng. "The Politburo itself. With the new changes to our economy that the new currency will bring, it has surfaced that there has been widespread corruption among high-ranking Party officials in the Politburo. Those of us still loyal to China are making plans to have them all arrested, but it was important to have you here before we did."

Li felt his stomach plunge. Even with what he currently knew about the General, if he were to be arrested—

"Do not look so concerned, Comrade Li. Two days ago the Politburo decided to make you its twenty-fifth member in light of your service. You have the gratitude of our nation.

"As to the arrests to be made, the Politburo will be dropped in size from twenty-five to nine. We need to install people of vision who are loyal to China, and not the corrupting influences of the West." Deng proceeded to rattle off the names of those who would be joining. Among them was a fellow technocrat, a longtime friend of Li's. Two were close associates of Deng in the military and the other four were senior military officers who had been among those opposing escalation in relations with America. "Do you expect any problems getting your plan through this new Politburo, Comrade?"

"No, General. Your choices are superb ones. And I am most grateful that you would consider me worthy of being a member. I am happy to serve China. My presence would certainly ease the financial transition. There is a lot to do."

Deng smiled. Li would get his plan approved but Deng would control the Politburo. "As to the downsizing, the arrests will be made swiftly and without warning. But to prevent panic among the people, we must have the new Politburo in place to assure a smooth transition."

"General Deng, you have been most thorough." Li had more to say to Deng, but he needed a little time to process this new information about the Politburo. Besides, he was not about to call him Comrade yet. He decided to shift gears to buy himself some thinking time. "But I have concerns still about the safety of my family as well."

"As a member of the Politburo," Deng said, "you will have the best security available to both yourself and your family. I would be horrified if anything happened to any of you, and since I have access to the best in security, I will give very firm instructions to keep you all safe."

"I am sure you will. But as a member of the Politburo I would also have the privilege of directing security in situations like this. So from this point on the security detail reports to me and to my wife. Are we clear?"

"Comrade Li, you do not seem to trust me despite my complete support for your new monetary policy initiative."

There was the opening he was looking for. His thoughts now in order, Li said, "General Deng, I am not the only one who has been busy doing things in America this last week."

Deng put on a puzzled look. "I'm not sure what you mean."

"The dinner that my wife and I were supposed to have with Chairman Coleman and his lovely wife was abruptly canceled after Mrs. Coleman was kidnapped."

"Oh, yes. Most unfortunate. I received a memo about the incident a few hours ago. It certainly does not speak well of the level of security America provides its top people."

"Deng Wenxi." Li deliberately dropped all honorifics in addressing the man before him. "You did not need a memorandum to inform you of Bernadette Coleman's abduction, did you?"

Deng was shocked. In part it was the insulting nature by which he had been addressed, but his real worry was what Li might know. "Comrade. I am not sure what you mean. The memo I received said that it was the work of the Irish Republican Army. It seems that the Red Ninja has made a world full of people angry with her. Though I will admit she is not my favorite person—"

Li cut him off. "Let's cut the bullshit, Comrade Deng. Now that we are going to be comrades there is no room for that kind of lie telling between us. You have boasted of your reach, but you failed to recognize that I have reach as well. I know the man who abducted her was Sean O'Malley, a former member of the IRA. He is now an arms dealer with a very diversified client base. You have been one of his key suppliers throughout his career."

"I have no idea what you are talking about," replied Deng.

"Oh, but you do, Comrade General. I have the web traffic to prove it. And I know a little bit about your blackjack side bet habits. You have a love of capturing queens." Li studied the look on Deng's face. "Don't worry, Comrade General. The Americans have no idea. At least not now—"

"I suspect they never will, Comrade Governor." The sarcasm was evident in Deng's voice. "Especially not with your lovely wife and daughter in that country."

"That is where you're wrong, General. If anything were to happen to them, then the evidence that I have will be delivered to Chairman Coleman. Physically it already has. He just doesn't know the encryption code or the contents of the zip drive. But he knows where to find it in the event anything happens to me or my family. He and I have developed a high level of trust. He will not breach the confidentiality prematurely. He has too much at stake to do it. And I will not lift a finger. But if my fingers for some reason cannot be lifted ... he will know what to do."

Deng went back to the chair behind his desk and sat. It was a play for time. But his mind sensed that he was defeated. He could not believe that Li had him. But why take the chance over such a trivial matter? "You are absolutely correct, Comrade. Any member of the Politburo has the right to control his own security detail. And if you wish the same for your family then who am I to stand in your way?"

"Thank you, Comrade. I knew you would understand. Now there is one other issue I would like to discuss."

Deng looked at him quizzically.

"I agree that a new Politburo is of critical importance at this juncture. But we need far more technocratic talent than you proposed on your current roster. They have diverse expertise in economic and social management. You have selected several fine members of the military, but they are overrepresented relative to China's most pressing needs. They know very little about technocratic management. A balanced coalition of technocrats and those with military experience seems ideal. I believe the following individuals have those needed skills." Li began ticking off a list of six names, counting them on his fingers as he went.

Deng did the math. They were all longtime allies of Li's. This would give him an upper hand within the Politburo. *What an uppity bastard.*

He chose to negotiate. "Sorry, Feng and Shen will not fit in well."

"Comrade, there are many things that might not fit in well with your plans. Or be in the best interests of China, such as exposure of your links to O'Malley. Or your responsibility for ordering the kidnapping of the wife of the Chairman of the Federal Reserve, a man we are counting on to save China economically. The evidence I have suggests that you were going to have her killed, this woman who is a trusted adviser to the head of the CIA and the best friend of the First Lady of the United States. Even if what I have does not definitively prove it, how will this be received with our new partners in prosperity?"

Deng had never seen this side of Li's personality before. Knowing he was cornered, he assumed a rigid military posture. "Very well, Comrade. If you feel that a more technocratic Politburo is necessary for China's success, then who am I to stand in the way? We obviously both care about China first and foremost."

¥ $ €

Nothing could have prepared Ben for the reception he got in Beijing. There was the red carpet with Governor Li. Other officials waited at the bottom of the staircase to shake his hand and thank him for coming. Li insisted that Ben ride with him in his limo to the central bank. "It will give us a chance to talk."

As they drove Ben said, "It is also giving you a chance to show off."

Li smiled. "I have learned a new skill. Organizing the equivalent of a state summit."

On every lamppost along the road there were small Chinese and American flags flying side by side. Every overpass had a banner in Mandarin and English of the agreed upon slogan: *China and America: Partners in Prosperity.*

By the time the road turned from a super-highway into a broad city street, crowds were forming along the route. At first they were in small bunches. Then the entire street was lined with a single row of citizens, most holding flags, some holding banners. When they were within half a mile of the Central Bank the crowds were clogging the sidewalks four and five deep. Everyone in the crowd was clapping.

"What did you do?" Ben said. "Give everyone the day off?"

"Actually, no. But we did provide the likely schedule of the motorcade to both the citizens and the businesses. Almost all the businesses encouraged their employees to take an extended lunch hour. You are right, I am showing off. I do hope you are impressed. This is how much your idea means to me and to China."

"It was your idea too," said Ben.

"No. Remember at the Metropolitan Club? All I said was that I read your mind and your past speeches and knew where you were headed. This is all Ben Coleman."

"Please don't say that in public. This is President Turner's plan. As they say in Washington, you can only get things done if you don't care who gets the credit. I am sure the same principle applies here."

Li said, "In Beijing we get this done giving you the credit for delivering America. You brought the American president along and you are giving your imprimatur to China's new currency. If we didn't have you, we would be bickering among ourselves as to who to give the credit to."

The entire plaza in front of the People's Bank headquarters was packed with throngs of people. All were cheering wildly and waving American and Chinese flags. Across the circular portico that shielded arriving cars from the elements hung a massive version of the *Partners in Prosperity* banner, at least twenty feet high, the Mandarin about three times as high as the English.

The massive entrance hall was packed as well. At the front sat a raised dais with a table and two chairs. Microphones were placed at each chair. In front of the dais stood the press with its bank of cameras. The room thundered with applause as Ben and Li ascended the stairs to the dais. Both men acknowledged the crowd and then took their seats. Ben noticed most of the people in the hall wore earpieces, which meant that simultaneous translation would be taking place.

Li's talk was about his close working relationship with Chairman Coleman. What a brilliant and thoughtful man Chairman Coleman was. How he and Chairman Coleman had come up with this plan to have both countries launch gold coins. On and on. Ben did not bother with the earpiece. He knew a smattering of Mandarin and besides, the name Coleman was used over and over. Not wearing an earpiece was a way of encouraging the people watching to overestimate his fondness of China. This, like his now-famous nickname, was one of those times when overestimation easily trumped the advantages of being underestimated.

He heard his full name and Li turned to face him. He rose and the entire hall delivered a standing ovation. *Game time*, he thought, and began to speak, giving pause between sentences for the translators to keep up.

"Thank you so much, my good friend. Your comments were far too generous. If credit is to be assigned for this momentous agreement, then it should go to Li Xue. His sage wisdom and desire to produce an outcome that was in China's best interest guided us away from a course that would have led to disaster for China and for the world." Ben turned and applauded Li and again the entire room rose to its feet in a long, standing ovation.

"Thanks to his efforts, the people of China will now be able to put their money in the banks with complete confidence that it is sound." Ben paused for applause.

"The poor and the elderly here in China will no longer have to worry about rampant inflation destroying their ability to make ends meet." More applause.

"Investors in China can have renewed confidence in their ability to successfully make a profit and workers will find jobs plentiful and wages rising." Another standing ovation.

"This is also important for the world. Not only for the global economy, but for global peace. America and China will now be working together. As the banner says above the entrance, 'China and America, Partners in Prosperity.'"

Wild applause followed with repeated chanting, "Partners in Prosperity."

With help from Bernadette, Ben had memorized the last sentence of his speech in Mandarin. "Fellow citizens of planet Earth, today we usher in a new era of peace and prosperity for all mankind."

This time Li rose to his feet and shook Ben's hand. Then both men embraced in a hug.

Two men came on stage, each carrying a leather-bound document holder containing the agreement for the swap of gold coins. The document was solemnly presented to each man to sign. Then they were switched for the matching signatures. After Li and Ben had each signed both documents, they closed the document holder, shook hands, and exchanged holders once more. The room broke out in applause and more chants of "Partners in Prosperity." The two men descended the stairs from the dais as the chanting continued.

"That went well," said Li.

"I hope it will go as well this evening at dinner," said Ben.

"I am quite confident that it will."

¥ $ €

Ben and the ambassador got out of the elevator at the top floor of the Party headquarters.

"Never been here before," said the ambassador. "I guess I need to accompany a world celebrity to make the cut." He smiled to show he spoke without malice.

Ben saw General Deng approaching them, accompanied by his nephew, Deng Fei. The younger man wore a cheap suit and no tie. Ben could barely hide his shock. Then he saw Li standing off to the side but within listening distance and with a clear view of the proceedings. General Deng stopped about two feet away from Ben and extended his hand. Suppressing his visceral dislike for the man, Ben grabbed it and shook.

Then the general grunted and Deng Fei fell to one knee. His head was bowed, and his hands crossed over the other knee. Ben could understand the General's brief phrase to his nephew. "You may speak."

Deng Fei spoke perfect English, though this time it was obviously rehearsed. "Most noble and distinguished Chairman. I humbly beseech your forgiveness for my behavior in your country. Truly, I never meant any harm to your wife or to the First Lady. I beg your forgiveness and ask that you will convey my deepest apologies to both of them as well."

Out of the corner of his eye Ben spotted Li shooting video of the scene with his iPhone.

General Deng motioned to his nephew, telling him to translate as he spoke. "My nephew is a good man, Mr. Chairman. But he had the easy life like so many in his generation. The public calls them 'the Princes' because everything they have is due to family. He never had to learn humility. Nor has he ever had to face a worthy adversary. He obviously was bested by your most accomplished wife. His arrogance made him careless. And as a result, he embarrassed himself, his family, and China."

Ben thought how humiliating it must be for Deng Fei to have to translate this string of insults from his uncle. On bended knee and to a Westerner much less. China had always been a face-based culture using shame quite liberally as a disciplinary tool.

Deng continued with the humility. "I am actually grateful to you and your country for teaching him a lesson. Li will tell you that once I received his letter and the one from your president, I thought I might not have minded some slightly harsher treatment. I hope you will convey my sentiments to your wife, the President, and the First Lady." General Deng extended his hand again.

Ignoring the nephew as Deng had, and using him merely as a translator, Ben said, "General Deng. I will be happy to convey your sentiments to all concerned. As you know your nephew's pardon is conditioned on him never returning to America. Should he ever return I can assure you that the President will make sure that his next visit to one of our prisons will be more memorable, and if the President is feeling generous toward me, he may let me beat the crap out of him before he goes there."

Deng said through his nephew, "If he is that careless again, I will be happy to toss a coin with you on who gets to beat the crap out of him first."

General Deng grunted again, "You may rise." Deng Fei did so, his head still down, and backed away from the three as a servant would. In a moment he had disappeared into an elevator while his uncle moved on to another circle of attendees.

Li approached, saying, "I told you that I was confident the night would go well. I hope that this humiliation of Deng Fei helps convey the depth of my gratitude." He handed Ben the cell phone he had used to record the interaction. "I got this just for this occasion so that you might take it with you without our having to pass on this information in a way that all of the intelligence agencies in the world see." But Li knew that all the right people would see it. He was counting on it.

¥ $ €

Ben headed straight home after his flight landed in D.C. He'd had a few drinks on the plane and then promptly slept for almost seven hours. He knew he was about to be debriefed by the best and in a very intimate way. The last thing he wanted to do was fall asleep during the debriefing.

"The conquering hero," came from the living room as Ben opened the door. That was quickly followed by the kind of kiss welcoming heroes are supposed to get on their homecoming. "The media coverage here has been extremely favorable. You wowed them. The cognoscenti are all calling you a man who bridged a great cultural divide."

Ben peeled himself from Bernadette long enough to take a theatrical bow. "So what does a conquering hero have to do to get sex around here?"

Bernadette starting unbuttoning Ben's shirt. "I guess that my Chairman Stud has even more energy than I thought he would after such a long flight." Bernadette unbuckled his belt and unclasped his trousers.

"Do you mind if we continue this conversation upstairs?" Ben grasped his pants to hold them up and proceeded toward the stairs. "We have a lot to talk about."

Bernadette followed Ben up the stairs but more slowly. She was still a bit sore, but certainly not enough to forgo the home coming celebration. Then she noticed that he had left his luggage by the door. *It can wait I suppose*, she thought.

By the time she got to the bedroom Ben was in his boxer briefs, lying on the bed. He held a cell phone in his hand, but it didn't look like his.

When he showed her video of Deng Fei's apology, Bernadette grabbed the phone, turned it off, and hurried to her dresser. She pulled out a leaded case that blocked all wireless access to the phone. "Who gave you this?"

"Li. He was the one who shot the video."

"I love it, but that might have not been his sole purpose in giving you the phone. You never know. He doubtless wanted you to show it around." She put the phone into the case and clicked it shut. "Let me run into the office for a bit tomorrow and get the phone checked, have the video downloaded in a secure way. We will want copies to pass around tomorrow night."

"No. Whatever it is. I need a break."

"Yes, but not tomorrow," Bernadette insisted. "It's dinner at the White House. In the State Dining Room, no less. All the people who were involved in the victory you just consummated. That includes the two young men who got the goods on General Deng. They are being honored. As for you, Chairman Coleman, you are ordered to stay home all day tomorrow until it is time to go to the dinner."

"Ordered by whom?" asked Ben.

"Well. Let's start with Peggy. Then there's me. Then there is Cynthia. And lastly, there is the president of the United States. Any more questions?"

"I know when I am beaten. Hope we can start our own celebration sooner than tomorrow night. Like now?"

"Absolutely."

Bernadette pulled off her outer garments and landed right on top of Ben. "I love you, Ben Coleman." That ended the oral communication for the evening until Ben fell asleep quite exhausted.

¥ $ €

Bob Franks and Tom Butler rode to the dinner with Director Lopez. It made clearance at the White House easier. Hector briefed the two young men on the way. "Gentlemen, here's the protocol. The President and the First Lady will both imply that it is okay to call them by their first name, but it isn't. It is *always* Mr. President and Mrs. Turner. In fact, you should address the other attendees by their title until they invite you to be on a first-name basis. Then it is okay, and you should honor their request."

"Roger that," Bob said.

"I should also let you know that everything that happens tonight is classified. I mean it. For the record, tonight never happened. I told you at the outset there would be no medals and no ticker tape parade to honor your heroism. This dinner and a meeting with the President are all the reward you will get. Your exploits are to remain highly classified, though everyone tonight has clearance and if asked, you should feel free to speak to them if you want."

"This is honor enough, sir." Bob said it first, but Tom felt the same way.

The three were waved into the Oval to find the President, Secretary Reynolds, and a White House photographer already there, snapping pictures as they entered. The President came forward to meet them and shook Bob's and Tom's hands with eagerness.

"Gentlemen, I can't tell you how honored I am to meet you. It is rare in Washington to meet genuine heroes. And you two are the real thing. On behalf of a grateful nation, I want to thank you for your service."

"Mr. President, the honor is ours."

"Now let's take get some official photographs."

When the President said photos, he meant it. There was a pose with each of them shaking hands with the President in front of the Resolute Desk. There was one with the President in the middle with Bob on one side and Tom on the other. Then one with Bob in the middle flanked by the President and Lopez and one with Tom in the middle flanked by the President and Secretary Reynolds. Finally, there was one with all five of them, the President in the middle, Bob and Tom flanking him, and Lopez and Reynolds on either side.

The photographer left the room and the President said, "Glad that's over. Please, come and sit down." He motioned for each man to sit on one of the couches on either side of his chair and for Reynolds to sit next to Tom and Lopez to sit next to Bob. A waiter appeared, offering each attendee a drink.

"Tito's on the rocks, gentlemen?" he asked.

Both men looked at the President quizzically.

"How did I know? I have some of the best intelligence anyone can gather. In this case we checked the mini-bar on the plane that brought you to Australia to see what was missing." The entire room started laughing.

"Gentlemen," continued the President, "I checked the rules on all the medals a president is allowed to convey on civilian heroes. The problem is that each requires for the public record an explanation of why the medal was being given. The situation we have with China is very delicate right now, and we can't have any questions emerge about what may or may not have happened in Laos.

"Suffice it to say, your photos went straight to Governor Li of the People's Bank of China. He now holds all the cards on Deng. The General is still an evil bastard, as bad as they come. But at least now he is now *our* bastard.

"Now. As you've no doubt been told, there may be no medals, but your actions will not go unrewarded." He motioned to the Secretary of State.

Dianne Reynolds stood and approached them. "Tom, you brought Deng's behavior to Bob's attention and thereby to ours. You put yourself on the line in a truly heroic way. That proves commitment and dedication to a cause that rises well above one's own self. The State Department needs people like that. We have a job titled Deputy Assistant Secretary of State for Advancement of Human Rights. Chief on the job's list of responsibilities is to combat sex trafficking around the world. Will you do me and the President the honor of taking that job?"

Tom swallowed hard, then found the presence of mind to pick up the cue. "Mr. President, Madame Secretary . . . I would be deeply honored." His words were genuine, but his brain was spinning about what had just happened.

The President spoke. "Hector, your turn."

"Bob," said Hector, standing, "let me cut to the chase. The President threatened to hire you away from me. I told him that I was eligible for early retirement and would retire in protest on the spot if he did. So he said, 'Well then, make the lad a better offer.' See the kind of businessman he is?"

Laughter all around.

Lopez continued. "Bob, you know that I value all that you have done for me enormously. But what you did in Laos has made me realize that I am underutilizing your talents. I would like to offer you a new job—assistant to the Director. You would have someone working under you to do your current clerical duties. Your new job would include full access to me on any matter. You will go from a GS-12 to GS-15 rank with the appropriate bump in salary. It's not a medal but it is a way of making a better use of your talents."

"Sir, how can I say no?"

"All right, men," the President said, "I've heard what I needed to hear. I am going to be announcing your new jobs at the dinner tonight. And I for one am hungry."

¥ $ €

When they reached the State Dining Room, the President gestured to a smaller room off to one side, intended for more intimate functions of state. He motioned for Bob and Tom to go first, and as they entered the room the other guests rose and started applauding. All rushed up to shake the young men's hands.

"These are our guests of honor," the President announced, joining the others in the applause along with Hector and Dianne. When it died down, he pointed them to their seats and invited everyone to place a drink order. As soon as the waiter had placed a glass in front of each guest with their preferred beverage, he rose.

"Tonight, we gather the people who were most critical to our successful resolution of the China currency war. Two months ago, the People's Republic launched an economic war on us designed to disrupt our markets and displace the dollar as the world's leading currency. Tonight, the dollar remains the world's currency of choice. It is now supported by legal changes that make it far more difficult to inflate away its value, and the much-needed fiscal changes our country needs are well on their way to enactment." He raised his glass and others raised theirs to a round of "Hear, hear."

"In this war, most of us at this table were senior government officials who were doing the jobs we were supposed to do. But three people in this room went above and beyond the call of duty and volunteered to help this country outside the norms of their daily lives. Some did work so extraordinary that I cannot publicly recognize it in any ordinary way for their efforts must remain secret.

"But one person I can recognize in the usual way is Bernadette Coleman, to whom I am going to present the Presidential Medal of Freedom. Bernadette, would you join me?"

Bernadette stood, demurely smoothed her dress, and took her place at President Turner's side.

"The Presidential Medal of Freedom was established by President Kennedy," he said. "It is the highest award a president can give to a civilian who has made an especially meritorious contribution to the security or national interests of the United States. Bernadette Coleman came out of private life to advise the Director of the CIA and the President of the United States on how to deal with the Chinese challenge. She is the world's leading expert on the organizational behavior of the Chinese government and on individuals within that government. Bernadette, we couldn't have done it without you." The President displayed the medal with its distinctive blue ribbon to the people at the table and then hung it around Bernadette's neck.

She stepped away to leave, but Turner caught her by the arm.

"One additional thing," he said. "Ben, you undoubtedly know how hard it is to say no to your beautiful bride. I experience the same thing with Mrs. Turner. And when these two put their two heads together, well . . . let's just say it leads to moments where I wonder who is really running the country."

There was appreciative laughter all around.

"So Mrs. Coleman and Mrs. Turner, you will be happy to hear that Congress has approved your latest joint venture. As a result, I will soon be awarding Deputy Valeria Evans of the Jefferson County, West Virginia, sheriff's department the Public Safety Officer Medal of Valor for saving the life of a valuable CIA asset and allowing The Turner Plan to be implemented without a hitch."

Bernadette said her thanks to the President and was seated, after which he continued. "The next two men are genuine heroes. They gave up the safety of their jobs in Washington and put their lives at risk to entrap one of the most dangerous and evil individuals on the planet. Their actions set in motion a chain of events that forced radical changes in the government of the People's Republic of China, which in turn led to our ability to reach a successful resolution of the conflict between us. The American people owe them a debt of gratitude. Robert Franks and Thomas Butler, will you join me?"

As the men stood, he presented each with a framed, handwritten letter of thanks, ambiguously worded so their actual actions were not revealed.

"This incident brought to our attention that the talents of these two gentlemen were being seriously underutilized by this government. I am pleased to announce that just before this dinner, we have addressed that issue." He went on to describe the new positions given to Franks and Butler, followed by hearty applause. The two men moved to sit, but Ben Coleman rose, and the President motioned that they should remain standing.

Ben took a place between Bob and Tom. "Gentlemen, the President can't give you a medal, but someone else can. You should understand that what I am about to present should not be prominently displayed after tonight, and your story should not be discussed, except within this room."

Ben produced four gold coins, each attached to a ribbon, from the pocket of his jacket. "These are presented on behalf of the Governor of the People's Bank of China and the Chairman of the U.S. Federal Reserve to two men whose extraordinary efforts have done more to assure the stability of the world monetary system than anyone else Chairman Li and I can think of."

Ben hung two coins—a yuan 100,000 gold coin and a U.S. $10,000— around the neck of each man. "I brought these back last night from

China. Governor Li had them made over there as I wanted to keep them secret, and it is far easier for me to keep a secret from this crowd in China than here in the U.S." He stared straight at Bernadette and the entire table laughed.

"Governor Li was exceptionally gracious. He could have chosen our \$5,000 gold coin instead. But as he said to me, 'Your \$5,000 coin is smaller than our yuan 100,000 and that would cause you to lose face to China. You have given both China and me personally tremendous face, and so I return the favor by using an American gold coin that is larger than the Chinese version.'"

During the next round of applause, he pulled four envelopes from his inner pocket and handed two to each of the gentlemen. "These are personal notes from Li and I. Thank you very much for your service and your sacrifice." He nodded, and Bob and Tom took their cue and sat down.

"Ladies and gentlemen," Ben said, "I have returned from China with one more award. This one gives me particular pleasure to present since it represents a very rare event in my life. Unless she is trying to make me feel good, I do believe I have managed to keep a secret from my wife. Mrs. Coleman, would you be kind enough to join me?" Bernadette rose and gave Ben one of those looks that meant he had succeeded in surprising her.

"Bernadette Coleman, I present this to you as a gift from Governor Li and the People's Bank of China for your extraordinary service in bringing a peaceful resolution of our disagreements." Ben hung the 100,000-yuan gold coin around her neck. Unlike the ones for the men, this one was attached to a finely braided gold chain. Ben gave Bernadette a peck on the cheek when he had finished to more applause from the table.

"Ben Coleman," she said, "you actually surprised me. That does not happen often and is a bit of an affront to my skills in my chosen career. So be on notice that I am going to remember you pulling one over on me—and I have a *very* long memory." The whole table laughed, and the President signaled the waiters to begin serving the meal.

The President and First Lady climbed to the top of the stairs in the front hall after bidding their guests farewell.

Cynthia squeezed her husband's hand and said in a low voice, "Don't you dare let her go."

"Who are you talking about? And go where?"

"Will Turner, remember your first campaign speech? It was about stopping the brain drain. You're letting one happen right under your nose."

The President looked at his wife.

"I'm serious. Bernadette told me there's talk in Britain of bringing her back to head MI6."

"You know as well as I that talk is cheap."

"Even when it comes from Edith Spensley?"

The President sighed. "Why is it that whenever I hear that woman's name, I no longer feel like the most powerful person on the planet?"

"There's election talk in Britain, and depending on the outcome, Doris Billingsley will be kicking rocks down the road."

The President squinted his eyes at her. "But Bernadette? She's been out of the game for—"

"I know," said the First Lady. "But consider this. With this brave new world you've created with our new Partners in Prosperity, our closer relationship with China threatens the level of our relations with existing allies. The Brits need someone who is close both to China and America. And who is the best analyst in the world when it comes to China and has outstanding relationships here?"

"She'd never leave Ben."

"No. But who is to say that Ben wouldn't leave *us*?"

"Cynthia, I love you, and your analysis may be flawless, but I'm not sure what I could offer them that would keep them in the country. Some things are above even my pay grade."

"I disagree."

"I don't believe this. I thought you would be the last person to argue that a woman should sacrifice a career move like this for her husband's career. She has sacrificed for him. In this modern age isn't it proper that he return the favor at the right moment?"

"I would never ask my best friend to make a sacrifice like that," Cynthia said.

The President looked at her quizzically. "I'm not sure I get where you're going. What could possibly be more alluring to her than MI6?"

"My dearest love, sometimes you are so dense. Hector Lopez is due for retirement at the end of next year."